RESTLESS COFFINS

RESTLESS COFFINS

M.P. Wright

BLACK & WHITE PUBLISHING

First published 2018
by Black & White Publishing Ltd
Nautical House, 104 Commercial Street
Edinburgh, EH6 6NF

1 3 5 7 9 10 8 6 4 2   18 19 20 21

ISBN: 978 1 78530 158 2

A CIP catalogue record for this book is available from the British Library.

Typeset by Iolaire, Newtonmore
Printed and bound by Nørhaven, Denmark

Dedicated to Tony R. Cox, John Martin, Ken Hooper
and to Abby Jayne Slater-Fairbrother.
JT and I are indebted to each of you.

PROLOGUE

Ginger Bay, St Philip Parish, Barbados
9 August, 1934

The boy and girl walked without speaking to each other, each carrying thin bamboo cane fishing rods across their slender shoulders, languidly kicking at the pale, dusty ground with their toes as they travelled from their chattel home out along the edge of the dirt track road, north towards the sea. The midday sun hung high in a cloudless, turquoise sky behind them, its heavy rays already stinging the backs of their heads and necks. The sticky humidity clung to the insides of their T-shirts, the steamy air around their faces, fuggy and still. As they walked, they could hear, lost in the thick hedgerows, the hypnotic sound of cicadas chirping. Above their heads, hanging from the branches of the grizzled gum trees that lined either side of the road, fell long strands of rotting moss. The fecund earthy scent of decay seeped from the flowing green-tinged boughs, its fusty odour drifting downwards towards the sticky haze that skirted out in front of them.

The children's daily journey down to the cove where they played was a familiar one and the young boy always set the pace, his barefoot strides quicker than those of his younger sibling. Unable to match her brother's whirlwind gait, she abruptly stopped on the roadside, defiantly rested her tiny hands onto her hips then yelled out to him. "Will yuh slow down, Joseph?" The boy, accustomed to his sister's daily request, took no notice of her whine and immediately quickened up, deliberately taking another half-dozen lengthy strides, only stopping and turning around after the girl had bellowed out again for him to wait for her. The boy stroked his chin with the tips of his fingers and began to tap the ball of his right foot impatiently on the ground. He stared back down the road then wiped his thin forearm aggressively across his sweating brow whilst he waited for his dawdling sister to finally catch up.

The little girl smiled to herself then ran the remaining few yards to reach her disgruntled brother. She came to a weary halt in front of him and stood panting like an overheated puppy. When she'd finally caught her breath, the little girl raised her makeshift fishing rod in the air and defiantly shook it over her head.

"Joseph, I'm gonna catch me a big bonefish today."

The boy looked down at his sister, shaking his head. "Girl, don't be talkin' doh'tish. Yuh ain't catching nuthin' wid dat tatty rod at all."

The little girl shot her brother a pained stare. "Yeah ... well, jus' yuh wait, I'm gonna show yuh." Joseph sneered back at her, spat a thick wad of saliva at his feet then prodded a damnatory finger into his sister's face.

"Bernice, quit lick moutin'. Yuh ain't showing me nuthin'. Pickney, I bin dropping a line in de water since befo' yuh bin suckin' on Mama's titties!"

Bernice cursed at her brother under her breath then sucked in a stream of warm air through the thin gap in her front teeth. She looked back up at her brother, her eyes squinting into severe slits from the glare of the sun, her face crinkled with childlike anger.

"Well, yuh look like Mama's titties!"

Joseph stared back blankly at Bernice then raised his right hand out in front of his sister's face, his middle digit fully extended, giving her the bird, then turned sharply on his heels and continued walking briskly along the road.

The vexed little girl gave a deep sigh then slung the cane rod back over her shoulder and chased after her testy brother, the pair not stopping again for another half-mile until they reached the junction of a crossroads. Joseph took hold of Bernice's wrist, drawing her close to his side and scanned his eyes diligently along either side of the desolate highway for the remote possibility of an approaching passing car, bike or truck. With no approaching vehicles in sight, Joseph dropped his hold on his sister's arm and the two of them quickly crossed over the scorching tarmac and made their way along the unpaved sidewalk until they reached a steep, parched soil embankment which fell away from the road. Without turning around to her, Joseph again reached out behind him with his left arm and held out the palm of his hand and waited for his sister's slender fingers to grasp hold of it.

The two children climbed down the heavy earth mound into a dense undergrowth of hanging tamarind branches, bright crimson caesalpinia bushes and sweet-smelling magnolia shrub and began to walk through the dense canopy of green foliage until they came to a thin sand-blown track between the shaded arch of a row of bowed silk cotton trees. Above their heads they could hear the loud, discordant cries of flock shearwaters and storm petrels as they flew out to sea. Joseph stopped for a moment and looked up at the swooping birds then let go of his sister's hand and broke out into a sprint along the remainder of the path and down to a thin row of grassy dunes. He climbed up on to the sandy knoll and stood motionless looking out to sea waiting for Bernice to arrive at his side. When she finally joined him on top of the dune, the two children gazed down on to the white powdery sand and shady swaying palms and smiled at each other, content in an unspoken mutual reverie. They had returned again; back to their secret, hidden world.

The sheltered bay with its tranquil shoreline was nestled between two imposing limestone coral rock structures which towered up either side of the secluded basin. Joseph and Bernice ran off the dunes on to the beach and across the baking hot sand down to the sea, dropping their fishing rods at the cooling water's edge. Even at low tide the impressive-looking, small, white-tipped waves had a menacing presence about them. The crystal-clear water gracefully ebbed and flowed around the tops of their legs. They both waded excitedly out into the alluring azure-tinted ocean until the sea reached their stomachs then started to swim along a short stretch of the bay, neither forgetting the dangers that lurked beneath them nor the strong currents and dangerous swells and undertows that swept undetected through the cove. The unseen deadly tides were a constant reminder to the two children of their mother's sombre caution to them each time they left to visit the deserted beach: "Child, yuh mind dem waters ... De sea, it e'n got nuh back door. It tek yuh; yuh gon' fo'ever, you 'ear me?"

They swam and dived in the shallow waters for the next hour, finally returning to the shore after Bernice had begun to complain that she was cold and tired. The little girl followed her brother out of the sea, trooping back up on to the beach then dropping down with a heavy thud at Joseph's side. She threw her gangly legs out in front of her, accidently kicking sand over Joseph as she shook droplets of water and grit from her feet. Joseph shot her a dirty look. Unruffled by her brother's irritation, Bernice stuck out her tongue then hitched herself a few inches away from him, pulling her knees up towards her chest, tucking her arms around her shins then resting her chin on top of them. She huffed indignantly to herself then stared solemnly out to sea.

The two children sat in silence, letting the afternoon sun dry the saltwater from their bodies. Joseph was the first to break the stillness with a question.

"Yuh ready to go fish, then?"

Bernice kept looking out at the ocean and slowly nodded her head, then quickly got to her feet, collecting her fishing rod as she did so and began to walk slowly through the surf towards the blue hole caves further down the beach. Joseph shot up off the sand and ran to Bernice's side, noticing the inch-long crimson scar on his sister's lower calf as he edged in front of her to take the lead once again. The claret-coloured lesion had been caused by the toxic sap from a manchineel tree which Bernice had climbed the previous summer. The fiery plant juice had grazed her skin, burning the flesh and leaving an ugly welt; a painful reminder that she should never attempt such a foolhardy pursuit again. Joseph looked at his sister and smiled to himself, quietly registering in his mind that it wouldn't be the last time Bernice did something foolish.

*

They stood on the jagged rocks above the caves, on a low promontory that jutted out between a series of deep pools, casting their fishing lines out into the sea. By late afternoon they had caught and thrown back over a dozen bar jacks and mahogany snappers. The sky had begun to turn a darker blue and at the furthest edges of Joseph's vision he could just make out the portentous darkening heavens of an approaching storm. The gulf waters below were still lime green but had become streaked with threatening whitecaps, darker patches of deep water, like clouds of ink, had begun to drift across the coral reef; another sign to the young boy that bad weather was brewing. Joseph and Bernice collected up their rods and lines and trudged down the steep cliff path back on to Harrismith Beach then headed south towards the coast road.

They walked quickly over the soggy sand, the seawater washing away their footprints before heading back away from the beach, climbing over rocks which were scattered across a series of interconnecting lagoons. In the distance, Joseph could see the multicoloured fishing boats moored up on towlines in the harbour at Deborah Bay. A thick, fetid odour suddenly blew in off the gathering tailwind. It wafted across the children's faces, making Bernice grimace.

"What's dat?"

"Probably yuh breath," snapped Joseph.

"Yuh shut ya mout'!"

Joseph cackled loudly, pleased with his cruel jibe and his sister's tetchy response to it. Bernice retaliated quickly by splashing water at her brother's back. The two children continued to taunt and sneer at each other as they pushed on, out across the lagoon away from the blackening clouds in the bay behind them. Joseph continued to walk a few feet in front of his sister, the sour smell becoming more intense as they crossed over into an ankle-deep inlet which stood between them and the path across to the next cove. They trod carefully in the shallows, both navigating their footsteps away from the sharp coral and the spines of semi-hidden sea urchins. A floating island of kelp bobbed in the water in front of them as they climbed over a sandbar into another rock pool. That's when the putrid hum hit and Joseph, out of the corner of his eye, saw a few yards in front of him just what was making all the stink.

Underneath the overhanging branches of a palm, nestled in a stagnating saltwater-filled depression, was the body of a man. The corpse, crawling with ghost crabs, lay face up and was partially dressed in a tattered blue uniform. The head was snatched back, the eyes sunk deep into his skull and covered in a thin milky film. A thin web of dried algae and seaweed was interwoven through the damp, matted blood-stained grey hair. The skin was as thin as parchment and the colour and texture of tanned, wrinkled damp leather. The arms and hands were liver-spotted and etched with dull, sunken blue veins.

Joseph held out his arm behind him, the palm of his hand flat as Bernice approached.

"Yuh stay there!"

"Why, what yuh seen, Joseph?"

"Nuthin! Jus' do as I say." Joseph swallowed hard then took a couple more steps through the water towards the body. He stared down at the man's bloated face, which was burnished with heavy, dark bruising, the mouth yanked wide open, a silent scream emanating from ruptured lips, tarnished a deep purple; the colour of rotting hog plums. The throat stretched taut, revealed a gaping slit which had been carved deep into the flesh above the Adam's apple. Further down the body, barely covering the torso, a buttonless shirt with silver insignia decorated on each lapel was torn open at the midriff, exposing a beaten and bloated stomach which hung down towards the man's thighs like a water-filled balloon.

7

"Lemme see what it is, Joseph . . ."

Joseph, his mouth dry, hesitated before faltering back to his sister. "No, I said stay there."

"But I wanna see."

Joseph, without taking his eyes from the distended cadaver, stabbed his finger back at his sister. "No pickney should be seeing dis." Bernice took no notice of her brother's warning and rushed through the water, clambering over Joseph's shoulder, looking down to where the man's decomposing remains lay. Joseph immediately felt Bernice's body stiffen then shudder next to his, her voice was muted and crackled with fear when she finally spoke.

"That fella a redleg, Joseph?"

Joseph shook his head and took a step backwards. "He ain't no crook . . . Dis fella, he a po'lice man."

Another flurried gust lifted the unmistakable musk of death up from the water-soaked ground at their feet and draped itself over the children's faces like the cursed cloak of a dark angel. Joseph felt a wave of panic shoot through every fibre of his being, the inside of his head felt woolly and began to spin as he heard his sister repeating the words he'd just spoken. He quickly turned back to look at the foreboding, low grey canopy in the darkening sky, the burgeoning storm was now anchored a few miles out in the bay behind them. The palm fronds whipped in the wind above their heads and the sea had begun to turn choppy, the aggressive tide starting to inch its way further in towards them. The approaching waters carried on its spiky edges a thin, white line of surf, its spray spitting violently up into the air. Lightning suddenly forked out in the distance like a shard of fine glass followed by the faint rumble of thunder which trembled inside the gathering clouds.

The two children stood over the dead man's body, a fine sea spray blowing in their faces, the ebony-tinged sky above them growling. The clouds sparked inside, their mantle imbued with a blood-red stain. Joseph dropped his fishing rod into the water and reached down for his sister's hand. They began to run, never once looking back. They heard the racked screams of the Obeah unleashed from the floor of the rock pool behind them, its tormented howl swiftly gathered up in the squall which blew in across the cove. The cruel wind clawed at their backs like the hands of the grasping undead and screeched across their path as they bolted back across the dunes; the hot sand underneath their feet stung at their soles like crushed diamonds.

1

The early morning March air was cool and tinged with the unmistakeable tang of the sea. It was a comforting and now familiar scent; a welcoming aroma that would, often as not, greet me as I woke and then gently cosset me as I fell asleep late at night. In the winter of 1967 I had moved out of my digs on Gwyn Street in St Paul's, and discreetly relocated down by the waterside of Bristol harbour and settled on a narrow beamed Dutch barge, which I began renting from the Avonmouth Port Company.

The old vessel had seen better days and was now permanently moored out at Nova Scotia Place on Spike Island, close to the busy Cumberland Basin and the bustle of the town. Despite its unusual location, and rusted and haggard exterior, the ancient boat allowed me and the ghosts I carried around a tenuous sense of privacy. It offered a retreat from the outside world; a place I often found to be inhospitable and one I occasionally struggled to understand and cope with. The barge was well over eighty years old and certainly not most people's idea of the perfect domicile; but for me, despite all its cosmetic flaws, the tatty tub was somewhere I finally felt safe. I'd become happy to call the narrow boat my home; something I'd felt I'd never truly been able to since moving from Barbados to Britain some four years earlier.

It was the day before Good Friday, just after 8am and

the low rising sun was misty and soft in the trees. I'd woken early and was sat outside, barefoot in my vest and trousers on a short-legged, wooden stool at the furthest edge of the bow of the barge, clasping a battered blue and white enamel mug filled with coffee. I took a sip of the fragrantly hot liquid and looked out at the smooth water around me then briefly closed my eyes, the cool ozone-scented breeze touching my face and bare shoulders.

Herring gulls squabbled in the sky, their choking calls echoing loudly across the dock. I took another swig of coffee, rested my back against the cabin wall and watched a pair of young water voles swimming between my barge and a small tug boat on the opposite side of the dock. Driftwood bobbed and floated aimlessly across the top of the dark water's surface, its brackish iodine odour mixing with the scent of the Mexican fleabane and bright purple bellflowers which grew in abundance along the harbour walls. A cyclist rode towards me along the towpath. I watched the rider approach, finally recognising a familiar figure distinguished by his well-pressed Royal Mail uniform.

Harry Parkin was my local postman, whose delivery round took in parts of St Paul's and, occasionally, the dockland district. I watched him come to a halt at the side of the boat. He nodded his head at me politely then leaned on the crossbar, where a pair of rabbits, recently shot and freshly gutted, hung from the stem.

"How you doin', Harry?"

"Not bad, not bad at all, Mr Ellington." Harry winked at me then stuck his hand in his jacket pocket and took out a brass pot of Will's snuff. He opened the small tin box and ground tobacco leaves between his thumb and forefinger, placed it carefully in two small heaps on to the back of his

12

hand then inhaled it sharply into both nostrils. Harry threw his head back, wiped at the end of his nose with the back of his hand and coughed loudly after delivering himself the swift hit of nicotine. Harry Parkin was a plain-speaking man, good-humoured, kind-hearted and a natural born crook. He was thin as a rake, with skin as pale as Banquo's Ghost, his lumpy battered face betraying the pain and suffering that he'd survived in his youth.

He was fifty or more years old, balding and had seen his fair share of hardship, mainly across the theatre of war as a sapper with the Eighth Army at places like Tobruk and then Italy. I liked Harry. He wiped again at his nostrils with the edge of his finger then gestured with his head towards the mail sack hanging at his side.

"I bin an' delivered a telegram up to your place o' work this morning."

"A telegram?"

"Yeah, I gave it to that old witch you got working on the door."

"Old witch? You mean, Mrs Pearce?"

"I don't know the biddy's name, I just know she's got a bloody sharp tongue in her head."

I smiled to myself, fully aware of my old neighbour's fearsome reputation and her fiery disposition. "Having her about is cheaper than keeping a guard dog, Harry."

Harry winced at the thought. "I bet she is ... Anyways, I don't often deliver telegrams. I was down this way, thought I'd tip you the nod."

"Thanks, Harry, that's real good of you. It must be my lucky day. Perhaps the queen's gone an' knighted me?"

"You, a knight o' the realm?" Harry smiled then shook his head doubtfully.

13

I shrugged my shoulders at the mailman. "Stranger things have happened, look at Learie Constantine. He got one."

"Constantine was a bloody good cricketer. You, and what you get up to: I don't think so, matey. The queen ain't in no hurry to send you no medal; not unless Her Majesty's gone all soft an' moved out to the colonies, she ain't."

"The colonies, what you talkin' 'bout?"

"That telegram o' yours, sent from Barbados, it was." Harry raised his eyebrows at me then sat back on the seat of his bicycle, put his feet through the pedal straps and began to proceed back up the towpath. He called after me, his voice crackling with suppressed laughter.

"Either you're being deported, old son, or somebody needs to get a hold of you pretty sharpish. I'll be seeing ya."

I waved farewell to Harry and watched him ride off then closed my eyes again. I listened to the chimes from Holy Trinity Church striking the half hour and to the swallows as they swooped down from the warehouse eaves around me and glided across the still canal water. I shuddered. From out of the darkness behind my eyelids, somewhere in the furthest recesses of my mind, I thought I could hear the sage, foretelling whisper of my long-deceased mama's words calling out to me.

"Boy, yuh 'member, nuthin' travels faster than bad news."

★

I sat thinking about what was contained in the wire that was waiting for me back in St Paul's. I mulled over the possibilities whilst I drank the last of my now cold coffee then went back inside and put a kettle of water on top of the wood stove and waited for it to boil. Twenty minutes later

I'd washed and shaved. I brushed my teeth, ran Bay Rum through my hair, splashed a palmful of English Leather aftershave across my jaw then dressed in a white cotton shirt and grey herringbone tweed suit. I stood in front of the mirror and knotted a dark blue satin rayon tie around my neck then slowly ran my thumb along the small half-inch scar that ran down the left side of my brow and smiled to myself. The faded cicatrix was an old war wound given to me by my younger sister, Bernice, who had, in a fit of temper, thrown a broken conch shell at me when we were kids. I sank back the remainder of a second mug of coffee, pulled on and laced up my black Oxford brogues, threw on my old Aquascutum overcoat and fitted my black felt trilby on to my head, drawing it down low over my eyes.

I locked up the outside cabin door of the barge and made my way across the wharf and back along the chocolate block stone path towards St Paul's. As I walked, I recalled an observation Lord Learie Constantine had once made more than a decade earlier which aptly summed up the world around me:

"Almost the entire population in Britain really expected the coloured man to live in an inferior area … areas devoted to coloured people … Most British people would be quite unwilling for a black man to enter their homes, nor would they wish to work with one as a colleague, nor stand shoulder to shoulder with one at a factory bench."

An uninvited anger aroused me as I thought about Constantine's sombre sentiment and I reflected on how little I now missed the rundown ghetto I had recently left and where so many of my fellow émigrés still resided; most living

15

in rundown slum properties, paying criminally high rents to wealthy white landlords.

I climbed a series of steep concrete steps out on to Hotwells Road, stopped for a moment and stared at the magnificent Clifton suspension bridge raised high above Avon Gorge and across to the wealthy city of Bristol; my gaze finally drawn out towards the port town's poorer neighbourhood, St Paul's. Thirteen years on since Learie Constantine uttered his bleak declaration of our migrant plight and his disquieting words were still ringing true ... Some things, I feared, just weren't meant to change.

*

I shared my place of work with a two-ring boxing gymnasium. Vic's Gym was a rundown, three-storey Georgian building on Gloucester Road in the heart of St Paul's. It was just after 10.30am by the time I'd climbed the fire stairs at the back of the gym and walked into my office. There were already a dozen or so punters either working out on the heavy bags or sparring with each other. Fighters of all stripes and experience yelled instructions and bawled obscenities as they lifted weights, shadow-boxed, hammered speed bags or punished their muscular bodies with a regime of sit-ups, medicine ball circling or rope-jumping. Most of the men were black; many were aimless young souls who came to Vic's to hone their anger to a fine point of violence in a crude attempt to shed the skin of unemployment, poverty and future lives spent on the shady margins of small-time crime; young lives that would mostly likely be wasted enduring lengthy periods of time holed up in local police jails or rotting in prison cells across the land.

I took off my trilby and overcoat and hung them on the

teak coat stand by the entrance to my office door and went to seek out Mrs Pearce. My former neighbour and friend had in the past six months taken it upon herself to become my personal secretary and office cleaner, as well as providing me with a host of nourishing meals, a quality laundry service, and business and personal advice, whether I wanted it or not.

For a woman in her late seventies she was unusually spritely, adept at problem-solving and annoyingly efficient. We shared a love–hate relationship and, in truth, she was the closest thing to a friend that I possessed. The old girl had already sensed my presence in the building, hotfooting it from less important duties downstairs. She was standing like the Sword of Damocles in the shadows at the end of the hallway staring down at her wristwatch.

"Good morning, Mr Ellington. And what time do you call this?"

I looked back at the clock on the back wall of my office. "'Bout the time I be needin' you to brew me a cup o' your tea." I smiled at her and she stared back at me stony-faced. I nervously cleared an imaginary frog from my throat and looked at the telegram clenched in Mrs Pearce's right hand. I pointed sheepishly at the yellow-papered telex like a child awaiting bad news from an unwelcome school report.

"I'm assuming that's fo' me?"

Mrs Pearce nodded and handed me the envelope. "It certainly is. Delivered first thing this morning by that awful postman you drink with in the Prince of Wales public house."

"How'd you know I drink with Harry Parkin in the Prince o' Wales?"

"Because the man reeks of snuff. You may wish to remember that I wash your clothes, Mr Ellington. He must

17

get a half ounce of the stuff down the front of your shirt every time he sneezes. Disgusting pig."

I took the telegram from her and nervously held it by the tips of my fingers, staring down at my name on the front of the envelope, unsure if I wanted to open it for fear of what may be contained inside. Mrs Pearce jabbed at my side with her bony hand.

"Well, come on then, man, I haven't got all day ... open it."

I turned the envelope over and slipped my thumb underneath the seal flap and tore it open. I pulled out the wafer-thin sheet of paper and read the words which had been typed across it.

22nd March 1967

Bridgetown. Barbados. 33 9 1527

Joseph **Stop** I sincerely regret to inform you of the death of your sister Bernice May Ellington **Stop** Request you make urgent travel arrangements to return to Barbados to settle affairs **Stop** Expect Telephone Call At Grosvenor Road With Further Details and Instructions **Stop** Thursday 23rd March at 19.00GMT **Stop** V **Stop**

I felt the tears well up underneath my eyes and a cold pall wash over my body. A bitter metallic taste rose up from the back my mouth and crept across my tongue as the all too familiar and unwelcome revenant of death entered my being once again. Its hidden, wraith-like presence clung at my insides like a craven succubus. My arm fell like a lead weight at my side and the telegram dropped from my trembling fingers and fluttered downwards, landing at my feet. I left Mrs Pearce standing outside of my office door and, without speaking, walked down the hallway and stood on the balcony at the top of the fire stairs. I knew that, behind me, my old neighbour would be picking up and reading the cable sent from my cousin, Victor. I also knew that, at that moment, I did not want to hear the septuagenarian offer her well-meaning words of condolence. My insular anguish was eager to rebuff any reassuring pats on my back or biblical sentiments of solace.

I'd learned since the death of my wife, Ellie, and young daughter, Amelia, that grief was a painfully private and, at times, all-consuming and cruelly bleak emotion. Back then, grief had chosen me very early on as its repository and I found it didn't share itself easily with others.

Outside, it had begun to rain, the water dripping from the roof above me and running in rivulets off the cracked guttering down onto the ground below, collecting in pools across the red bricks in the yard. The sky had darkened and a cool, sharp wind blew across my face, whipping the falling tears from my cheeks and dissolving them into the rainfall. My head throbbed and became woozy, my body light and strangely disconnected from the world I normally existed in. My bleary eyes tried to focus on the row of whitebeam trees which stood behind the wall at the back of the gymnasium, their branches overhanging and laden with clusters of small ivory-coloured flowers. In the greying light, the trees seemed to bow together, their interconnected boughs resembling the entrance to a strange subterranean tunnel to another world. I felt myself being drawn towards the unearthly ingress and gently ushered to a place I could be reunited with those I'd lost. Inside, in the distance I could hear my little girl call out my name. I could not see her, but felt her take my hand in her own and slowly walk me through the darkness to a cold and solitary chamber where I knew wounds healed themselves, mortal flesh would not rot and where sealed coffins could be opened to reveal the wonders of the undead.

2

I'd never known a longer wait. Eight hours where my mind succumbed to a theatre of free association, allowing me to reside in a sunken, grief-stricken abyss. The strangest thoughts and emotions ran through my addled brain as I struggled to make sense of what I read in the telegram. Mrs Pearce had stood silently at my side on the balcony of the fire escape as I sobbed; my weeping masked by the heavy deluge of rainwater falling out of the heavens. My elderly friend had eventually brought me in out of the rain and we'd returned to my office, where, overcome with shock, I'd dropped into my chair and slumped behind my desk for the rest of the day, either staring into space or watching the hands on the wall clock tick themselves away into oblivion as I waited anxiously for the telephone to ring.

By 3pm the rainstorm had begun to subside. I'd knocked back a few shots of Mount Gay rum earlier, which helped to settle my nerves. Mrs Pearce had taken offence to my drinking liquor so early in the day and had left me with my glass of hooch, malcontent and mumbling to herself, only to return an hour later with freshly made cheese and onion sandwiches and a steaming pot of her darkly brewed tea. To show willing, I took a couple of mouthfuls of one of her sandwiches and, when the old girl wasn't looking, reached down to my bottle of copper-coloured spirit and laced a hefty shot of rum into the mug of tea and began to sip at it like a cat licking at sour milk. I leaned forward in my chair, staring down at the top of my teak desk, my watery eyes following the spiralling, dark grain in the wood, my head lost in a mournful reverie of old memories; melancholic brooding which conjured up long-lost images of my sister, Bernice, our deceased parents and the life we'd once led on a sun-washed island over four thousand miles away.

★

My father, Clifford, had been dead for over twenty years. He'd worked as a labourer at the Portvale sugar factory in St James Parish on the island of Barbados since he was a young boy and had a fearsome reputation with his fellow workers and in our community as a brawler and hard drinker. My papa was a solitary man to his family, with few friends. He had a mean temper whether he was drunk or not. He could not read or write, except for his own name and had difficulty recognising numbers, and hadn't left the island he was born on, knowing nor caring of home or world events. Never one to consider the welfare of others, Clifford Fitzroy Ellington would spend what little money he earned, gambling in card games, on dominoes or betting on any beast that could run, swim or crawl. My papa was also fond of late nights in the company of mulatto women whose names he had no care to know and he would more often than not return home, worse for the bottle, and take his belt to me and my sister and then his sizeable fists to my mama, simply because he could.

The four of us lived just outside Six Cross Roads village, close to the sea in a wood-built chattel house that was set up off the ground on concrete blocks. It was a one door, one window shack with no toilet, no electricity and no running water. It wasn't much to look at or to live in, but it was home.

My mama, Cora, was a gentle, soft-spoken woman of staunch Christian beliefs who worked as a housemaid and cook for the Lewises, a wealthy white family whose head, Colonel Matthew 'Monk' Monroe, had made his fortune exporting rubber and cocoa overseas. Mama worked from sun-up until sun-down for sixty cents an hour, rising early in the mornings, leaving her bed in darkness to walk to the 'big house' to prepare the Monroe family's breakfast and strip the bedding in the house's many bedrooms. She would stay on there working her fingers to the bone, often late into the evening to dish up the colonel and his kin's evening meal.

For a weekly pittance, she washed their clothing, scrubbed their floors and cleaned up after them. When she'd finally return home, tired and hollow-eyed, she had little time and energy for either Bernice, me or her intemperate husband. The back-breaking work she undertook, often a seven-day job, aged and diminished her good looks and ardent love of life quickly, her daily working existence reducing her to little more than a slave to wealthy landowners who never cared less how she or we, her family, lived, just as long as their own needs were met. My papa, in a booze-soaked haze, would often violently admonish his wife, yelling that she was never around and that she was both lazy and uncaring. "Wom'an, yuh clean fo' 'fancy white folk' an' yuh bubble a pot fo' 'em in da kitchen, an' all I git is mush an' a sour face outta yuh!" His bitter accusations were both erroneous and misplaced. What was often true was that she would return home, finding little if anything to feed us from the larder, and would have to slap something together hastily out of meagre leftovers or from rusting tins. To her credit, out of the most scant and simple ingredients, she would always cook up something that was both hearty and flavoursome.

Once supper was ready, she'd summon us all up to the table sheepishly with a worn-out "Ya food here!" Bernice and I would rush to our seats and say grace with Mama whilst we waited for my father to stagger in. On the good days, my old man would flop down in his chair next to us and look disdainfully at the meal in front of him, raise merry hell with his wife and throw his plate of food at the wall. On the bad days, he'd beat our mama to a pulp in front of our very eyes.

"I'll take a penny for them?" The sound of Mrs Pearce's gentle voice pulled me away from my gloomy daydream.

"For what?" I grunted, my head down, my eyes still fixed on the tainted pattern in the wood of my writing desk.

"Penny for your thoughts ... I was asking what you were thinking about?"

I sighed and looked up at my friend. "Marjorie, ain't no way in the world you wouldn't wanna pay fo' my damn memories."

"Perhaps not, but memories, even the bittersweet ones, are better than nothing."

I nodded my head. "Is that so? Well, most of my recollections have led me to a helluva lot a bad luck. Perhaps I should 'a bin a bit more cautious 'bout which roads I took a stroll along in life?"

The old woman walked over to me, leaned forward and gently kissed the top of my head. She drew away and spoke to me again in a hushed tone. "Joseph, the hardest thing about the roads not taken is that you never know where they might have led. Be grateful for the ones you did get a chance to journey along."

I watched Mrs Pearce walk out of my office and disappear back down the hallway. Inside, away from my grief, her sage words had made me feel like a man lost in a dream filled with wealth and great riches; the treasure in my hands melting like a mist between my fingers.

★

At precisely 7pm the telephone rang. I listened to it ring several times before picking up the receiver. I put the phone to my ear and waited for Vic to talk to me. The voice I was longing to hear never spoke, instead a woman's voice, husky and cool, purred down the line, her American accent, genial and songlike.

"Mistah Ellington?"

"Yeah, this is Ellington, who the hell are you?"

"My name is Evangeline Laveau, I'm a good friend of your cousin, Victor. He asked me to call yo' on his behalf. I'm real sorry to hear 'bout your loss."

"Thanks, where's Vic at?"

"He outta town, sugar."

"Outta town ... Lady, I need him on the phone right now."

"Your cousin ain't here to speak wid you right now. He ax' me to be his go-between."

"Go-between? Look, I wanna know from him what happen to my sister."

"I know you do, an' I sympathise, I truly do, Mistah Ellington. It's like the cable Victor sent you said; she gone. All I can say fo' now is that the po'lice said your sister was involved in a tragic accident."

Tears begin to roll up in my eyes and cloud my vision. The woman on the other end of the line hesitated for a moment, somehow sensing my sadness. She cleared her throat then continued to speak. "I feel fo' your loss, honey, I surely do, but how your sister died ain't sum'ting yo' need to be hearin' on the end o' no phone. You git me?"

I nodded in reply to Evangeline Laveau's question, then grumbled, "Uh-huh."

"Look sugar, I just bin tol' by Victor to say, that you needin' to git back home quicker than the crow can fly. He tol' me that if you was to give me any truck 'bout what you gotta do then I was to say the name Monroe to you. Said you'd know what he meant."

"Monroe, what's he gotta do with Bernice?"

"I don't know nuthin' 'bout the fella or what he has or ain't gotta do with any'ting. It's just like I said; Victor tol' me to mention this dude Monroe's name if you got vexed at me. You got vexed an' I give you the name."

I breathed hard down the phone, trying to take in everything the American woman was telling me. I rubbed at my scalp frantically in frustration as I tried to weigh up the situation. "Lady, even if I wanted to, where am I supposed to get the cash to get myself on a boat home?"

"Boat?" Evangeline Laveau gave a hearty belly laugh down the phone line. "You ain't taking no boat, sugar. Victor, he gone an' made all the arrangements on yo' behalf. Yo' flying out tomorrow. All yo' gotta do is pack light an' get yo'self to London for a 6.45 flight out to New York."

"New York ... flying, what the hell you talking about, woman?"

I listened to Laveau strike a match then pull on a cigarette before she spoke again. "I'm talking 'bout your travel arrangements, sugar. How else you gonna git here ... walk it? You got yourself a pencil an' paper handy there?"

"Yeah." I reached across my desk and pulled a jotter pad and biro towards me and waited for Laveau to start speaking again.

"Okay, you need to git your ass to the Oceanic Terminal

at Heathrow Airport an' check in at the BOAC Cunard desk by 4pm. There's a return ticket in your name an' a envelope full o' American Express traveller's cheques waiting fo' you to pick up."

"And then what am I supposed to do?"

"Baby, other than git on that damn aeroplane, you ain't gotta do nuthin'. I'm gonna be takin' care o' every t'ing. I'll be waiting fo' you to arrive at this end. Victor he tol' me to make sure you comfortable when you get in. He even gone an' left me some travellin' cash fo' yo' too. Yo' ain't gonna need to be paying no mind to any money worries while you here. It's gonna be a pretty tight schedule you is on, so git some sleep on the flight over. Vic says to tell you that he's gonna be waiting fo' you back on your home turf in a few days' time."

I looked at the instructions I'd just written down on my jotter pad and felt my guts churn over when I reread what I was being asked to do. I shook my head as I considered the madness staring back up to me from my own handwriting. I spoke into the receiver, my voice crackling with hesitation, a timbre of suspicion lay heavy in my tone.

"You seem like you got all this pretty well figured out, ain't you, Miss Laveau."

I heard Evangeline Laveau laugh again. "Oh, yeah, sugar, I sure got it all figured out ... Now just don't you go missin' that flight."

It was the last thing I heard her say before she put the phone down on me.

3

It was just after eight by the time I'd finally locked up my office, said my goodbyes to Mrs Pearce and walked out of the gymnasium's main doors on to Grosvenor Road. The moon was still down in the night sky and there was a distant rumble of thunder in the air. My head was filled with unanswered questions and throbbed with a burgeoning headache. My whole body ached; the muscles in my shoulders rolled into tight knots. The skin on my forehead and cheeks felt hot and was dry to the touch. As I walked, I thought about my sister, Bernice, my mind trying desperately to fathom what could have happened to her. The telephone call I'd just taken and the strange conversation with the mysterious American woman, Evangeline Laveau, had thrown little light on the situation. And then there was Vic; the hairs on the back of my neck stood on end as I considered what part he might possibly play in all this mayhem.

No one had heard from my cousin since he disappeared nearly a year ago.

Many thought him to be dead, but I knew that was not the case, and so did his elderly parents, my Uncle Gabe and Aunt Pearl. It was our secret and one which, if required, we intended to take to our graves. Their son had gallantly saved my life, but had paid a high price for his courage. His fearless actions in stopping the bullet that would have torn through my body and killed me had, in effect, banished him to a distant and uncertain existence. On the evening that Vic had shown such nerve and daring, fate had been cruel and bitterly welcome to both of us. In saving my life, Vic had killed a number of corrupt police officers and, in doing so, exposed to the local law his own growing criminal activities. The far-reaching effects of my cousin's valour were now etched deep in my memory.

The police, after an extensive search, had considered him dead; his body never found after he had fallen from the edge of Leigh Woods down into the deep waters of the Avon Gorge. A week after that terrible evening's events, I'd seen Vic, bruised and broken but very much living, as he stood leaning against the railings of the deck of a huge passenger-carrying Fyffe's banana boat, the TSS *Camito*, bound for Jamaica. He had bid his farewell to me with a single wave of his hand and then vanished into a crowd of passengers.

Now, to the rest of the world, Vic was gone. There had been no funeral to lay him to rest, no grave for our community to pay their respects or to lay flowers at, and his memory was only ever spoken of in hushed and deferential tones; the fear of his vengeful duppy never far from people's minds. More than ten months had passed without any word from him. I thought of him daily and missed his presence by my side. When I slept, my cousin would often visit me in my dreams and sometimes, whilst I worked during the day, I thought I heard him speak to me. But these were illusions; vapour-wrapped hallucinations as fleeting and as inadequate as a kiss from a restless spirit.

★

My Uncle Gabe and Aunt Pearl's home was a small Victorian-built, double-bay-windowed terraced house on

29

Banner Road in the heart of St Paul's, which they had rented since Gabe had been demobbed from the army in 1949. I walked through the dark green, slatted-wood gate and made my way up the short path to their front door, knocked, then walked on in. The inside of my aged kin's house was always kept spotlessly clean. The wood floors were scrubbed and polished until they shone, the furniture always dusted, their kitchen neat with not an unwashed pot or pan to be seen. I made my way along the hall, the smell of stewed-down salt fish wafting enticingly at me as it bubbled on the hob of the stove, and found Pearl alone in their small living room.

She was sitting on their ancient purple couch listening to the BBC light programme on the transistor radio. Imitation lace doilies were spread on the arms and headrest of the couch, making the tired-looking settee appear less worn out than it actually was. By the door stood an antique Welsh dresser, its shelves covered with cheap porcelain figurines, worn paperback novels, Bibles and borrowed library books. On the wall above the fireplace were three framed black and white photographs of Pearl and Gabe on their wedding day. All three had yellowed at the edges, but showed a couple as much in love then as they were today.

"Yuh bin drinkin'?" Aunt Pearl barked at me as soon as I showed my head around her living room door. She sniffed into the air like an old bloodhound tracking the scent of an escaped convict. I didn't think I smelled of booze, and I sure hadn't drunk enough to be staggering, but that was a scary thing about Pearl; apart from having the wisdom of her ageing years, the old woman knew me too damn well.

I walked in sheepishly and stood on the rug in front of my aunt with my hands stuck deep into my pockets. "Yeah, I had me a couple 'a shots a' rum."

30

My aunt rose up out of her chair, shaking her head, and stood toe to toe with me, staring up into my eyes like a prize fighter ready to sling that first hefty blow.

"So, why yuh come me home all liquored up, Joseph?"

"It's bin one 'a those days, Aunt Pearl."

"Pickney, it always one o' dem days fo' yuh. What new?"

My head sank to my chest as I dug a little deeper into my overcoat pocket and pulled out the telegram from her son, Vic, and handed it to her. Pearl's face was suddenly filled with a look of disquiet and uncertainty. She held onto the yellow paper telex in her frail fingers for a moment before unfolding it then reached down for her reading glasses which were sat on the arm of her chair. I watched as her lips began to tremble as she mouthed each word that was written on the crumpled sheet, then stood helplessly as she stumbled backwards, falling down into the armchair behind her. She gripped at the telegram in her hands, tears suddenly streaming from her eyes, and called out frantically for her husband.

"Gabe ... yuh 'ear me, Gabe?"

Gabe had heard alright; I listened to my vexed uncle in the next room as he raised himself noisily out of the kitchen chair he'd been taking a nap in, muttering obscenities under his breath as he did. Moments later, he ambled into the living room, a copy of the *Bristol Evening Post* under his arm; his face filled with sleep and puzzlement. He looked at me and smiled then shot a withering stare across to his wife.

"Wha' yuh hollering de house down fo', woman?"

Pearl shook the telegram at her confused spouse. Her voice quivering with a strange mixture of grief and thinly concealed relief. "Look, dis come from de boy. It's Victor, he gan an' wrote."

31

Gabe snatched the telegram from his wife's hand and began to read it. I watched as the old man began to shake his head, his face stony.

"Dear, sweet Jesus, no." I watched as Gabe bit at his bottom lip. His eyes coated with a watery film. He stood silently, staring at the letter in his hand, sniffing back tears that he refused to let fall. He composed himself then looked at me and gently rested the palm of his hand on my arm. "What Vic say happen to young Bernice?"

I shook my head despondently. "I don't know, Gabe."

Pearl wiped at her eyes and cheeks with a handkerchief and shook the telegram at me. "Don't know ... but Vic, he call yuh yes, like he said he would?"

"I got the phone call, but it wasn't from Vic."

"Then who call?" snapped Pearl.

"Some American; a woman calling herself Evangeline Laveau. She called on Vic's behalf."

Gabe slapped his newspaper into the palm of his hand. His face now filled with anger and bewilderment. "What da hell a Yankee doin' making a telephone call fo' Vic fo'?"

"To tell me that I gotta go home, back to Bim."

I saw Gabe's fists ball, the telegram scrunching up inside his hefty fingers. "Barbados? Why yuh going back there? Yuh know dat place only gonna be a world 'a trouble fo' yuh?"

"Like the telegram said. I need to go back an' settle Bernice's affairs."

Gabe gawped back at me in dismay. "What damn affairs? The poor child had nuthin' cept the clothes on her back. What more there to settle?"

"I don't know, Gabe, but none o' this feels right to me."

Gabe stared back at me bitterly. "How can it be right, if Vic be meddlin' in all dis misery from in de shadows?"

Gabe rubbed at his mouth and chin and looked at his wife. "I tell yuh woman, sum'ting not right. What our boy gettin' himself inta now?"

Pearl came and stood next to her husband and took his hand in her own and I watched as she gave it a gentle squeeze then smiled at him. "I don't nuh, but if I know Victor, it'll be most likely trouble he up ta. Same as he bin doin' since he was a pickney."

Pearl shook her head and looked at me. "Yuh stay an' eat with us, yeah?" My aunt didn't give me chance to respond to her request. She left the room without saying another word, only letting go of her husband's outstretched arm when she neared the door.

*

The kitchen smelled of smoke and scorched wood pulp mixed with the welcoming aromas of my aunt's home cooking. Whilst Pearl set the table, Gabe and I set about reigniting the embers in the grate. Firewood had been stacked carefully at the side of the large black range. I collected three logs from the top of the pile whilst Gabe broke up kindling from an old orange crate and placed it in the fireplace under balls of crumpled up newspaper. My uncle took a match and lit the paper and the two of us watched as the kindling caught; a bright red cone of flame curled into the air and began to rise up into the brick chimney. Ten minutes later, we had ourselves a roaring fire. The three of us sat at the kitchen table and ate in silence. Pearl's salt fish stew was as delicious as usual, but I had no appetite and, rather than eat, I simply played with the food on my plate with the tip of my fork. Gabe finally broke our mutual taciturnity, his question to me brutally blunt.

33

"When yuh leave fo' Bim?"

"Tomorrow, first thing. I'm catching an early train to London." Pearl looked up at me in surprise.

"London, why yuh goin' London?"

"To get myself to the airport."

Gabe slapped his knife down on to the kitchen table and looked at me.

"Yuh flyin' ta Bim?"

I shook my head. "No, to New York."

Gabe choked a mouthful of food down, his eyes nearly popping out of their sockets. "New York! Wha' the hell yuh doin' flyin' ta New York fo'?"

"Vic's there. We leave for home after I meet up with him."

Aunt Pearl sat back in her chair, her face pained with worry. "Wha' in the name o' mercy is ma boy doin' over in a place like New York, Joseph?"

"I ain't sure what he's up to, Aunt Pearl. All I know is that Bernice is dead and that Vic somehow needs my help back home. I know he ain't telling me the whole story, and that's why I gotta go find out for myself."

Pearl nodded her head passively at me then placed her knife and fork at the side of her plate, her meal only half eaten. Gabe, his face flushed with emotion, got up out of his seat and walked out of the kitchen. I looked at my Aunt Pearl and took her hand. The two of us sat, paralysed with a grim sense of mutual impotence, and listened as her husband climbed the stairs, his weeping quietly resonating back along the hallway towards us.

A short while later Gabe returned to the kitchen whilst Aunt Pearl and I finished up washing and drying the dishes. He stood quietly behind the two of us, his hushed presence and the feeling of his escaping inner pain searing into my

34

back like the blistering head of a blacksmiths tongs. I turned to face my uncle, who looked down at his feet and shuffled in embarrassment. He remained silent and held out his hand to me; looped between his fingers was a thin gold chain with a locket attached to it. Pearl reached over to her husband, kissed his cheek, took the necklace from him and handed it to me, closing the pendant in my palm and then squeezing my hand. She looked at me and smiled, tears forming once again at the corners of her eyes. "Dis was yuh mutha's, Joseph. Yuh put it close to wherever Bernice's laid ta rest. Then when yuh sorted dis mess out, yuh bring yuh'self an' my son home: yuh 'ear me now?"

I nodded my head, unable to speak. I walked over to the kitchen chair where I'd left my overcoat and trilby, put them on, then returned and hugged and kissed my aunt and uncle. As I walked back down the hall, Gabe called out to me.

I turned back and saw the old man stood in the kitchen doorway, his bulky silhouette highlighted by the light from the kitchen fire behind him. He nodded to me, raised his arm and held up the palm of his hand to bid me farewell.

"Yuh mind yuh step out there, Joseph. Yuh know what dey say 'bout funerals?

"No, whadda they say, Gabe?"

"Dey's always somebody by the damn grave catches his death."

★

It was just after 11.30pm by the time I stepped back onto my waterside home down by the harbour. Inside, the old boat felt cold and damp. I took off my overcoat and jacket and boiled up a kettle of water and made myself a mug of coffee then took a wash and shave in the remaining hot water. I collected together my passport and driving licence from the galley cabinet drawer then fished out a small brown leather suitcase from the storage compartment underneath my bunk, then, just as Evangeline Laveau had instructed me to, I went to the small fitted wardrobe at the foot of my bed and began to pack light. I filled my washbag with a toothbrush and paste, a razor, some spare blades, a shaving brush and soap stick, as well as a bottle of English Leather aftershave and Bay Rum, then sat the suitcase by the foot of the cabin door.

I polished my black brogues, brushed down my trilby and hung my best charcoal grey worsted suit on to the front of my wardrobe door, dropping my favourite Puma penknife into the inside pocket of the jacket. I took a seat on one of the wooden galley chairs and sat staring at my suitcase wondering what the hell I was about to get myself into. I set my alarm clock for 6.30am then, finally succumbing to fatigue, got undressed and crawled into bed, my body cold and shivering. Exhausted by the day with my mind still racing, I eventually allowed the shadow of sleep to welcome me to its bosom. Without my prior knowledge, the slumber I desperately craved would be both fitful and plagued by an unwelcome and spiteful incubus.

*

In my dream, Bernice and I are sat alone close to the waters' edge back home on Ginger Beach. It's a beautiful, sunny afternoon, no different from any other summer's day when we were kids. I feel the comforting heat of the day wrap itself around my body, embedding its warm caress deep inside me. Above our heads, the hot wind swirls through the palm fronds and sends ripples across the surface of the sand at our feet, spitting the grains into the air and blowing them out towards the sea. A will-o'-the–wisp haze surrounds us as I look at my sister, who is motionless, staring down at the gold-coloured ground, her face hidden from my view.

"Will yuh come see me, Joseph?" I hear Bernice's words in my head but cannot see my sister speaking them. Her whispering, brittle voice seemingly spoken to me from an unearthly threshold.

"Come see yuh where?" I ask.

"Here, in the dark place." I hear my sister's voice crackle then listen as she begins to cry.

"What dark place yuh talkin' 'bout?"

"The dark place where it hurts ... I need yuh ta mek it stop hurtin' fo' me, Joseph. Can yuh mek it stop, please?"

"I don't understand. Mek what stop hurtin', Bernie?"

"This ..." My sister looks up at me, her face iridescent with humidity, the tiny beads of sweat falling from her brow. A bullet hole shows wide and deep in the side of her head. The smell of charred flesh and hair seeps up into my nostrils. I want to be sick and feel the bile rise in my throat. The skin across my lips starts to crack and the inside of my mouth dries.

"Who did this to yuh?"

"It don't matter none who did it, Joseph, just why."

I watch in horror as a thin line of blood begins to drip from the gaping wound in my sister's skull and then run in crimson streaks down her face. Bernice smiles at me, the blood and black spittle trickling from the corner of her mouth. I watch as her hand reaches out to take mine and snatch my own arm back away from her, my feet digging frantically into the sand to push myself out of reach of her grasp. Bernice begins to sob uncontrollably, then rises slowly to her feet and stands over me. My fingers grip into the sand and I look up at her and watch as she turns and walks down to the shore and out into the sea. Tears begin to run down my face and I feel my muscles stiffen then lock tight, my childlike body fixed to the ground as I stare helplessly as Bernice wades further out across the reef, her body sinking deeper into the bloodstained, bright-blue water.

As the red-tinged foam and waves strike at the tops of her legs, the sun above her head flares across her back like someone has held a lit match to her skin, blurring her from my weeping vision. The lids of my eyes snap shut as a savage glare erupts across the horizon. When I finally pluck up the courage to look back towards the ocean and the shrinking solar burst, my little sister is gone.

It's my screaming out of Bernice's name that awakens me from my night terrors. I pull myself bolt upright in my bed, arms stretched out in front of me, my fingers clawing at the night air, my eyes searching into the blackness of the cabin of the Dutch barge, hoping to catch one last evanescent glimpse of Bernice's spirit as it fades into a faraway and impenetrable perdition. I shake my head and rub the perspiration from my scalp and face, and immediately feel the sweat-soaked sheet underneath me and the cold air washing across my bare legs where I had kicked off my blankets.

I swing both legs out of bed and rest the twitching soles of my feet onto the draughty wooden floor and breathe deeply, desperately trying to dismiss the aching clutch of fear in the pit of my stomach as being part of the nightmare and not a portent of the uncertain and dark days which lie ahead of me.

4

I needed to catch the 8.27am from Bristol Temple Meads Station to London Paddington. I was up, washed and dressed by 7am. I sat out on deck, a plate of toast balanced on my knee, and ate my breakfast to pass the time. After swilling my breakfast dishes under the tap, I locked up the barge and walked up to Hotwells Road. I hailed a passing taxi cab which got me to the station for just before 8am. After I'd waited at the kiosk to buy a ticket, I went into the newsagent's and bought a copy of the *Bristol Observer* to read on the journey and a half-bottle of Johnnie Walker Red Label whisky, then climbed the stairs and walked along the enclosed overhead corridor towards the waiting train. My footsteps echoed as the soles of my shoes clicked heavily on the hard, wooden flooring. The diesel locomotive was already humming on the rails. I shot along the busy platform and got in. I slammed the door behind me and looked down the nicotine-tinged aisle of the busy carriage. There were about half a dozen passengers all with their backs to me, all frantically searching for somewhere to sit.

I continued to plod along the carriages until I found a seat in an empty compartment. As I sat down, a middle-aged white man slung open the compartment door. He looked at me in shock for a second then hesitated to take another step inside, his confused little brain now working overtime.

Desperate to seek another compartment, he began to

quickly reverse out into the corridor, but his intentions were curtailed by the shoving hand of his enormous wife, who pushed him reluctantly back inside. When she waddled into the compartment and saw me sitting there, her face quickly turned to thunder. The uneasy couple, now at a point of no return, shuffled unenthusiastically around each other in the carriage for a moment, and grudgingly took their seats opposite me. I watched as the woman squirmed up close to the side of her old man, clearly unimpressed to have me as one of her new-found travelling companions. I smiled across at the two of them, but got no response. I leaned back and stuck my hand in my jacket pocket and pulled out the half-bottle of Johnnie Walker. I weighed the glass flask of whisky in my palm for a moment then cracked open the cap, put the bottle to my lips, took a couple of swift nips of the strong caramel-coloured liquor and stuck it back in my pocket. Across from me, the plump, hard-faced woman, who was probably in her mid-sixties, stared back at me in disgust then scowled over at her mousey-looking husband, who had by then taken out his copy of *The Times* and was tearing open the pages of the paper to begin reading.

I smiled to myself, shuffled across my seat and leaned against the window, waiting for the train to depart. Warmed by the alcohol in my belly, I closed my eyes and let myself relax a little. A short while later, the locomotive began to pull away and we slowly rolled out of Temple Meads. I watched the city streets start to roll past. Each blue-tiled building had its back turned awkwardly towards the train lines. It offered me a steady view of rusting drainpipes, condensation-saturated kitchen windows, damp laundry hanging on washing lines in red-brick yards and badly maintained gardens.

Thirty or so miles into my journey, an inspector, resplendent in his new blue British Rail uniform, opened up the carriage door and stepped inside. He gave me a chary look, then switched the bearing of his character and politely asked the passengers opposite for their tickets. The man facing me lowered his enormous newspaper and reached into his jacket and presented the inspector with the requested travel passes. The toady official gave the tickets a perfunctory glance, then swiftly punched each piece of card, returning them to the passenger with a fawning upper body bow and another toothy grin. He turned to me and immediately lost the air of courteousness. He stuck his arm out and unfurled the palm of his hand in front of me like an expectant hotel doorman awaiting a generous gratuity.

"Ticket." I looked up at the churlish rail official then slowly raised myself a couple of inches off the seat and stuck my hand in the back pocket of my trousers and pulled out my wallet. I opened it up, took out my train ticket and handed it to him.

The conductor looked at it warily. "Where you alighting, sonny?"

I heard myself sigh loudly. I scratched irritably at the back of my neck with my fingernails then gestured idly with my head towards the card pass the dour rail man held in his hand. The innate accent and patois of my early years rolled up from my voice box and began to trip off my tongue.

"Just where it say on there."

The conductor stunned by my tetchy response took a step back. He rolled his shoulders defiantly, and squared off his hoary body at me. "Don't you give me any of your lip, sonny Jim."

I sat back in my seat. "You ain't gettin' any lip. You can read, can't ya? Every'ting you need ta know is printed on the front o' that ticket, mister."

My vexation started to bubble up and began to fester beneath my chest. My anger barely curtailed, I looked back out of the window at the rain-soaked terrain and down towards the deep railway gully that the fast-moving train was racing past. I glared back up at the inspector who was still examining the ticket like I'd just stolen it from a member of the landed gentry. I snapped up at him like a mongoose snarling at a circling cobra.

"Hey, fella, are yuh gonna punch that ticket o' mine or yuh gonna tek it away an' git it framed fo' me?"

The inspector lifted my ticket up in front of his face and snapped a hole in the left-hand corner then slung it down into my lap. As he began to walk out of the carriage, he muttered some obscenity under his breath. I watched him as he stood and glared backed at me from the carriage of the train. One look into his rancorous old eyes told me the whole story of what he truly felt about a man like me.

*

It was just after lunch by the time the train pulled into Paddington. I handed in my ticket to another fusty-looking collector on the platform and walked through the barrier out to the front of the station. It was my first time in London and the busy city immediately put me on edge. Heavy rain poured out of the sky on to the granite pavements and the old stone buildings around me. The downpour hammered down onto the fast-moving and hunched-up folk who rushed past me, their wet heads bent down, eyes averted from each other, their fixed and jaded expressions stating they wished they were somewhere else. I pulled my trilby over my face, crossed over the road and began to walk briskly along a lengthy office-filled avenue called Chilworth Street.

Two minutes later, I found myself standing outside a pub that was within spitting distance of both the taxi rank and the Tube station.

The Cleveland Arms hadn't been open for its afternoon business for long. It was the kind of place I knew I had no right stepping into, but I had time to kill and the lousy journey, combined with the way I had been treated by the inspector and my fellow travellers, had put me in a peppery mood. Despite my immediate wariness to step inside, I needed to get out of the rain and slake both my thirst and my ill temper with a pint. Inside, the tatty ale house truly lived up to my wary expectations. Staggering by the door, a ruddy-faced chap, clearly already the worse for booze, attempted to stab pennies into the thin aperture of a fruit machine. The drunk lifted his head up from the slot machine, gave me a pie-eyed once over, then spat a thick wad of green phlegm onto the cheap threadbare, patterned carpet. The place looked almost empty, was dimly lit and stank of stale cigarette smoke, sweat and stagnating ale.

Across the room an old man was nursing a half-pint of bitter, his head stuck inside the *Racing Post*. He sat next to a mean-looking elderly woman who was dressed in a lime green trouser suit and scuffed, strappy, high-heeled sandals. She gawped at me as I stood in the doorway, then nudged her old man, who ignored her; his only interest being the inside pages of his betting rag. The badly dressed harpy crossed one leg over the other then looked me up and down and sniffed indignantly into the air. She shook her head in obvious disgust at my being in the same room as her, and lifted a partially drunk pint of mild up to her mouth. The old girl took a swig of her beer and dropped the glass back on the table leaving a smear of cheap crimson lipstick around

43

the edge. She watched me warily as I casually walked over to the bar.

I rested my suitcase down on the floor and nodded a friendly greeting to a young fella who was sat on a stool next to me. The man reeked of what he'd been drinking. I watched as he truculently bit at his bottom lip with the tip of his tooth. He stared blankly out at the spirit optics in front of him, taking no notice of either my presence or my expression of goodwill.

Further down the bar, a big-set man, who I assumed to be the landlord, sat counting out a pile of one-pound notes onto the brass top. A scrawny barman was leaning against a large, ornate Fullers Brewery mirror, polishing a jug-handled glass. He looked about twenty years old, but had the kind of icy veneer etched across his mug that told the world and me that he'd been in a bad mood since birth. His pock-marked face was gaunt and his deep-sunk eyes were haggard and cavernous. On top of his pointy head was a well-greased mop of dark hair, the sides slicked back from the temples, the heavy quiff at the front of his scalp stuck thick with Brylcreem. I looked over at the surly barman to try and get a little service. When he didn't move, I pointed at the hand-pull beer pump in front of him.

"Pint of stout, please."

The barman looked at me, then over to his fat boss who was still counting the cash. The young bartender cleared his throat loudly to get his guvnor's attention then, when he had, slung his thumb in my direction. "This coon 'ere wants a pint of stout. That alright wi' you, gaffer?"

The fella on the stool next to me clearly liked the term *coon* and threw his head back and gave a short, hard laugh. He lifted his glass to his mouth and sank the remainder of his whisky then looked across at me, his fists balled, his eyes filled with enough hatred to fire up a Ku Klux Klan rally. The landlord ignored the cackling customer at my side and looked me up and down suspiciously. He tapped his chubby fingers rapidly next to his mounting stack of dough as he considered his skinny minion's question.

The landlord shot out his arm and stuck his index finger in the direction of my face: "We don't want no nig-nog trouble, you 'ear me?"

I slowly nodded my head. "Sure. Yuh ain't gonna git no trouble from me, mister. It's just the pint I'm after."

The landlord gestured at the barman with a flick of his head. "Just the one then. Alright, Keith, give the sambo his drink."

Keith the barman reluctantly let his arms unfold. He reached out under the counter for a pint mug and made his way to the ceramic handpumps and grudgingly began to pull my pint. A few moments later, he slid the filled glass across the bar towards me with his scrawny fingertips. I stuck my hand in my trouser pocket and drew out some copper and silver change and spread it out across my palm.

"How much?" I asked without looking up.

"One an' ten."

I gave the barman the correct money, thanked him, then put the rest of my change back in my pocket, picked up my suitcase and went and found a seat in the enclosed snug on the far side of the pub, where I hoped I would be able to drink alone and in peace. I sat down on one of the red velvet cushioned seats, tipped my trilby to the back of my head then rested myself against the wall and took a long swig of my stout, sinking half the pint in a couple of gulps. Outside, in the main bar, I heard the jukebox being fired

45

up. *The Tremeloes'* 'Even the Bad Times Are Good' began to play through the cheap speakers above my head. I took another swig of beer and thought to myself how much I hated the song. I looked down into the dregs of my glass and considered going back to the bar and chancing my arm for another. I shook the stupidity of such a thought out of my head then heard the snug door creak open. The chuckling whisky drinker from the bar had decided to crawl away from his usual place at the watering hole and come and join me. Stony-faced, he strode over and stood in front of the table then stuck a tobacco-stained finger in my face.

"This ain't no nigger's watering 'ole. Sup up an' sling ya bleedin' hook."

I sat my glass on the table and looked up at the man. "I beg your pardon?"

"You heard me, sambo. Sink what's left o' that fackin' jungle juice an' piss off!"

The man stepped back to prove he meant business. He thought the movement would make him look tough, but all it did was to make him look stupid and slow.

He foolishly bent down towards me to offer up a more intimate show of force and to let me smell his nasty, whisky-soaked breath.

"I won't tell you again, coon. Git your arse out that door."

The man snatched up my beer glass and threw it against the wall. I saw a flash of red erupt across my eyes and felt myself quickly sink down low in my chair. As the man went to grab me I squared off my right shoulder and hit him hard in the stomach. My fist buried itself deep into his sternum. Spittle flew up from his mouth and slung itself across the tabletop. I shot up out of my seat and rained a hammer blow down across his left eye. I saw the skin break against the bone and well with blood. The man tried to regain his balance and raise himself up and take a swing at me, but I yanked him back up, slinging him sideways by the scruff of his neck and drove another heavy blow into his ribs. I watched as he dropped to his knees between two short bar stools. His bottom lip and chin dripping with blood which had begun to run from the deep laceration across his temple. I kicked at his shoulder with the sole of my shoe, knocking him to the ground. I wanted to stomp on his head with the flat of my heel but my wrath was suddenly sated by an overwhelming feeling that my luck was about to run out. Filled with a hearty sense of self-preservation, I hastily picked up my hat and suitcase from the floor and stepped over the subdued bigot writhing on the carpet. I coolly walked out of the snug and headed for the pub door. The fat landlord was half-heartedly crossing the bar. A fistful of cash in one hand and a cut-down pickaxe handle in the other.

I bolted out the door and hit the street like a greyhound out of a trap. Panic rushed through every fibre of my being. I sprinted across the road and headed for the taxi rank on the other side of the street. I jumped like a mad man into a black cab and slung my suitcase on the seat beside me. A startled elderly driver turned from the wheel of his car and nodded his head at me.

"Where to, mate?"

"Heathrow Airport, please."

"Heathrow, it is." I heard the driver turn the key in the ignition and the engine fire up then the motor quickly accelerated away from the curb. As we sped off down Chilworth Street, I turned around and looked out of the back window of the taxi. Behind me I saw both the landlord and skinny barman come to a halt in the road. They stood like a pair of shop window dummies and watched as the taxi drove me out of their reach. I saw the landlord sling the pickaxe to the ground in temper and kick it towards the gutter. I turned back to face the driver and slumped back against the leatherette seat. My heart was beating in my chest like a jackhammer. Sweat poured down my brow. I let my breathing begin to slow and closed my eyes for a moment. As we headed across London, my weary body began to relax. The pounding underneath my ribcage had begun to diminish and my raging pulse had slowly calmed. I took a deep breath and looked back out of the window of the taxi onto the capital's busy, rain-soaked streets. As the black cab navigated its way through the heaving traffic and my body started to unwind, my mind gradually freeing itself of the memory of my earlier hot-headedness and brutal behaviour back at the pub. My lightened repose was to be short-lived, as I suddenly became aware that I'd never set foot inside an airport nor had I ever flown on an aeroplane.

5

A light fog had begun to close in over the runways at Heathrow Airport. Cold drizzle carried on the wind washed against the glass as I looked out of the windows of the Oceanic Terminal towards the various aircraft lined up on the tarmac. Behind me, thirty or so passengers waited patiently for the next flight to be called. I'd been sat at the end of a row of interconnecting red cushioned seats since just after 2pm. I glanced at my wristwatch; it was 3.45pm; still another two hours before takeoff. My palms and under-arms were damp with sweat at the thought of getting onto the plane. I stared down at my shaking hands and felt the backs of my legs quivering. My breath tasted sour and trembled in my throat each time I inhaled.

I looked at the bustling terminal; the check-in queue for one airline snaked beyond the restrooms and the lifts which led down to the baggage claim area and out past the entrance of the main building before making a dogleg that stretched almost to the corridor leading to the next terminal. The stream of people wasn't moving much either. I watched as the queue of travellers kept getting longer, a conga line of disgruntlement and frustrated passengers replete with all manner of pained expressions and muttered complaints. People slumped forward carrying heavy baggage like Atlas trying to hold up the world, all maintaining a death grip on the handles of their various luggage. As time, and the line, stretched on, they sloughed their suitcases from their gripping palms and were reduced to nudging them along with their feet, as if prodding a recalcitrant pack mule down a stony trail.

I continued to gaze around the vast sterile expanse of the airport departure lounge simply to try and take my mind off the approaching aerial adventure which loomed heavy in my mind. I tried to read my copy of the *Bristol Observer*, bought cheap coffee from a vending machine and a bar of chocolate which I stuffed into my pocket and didn't eat. I paced the building like a soldier on guard and obsessively clock-watched until I was sick of seeing the hands aimlessly tick away minute by minute. I finally forced myself to return to my seat and then sat with my head in my hands looking through splayed fingers down at my feet, which tapped nervously on the black and white chequered floor.

At just before 4pm, as instructed by Evangeline Laveau, I walked across to the BOAC Cunard desk to collect my travel documentation and ticket. A blonde woman, attractive and in her early twenties, stood behind a chest-high counter. I watched as she wrote on a lined pad with a blue-ink biro. When she had finished scribbling, I cleared my throat to get her attention. The woman looked up from her desk, took a double-take when she saw my face, then gave me a one-eighth nod and a frigid grin.

"Can I help you, sir?"

I returned the smile. "Yeah, I'm hoping so. My name's Joseph Ellington. I believe you have a ticket reserved for me on the 6.45 flight to New York?" The woman, caught off guard by my statement, flashed me a wary smile then cleared her throat.

"Mr Ellington, you say?" I nodded my head back at the circumspect desk clerk. The expression on her face a little flintier than when she'd first clapped eyes on me. "Right, one moment sir, I'll see what we have for you over here."

The blonde got off her seat and walked across to a grey office filing cabinet. I watched her open the top drawer and begin to riffle through its contents then pull out a large white envelope. She returned to her work station and tipped the contents out in front of me. "Here we go." The clerk cautiously leafed through the various paperwork on her desktop, separating the different documents with nimble fingers then looked back up at me, the expression on her face less severe than it had been.

"So, we have one return ticket, BOAC flight 117 to New York and I have a currency release for you to sign." She tapped her hand on the counter. "Could I have your passport please, Mr Ellington?"

"Yeah, of course." I stuck my hand into the inside pocket of my jacket and pulled out my passport and slid it across the counter towards the attractive airline ticket clerk. The young woman picked it up and opened it then read the details inside. She looked up from the passport and scrutinised my face for a short while then returned to the open travel warrant to look again at my photograph pasted inside.

"That all seems to be in order." The clerk handed my passport back to me then fanned out two white sheets of printed paper on the counter in front of me and placed her biro on top of one of the documents. "If I could just ask you to pop a signature at the bottom of each of these forms. We can then release the American Express traveller's cheques which have been left with your ticket."

I did as I was told and signed both sheets of paper on the dotted line and pushed them back across the counter. The blonde checked the paperwork I'd just slapped my name on then studied my ticket for a moment. I saw her shoulders shrug slightly before she looked back up at me and offer another of her comforting smiles. When she spoke, there was a hint of surprise in her voice. "So, you're seated in first class, Mr Ellington."

I stared back across the counter, my mouth agape, my jaw almost touching the Formica top.

"Say what, miss?"

"You'll be travelling with us this evening in the first-class section of the aircraft; a window seat, 6A." I stood staring up at the desk clerk, still trying to process what she'd just said to me. I tried to talk but my throat had seized up.

"Are you alright, Mr Ellington?" I nodded back up at the bemused airline official.

"Yeah . . . Yeah, I'm fine, thanks." The clerk leaned across the counter and handed me the white envelope, clearly eager to get rid of me. "Here's your tickets and currency, sir."

I stuck my hand inside the envelope and looked at the ticket and then fingered through the book of American Express cheques. I counted each of the $100 cheques twice. $1,500 in total. I thanked the clerk again, then staggered from the desk. I folded the envelope and stuffed it into my jacket pocket, then walked slowly across the terminal to the huge glass window that looked over the runway and stared back out across the wet tarmac at the darkening sky. My cousin Vic was clearly prepared to pay a high price to get me home. I just couldn't work out at that moment what the cost might be to me when I arrived.

*

With my suitcase checked in and stowed away onboard the jet airliner, I sat alone in the BOAC departure lounge for another hour and a half, my head filled with trepidation at the thought of the ensuing flight, my thoughts occasionally focusing on the huge wad of cash in my pocket and what kind of roguery my damn cousin Vic might be involved in back home. By 6pm everyone onboard my flight had been escorted down to Gate 3. I sat staring into space, waiting for the flight to be called amid the stares of at least two dozen or so perplexed first-class passengers. At precisely 6.30pm, we were informed over the tannoy that the plane was ready to board. I watched a few passengers rise from their seats before getting up and making my way along a labyrinth of corridors towards a covered concourse which led down to the aircraft. A young female flight attendant, wearing a blue dress with a red bow and high-heeled shoes, stood at the door of the Boeing 707 and smiled at me. She held out her slender palm by way of a greeting as I walked inside.

"Welcome aboard, sir."

I thanked her then handed my boarding card like a schoolboy handing over an illicit note to a teacher. The flight attendant gave the card a cursory glance then ushered me towards my seat at the front of the plane. Inside, the aircraft was truly an impressive beast. Every traveller, it seemed, was to be treated as an explorer in opulent luxury. I looked around and took in the subdued lighting and felt the air-conditioned ventilation cooling my face. I followed the attendant along the cabin, which was already filling with passengers, each taking their plush seats in relative silence. The interior colour scheme was pale and muted, the carpeted walls which flowed down to the floor plush and warm, the décor a mixture of chrome and American chintz. I was shown to seat 6A and sat down nervously next to the window. The cabin resonated with the excited chatter of boarding passengers. A handful of the stewardesses mingled between the passengers, assisting and greeting. Each was a sexily stunning mixture of pure 'Coffee, Tea or Me' professionalism. They resembled avian goddesses, their graceful demeanours showing no haughtiness; just a crisp, competent cheeriness normally befitting the manner of a well-meaning doctor or your favourite school teacher.

One of the pretty attendants stopped in the aisle next to me, smiled and leaned across my lap. I watched as she gracefully collected up the seat belt at the side of my seat and proceed to fasten me in. She rested her arm on the headrest in front of me and opened up the overhead compartment and pulled out a red blanket and pillow which was wrapped in a clear plastic bag. The stewardess handed me the bedding and gestured towards my feet with her head.

"Here we go, sir. Just pop these under your seat for later. It can get a little chilly during the night."

I did as I was told and bent forward, stuffing the blanket and pillow out of sight with the heel of my shoe. Ten minutes later I heard the large cabin door shut. I immediately felt my lungs begin gasping for air. I don't know which made my heart panic most: the intrusive search through my bag earlier or now being strapped to my seat by a tight belt.

The massive airliner began to reverse away from the terminal then slowly taxi across the concrete towards the runaway. Six or seven minutes of gentle cruising across the tarmac and the Boeing came a sudden halt. Out of nowhere, the engines kicked in and started to roar. The aircraft suddenly surged forward and accelerated. The huge aeroplane shuddered and rattled, I closed my eyes and gripped the arm rests of my seat in fear, the tips of my fingers almost poking through the expensive leather upholstery. The aircraft lifted off the ground and the engines began to scream out loudly. The plane began to lumber into the air then started to make a wide circuit, gathering height as it crossed over Heathrow and the surrounding towns and villages.

As we climbed higher, through the din of the engine I heard the mechanical whirring of the front wheel being lifted up into the undercarriage of the fuselage, a heavy thump underneath me as it found its place underneath the wings, the flaps closing angrily behind. I suddenly felt my ears block as they filled with pressurised air. I swallowed hard and kept gulping until they finally popped and the buzzing sensation in my head disappeared. I was still clutching onto the arm rests for dear life with my fingertips, the inside of my mouth as dry as sandpaper. I nervously stared out of the window and immediately wished I hadn't. Despite dusk quickly approaching, I could just make out the ground a few thousand feet below me. My stomach turned over. I took a deep breath and snapped my eyes shut and sank my head to my chest, my chin resting heavily against my body. The sound of my thumping heart echoing inside my head.

Fifteen minutes later and the plane began to finally level out, but I still felt as jumpy as hell. I nervously peered out of the window again and looked out through the darkening sky. A striking sunset began to fall in the dimming early evening sky and not being able to pick out the ground below me as easily somehow calmed my nerves. I watched as one of the cabin staff approached me. She offered a friendly "Good evening", then proceeded to lift a small extendable table from the seat next to mine and opened it out at my side. A china plate was then sat on top, along with silver cutlery and a white linen serviette. In front of me, flight attendants had begun to serve chilled champagne in crystal goblets and bring trays of canapés to each of the passengers. I was stunned to find out that everything on offer to me was completely complimentary. While some stewardesses handed out an array of finger food, others sauntered along the aisle and casually served up the first of the free booze on offer; booze which I soon found out would just keep on coming throughout the flight.

I was comforted by the fact that I could drink as much of the stuff as I damn well pleased and it wasn't going to cost me a penny. If nothing else, knocking back glass after glass of rum would settle my nerves and keep me entertained in a partially drunken but happy stupor for the rest of the flight. Around me, passengers began to light up cigarettes, pipes and cigars. I coughed as I took in a hefty nostril full of tobacco smoke. The idea of being sealed up in a metal cylinder of nearly everyone's second-hand fumes wasn't my idea of fun, but from the look of all the grey smog smouldering above my head it was a necessary evil I'd simply have to get used to.

A young stewardess came down the aisle and stood at the side of my seat. She was holding a silver ice bucket with a huge green bottle sticking out of it. I could just see the pretty gold and purple label on its side. It was a stamp that smacked of being both exclusive and expensive. "Champagne, sir?" I nodded politely and watched as the stewardess lifted out the heavy bottle from the bucket and pour me a goblet full. I watched the bubbles rise hypnotically in my glass, then swigged half the sparkling wine back and winced as the acidic vino hit the lower part of my throat. I quickly grabbed a shrimp vol-au-vent off the plate on the tiny table at my side and stuffed it into my mouth to try and get rid of the tart taste.

I rolled my shoulders and tried to relax a little, stared around the aeroplane cabin and watched the other passengers eat and drink. It appeared that I was the only black man onboard. Back home on Barbados, if you saw a black person at an airport they were almost definitely a porter, not a passenger. The idea that a person of colour would actually get on board an aircraft and be able to fly on it was thought to be almost absurd. Only white people flew. On Bim, the average white fella was paid nearly five times as much as his coloured counterpart, and since air travel was still such a luxury for many, few black folks could afford to take to the air.

In the next two hours I was afforded every luxury. Rounds of drinks were brought to me at varying intervals, along with a three-course luncheon which I picked at. I sat back in my plush seat and listened as the Boeing whispered through the night sky. Three hours out of London and I had tired of edgily looking out of the window into the blackness of the night sky. It began to dawn on me that flying was both scary and boring: I was sealed in a droning metal tube for over eight hours and I was then expected to just sit there, staring at the back of the seat ahead of me and possibly get blind drunk on free drink. I looked down the cabin at the other passengers who all appeared to be smoking and drinking, many using their in-flight time to either write letters or postcards to folk back home on the ground, describing their trip and the wonder of the flight, or reading magazines, newspapers and books.

From the galley I watched a stewardess wander along the cabin, a tray of empty coffee cups in one hand. She moved slowly along the aisle, checking on her passengers. Around me, some of my fellow travellers were swaddling themselves in comfy blankets, each shod in airline-embossed slippers. Here and there I could see the brighter lights of reading lamps, some silhouetting businessmen poring over company papers and journals and, behind me, a mother reading a novel, her sleeping children gathered at each side of her, faintly conscious of the aircraft's vibrations and the distant murmur of its engines.

The cold, stale air from the vent above my head had begun to make me feel nauseous and chilly. I bent down and pulled out the bedding I'd been given from under my seat. I removed the red fleece blanket and pillow from the plastic bag and wrapped the blanket around my body. It felt prickly but warm. Then I reclined my seat all the way back and wedged the tiny white pillow somewhere between the armrest and the window and put my head down. I closed my eyes and tried not to think about the fact that I was suspended in a luxury metal tube more than six and a half miles up in the air, nor the amount of distance I still had to travel before I finally reached my home. As I lay huddled up with the blanket tucked underneath my chin, my arms and legs became heavy and I suddenly became light-headed. The effects of the alcohol I'd consumed starting to work its dark magic. The cool, air-conditioned breeze spun its icy shadow against the side of my face. A dull weight descended over my body, it latched on to my weariness then drew me slowly towards the slumber I craved so desperately.

6

The BOAC Boeing touched down on the asphalt runway of John F. Kennedy International Airport at a little after 11.45pm. The landing of such a huge aircraft had felt light and effortless, my fears of being up in the air finally allayed as the powerful jet taxied towards the huge glass and steel structure of terminal building one. The flight, whilst long and tedious, had passed without incident. I'd thankfully managed to get a few hours' sleep under my belt, spending the remaining few hours reading a handful of glossy brochures about the famous East Coast city I was soon to arrive at and watching an old Abbott and Costello movie. For the first time, a gentle shudder of excitement crept through me as I thought about arriving in the United States. Butterflies hung in my belly like a child excited by the prospect of finding presents on Christmas morning. I'd not felt such a feeling since arriving at Southampton docks three and a half years earlier.

After disembarking from the Boeing, I followed the rest of the first-class passengers along a maze of plush-carpeted corridors and ceiling-to-floor glass-panelled walkways, and waited for fifteen minutes at immigration to show my passport to a port authority guard. I then stood around for another twenty minutes for my suitcase to appear from behind the partition wall of the baggage bay. My eyes began to sting as I watched my case finally trundle along a lengthy and noisy circular carousel towards me. From there I humped my one piece of luggage over to customs and queued once again to have my bag opened by one of the surly-looking immigration officials. Finally, my turn came and a spotty young man, in his mid-twenties with a severe crew cut, turned-up top lip and a sparse blond moustache, which gave him the expression of a belligerent hamster, called me over to his waist-high work space with the crooked end of his thorny-looking index finger. I walked up to the white Formica counter, lifted up my suitcase and laid it on top in front of the inspector.

The official cleared a frog from his throat then laid the palm of his hand out in front of me. "Passport, please." I dug inside my jacket pocket again and handed over my travel document, then watched in silence as the customs officer began to leaf through its pages. The airport bureaucrat sniffed indignantly a couple of times as he studiously read my personal details then snapped the passport shut and sat it next to my suitcase, finally sliding it back across the counter towards me with the tips of his fingers. I then watched as he flicked up the brass clasps of my case, opened it and begin to methodically rummage through my clothing and wash kit, examining the contents of my bag with the scrupulous determination of a prison guard. The youthful customs officer looked up at me with an insincere smile. "What's the purpose of your visit to the United States, sir?"

I watched his mouth form the words around a huge wad of gum that he was chewing. "I'm visiting my cousin and his friends here in New York for a few days before we all travel on to Barbados for a family funeral."

The customs man nodded his head slowly to himself, digesting the answer I'd just given him. He sniffed to himself again then looked down inside my case for a while longer before quickly dropping the lid down and pushing it away to the side of him. "I'm sorry for your loss, sir. Welcome to the United States." The official did not make eye contact with me again. He looked over my shoulder and waved me along with the back of his hand, pushing out his uniformed arm and beckoning the passenger behind me to approach the counter with their luggage. I did as I was told, moved out of the way and attended to my case, quickly closing the clasps. I lifted my case down off the counter and turned to face a large, unfurnished, frosted-glass partitioned, barren-looking room. I looked around me and noticed a sign to my left with the word Arrivals printed in bold, black lettering. A large arrow pointed towards two double swing doors on the other side of the room. I walked across the black and white chequered floor, put my shoulder to the edge of one of the swing doors and heaved myself and my well-inspected case through it into the unknown. What I found waiting for me on the other side fair took my breath away.

*

The strikingly beautiful black woman stood out amongst the sizeable crowd of white folk that were stretched out in an excitable line in front of me. I saw her eyes lock on to mine, then I watched as she broke out of the busy throng of waiting souls and began to walk across the arrivals lounge towards me. I headed across towards her, the two of us finally coming to a sudden halt only a foot away from each other. The woman's heady perfume hit me at about the same time her mischievous smile did.

"Mistah Ellington?"

I nodded my head. "Yeah, that's me."

61

The woman, continuing to hold me in her gaze, held out a gloved hand towards me in greeting. "I'm Evangeline Laveau, pleased to meet you."

"Likewise." I reached out and took hold of her hand then immediately felt the cheeks of my face heat up and my stomach flip unexpectedly as our palms intertwined to welcome each other. Evangeline Laveau was dressed top to toe in black. A black leather trench coat hung over her slender shoulders, underneath it she was attired stylishly in a tight-knit woollen skirt and sweater, black stockings and high-heeled, knee-high leather boots. Her thick black hair was held back in a bun with what looked like a pair of ebony chopsticks. In her left hand she held a silver-handled, polished cane, her petite fingers encased in expensive Italian leather gloves. She was no more than thirty-five with a thin, graceful body that appeared almost gaunt, her breasts barely discernible beneath the heavy folds of her expensive sweater. A gold clenched-fist medallion hung around her neck on a simple chain. Her eyes were cat-green, set in a warm, angular Creole face. They burned out at me beneath dark, heavy brows. Our grasp instinctively broke way with the sudden, hushed appearance of a huge black man who came up and stood directly behind Laveau. I looked across at him and watched as his massive head moved in a slow side to side sweep of the floor around us; his eyes scanning the building from behind silver-rimmed military-style sunglasses. Laveau ignored the man's presence and continued with the pleasantries.

"So, you have a good flight?"

"It was my first." I watched as Evangeline Laveau's face suddenly broke into a look of surprise.

"Really? Your first time? Must 'a bin a real thrill, yeah?"

My face secretly flushed with embarrassment again. "No, not really, I spent most of it scared witless and sinking as much free booze as I could lay my hands on."

Laveau smiled again and took a step forward to look up at me. "So, you're a gumshoe who's scared to fly, eh?" Her voice had a husky Yankee drawl to it, with an added icy vibration to its timbre that sent chills deep down through my shoulder blades and into my gut.

"I've been called a lot of things in my time, but never gumshoe."

"That right? So whadda ya like to call yourself, Mistah Ellington?"

I rubbed at my chin and mouth nervously with my fingertips. "Well, it says *Enquiry Agent* on my office door, but I'm just a guy who's paid to snoop around. My cousin Vic calls me JT, but most folk call me Joseph."

"And what 'bout the scared part, Joseph?"

"Oh, I get scared all the time ... I just try an' hide the fact." The mute black fella let out an all too brief snigger that he quickly reined in after Laveau glared back at him bitterly. I heard her take a deep breath and watched as she raised her arm up towards the big man and held the palm of her hand out in front of herself.

"Joseph, I'd like to introduce you to my right-hand man, Clefus Hopkins." Laveau stood to one side and the sizeable black fella walked out from behind her and took a couple of steps forward to greet me. At well over six and a half feet, Clefus Hopkins' hefty frame hung over me like an unwelcome threat. He nodded his huge head then outstretched his arm and I reached and took his big mitt in mine. His thick fingers gripped tightly at my palm as we shook a brief, wordless greeting. Like Evangeline, Laveau's bodyguard was also dressed to impress, kitted out in a navy blue cashmere coat with hand-stitched lapels and patch pockets which were unbuttoned to reveal an expensively cut dark blue, soft chalk flannel suit. His shirt was hidden by a black silk scarf which was looped around his sinewy neck. A wide-brimmed black felt fedora was pulled low over his shaded eyes. Hopkins had a broad, blank-looking pockmarked face which was made more severe looking when he smiled at me; two striking gold caps covering each pointed canine shone like miniature suns between his otherwise pearly-white teeth.

"Should we get you back to the car? A three an' a half thousand-mile journey is gonna knock the wind outta most folk; let's git you back to the hotel. You must be dead beat?"

I nodded my head in agreement and felt the palm of Evangeline Laveau's hand gently cup itself underneath my elbow. "Clefus here will take your case." The muscle man leaned across me and carefully prised my luggage from my weakening grip. As we began to walk across the airport terminal towards the main doors, I was hit with an overwhelming sense of weariness. Evangeline Laveau hooked her arm through mine and the two of us followed Clefus Hopkins out of the arrivals building and into the New York night. The air smelled fuggy and alive; a mixture of petrol fumes, damp pavements and musky body odour. Light rain fell from the evening sky and mixed with a gentle warm breeze, which blew against my face as I was guided along a concrete concourse down towards a black Cadillac limousine, which was waiting directly outside the arrivals building.

The huge motor sat idling on the kerbside, its headlights blazing, the strafing beams gleaming out in front of the bonnet, the windshield wipers clicking back and forth.

Clefus Hopkins snatched the handle of the rear door of the limo and opened it up for Laveau and myself, then walked round to the trunk of the car, popped the boot and dropped my case inside. He came back around to the front passenger door and heaved his huge muscular frame inside. Evangeline Laveau got in and slid herself across the leather upholstery then tapped the palm of her hand on to the seat next to her. I climbed in and fell back into the plush seating of the flash motor, then caught sight of the fella up front.

Sat behind the wheel of the car cleaning his fingernails with a tiny silver-handled penknife was a severe-looking, clean-shaven black man, no more than thirty years old; the only distinguishing feature on his blank face was the pencil-thin scar that ran in a jagged line from his temple down the left-hand side of his face to the edge of his smooth, chiselled jaw. Scarface looked backed at me suspiciously through the rear-view mirror and made a sucking noise through his clenched front teeth but quickly diverted his eyeballing gaze when Clefus Hopkins opened up the passenger door and sank down into the seat next to him. Hopkins looked at the driver and grinned his gold teeth at him, then looked over his muscular shoulder at me.

"The ugly brother 'ere giving you the evil eye name's Pigfoot." The flinty driver shrugged off Hopkins' cruel introduction with a stiff nod of his head and continued to stare out blankly through the car windscreen into the night. Pigfoot sat in silence. He didn't look bored, nor did he look impatient to make a move, he just looked like a man who knew that waiting was part of his job. I saw Clefus Hopkins gesture with a sharp nod of his head towards the driver. Pigfoot fired up the ignition on the Cadillac, swung the car out into the road and hit the gas.

As we drove out of the airport and onto the highway, a wave of heavy fatigue began to wash over me, the muscles in my neck and back tightened, my arms and legs stiffening, becoming like lead weights hanging desperately from my tired limbs. My eyes misted over and started to water. I wiped at them with the back of my hand and yawned again. I turned to Evangeline Laveau and watched as she moved herself smoothly across the back seat, then leaned her lithe body in close to mine and smiled at me. I got another hit of that intoxicating perfume and the heady scent of the patchouli oil in her hair as she nestled in next to me. I watched as she brought her arm up towards my chest and begin to run the back of her hand along the side of my arm, finally bring her palm to rest on the back of my hand.

"It's only a short drive into Harlem. Enjoy the ride, baby. Vic wanted you to be taken real good care of."

"Oh, I bet he did."

Laveau's eyes widened a little, clearly unimpressed with my weary sarcasm. "You must have a lotta questions, Joseph?"

"A few, like where the hell is my cousin for a start?"

Evangeline Laveau smiled again and moved in a little closer towards me, her hair brushed gently against the side of my face and her lips touched the side of my ear as she whispered into it, "You'll git all those answers in the morning, honey. That's a promise." Evangeline's hand squeezed onto my arm and I felt the comforting warmth of her body against my own. A strange hollow feeling surfaced inside my chest. I swallowed hard as I listened to my heart pound away. It felt like fear, but not a fear I'd ever experienced before.

As the car accelerated, I turned and looked out of the window and watched the orange flare of street lights flit past me, blurring against road signs I could not read. Ahead of me in the distance I thought I could just pick out the iridescent glimmer of the night time Manhattan skyline. I tried to speak but no sound would leave my mouth. My eyes twitched and jumped and began to sting again, the lids becoming heavy. I shook my head from side to side and fought to keep my self awake, I did not wish to go gently into the night; I wanted to rage against it, to remain conscious and in control and not allow the sandman to have his way. The car rocked me with its speeding lullaby and, like ash in the wind, I once again succumbed to a nocturnal slumber I could no longer make truce with.

7

The world came back into focus slowly as I opened my eyes. My heavy lids blinked madly as I tried to acclimatise myself to the new surroundings I had woken up in. My ears echoed with a dull hum and my head felt light and otherworldly, like a shadow stalking itself into new-found light, my conscious self struggling to drag itself out of the heavy dream state I had been dwelling in. I rubbed at my face then saw the sunbeams that were creeping through a gap between a pair of large dark purple window drapes. The thin rays cut through the duskiness of the strange room and were lost in the dimness behind me. The room was hot, the air stale and clammy.

I was lying on my side in a large double bed, the mattress soft and comforting underneath my sweating body. My legs were nestled in among a bunch of tangled sheets and blankets, my arms underneath the covers, the crisp linen tucked around my back and buttocks. It all felt very slumberous and sensual, but I had no memory of how the hell I had got there.

"Sleep well?"

I turned over to face the voice speaking to me. "Yeah, like a log."

Evangeline Laveau stared down at me. My memory may have been shot, but I easily recollected the beauty standing over my bed. Laveau was dressed head to foot in black leather, a black beret was pulled down tight across her head and was pulled down low across her brow, the gold clenched-fist pendant she'd been wearing previously was again hung around her neck, the charm cosied up at the base of her cleavage. She smiled then sat down on the bed next to me and slid her hand across the mattress. "That's good cus you got a real busy afternoon ahead of you."

I looked around the room to try and find a wall clock. "Afternoon, what the hell time is it?"

"Mistah, you managed to sleep until almost noon!" A man's voice boomed above my head. Heavy footsteps stomped across the room and then I heard the dramatic swishing sound of the window drapes being drawn back. I looked into the brightness and saw the huge frame of Clefus Hopkins standing in a halo of sunshine. I raised myself up onto my elbows and looked around what appeared to be a snazzy-looking hotel room.

"How did I get here?"

"I carried yo' sorry black ass inta bed, that's how!" Clefus Hopkins stood away from the large bay window and grinned at me, then walked back across the room and stood with his back against the door. Evangeline laughed, hitched herself across the bed, placed her finger underneath my chin and stroked at the stubble with a long, manicured red nail.

"Flying an' moonshine, they don't mix, baby."

"What?"

"I'm talkin' 'bout all that hooch you sank whilst gittin' over here and the time difference. You got yourself a nasty case o' jetlag. Dead to the world before we crossed the Kennedy Bridge."

I rubbed at my eyes and stared up at Evangeline. "I'm sorry, everything's kind of a blur. I remember getting into the car last night then the rest's just a blank."

"Ain't no need to go apologising. Everything's cool. Like we promised you, you're gonna be well looked after during your short stay with us. Welcome to the Hotel Theresa. If it's good enough for Castro, it's damn sure good enough for Joseph Ellington."

Laveau laughed and got up off the bed. With my head resting against one of the pillows, I watched as she slinked her way across the floor towards a large wardrobe. She hooked the fingers of her right hand around the lip of the door and opened it up to reveal a collection of men's clothes hanging neatly from the polished brass rail. Laveau brushed the back of her hand admiringly across the clothing.

"Your cousin Vic called an' gave me some idea of your measurements. Hope none of it's too snug. I chose it myself." She smiled again then closed up the wardrobe door and walked back across the room to join Clefus Hopkins. "We're gonna leave you to freshen up and change. Be back for you in an hour." Hopkins and Laveau turned and began to walk out of the room.

I quickly sat up, leaned my back against the velour headboard and called out after them, "Where we going?"

Evangeline stopped in her tracks and looked back at me. "You're goin' to church, baby. Sending you uptown. We're gonna find you a little sweetness on 135th Street."

★

The bathroom was white-tiled and shone with a pristine newness, the likes of which I had never seen before. The perfume of lavender and newly cut flowers scented the air. I walked into a large glass and ceramic cubicle and showered under hot water, the sharp spray knocking the life back into my soporific soul. I shaved then toweled myself dry and went

70

back into the other room and opened the wardrobe. Inside I found a selection of silk ties, three cotton short-sleeve shirts in white, light blue and cream, along with three pairs of worsted trousers in dark grey and brown and lightweight casual jackets to match.

Unsurprisingly, everything I tried on fitted me. I'd always known that blood was thicker than water and Vic had sized me up well, but then again, my devious cousin always could. I put Vic out of my mind and changed myself into a white shirt, pulled on a pair of grey strides, slipped on my brogues and tied them, then looped a navy blue tie around my neck and knotted it smoothly underneath my Adam's apple. I splashed my favourite English Leather aftershave on my face then took a grey jacket from off its hanger and slipped my arms into it and stood in front of the mirror and admired my new look. As I stared back at myself, I caught sight of the small half-inch scar again and thought of Bernice. The circumstance of her sudden death was still a mystery to me, my painful reverie of her loss suddenly brought into focus by the old wound. My sister's death and Vic's sly methods to get me to the States had become unwelcome, hidden ushers, latent relatives drawing me into another clandestine realm I knew I had no place venturing towards. My destiny was in the hands of the dead and the morally impure.

As promised, within the hour Evangeline Laveau and Clefus Hopkins were back. I picked up my raincoat and trilby and followed them down an elegant hallway and into an elevator which took the three of us down four floors to the hotel lobby. Laveau stuck her hand into her jacket pocket and handed me a brass key which was attached to a silver fob with the number 216 etched into the centre of it. "Here's your room key, you'll be needing it later. Don't go losing it now." Evangeline winked at me and strutted on in front.

Clefus Hopkins nudged me in the ribs with his bulky elbow and laughed. "I see that look on yo' face, brother. Shit, yo' betta watch it, you'd be fuckin' with a heavyweight there. She eat you up an' spit you out fo' sure, niggah."

I stopped in the middle of the lobby to ask Hopkins what the hell he was talking about, but the big man was already moving away, chuckling to himself, his vast shoulders rolling back and forth as he walked out of the hotel's main doors.

Outside in the street, pulled up on the kerb side, its engine running, was the flash-looking Cadillac that I remembered picking me up from the airport the night before. Clefus Hopkins was still sniggering to himself as he stood by the open rear door of the car. I climbed in next to Evangeline and the bulky minder slammed the door shut behind me. Hopkins got into the front passenger seat and looked across at the driver then back at me, a big smirk running across his face, the gold caps on his teeth glistening menacingly.

"Don't tell me all that airline booze made you go an' fo'git 'bout ole Pigfoot 'ere too?" Pigfoot ignored Hopkins and sat picking his teeth with a wooden toothpick. Laveau smacked her hand on the back of Hopkins' seat.

"Enough of this shit!" Laveau sighed heavily and sank back into her seat then looked over at the scar-faced driver. "Pigfoot, drive."

Pigfoot obediently nodded his head back at Evangeline. "Yes, ma'am."

"So, are you gonna actually tell me where we're heading to?" I asked.

"The MAME."

I shrugged my shoulders at Laveau. "Say what?"

Laveau grinned playfully back at me. "The Metropolitan African Methodist Episcopal Church, on a Hunnerd an' Thirty-fifth, just like I'd said."

I shook my head slowly in disbelief. "I don't like being messed with, Evangeline. Something about all this..." In the rear-view mirror I caught Pigfoot giving me the evil eye. Evangeline Laveau smiled at me and shuffled nervously in her seat then offered her hand on my sleeve by way of reassurance.

"Ain't nobody messin' with you, Joseph. It's just like I told you last night. You gonna git the answers you lookin' for real soon. Have a little faith."

"I gave up on faith a long time ago."

"Well, maybe faith ain't ready to give up on you just yet."

*

The brightly lit frontage of the Metropolitan African Methodist Episcopal Church came as a real shock. It didn't look like any kind of place of worship that I'd ever set foot in, more like a swanky motel than a house of the Lord. We parked up on an unpaved lot next to the church and Clefus Hopkins got out and walked around the other side of the car and opened up the door for his boss. Pigfoot switched off the ignition and pulled up the handbrake before opening his door. He turned to address me for the first time, his eyes shifting from the simple pleasantries expected of a driver to the deadly intent of a lethal assassin with barely a twitch. When he spoke, his voice resonated with a familiar sounding deep Bajan accent. He pointed with his finger back towards the church.

"The Obeah inside there, he wanna tell yuh sum'ting real

important 'bout yuh kin folk. Best yuh listen good to what he gotta say. Understand?"

"What Obeah?" I looked back at Evangeline Laveau. "What about my family? What the hell's this guy talking about?"

The driver leaned forward and grabbed hold of my jacket lapel, pulling me hard towards his face. His rank breath hit me full on. It smelled of a foul mixture of stale reefer and sweet Parma Violets.

"The woman know nuthin'. Your bid'ness is back there wid the Heartman. Yuh best not keep him waitin'." Pigfoot let go of my jacket and I snatched myself back away from him. The scar-faced Bajan turned back and looked blankly out of the car windscreen across the lot. I flung open the door and pulled myself out of the back of the car and walked across the lot to join Laveau and Clefus Hopkins, who were waiting for me out in the street. Hopkins gestured with his head towards the direction of the church.

"Let's git this crap over with, Evangeline. You know how much I hate this voodoo shit!"

We walked the short distance along the pavement to the steps of the makeshift church. Hopkins climbed the steps and opened the door, allowing me and Evangeline to enter first. Inside, a gaudily decorated lobby greeted us. Several large crucifixes hung at various heights from the walls, religious gold icons and brightly painted biblical statues adorned a series of black velvet tables which resembled the gothic shrines of a less enlightened time. The whole place reeked of the pungent odour of burning incense sticks, the cloying hum catching the back of my throat, forcing me to hack like a sixty-a-day smoker.

On the far right-hand side of the lobby, leaning against a

waist-high wooden counter, stood a Creole woman in her late fifties. She had large breasts and slim hips and emphasised them with a pink angora sweater and tight black pencil skirt. Her hair was pulled back from her forehead in a ponytail, the tight curls of a combed-out afro escaping from a tussle of copper-coloured ringlets. As we approached her, I could see that her bright, azure-tinted eyes flickered and wobbled from side to side. The woman looked out across the room as if unable to make actual eye contact with us, her milky white pupils darting uncontrollably in all directions. Clefus Hopkins turned and pointed his finger at me.

"This man here has an audience with the Obeah."

The woman's face grimaced and contorted as if it were possessed by demons. She took a step forward and directed her racing eyes towards me. "Yuh Ellington?" Her voice was distinctly Bajan, the timbre and lilting tone almost identical to my sister, Bernice's. The uncanny similarity poleaxing me for a moment. The woman broke me from my trance-like contemplation by snapping her question back at me. "I ax yuh if yuh Ellington?"

"Yeah ... yeah, that's me. I'm Ellington."

The woman turned her head away from me and raised her arm and pointed with her a crooked index finger across to the far side of the lobby. As she held her arm up in the air, I could see that it was the only finger that remained on an otherwise cruelly butchered hand. "Yuh tek da elevator. Fourt' floor. Room 444. Yuh need ta knock on da light switch when yuh go in. Obeah be in da back room. Only da Bajan go in."

As the three of us made our way across the lobby, we passed a small group of elderly black women, all dressed in black clothing, each was sat silently around a small green baize table reading from small leather-bound Bibles. The women didn't look up as we walked past. The elevator doors were made of hardwood with hand-carved gilt inlay in the centre of each. Clefus Hopkins pressed a button and we all stood in the lobby in silence, waiting for a car to come down from one of the floors above. A few moments later, a muted chime sounded and the elevator doors opened. Hopkins held open the door for his boss with the flat of his hand. Evangeline Laveau slinked her way past her bodyguard and I followed. The inside of the elevator car was old looking but still stylish with lobster-pink velvet walls. An ornate crystal chandelier hung above our heads, the low-watt bulbs offering a hazy glow rather than a burning bright light. The fittings inside were all gold-plated and well-polished. Hopkins pressed one of the buttons on a panel on the lift wall and I watched the doors close up swiftly, like a scared snail drawing itself back inside its shell. The car's elderly winch mechanism kicked in and we began to climb slowly. I closed my eyes for a moment and breathed in deeply, glad to be free of the choking whiff of incense. As I sniffed in the new air, I got a hit of Evangeline's expensive scent, the heady perfume filling my nostrils and making my head spin a little. The elevator ride was brief, the lift came to a sudden halt and the three of us got out on the fourth floor. This had a wide landing interspersed by numbered room doors which looked like they were made of heavy oak. Evangeline turned and smiled at me, she held out her hand to her left then began to slowly walk down the hallway. Against my better judgement, I continued to chase Laveau's tail down the dimly lit landing. On either side polished brass light fittings adorned the length of the flock-papered walls, the carpet a complex design of purple and gold squares.

We found room 444 midway down the hallway. We stood outside for a moment then Clefus Hopkins gave a single knock at the door and stepped into the darkened room, and that's when the stench hit us. Clefus turned and looked at Evangeline and me, his face puckered up from the putrid smell. "Shit, this damn place is as funky as a fat man's drawers!"

I watched from the landing as Evangeline Laveau's minder ran his hand along the wall, the room barely came alive when Hopkins finally knocked on the light switch. Two tiny wall lamps offered little by way of a warm welcome. I followed Hopkins and Evangeline inside. The place steamed like the inside of a slaughter house. I covered my mouth and gagged and watched both Laveau and Hopkins heaving into their palms. At the end of the room was a large sash window, the panes of glass covered with oiled brown paper. A coal-burning pot-bellied stove was unlit, its grate still filled with ash. A white porcelain washbowl was plumbed in on the back wall, a rusting tap jutted out from the wall above the tired-looking sink. A ceramic blue and white pitcher sat on a small square table next to a double bed with a white enamelled frame sat in the left-hand corner of the room. The only covering on the bare wooden floors was a threadbare rug. Four white candles flickered on saucers set at each of the corners. To the left of the bed, a line of dull light showed under a closed door. I went over to it and knocked.

"It open," a voice called.

I turned the knob and looked into a small, bare room. Sat in the corner on a huge cushion on the floor was an elderly black man. An odour of sweat and sadness hung in the air. I walked in, leaving the door open. The only illumination came from a dingy skylight above my head, which offered sufficient light for me to see the old man's face, which had the cracked complexion of the hide of a dead alligator. The old fella looked up at me and smiled.

"Mistah Ellington?" Another Bajan accent hit me. This time croaky and whisper-like. The voice made me feel like I was truly back home.

"Yeah, that's me."

"Sit, Mistah Ellington."

I did as the old man asked, crouched down on my haunches and sank my buttocks onto the wooden floorboards. The old Bajan drew himself forward so that his face was lit a little by the skylight above us.

"Yuh po'liceman on Bim, yeah?" the Obeah whispered at me.

I nodded my head back at him in the semi-darkness. "I was, some time back."

"Yuh jus da overseer's lackey, yuh?"

"I've bin called worse."

The Obeah laughed to himself hoarsely then spat back at me quietly. "Overseer, white master, po'liceman... Monroe!"

"Wha? What did you just say?"

"Yuh hear mah, Mistah Po'liceman. Hear mah good. Yuh recollect dem name outta yuh past like a dog sniff outta a bitch's pussy on heat."

The sweat began to rise under my arms and on my back. The droplets slowly ran along my skin, soaking into the fabric of my shirt. "What do want with me? Why have you brought me here?"

The old man drew himself back into the shadows. "Da Heartman call yuh 'ere. Me, I'm just his messenger."

"An' what's the message?"

78

"Yuh is as impatient as yuh is petulant, Mistah Ellington ...
Ere's the word I bin ax ta serve upon yuh."

I watched the old man's arm reach out of the gloom and
slide something across the floor towards my feet. I let it sit by
my shoe for a moment then grabbed up the object and held it
in my shaking hand underneath the dull glow of the skylight.
It was a strangely shaped box, weighing no more than a few
ounces and some eight inches long. I held up the box, moving it
closer towards my face, my eyes slowly becoming accustomed
to the lack of light. I turned the box at an angle, catching a thin
arc of light that rained down faintly from the glass ceiling lamp.
Between the tips of my fingers was a white, alabaster coffin. I
spun it around so that the lid was facing me. I could just pick
out a gold-painted pentangle etched into the stone. I looked
back into the dark.

"What is this?"

I heard the Obeah sigh heavily.

"Only a fool ax a question like dat. What yuh need ta be
axing is why yuh bin given it."

"And why I have I?"

"Right man, right time."

"You're not making any sense."

"Da sense yuh looking fo' come from inside dat casket. It
ain't fo' my old eyes ta know 'bout it. Jus' yuh. Yuh open it
when yuh leave. Nah be on yuh way, po'liceman."

I heard the old man's breathing become crackly and
shallow and then felt the room suddenly become cold. I
stuffed the coffin into my jacket pocket and drew myself
onto my knees and leaned forward towards the Obeah.

"I was told you may have information about my family,
perhaps about the recent death of my sister. What do you
know?"

79

I could hear the rasping sound of the witch doctor's erratic breathing. I stuck my neck out a little further into the blackness. The Obeah shot his head out towards me, his face only inches from my own.

"She in the flame wid the rest o' yuh kin folk. Mind yuh tek care when yuh reach out to drag 'em from dem fire, yuh sure ta be pulled in ta burn wid 'em, fool."

I watched as the old man fell back into an obscure, veiled world I had no wish to explore. I heaved myself to my feet and slowly backed out of the room into the light. I closed the door and rested my shoulders against it, locking away the madness held within. When I finally found the strength, I walked back and rejoined Evangeline and Clefus Hopkins. All that I could hear were the searing cries of my wife and children screaming in my ears.

8

Evangeline Laveau, Clefus Hopkins and I took the short elevator ride back down to the lobby without uttering a single word to each other. The putrid stink from room 444 lingered in our nostrils and on our clothing like ripe pig shit in a pen. I put my hand into my jacket pocket and gripped at the Obeah's strange gift he'd bequeathed to me. The alabaster coffin suddenly felt fiery hot in the palm of my hand. Surprised by the heat, I snatched back my hand, leaving the gypsum box inside the dark recess where it so clearly wished to remain. I looked down at my hand and rubbed at a small blossoming red weal that began to swell in the centre of my palm. The tiny welt stung when I touched it. I clenched my fist open and shut in quick succession to try and numb the hot throbbing pain, but it did little good. When the lift door opened, the one-fingered woman was standing at the reception desk waiting for us. She looked at Clefus Hopkins, hawked up a wad of phlegm from her throat and spat it out on the carpet at his feet. "Yuh find what yuh lookin fo' at dem Harlem river houses on West One Fifty-six, 'partment t'ree. Vic, he say ta give da money to de Bajan ta bring him."

I watched Evangeline's eyes dart suspiciously at Clefus Hopkins before addressing the woman. "You can have Mr Ellington's payment when we collect the merchandise, just like we always do."

81

The woman shrugged her head towards me. "Like I say, dis time de Bajan tek it ta Vic."

Evangeline took Hopkins' arm in her hand and drew him closer to her. "Go out to the payphone on the corner and make the call. Get the merchandise picked up, tell the guys we'll be there shortly; make sure everything's in order, then they can take it to Minton's. Got it?"

Clefus Hopkins nodded and pushed past the woman and walked back across the lobby and out into the street. Evangeline turned to me and smiled. "Okay, we can go. Our business here is done."

She began to make for the church doors; I grabbed hold of her elbow and yanked her back. "Like hell are we done."

Evangeline snapped round on her heels, ripping her arm from my grip. "Don't fuck around with me in here, brother. Take ya shit out back to the Cadillac in the lot."

Laveau swung around and stormed towards the exit. I followed her sheepishly out into the street and back to the Cadillac parked at the side of the church. Evangeline tore open the back door of the limousine and gestured savagely with her hand for me to climb aboard.

"Git in the fuckin' car!"

I stood my ground, shook my head and pointed a finger in Laveau's face. "Not until you start playin' straight with me, I ain't."

"Play straight? You some kinda fool? Baby, ain't nuthin' 'bout this shit that's straight. I ain't 'bout to start talkin' my fuckin' business with you out here in the damn street. You wanna talk to me, git in the motor!"

Laveau spat out her words like she was chewing on poisoned food. She eyeballed me with the look of the devil, then snatched at the door again. I shook my head to myself, the stark realisation that I wasn't going to get my way now staring me in the face. Evangeline Laveau spoke again through gritted teeth. "Haul it, Joseph."

I submitted to the woman's will and bad temper and did as I was told and got inside. Laveau quickly followed, slammed the door to and looked over at her Bajan driver. "Pigfoot, slide up the glass, brother." I watched the scar-faced chauffeur flick a switch on the dashboard then settle back into his seat, his beady eyes watching me through the rear-view mirror. A frosted glass partition slowly rose out of the leather upholstery, sealing Laveau and me in the back in private. Laveau stared back at me, her face like stone.

I bit at her like a crabby adolescent. "What the hell you got going on here, Laveau? Why's my cousin gettin' cash sent to him by you and your damn cronies?"

"We got ourselves a business agreement!"

"The only bid'ness my cousin deals in is the bad kind, an' from the sounds of things, I'm about to get my sorry ass dragged into some of it again."

"You've mistaken me for someone who actually gives a fuck 'bout what you an' yo' kin git up to!"

I moved in a little closer towards Laveau and felt the hackles on the back of my neck rise and my fist clench in fury, my fingernails dug into the tender weal on the palm of my hand, making me wince. I was about to lose it when Clefus Hopkins flung open the door next to me, stuck the top half of his massive body inside and heaved me back against the limo seat.

"What the fuck is goin' down here, niggah?" I flailed my arms about and tried to struggle out of the big man's clutches but that only got Hopkins angrier. He pinched at my neck with a vice-like grip, sending a shooting wave of violent pain up into my skull and down my back. Evangeline Laveau slammed her hand against the passenger door.

"Enuff o' this shit! Let the brother go, Clefus." I felt Hopkins' grip on my neck loosen immediately. I shook myself out of his grasp and straightened my collar and jacket whilst the minder hung over me, waiting for his next order. "Clefus, git up front an' git Pigfoot to drive us over to the projects. Tell him to play it cool and keep his foot off the damn gas."

Hopkins reversed his bulky frame out of the back of the car and got into the front seat. I watched Pigfoot listening to Hopkins' orders then felt him fire the Cadillac up and circle the big motor in the lot and drive carefully back out onto the street and slowly start to accelerate up the road. Evangeline Laveau looked across at me. "Let's go git those answers you keep axin' me 'bout, fella. Maybe then you'll cool that bad vibe you got runnin' up yo' ass."

I shuffled irritably in my seat and looked out of the window. "All I'm asking for is the truth."

"Well maybe you axin' fo' too damn much, brother!"

I heard Evangeline Laveau suck air sharply through her front teeth. It sounded like a razor blade slicing through silk.

★

We drove slowly in the dimming afternoon sunshine, the Cadillac entering the segregated mid-realm of Manhattan at an almost funereal pace. I looked down at my wristwatch, it was just after 3.30pm, then continued to look out of the now open window of the limousine at the varying styles of old brick and wood-slat buildings that made up such an infamously neglected area. I saw children playing on pavements and in the gutters, their laughter echoing after us as we travelled past them. Woman chatted to each other on door fronts or leaned against shop fronts, whilst elderly negro men sat outside of slum clubs and corner bars, playing cards, dominoes or craps. To me, as a black man, the streets appeared to have a friendly feel to them, almost homely, but it was also clear as we motored along the pot-holed, unmaintained road, that this was an isolated and much discriminated neighbourhood, the residents of this clearly deprived district of such a wealthy city observing, perhaps, that those who dwelt in the rundown urban ghetto of Harlem were mysteriously as dark in skin as the area was in the minds of their white supposed betters.

The Harlem river houses project on West 156th wore its old age badly. A veil of springtime green floated like a cloud over its many tired courtyards, where the plane trees grew higher than the seven small red-brick apartment buildings that the Cadillac pulled up outside of. A large truck was parked up a little further along the road. The four of us got out of the car and Pigfoot walked over to the lorry and began talking to the driver in the cab. I stood on the dusty sidewalk and looked along the street at seven five-storey homes that ran the length of the road. Each block of apartments was arranged in squared-off serpentines with intricate concrete pathways that spurred off in all directions. Many homes had their windows boarded up; litter was strewn everywhere, graffiti etched on the walls of homes that had never seen a lick of paint or a mop in years. The place was nothing more than a bricked-up maze, the perfect setting for any kind of festering criminal activity. I felt right at home. Clefus Hopkins stood at my side and flashed his gold teeth at me, then pointed over to the rundown tenements. "Welcome to the projects, Mistah Ellington. They sure are sum'ting, ain't they? You know, African-Americans weren't allowed to rent these damn places till 1933. When niggahs finally got inside these rat 'oles, they wus payin' top dollar fo' the privilege, an' they still coughin' up the same big bucks to dis damn day!"

"Something's never change, Joseph, and that is the truth!" Evangeline Laveau joined the two of us on the pavement to admire the squalor of the shabby buildings just as Pigfoot returned and walked round to the trunk of the car and opened it up. Even with my back turned to him, I could guess what he was doing. I heard the all too familiar and unwelcome clack of a metal sliding against metal as a cartridge casing was chambered into a pump-action shotgun, then I watched as the taciturn Bajan took off down one of the concrete paths towards apartment number 3 with the lethal firearm hung lazily in his right hand. Clefus Hopkins stuck his hand in his jacket and pulled out a black, lacquered Colt .45 and chambered a round into the breach. He winked at me as he weighed the pistol up lovingly in the palm of his huge hand. "You can never be too sure 'bout these island monkeys. Those niggahs'll stiff you quicker than shit through a goose!"

Hopkins laughed to himself, holstered the pistol, then followed after Pigfoot. Laveau walked on after him then turned to me. "Answers you lookin' fo' are in that apartment building down there. You ain't gonna like what you see, but at least it's the damn truth." I trailed on down the path after Evangeline Laveau, my stomach as heavy as if it had just been lined with concrete.

Two black men stood guarding the entrance of the ground-floor flat. Inside, the apartment the floor was pitted linoleum, light blue where it had kept its colour, grey where it had worn through. Wallpaper had been stripped away to reveal clammy, punched-out plasterwork. I walked into the centre of the room and looked around at the hovel that was disguising itself as a home. There was a card table for dining and a fold-up plastic chair for a seat. A light fixture above the table had a sixty-watt bulb flickering in it. Empty beer cans, used syringes and cigarette ends littered the floor. To the left of me was a kitchen big enough to house a small man with a stooped back. Shelves that were once cabinets hung in lopsided fashion on damp, mildew-tainted walls. A few chipped, blue earthenware mugs sat on top of them. Below the makeshift shelving, a stained, cream-coloured ceramic sink was filled with mouldy plates and bowls, a single, cold water tap dripped lazily onto rotting dishes. A rusting hot plate rested on the draining board and various items of worn-out cutlery were strewn next to it. These seemed to be the only luxuries on offer.

From what I could see, all the interior doors had been torn off from their frames and burned as firewood. The place stank of piss, illicit sex and stale ganja. At that moment in time, the four of us were the only folk about, but I was pretty sure the place came alive after dark. Clefus Hopkins and Pigfoot had already walked through into what I could only imagine to be the bedroom. Evangeline prodded me sharply in the back with her fingers. "Go take a peek inside there, Joseph."

I walked nervously across the sticky floor to join the two other men in the next room. Clefus Hopkins and Pigfoot stood in the windowless room next to three wooden pallets. On top of each pallet were stacked around fifty or more large hessian sacks. The room recoiled under the intoxicating perfume of well over a ton and a half of top-grade marijuana.

87

"Ah, Jesus Christ." I shook my head in disbelief, then squeezed my thumb and forefinger across my tired eyes and pinched sharply at the bridge of my nose.

Clefus Hopkins laughed. "Niggah gotta mek a dollar, brother."

I continued to shake my head and turned around and found Evangeline Laveau standing in the doorway.

"So now I know why there are more damn Bajans in these parts than back home." I pointed back at the sacks of hemp. "This is how my cousin is making a living is it, supplying our island's grown sinsemilla to you?

"Not to me, brother. To the BPP."

I shrugged my shoulders back at her. "What the hell is the BPP?"

"The Black Panther Party," Clefus Hopkins' thunderous voice interrupted from behind me. "The Panthers are a revolutionary group. One that's waging a racial war against the state."

"Vic's supplying drugs to revolutionaries. You gotta be kidding me."

Laveau joined Hopkins and Pigfoot by the pallets of grass. "Joseph, we're more than just freedom fighters. We speak out for the oppressed black man and woman. We have four simple desires: equality in education, in housing, employment and civil rights, and we aim to get those liberties at any cost."

"That's all very noble, but I still don't get what it's got to do with me."

"It doesn't concern you one bit. Only your current situation involves us."

"My current situation? I don't understand?"

"Look, we pay your cousin Victor to supply us on a

monthly basis with enough Panama Red to knock out more the half the Eastern Seaboard. Revenue from the sale of this hemp funds our cause. It's as simple as that. We've never had a problem with supply or payment since we first starting trading with your man more than six months ago. Two weeks past, I get a call from Vic. He tells me that the next shipment of merchandise would be coming in today and that the cost would be the same. The only thing that would differ is how we stumped up fo' it. Said that you would be flyin' and we had to treat you real special. Didn't say how we'd actually make the payment though. Well, now we know. From what that one-fingered witch said, it looks like you gonna be your kin's new bag man."

I ran my fingers through my scalp and pinched at my temples with my fingertips. "He must be insane."

Laveau shook her head. "Oh, far from it, Joseph. I think your cousin is playin' with a very full stack. The brother's got himself a very tight operation going down. Very cool, no jive, never any slip-ups. Always a different venue fo' each drop, never stiffs us on the merchandise, and he uses his own people here in the States to make sure things run real smooth. He even loans us ol' Pigfoot here as a special kind of security."

"Oh, I bet the hell he does." I looked across at Pigfoot and the 12-gauge, pump-action shotgun sat in his scrawny black mitts and felt my guts tighten.

I looked back at Laveau. "An' what 'bout all that shit that has just gone down back at that shifty chapel we just left?"

"The MAME? You tell me, superdick, 'cause I ain't got a fuckin' clue!" I felt my hand run down my side and touch my jacket pocket and the alabaster coffin inside. The stone box now felt as cool as a tide-washed pebble in between the cloth and my palm. Hopkins smacked the side of one of the bales of dope with the palm of his hand.

"We need to git this shit shifted outta this cesspool and off the street."

Laveau nodded her head in agreement. "Git it loaded up and see you back at the club." Laveau turn to me and smiled. I felt that heavy feeling hit my guts again. "Come on, Sam Spade. I promised you a little sweetness earlier. I think it's 'bout time you got to sample it!"

I hadn't a clue what the woman was talking about. I watched as she walked out of the apartment. I felt my mouth turn dry and my heart thumping away in my chest. I looked back at the mountain of cannabis stacked up behind me and sighed until I had no more exasperated breath to expel. I thought for a moment about Vic and what kind of mayhem he was about to get me into then, resigning myself to an unknown fate, slowly followed Evangeline back out into the street, like a dazed lamb being taken off to the slaughter.

9

The huge sign hanging over Minton's nightclub on the corner of Lenox Avenue in Harlem read God Gets the Glory and was illuminated by what had to be over a hundred tiny white light bulbs. Pigfoot had pulled the Cadillac up on the pavement outside of the club's main doors and, although it was only just after six in the evening, a queue of black folk were already lined up halfway down the street trying to get in. Laveau leaned across towards Pigfoot. "Park her up then come an' join us, okay?"

The Bajan driver offered up a nod. The two of us climbed out of the back of the Cadillac and watched the motor drive off down the street. Laveau hooked her arm through mine and walked me across to the club. A young, well-dressed coffee-coloured man stood on the gate door and smiled a toothy grin at the two of us. "Evenin', Miss Laveau."

Laveau gracefully pulled her hand out of her coat pocket and slipped a folded banknote into the doorman's eager hand. "Good evenin', Fenton."

Fenton beamed back at her and swung open the door for us. "Thank you, Miss Laveau. You two have a good evenin', now."

The muffled hum of music throbbed as we climbed down a thin, poorly lit stairwell and walked through two heavy double doors into the dusky subterranean speakeasy. Inside the club was plush and dark. A haze of cigarette smoke hung in the spotlights that glowed in the arched recesses of the cellar walls. There was a comfortable enclave of black folk socialising, teasing, drinking and playing pool. The booze-littered tables around the bandstand were crowded with couples. Men getting up close and personal with their women, their bare arms glittering in a rainbow display of sequined strapless dresses, sat listening to a three-piece blues band. Laveau and I walked over to the bar and she perched herself on a stool. The bartender, a stout negro with greying temples and hangdog eyes, sauntered over and wiped the bar clean in front of us with a soggy cloth.

"What'll it be?"

Laveau didn't hesitate with her order. "Give us a couple 'a cold Miller's."

The bartender left then returned with two long-necked bottles of beer. I stuck my hand in my hip pocket and pulled out a fold of notes. The bartender looked admiringly at the cash in between my fingers.

"Be two bucks an' a quarter, bro."

Laveau looked at the bartender disapprovingly and pushed one of the bottles down the bar towards me without taking her eyes off him. "Put ya dough away, Joseph. I'll run us a tab." The bartender nodded at Laveau apologetically and went back to mopping his worktop. She raised her bottle and chinked the neck against mine then put it to her lips and sank half the beer inside; she swung around on the stool and threw both arms out in front of her, a huge smile bursting out across her face.

"Sweetness, my man!" I turned and saw a fat black man in his early sixties swaying towards us. The tubby man clapped his hands then rubbed them together gleefully, before taking hold of Laveau's fingers and kissing the back of her hand. The big man looked his guest up and down lustfully. "Miss Laveau ... yo' is a sight fo' sore eyes, sister. Always a pleasure ta have yo' visit ma place." The jovial host pawed at Evangeline Laveau's fingers a little longer then turned his attention to where I was standing. "An' what a' we got ourselves 'ere then?"

Laveau wrestled herself out of the big man's slimy grasp and stood up off the stool to introduce me. "This is Mistah Joseph Ellington; he visitin' all the way from England."

"A limey niggah, in my place? Shit, never thou't I'd see the day."

I stuck out my hand. "Pleased to meet you, Mr Minton."

Minton took my hand and shook it. His grip was pasty and weak. "Call me Sweetness, son. Practically every niggah in Harlem does."

Arnett "Sweetness" Minton had a friendly face as broad, dark and wrinkled as a slab of cured beef. His forehead was flecked with droplets of sweat; above his brow a thick, curly afro was the colour of cigar ash. He filled a shiny, tailored Italian silk suit to bursting point; his huge feet encased in a pair of shiny two-tone winkle-pickers. He backed himself up against the bar between Laveau and myself and shouted over his shoulder at the barman to pour him a double bourbon on the rocks. A sudden smile split his dark face when he saw Pigfoot approaching across the floor towards us. The nightclub owner took a couple of steps forward as Pigfoot drew in close and laid out the palm of his hand in front of the Bajan.

"Hey there, ugly brother, you gotta gimme five!" Pigfoot, unimpressed with Minton's comment about his face, drew himself up to his full height, tensed his shoulders then, realising he was being played, sighed impatiently and visibly

93

relaxed. I watched as he slowly held out his hand flat in front of Sweetness and the two men laid some skin on each other. Minton pushed the tetchy driver for a repeat greeting. "Now, gimme ten, yuh gimme twenty." Sweetness suddenly snatched his hand away, letting Pigfoot's palm fall through the air. "I would give you thirty, but ya ass too dirty!" Milton roared and slapped his knees, the rings on his stubby fingers flashing underneath the dim lights. Pigfoot's face looked like it was about to explode with rage.

Minton chivvied back at the Bajan. "Muthafucka ... Pigfoot, would it hurt yo' ass ta smile once in a while? Damn, you gotta mug like a pig pissin'!"

Sensing Pigfoot's displeasure, Evangeline Laveau stood in between the two men in an attempt to dampen some of the heat that was being generated. To diffuse things further, she turned to the portly club owner and squeezed hold of the side of his arm. "Sweetness, baby ... how's that lazy, good fo' nuthin' brother o' yours doin'? He still wid dat skanky wop out at Queens?"

Sweetness Minton's top lip turned itself up in disgust at the very mention of his kin. "That stupid muthafucka, he nevah gonna change. Proposed to that Eyetie bitch four damn times already, said he would leave his wife and kids and convert from Baptist to Catholic. Shit, you know that's gotta be some mean pussy to make a man change gods like that."

Laveau laughed and moved in closer to the club owner, stroking the side of Sweetness's perspiring cheek. "Baby, we is famished. Can we git ourselves one o' your tables at the back o' this joint an' git sum'ting ta eat?"

Minton hooked his head back and cocked a wry smile at his attractive guest. "Of course you can, honey. Let me git one o' my girls on it right now." Sweetness backed away from the three of us and winked mischievously at Pigfoot as he walked away. I watched the Bajan bite at his bottom lip, his temper only being reined in by the pain his was inflicting upon himself. Laveau also saw her driver's displeasure.

"Pigfoot, go git yo'self a Coke and then give Clefus a call at Swindler's Cove. See how he's doing."

I watched the Bajan walk back to the bar and turned back to Laveau. "He don't say a lot, does he?"

She shook her head and looked knowingly across at her Bajan chauffeur. "Nah, he ain't too good with words, ain't Pigfoot."

"What is he good at?"

Laveau moved in close and spoke softly into my ear. "Drivin', an' killin'; Pigfoot's real good at drivin' an' killin'."

I stood back, shocked at what she'd just said. Laveau began to laugh, then put her bottle of beer to her lips and knocked back the remaining dregs. A waitress arrived, breaking the tension between the two of us. She was a young Creole-looking girl, no more than twenty years old, dressed in a black trouser suit, with menus tucked underneath her arm. She smiled sweetly at both of us and gestured with her hand that we follow her. She walked the two of us across the club and showed us to a table at one of a series of secluded booths at the back of the cellar bar. As I sat opposite Evangeline Laveau, I ran my hand nervously across the outside of my jacket pocket and brushed my fingers against the coffin-shaped box the Obeah had given me earlier and felt myself shudder. The waitress laid out the menus in front of us and smiled.

"Can I git you both somethin' ta drink?

"Two more Miller's, an' a shot of dark rum fo' the gentleman." I raised my eyebrows in surprise and stared across the table at Laveau as the waitress disappeared into the darkness."

"Don't git freaked out, Joseph. I ain't psychic." Laveau picked up her menu, opened it up then sank back into her seat; she peeped over the top and laughed. "That insane cousin o' yours told me you had a fondness fo' rum. Said you drank it by the bottle when you were pissed at something or someone. I thought now was as good a time as any to let you start drown in ya' damn sorrows."

Over the noise of the band, I could hear Evangeline Laveau sniggering at me from behind her menu, her mocking laughter the least of my concerns, my harried brooding at the curious gypsum sarcophagus that lingered in my pocket a far more vexing concern.

*

The rum tasted real good as it hit the back of my mouth, ran down my throat and warmed the pit of my belly. Evangeline ordered us a couple of chicken-fried steaks with fries and a green salad and made sure both the cold beers and the rum kept on coming. We spoke very little as we sat and ate; without the pressure of heavy conversation I felt myself start to relax. The food I was chowing down on and the company I was keeping were both good. Laveau was a dark horse for sure and perhaps that was what was sparking my interest in her. I'd not looked at a woman with any kind of emotional interest or attraction since the death of my wife, Ellie, and as I sat admiring the beautiful woman in front of me, I felt a sudden harsh pang of guilt biting like an open sore deep in the pit my stomach. Although unaware, the anguish inside me was telling on my face and the truth I hid was all too apparent to Evangeline Laveau.

"Yo' married, Joseph? I don't see no ring."

On hearing her question, I sank my head down towards the table and looked at the empty plate, then took the final swig of rum from the shot glass. I looked back up at her and cleared the frog from my throat. "I was, but she passed some time back."

Evangeline Laveau smiled at me softly. "I'm so sorry to hear that." I watched as my pretty host considered what to say to me next. She moved forward in her seat and leaned against the table, about to ask me another question, but was interrupted by Pigfoot, who approached the table and dipped his head to whisper into her ear. After the Bajan driver had relayed his message, he stood back and I could see a look of bemused worry on Laveau's face.

"What's a matter?"

"Pigfoot can't getta hold o' Clefus. He's been trying the better part of an hour. Sum'ting ain't right. Hopkins always knows to keep in touch when he's shifting the merchandise." Laveau rose out of her seat, stuck her hand in her jacket pocket and threw a handful of ten-dollar bills onto the table. "We need to go." Laveau stepped out of the booth and she and Pigfoot started to hightail it across the club. I picked up my jacket and headed on after them, leaving Laveau's unasked question to me hanging in the air over the lonely banknotes she'd just scattered across the lacquered table.

Pigfoot drove us on darkening back roads that ran alongside what Evangeline told me was the Harlem river. The criss-crossing streets seemed to cut the black ghetto in half, with the skyline of downtown Manhattan sparking ahead of us. A dark forest of girders, broken down warehouses, shanty town buildings, gutted cars, graffiti-covered billboards and burned-out neon signs were the telling landmarks of the bleak neighbourhood we were travelling through. The Cadillac continued to follow the river a while longer, then the Bajan hung a left and followed a wide road that took us down to what looked like the harbourside; Pigfoot drove another quarter-mile over rough concrete roads, past warehouses and factories, finally pulling up outside a large blue-bricked four-storey building. On the wall about ten feet up was a sign which read, Swindler's Cove. Pigfoot jumped out of the driver's seat, the pump-action shotgun already in his hand. Laveau put her hand behind her back and pulled out a small black .25 Beretta and chambered a round. She looked across at me gravely. "You best stay here, whilst we go check this out.

I shook my head. "No, way." I then stepped out of the Cadillac and watched as Pigfoot walked carefully along a narrow alley towards the warehouse doors, the pump-action raised up in front of his scarred face. Without a gun or anything to protect myself with, I quickly regretted the stupidity of the false heroism I just displayed to Evangeline Laveau back inside the car.

I followed Laveau down the alley after Pigfoot, who was now standing in the road with the pump-action aimed towards the raised shutter doors of the warehouse. Inside it was pitch black. Pigfoot tightened his grip on the stock of the shotgun, forcing it tightly into his shoulder and slowly took a couple of steps inside. Laveau was close behind him and I followed the two of them into the pitch-black repository. Laveau moved to her left and grabbed hold of my arm. Pulling me against a wall, she raised the Beretta in front of her and edged along the smooth brickwork. I felt the flat of her hand suddenly touch my chest and stop me dead in my tracks, then heard the clicking of a series of light switches on the other side of the warehouse being knocked on in rapid succession. The huge storage place lit up in a wash of bright florescent light.

I stared out into the centre of the huge stash house and instantly felt my body go cold and my legs grow stiff and weaken. The hairs on the backs of my arms and at the base of my neck prickled and stood upright. My stomach gurgled and churned and I began to wretch, a bitter taste coating the inside of my mouth as I desperately fought off the desire to vomit. I shut my eyes then quickly opened them again, unsure if what I was actually seeing was real.

On the other side of the building, I watched Pigfoot spin on his heels, the shotgun held up high in his hands, his eyes frantically scanning the warehouse in every direction. Behind me I heard Laveau scream out the word '*No!*' I turned and saw her falling to her knees, her eyes looking upwards, her face contorted in horror and disbelief. I watched her fingers loosen and the tiny Beretta pistol drop from her hand then spin like a Catherine wheel across the ground towards me. I turned around and slowly took a half-dozen or so steps towards the centre of the warehouse and stared up towards the roof of the building.

Hung by a rope, headfirst below a metal parapet, was the naked corpse of Clefus Hopkins. Buried in the middle of his forehead was a short-handled axe. Fresh blood ran from his split skull down on to the concrete floor below and pooled in a dark sticky mass underneath his lifeless body. Both his hands had been severed at the wrists and they had been laid on top of his stained clothing, which had been carefully folded and left on one of the empty wooden pallets that had previously housed the many bales of marijuana. Next to Hopkins' severed body parts and clothes, stacked up crudely in a pile on the other two pallets, were the bodies of six other black men, each one had been shot in the back of the head, all of them stripped of their clothing. Behind me I heard Evangeline Laveau scream out Hopkins' Christian name over and over again, then I listened as she began to wail and sob uncontrollably. The smell of burned cordite, iodine and chopped raw liver permeated the inside of my nose and mouth, the foul unforgettable taste of death slowly coating my tongue and lips. I rubbed at my mouth with my fingertips and began to walk towards the piled up bloody cadavers, thinking to myself that I had seen this kind of atrocity many years before, back on an idyllic Caribbean island that I had once called home.

10

"What the fuck is goin' on?" The muzzle of Laveau's .25 Beretta was being pressed hard at the back of my skull, the cold metal parting through my hair, the barrel's tip burning at the skin underneath. My body stiffened with fear when I heard the hammer being cocked back. I looked across the warehouse and saw Pigfoot take a couple of steps towards me, the shotgun in his hands now pointed directly at my chest. I glanced sideways and out of the corner of my eye I saw Evangeline Laveau slowly take a few paces to her right. As she did, she dragged the barrel of the gun across my scalp then plunged it deep into the side of my neck. I swallowed hard and turned my face ever so slowly towards her. Laveau stared back at me, her watery eyes filled with pain and confusion, as if a terrible, indecipherable revelation had just been whispered cruelly into her ear.

"I just ax you a question, niggah, you betta git answering me befo' I end your cheating, sorry-assed life."

"I ain't cheated nobody."

"Bullshit!" Laveau jammed the muzzle hard into my neck. I could feel a slight judder from the gun barrel as her hand and arm trembled in anger. I tried to avoid swallowing again and attempted to keep my voice empty of the fear I felt running through my body. I closed and opened my eyes and blinked the sweat out of them.

"I'm tellin' you straight, I ain't played no part in all this slaughter." My eyes fixed on Laveau's dazed face and I saw her incisor tooth nervously bite down on her lip. I watched as she suddenly shifted her weight and glanced quickly across the warehouse, then quickly back over at me.

"You lying piece of shit. I knew something 'bout you stank! I wanna know what bastard carved Hopkins up and where the fuck the dope is?"

Laveau slid the barrel's aim a couple of inches down my throat and applied more pressure against my neck. "Did you and your fuckin' cousin really think you could stiff us like this?"

Laveau took a step toward me and gouged the Beretta sharply underneath my throat, her eyes glazed with fury. A sour metallic taste suddenly tainted my mouth and tongue, the skin around my lips tightened and my hands and my arm prickled with pins and needles. I felt my legs begin to buckle, then heard Pigfoot's gravelly Bajan voice sound out in front of me.

"Dis bloodshed ain't none 'a Vic's or his kin's doin', woman."

Laveau's eyes shifted from mine out across the warehouse. I looked straight ahead of me and saw Pigfoot now only a few feet away from the two of us, the pump-action shotgun raised high and now pointed directly at his boss's head. I let the fingers of my right hand clench up into a ball as Laveau, filled with rage and stunned at the betrayal that was seemingly unfolding in front of her, took a small step backwards. She swung the Beretta out in front of her, raising the gun barrel towards Pigfoot. As she did, I lashed out violently with my fist, catching her hard across the cheek and temple. Laveau's head shot backward, her body knocked off balance, both arms flailing helplessly either side of her.

I spun on my heels and, with every ounce of strength that I could summon, rushed at her with the full weight of my upper body, catching her mid-torso and instantly knocking the wind out of her willowy frame.

I heard the ear-piercing report as the gun went off, followed by a series of sharp cracks as the Beretta was wrenched from Laveau's grip and bounced across the concrete. I felt Laveau's footing give way and her knees cave from underneath her as we toppled headlong and careered across the floor. Her thrashing arms swung around me and she frantically clawed at my back with her fingers as we flew through the air, our bodies slamming savagely to the ground with a vicious bone- and muscle-wrenching smack.

The impact spun us apart like rag dolls, flinging me back against the warehouse wall. I quickly caught my breath then rolled over and perched on my knees for a moment and pulled myself up on to my unsteady feet, my head spinning. Ahead of me, Pigfoot was now standing over Evangeline Laveau, the toe of his boot pressing down hard on her right wrist, the shotgun directed down at her face. I heard her start to curse and swear at the scarred Bajan as I stumbled over to his side and looked down at his new-found captive. Laveau glared back up at the two of us with bloodthirsty ferocity; she gritted her teeth in blind temper then snatched open her mouth and spat a wad of white saliva up at the two of us. I tapped on Pigfoot's shoulder and nodded to him to ease up on the pressure on Laveau's arm. He obediently obliged and began to back off, but as soon as he lifted his foot Laveau started to thrash out at us with her legs. The Bajan snapped his body back towards her, letting the end of the barrel of the shotgun graze against her temple. Pigfoot shook his head at Evangeline Laveau disapprovingly and pulled the shotgun away from her face. He sucked through his front teeth disdainfully. "Yuh need ta calm da fuck down, lady."

Laveau cursed under her breath then gritted her teeth, her face contorting with anger and frustration at being overpowered, and the realisation that both her sudden desire for revenge against me and her own mercurial tendencies had allowed it to happen to her so easily. I watched as her body slowly relaxed, her arms and legs going limp against the cold concrete floor. I leaned forward and stuck out my right hand for her to take hold of, and her confused, scared eyes stared up at me for a moment before she reluctantly grasped hold of my palm allowing me to haul her up on to her feet. Laveau immediately let go of my hand and took a step back away from me, her shoulders rigid with muscle, her face stony. She looked at me blankly, as though she were seeing me for the first time, then spat in my face.

★

"Ellington 'ere ain't yo' problem fo' sure, Miss Laveau; same go fo' Mistah Vic."

Pigfoot was reaching down to pick up the .25 Beretta as he spoke. He turned and slowly walked back towards Laveau and held out her gun for her to take. Laveau snatched up the pistol and looked backed at Pigfoot, her face a picture of bewilderment. Pigfoot gestured with his head towards the Beretta. "Put dat pea-shooter away, Miss Laveau. Question yuh gotta be axin' yo'self is why wud da man tek from yuh wha' he already freely given?"

I took a step towards Laveau, my sudden movement clearly spooking her. Laveau swung the Beretta out in front of her and pointed it directly at my guts. "Stay right where yo' are, mistah!"

I slowly raised my hands out in front of me, my palms splayed out submissively for Laveau to see. "Just think about it. Pigfoot's right. Why would Vic steal all that dope when he's just gone an' shipped it out here for you ... an' he knows he's about to get paid fo' it too?"

"You're suddenly your cousin's new courier. Some ting ain't right. Mebbe you're part o' all this shit. Mebbe you cutting in on Vic's turf?"

"What? Woman, that don't make a blind bit a sense. How the hell could I have organised all of this carnage, what kinda animal you take me for?" I kept my hands out passively, my arms held high as I continued to talk. "You ever had any reason to distrust Vic or his people previously?"

Laveau swallowed hard then shook her head at me. Out of the corner my eye I could see Pigfoot nodding his head to himself, a wry smile arced across his normally sullen face. "Listen ta tha man, Miss Laveau. He talkin' da trute." Pigfoot stabbed his thumb over his shoulder. "All dis bloodshed, it's wuk o' Bajans fo' sure."

Pigfoot raised his arm and pointed his bony finger towards me. "But not him or ma boss man."

Laveau shot me a suspicious glare, her mind working through what was being said to her. She stared down at the gun in her hand, her fingers nervously squeezing around the grip of the Beretta. She stood silently for a moment, then clicked on the safety catch with her thumb and let her arm drop, the Beretta hanging limply at her side. She stared across the warehouse towards where Hopkins' corpse was hanging, her eyes swelling with tears. "If it ain't you or Vic ... then who'd do this and why?"

"I don't know, but I think what's happened here tonight may be connected to this."

I stuck my hand into my jacket pocket and pulled out the alabaster coffin-shaped box that the Obeah had given to me earlier and held it out in front of me. Laveau stared at my hand, her face filled with a strange sense of expectation and dread. She slowly walked towards me and picked the coffin out of my palm and raised it up in front of her face to get a better look. Tears slowly began to fall from Evangeline Laveau's eyes. I watched as they rolled down her cheeks and begin to drip from her jawline down onto the ground. Around us the air felt warm and fetid, the smell of drying blood and death seeping up my nostrils, turning my already queasy stomach over. The burning weal mark in the palm of my hand began to throb again, its pulsating, painful rhythm echoing my heart hammering savagely against my chest.

11

Pigfoot's true allegiance had come as something of a shock. The scar-faced, previously hostile Bajan wasn't a man I'd thought would come running to my aid if I'd found myself with a gun levelled at my head, but he had. Evangeline Laveau had told me earlier that Vic had provided Pigfoot as a "*special kind of security*" for her people. After the way the Bajan had reacted to Laveau pulling a gun on me, I'd quickly got the feeling that my cousin had installed one of his own minders within her organisation to keep a close eye on me, rather than the safety of either his narcotic shipments or the New York-based revolutionaries he was selling it to. It was the kind of advanced, sneaky battle-planning that I knew Vic always insisted on putting into place with regards to his illegal operations with fellow crooks or shady business dealings. My cousin never liked to find himself backed into a corner or losing the upper hand. Vic distrusted most people he worked with and rarely used a minion to do his dirty work for him. Pigfoot was clearly an exception to that rule, and that scared me. The fact that I didn't trust my own cousin as far as I could throw him gave me little confidence in my ability to place any faith in my new brooding protector.

The three of us had left Hopkins' bloody corpse hanging from the ceiling and taken bitter sanctuary in a dimly lit, but stylishly decorated, office at the rear of the waterfront warehouse. Laveau slumped herself down into a high-backed leather chair, which was behind a large oak desk with a baize green top. It was obviously her office. She drew a hand down her cheeks, stretching the skin beneath her eyes, and sighed heavily. I watched as she rested the Beretta on the desk with a trembling hand then went about making a telephone call to the nightclub owner, Arnett "Sweetness" Minton.

★

After a short, heated conversation, informing him of Hopkins' and the other men's deaths, and the loss of their merchandise, she'd hung the phone's receiver back on its cradle then stuck her hand into her jacket pocket and took out a packet of cigarettes and a gold lighter. She shook a cigarette out of its card box and placed it in her mouth, then snapped the lighter dryly several times, drawing hard on the filter. Laveau took in a full hit of nicotine then blew out a mouthful of curling smoke. I watched as the grey vapours whispered up in front of her face and floated aimlessly across the office. Laveau sat back in her seat and looked suspiciously at the alabaster box in my hand.

"Sweetness and some of my people are on the way. Understandably, they ain't too happy. We all gonna sit tight and wait." Laveau pointed to a wooden chair on the other side of the office. "Pull up a seat an' park ya ass down, Joseph. The boys ain't gonna be long gittin' 'ere."

I did as she asked, collected the chair and joined her, sitting myself at the right-hand edge of the desk, my back against the wall so I could see who was going to be coming through the door. Pigfoot stood on the other side of the room. He was looking out of the glass window in the door, the pump-action shotgun hung over his left forearm. He turned his attention towards me briefly. His eyes shifted from me and coolly began recceing the office, paying close attention to Evangeline Laveau's Beretta sat on the desk. In the poor light, the scar dripping down the

108

side of the Bajan mobster's face looked like a sliver of smooth red glass running underneath his pock-marked skin.

Laveau stuck out her hand towards me. "Can I take another look at that little casket?"

"Sure."

I leaned across the desk and slid the small white coffin across the green baize towards her. Laveau picked it up and turned it in her slender fingers, carefully inspecting each side and curiously eyeing the pentangle design etched into the lid of the pale, patina burial box.

"You evah see anyting like this before?"

I shook my head. "Nope, never."

Laveau rested the miniature coffin on the desk in front of her then flicked a switch at the base of an aluminium table lamp. She drew the bridge arm down so that the bright bulb was hanging only a few inches from the box. I watched as she turned the sarcophagus over on each side, examining every facet of the thing meticulously. Laveau turned the box back in her hand so that the pentangle design was facing her then drew it close up towards the light bulb and blew across the top of the lid. Specks of dust flew off the tiny gypsum casket, floating briefly in the air underneath the glare of the lamplight before slowly falling down towards the desktop. Evangeline Laveau positioned both her thumbs at the base of the box and carefully applied a little pressure to the foot of the stone lid. I moved forward in my seat to get a better look and watched as she pushed a little harder on the edge.

Slowly she began to prise up the thin alabaster cover, sliding the thin sheet of stone along the interior polished track until it came away, revealing the inside of the tapered, hexagonal box.

"Wha the hell . . .?"

Laveau looked up at me then back down into the minute

coffin. She carefully turned the casket towards her then put her thumb and forefinger together and pinched inside the coffin and withdrew a tiny paper scroll. A thin length of red ribbon, not much wider than the width of a human hair had been tied in a delicate bow around it. Laveau placed the scroll on the desk, untied the slender ribbon and unfurled the thin, sepia-tinted paper in front of her. She picked it up with the tips of her fingers and placed it under the bright beam of the lamp.

I watched as she studied the diminutive document, her head shaking slowly from side to side in a confused fashion. Laveau hunched up her shoulders and looked across the desk then cleared her throat nervously before handing over the tiny sheet of paper to me. I peered down in the poor light at the black ink script that had been carefully handwritten on the thin parchment and began to read. I mouthed the solemn words written of the paper as if I were silently reciting my own death warrant.

Dear Mr. Ellington,

There are three more caskets awaiting your collection, all for urgent transportation to St Philip Parish, Barbados. Please attend our premises personally at your very earliest convenience to conclude business in the above matter in regards the deceased, Bernice Ellington.

Sincerely,
Walter D. Odell
Odell & Bultman Mortuary Service
3338 St. Charles Avenue
New Orleans

★

"Muthafucka!" Arnett Minton's crude bark and bawling could have easily been heard on the other side of Upper Manhattan. I winced and listened as he cursed and swore his way across the warehouse and along the corridor that led to Laveau's office. When he reached the door, he stared in at me through the glass with angry, bloodshot, bulging eyes. Minton spat on the floor, then pushed open the door, letting it bounce back hard on its hinges towards him. He caught the edge of the door as it swung back at his bulky frame and cussed again, this time under his breath. Behind him stood two massive negro heavies, both looked like they had fallen out of the ugly tree and hit every branch on the way down. Both of the brothers were dressed in black leather jackets, military combat trousers and matching black berets. Sweetness clamped his jaw down so hard in agitation that you could see the bone sticking out under his ears.

"Who gone an' fucked up ma boys out there like that?"

I pushed myself hard back into my seat and looked up at Minton. "It's a mess fo' sure."

"A mess! Oh, dat's sum fuckin' mess alright, niggah. Yuh seen the bloodshed my men are gonna have ta be clearin' up? There's a helluva lotta muthafuckin' holes gotta be dug ta sort that kinda shit out."

Minton took a step toward me and stuck an accusatory finger in my face. "So, yuh tellin' me an' Laveau there dat Hopkins brains an' dem brothers' spilled guts dat's are sprayed across my warehouse flo' ain't the wuk o' dat fuckin' cus'in o' yours or mebbe yuh?"

I shook my head. "I ain't played no part in what's gone down here tonight ... an' I'm tellin' you that it ain't Vic's

111

way either." As I spoke, I immediately felt myself doubting the validity and truth of my own words.

Minton's arms shot up in the air in disbelief. "Not his way, shit! Who yuh tink yuh kiddin', boy? Yuh kin ain't no better than most o' dem peezy-assed bastard street-dealers I have ta thro' my pot in wid every day. I know fo' a fact that yuh boy Vic's fly n' mean wid it too. The fucka's sharper than a switchblade where bid'ness is concerned, an' don't try an' tell me it ain't so, brother. Shit, yuh cus'in could rob a stash a' cash from a niggah then sue his black ass fo' cryin' 'bout it!"

I felt my fists ball. I took a deep breath then sat forward in my chair and stared up at the bad-tempered club owner. "Minton, why the hell would Vic butcher Hopkins and six of your men then steal back a heap a' dope that he ain't even given you the damn chance to settle up for? It's like I said to Laveau back there, it don't make a blind bit a' sense. What the hell is in it for Vic? My cousin's in'ta some bad shit, but he sure has hell don't go 'bout stiffin' folk he does his business with. The man ain't no fool, Sweetness."

Sweetness turned to Pigfoot then pointed his stubby finger back in my face again. "Pigfoot, yuh vouchin' fo' dis niggah's shit?"

Pigfoot moved forward into the light and nodded his head slowly. "Don't matta wha cum outta his mout'. Yuh git Mistah Vic on Miss Laveau's phone der now. Ax him yuh'self. See wha da man have ta say when yuh call him a te'ef. Then yuh git da trute yuh lookin' fo'."

I watched Sweetness swallow hard, tiny beads of sweat began to protrude across his thickly lined forehead. He gestured with a sharp nod of his head towards Evangeline Laveau who was still sat behind her desk. "Hand me dat fuckin' phone."

Laveau leaned forward and slid the phone across the desk towards Sweetness, then sank back into her chair. Minton snatched up the receiver then turned and stuck it in Pigfoot's face. "Niggah, git yuh damn boss on dis phone fo' me now."

*

Sweetness Minton had to wait a helluva lot longer than he'd cared, to finally get to speak to Vic. Pigfoot had made the call at a little before 9.30pm. By the time the phone rang back, it was just after midnight. Minton did very little talking, my wily cousin saw to that. I sat back in silence and just listened. It had been the first time I'd heard Vic's voice in over a year. Even from a distance and though I wasn't holding the receiver to my own ear, I couldn't mistake either my cousin's deep Bajan accent nor the menacing tone with which he was speaking to Minton on the other end of the line. Less than ten minutes later, Sweetness Minton's telephone conversation with my cousin was over. I saw a tremor run across his hand as he quietly rested the receiver of the phone back into its cradle. The portly club owner looked over at Laveau, his sweaty face as lifeless as tallow.

"Evangeline baby, yuh goin' wid the private dick down sout'."

Laveau's mouth dropped like a lead weight under a hanging man's legs. "Down sout'? What you mean, I'm goin' down sout'?"

"I mean, I need yuh ta haul ya skinny black ass along wid Tess Trueheart over der, an' git ya self down ta New O'leans."

Laveau shot forward in her seat. "New Orleans . . . what the hell I gotta go down ta damn cracker country fo'?" Minton, the perspiration pouring like a torrent from the top of his brow and down his face, leaned across the desk and slammed his hand down on the green baize top.

"'Cause I fuckin' said so, that's why! Jus' do what I damn say fo' Christ's sakes."

Minton turned to the two heavies he'd walked in with and shook his head at them despondently, "Man, whatta niggah gotta do round 'ere ta git a bitch to do sum'ting fo' him other den blow his dick?"

Laveau bit at her lip, her eyes filled with disgust and loathing as she watched the two men across the room from her chuckle like a pair of shaved-down Neanderthals at their boss's cheap jibe. Minton laughed to himself, then blew out his cheeks, expelling a mouthful of air across the room before lazily slouching against the edge of the desk, his huge backside perching itself on the corner.

"Looks like our Barbadian brother's story's clean, same goes fo' him." Minton flipped a fat thumb in my general direction, then turned his face and his attention towards me. "Evangeline, I want yuh ta escort Mistah Ellington to da Bajan down in New O'leans. In return fo' his safe passage, we git our merchandise replaced, plus anutha fifty keys fo' our damn trouble." Minton sneered down at me.

"Fo' a crooked, backstabbing sonufabitch, yuh cus'in bin a real reasonable niggah. Reasonable an' damn generous wid it too. Brother says we don't gotta pay him a fuckin' ting, not till we got all our Mary Jane back under dis 'ere roof. Real sweet o' da man . . . real fuckin' sweet."

A smile broke out briefly across Minton's fat face, but quickly fell away as darker thoughts entered his head. "Ting is, I don't trust yuh cus'in's nasty lyin' ass one bit. Shit, if yuh man's as righteous as he's soundin' an' he keeps his word, then dat's cool. I'm gonna tek all ma misgiving 'bout him right back ... but if he don't." Minton waved one of his sausage-shaped fingers at me and began to shake his head from side to side like a dog with a flea in its ear. "Well, den dat muthafucka cus'in o' yours, he gonna re'grit he evah messed wid tha' Panthers or wid da Sweetness. Yuh 'ear me, niggah?"

I remained silent, knowing full well that Minton was yet to finish his sermon.

"Mistah Ellington, I'd like yuh ta meet my two associates." Sweetness Minton laid out the palm of his clammy hand in front of his men like he was introducing royalty. "This 'ere is Willy Love and Bumpy Edwards. I'm gonna be sendin' these boys along fo' da ride wid you an Evangeline 'ere."

Minton turned his attention to Pigfoot standing in the shadows. "Pigfoot, Vic say's yuh gotta be taggin' yuh raggedy ass along wid dem too, okay?" The Bajan gave a single nod of his head in acknowledgement.

"Good. Now all 'a these fellas are gonna be lookin' out fo' ma bid'ness interests in ma absence so ta speak an' they're gonna be keepin' a close eye on yuh ass too, Mistah Ellington." Minton dragged himself off the edge of the desk and brushed the lapel of his jacket. Her turned to Laveau and smiled. "Evangeline baby, git yo'self some beauty sleep. I'm gonna go arrange transportation fo' tha five o' yuh. Yuh all gonna need ta be up be fo' the crow starts crawlin'. There's only two Southern Crescents leavin' outta Penn Station tomorrow an' you all gonna be on the early one."

Minton sniffed into the air like a hound on a coon hunt. He pulled up the collar on his jacket then stooped his gargantuan head down low so that his double chin was almost touching his breastbone. He began to walk slowly towards the office door, his breathing heavy and laboured underneath his expensive silk suit.

115

He took hold of the handle and opened the door. As he was about to leave, he turned and grinned at me, then clicked his fingers together. "Oh, I nearly fo'got. Yuh cus'in said to tell yuh that..." Minton stopped mid-sentence and laughed to himself again, then closed his eyes and began to snap his fingers together again as if he was trying to recall a long-forgotten memory that was reluctant to be summoned back up to him. "Oh, dat's it, I got it ... Monroe. Vic said to say that Mistah Monroe will know yuh gonna be in town. Said I had to tell yuh that yuh gonna need to stay sharp ... said yuh'd know what he meant."

Arnett Minton nodded his head at me then slouched out of the office and began to tow his robust hide back along the corridor. He called back to me with a snide rattle in his voice that made me want to run down the hall after him and kick his fat ass out in to the street. "It's bin a real pleasure, Mistah Ellington, a real pleasure."

I looked across at Laveau and we both watched as Minton's henchmen followed on after him, as if they were oversized offspring chasing the tail of a burly parent. I closed my eyes and felt a prickly dread roll all over my skin. Behind my snapped-shut eyelids, I could see, in the darkness, the blurred, uninvited image of the man I knew as Conrad Monroe. A ghost from my past whom I feared and hated in equal measure.

12

It was just after 2am by the time I returned to my room at the Hotel Theresa. After leaving a group of Laveau's colleagues to clean up and remove the bloody remains of Clefus Hopkins and the five other dead men at the waterside warehouse, I'd sunk wearily into the back seat of the Cadillac limo next to Evangeline Laveau, along with the bulky, sweating carcases of Sweetness Minton's two minders, who had jammed themselves in either side of Laveau and me. I'd sat in silence on the journey back through Harlem while Laveau spoke in detail about her previous dealings with my cousin Vic.

The organisation she was part of had started its shady business relationship with my cousin after an introduction had been made between him and a nameless high-ranking, California-based Black Panther member some six months earlier. It soon became clear that it wasn't just top-grade Caribbean marijuana that Vic was importing into the States. Sweetness Minton and the black revolutionaries he was fronting were also buying in huge quantities of cocaine and guns from him. The Panthers' illegal shopping list was being ably met by Vic, who was successfully supplying what the organisation requested without hitch or hindrance. In return, Vic was being handsomely paid for his trouble.

Pigfoot and Laveau had dropped me and my new minders outside the main doors of the hotel. Laveau leaned out of the window of the limo and handed me a white slip of paper with a phone number which she said I could call at any time should I need her. She then warned me that she would be returning before 6.30am to collect me, and that our train to New Orleans would be departing early. I put the piece of paper I'd just been given into the inside pocket of my jacket and thanked Laveau, then said goodnight and climbed the steps of the hotel with Minton's hired help tailing close behind me.

The three of us walked through the ornate brass entrance and across the lavishly decorated lobby straight into the open doors of one of the waiting elevators. We rode up to the fourth floor to my room. With Willy Love and Bumpy Edwards in the hallway outside guarding, I walked back into my room and sighed heavily. I leaned against the door and blearily wrestled my arms out of my coat, then reached into the pocket and took out the small alabaster coffin. I stared down at the odd-looking box for a moment, my mind going over the horrors I'd witnessed back at the warehouse and what it might have to do with Vic and, more unusually, my deceased sister, Bernice.

I felt my shoulders slouch heavily against the door as a wave of fatigue ran through my body. I yawned and pinched at the bridge of my nose with my thumb and forefinger, then quickly shook my head from side to side in an attempt to keep myself awake a while longer. I kicked off my shoes and pulled my tie from around my neck then hung it and my jacket and overcoat over the back of a chair by the door. I took off my wristwatch and placed it on the bedside table with the white pot casket and turned on the night light. I grabbed my still unpacked suitcase from off the floor at the foot of the bed then walked over to the light switch on the wall next to the door and flicked it off. The dim glow from the night light behind me cast out an elongated, eerie shadow of my body as I made my way over to the wardrobe. I emptied the new clothing that was hung up inside into my suitcase then made my way into the bathroom and rested my butt on the edge of the sink, my head throbbing with confusion and exhaustion, my sluggish jetlagged body crying out at me to allow it to fall into bed and let it sleep.

I rolled a knot out of the muscles in between my shoulders and let my body go limp then closed my eyes for a moment and felt my head flop forward, my chin drowsily resting itself against my chest. Outside in the hallway, I could hear the deep, booming voices of Edwards and Love chatting away to each other. Their baritone chorus forcing me to stay awake and open my eyes. I drowsily pushed my body away from the edge of the sink and got myself undressed. I leaned into the shower, turned on the taps and waited a moment then climbed into the pristine white stall and drew the plastic curtain behind me.

I stood underneath the high-pressured spray with my hands propped against the tiles and let the hot water sluice over my head and aching body. The spray hammered against my knotted muscles. I held my face up into the rush of water and opened and closed my mouth like a guppy feeding in a fish tank. I washed my hair and soaped my limbs and torso, and rinsed myself then turned off the faucets and got out of the shower. I stood for a moment with my eyes closed, my head felt light and woozy, droplets of water running down my body on to the bathroom floor. I breathed deeply through my nose, wiping my face slick with the palm of my hand and forced my eyes back open. Out in the hallway Love and Edwards were quiet. I smiled to myself when I thought of the two weighty men bodyguarding me outside of my plush hotel room. I quickly dried myself off then wrapped the towel around my waist and walked back over to the sink, ran the hot water tap and wiped the condensation from the mirror. I took my badger-hair shaving brush and my razor from my washbag then lathered up my face and carefully shaved the hard, greying stubble from my jowls, top lip and chin. As I dried my face with a hand towel, I caught sight of my reflection in the mirror. I stared back at myself and again thought about Vic and his long-distance, foreboding warning to me. *"Mistah Monroe will know yuh gonna be in town."*

I rarely ever allowed myself to think about the man called Monroe. The mere mention of his name had sent a wave of horror, nausea and disgust through me earlier. Conrad Monroe was an evil man; a criminal overlord whom I would never forget or forgive. Monroe was the bastard who had casually ordered a group of his men to start a fire at my home and destroy my world. During the small hours of a misty September morning in 1964, whilst I was on duty, Monroe's men had travelled to my house and poured petrol across its wooden roof and its walls whilst my family was asleep inside.

They had then barricaded the front and rear doors and the windows, preventing my heavily pregnant wife, Ellie, and our daughter, Amelia, from escaping. The men had then torched our tiny beachside chattel house and let it burn. The Bajan gangland boss had ordered for me to be captured, beaten and then dragged kicking and screaming to my house to witness his brutal act of revenge against me. I was held on the ground by Monroe's cronies and made to watch as the searing blaze engulfed both my home and my beautiful family. Monroe had, in only a few hours, torn my life apart. His barbaric decision to murder my wife and children had been sanctioned in vicious retribution for my three-year investigation into his illicit criminal activities and my attempts to bring to a halt his brutal drug and money laundering operations. After being a thorn in his side for far too long, Conrad Monroe had tired of my snooping and the constant disruptions which I'd created for his criminal empire and his corrupt business dealings. Not content with murdering those I loved, Monroe had then successfully overseen both my personal and professional downfall and my disgrace from the force; fabricating a series of false criminal allegations against me whilst I was serving as a police sergeant back home on Barbados.

I stared back into the mirror and watched the tears well up in my eyes and roll slowly down my cheeks as I recollected those painfully bitter memories. I snapped my eyes shut and cleared the frog out of my throat then wiped at my face with the hand towel and hung it over the sink. I walked across the bathroom and turned out the light. My head and heart lay heavy with sombre memories, my already somnolent spirit now dampened by a heavy melancholic fug.

*

I felt the sudden cold draught sear against my naked skin two seconds after I'd stepped out of the bathroom door. I heard a high, thin whistling sound cut through the air in front of my face and, at the furthest edge of the vision on the other side of the duskily lit bedroom, saw a big-set figure rushing towards me. I instinctively bobbed my head down low then felt something fly out in front of my face. I panicked and dropped my knees a little, twisting my upper body away

121

from the door frame so that my right arm and shoulder could perhaps protect me from the impact of whatever was heading for me. Moments later, an explosion of bright light went off inside my head as a mass of solid muscle connected with tremendous force against my own body, the crushing impact spun me around on my heels, slamming me hard against the bedroom wall.

I felt the towel around my waist loosened and fall at my feet. My head cracked against the side of the wall and my eyes snapped shut. At the same time, a gloved hand gripped me tightly underneath my neck and, in a swift, single movement, began to lift me off my feet. My watery eyes shot back open and I glared back at a hooded man, dressed head to foot in black. I felt the man tense his arm then squeeze at my throat again, his vice-like grip pinching savagely underneath my jaw. As his huge fingers tightened around my neck, I managed to throw my arm out in front of me, my fist making contact with the side of the man's head. I immediately whipped my arm back and weighed into the side of his temple with another couple of desperate blows and felt the man's grip suddenly loosen for a moment. In that split second, I pushed every fibre of strength up into my shoulders and arched my back against the wall, kicking out at the man's guts with my foot, forcing him to loosen his hold on my throat. I dropped to the floor as my attacker stumbled backwards.

Adrenaline and fear surged through my body as I hauled myself to my feet and frantically slid along the wall to try and put some distance between me and my attacker. Whoever the hooded man was, he was like a wild animal; dangerous and strong. With hardly a breath lost, he flew back towards me and, as he lifted his right arm out in front of him, a cheese-wire garrotte came slashing out towards my body in semicircular patterns. I saw the garrotte swing round in the man's hand, his arm reaching high up above his head then come flailing back down towards my face. I immediately shot my body sideways to my left, snatching up my overcoat from off the chair next to me. I swung it around my lower left arm just as the garrotte cut back round through the air and connected with my wrist. The wire tightened itself around my coat, sending a sharp pain shooting up my arm and arcing deep into my shoulder. The masked man lunged at my face with his fist, I jerked my head to the side, his fist just grazing my cheekbone and smashing into the wall behind me. I felt the garrotte loosen from around my wrist. I pulled my arm back to wrestle it free of my coat and the wire but was stopped when I was hammered again at the side of my head. I snapped round just as the man threw another wild blow at my face. I ducked and pounded him twice in the midsection, making him wail out in agony. He was tough, but I knew the swift succession of those blows had hurt him.

The masked man came back at me and I took another heavy smack to my left shoulder where it did no real harm. I kicked out at his knee with the ball of my foot then quickly swung my right arm out, punching the man across the top half of his face. I felt my fist connect through the fabric of the hood, my knuckles impacting with the ridge of bone above the man's eye. The force of the blow threw both my coat and the loose garrotte off my arm, sending both flying across the room. My right hand instantly went numb with pain, my fingers stung in agony as if I'd just hit a stone wall.

I quickly shifted my weight, ducking and sidestepping the next couple of badly placed uppercuts. The man lumbered on, coming back at me, throwing hard, skilful jabs as he came. I hit him again, two nasty shots to the centre of his face made his knees buckle a little and felt his nose collapse like rotten fruit underneath the balaclava. As he stumbled backwards, I swung at him again, catching the back of his scalp with my knuckles. I came in towards him tight and low, hitting him underneath his ribcage and managed to get one of my feet hooked between his legs, pulling the two of us off balance. We fell down together, our bodies separating and sprawling across the carpeted floor like a pair of half-cut drunks. The man was now on his back, he moaned as he tried to pull himself up off the floor. Seeing me at his feet, he tried to aim a dirty kick sideways at my head. I caught his foot and yanked his leg away from me then lashed out with my heel deep into the centre of his groin. The man hollered a muffled cry underneath the mask as he doubled up into a foetal ball of writhing agony in front of me.

I pulled myself up onto my knees and sprang across the carpet at him before he had chance to recover, driving my fist into the side of his head and neck repeatedly, reigning down blow after blow. I yanked him onto his back and the man lashed out at my stomach with his elbow, clipping me underneath my ribs. Winded by the gut jab, I fell backwards on to my bare ass, the back of my head cracking against the wardrobe door. The man rolled back on to his side, his arm reaching out at something just above his head. His gloved hand stretched across the carpet, his fingers snatching out repeatedly into the dark. I hauled myself forward, slamming myself down onto the side of the man's body just as his hand suddenly shot back clutching the handle of the garrotte. The wire cut across the top of my head and bounced back away from me. I threw a short arm shot directly underneath the man's jaw then fell forward and slammed my forehead down into his face.

I snapped my head back and butted him again across the bridge of his nose, then fell forward and sank my front teeth through the wool balaclava, biting down deep into the flesh of his cheek. The man screamed out, letting the garrotte fly uncontrollably out over my back and head in a futile attempt to slice into my naked skin. I spat his blood out of my mouth and twisted my body to one side, my naked calves and feet twisted themselves around the man's thrashing legs, pinning them to the floor like a landlocked octopus. The man struggled to free himself from my grip, twisting his body and lashing out with his hands, elbows and upper arms. I pushed my right palm under his chin and levered his head back, quickly wrapping my forearm underneath his chin as we continued to frantically grapple on the floor. The man's hands gouged at my sides as I reached out for the deadly metal cord in his hand. I grabbed at one of the wooden handles of the garrotte, ripping it out of the masked man's palm then twisted the cord around his throat in quick succession and snapped my arms apart. The man's hands shot up into the air then dropped back down towards his whipping head. In desperation, his fingers grappled to loosen the ligature tightening around his neck. I yanked the cord tighter. His breath gasped and rattled in short, angry snorts, the blood and saliva gargling at the back of his gasping mouth spat out and fell back across my head and into my eyes. I felt his legs kick out wildly, his boot heels bouncing off the carpeted floor, every muscle in his body contracting and reluctantly relaxing as he fought to free himself. I gripped at the wooden handles of the garrotte again and yanked the wire as tightly as I could. The man's bladder gave way, his warm urine seeping down between his legs, soaking my stomach. I wrenched the thin cable tighter and he kicked out again, crying out through gritted teeth.

His body suddenly stiffened, his back arching up in the air violently then slumping down onto me.

I heaved at the cord again then heard the man's neck crack like someone easing his foot down on a dry stick. A warm jet of the man's blood sprayed out against the side of my face and trickled down my neck and shoulder and seeped down into the carpet. I felt the man's body go limp, his arms fell at his side and his head lopped towards the floor. I immediately released both of the garrotte's handles from my grasp. The cord did not uncoil itself easily from the dead man's neck. I pushed the lifeless body away from me and, as I did, heard a final breath weep up from deep inside his body. The rasping death rattle sounded like a tormented soul escaping a cruel purgatory; the condemned spirit unaware that it was about to be damned down into another fiery place of torment.

I dragged myself up off the floor and sat on the edge of the bed, my arms clenched across my chest, as if I had caught a chill. My naked body twitched and shivered, my hands throbbing with pins and needles that ran from my bloodied palms down into my fingers. My sweating skin was covered in the dead man's blood, saliva and his bodily waste. My mouth dry, the inside of my tongue was coated with a nauseating taste. The cruel stench of death and fear rose inside my nostrils and permeated itself into every inch of the room. I felt myself gag and covered my mouth, forcing myself not to vomit. I looked down at the body on the floor and felt my insides run cold. A wave of shame suddenly washed over me and I began to cry. I shook my head over and over and cursed at myself under my breath then put my face in my hands to mask my screams. My dazed, anguished mind unaware at that moment that my savage actions had surely saved me from an early grave.

13

A faint ephemeral curtain of light hung in the air of my hotel room. I kneeled over the dead body, my bloody hand trembling, pulled off the balaclava and looked down at the man whom I had just killed. The face staring back up at me was white and I guessed the man was no more than forty years old. He had tanned skin which glistened with moisture. His thick black hair was slick with sweat and shorn into a military crew cut. His empty eyes were the deepest blue, the pupils becoming dull, just minute black spots in the centre of his head that were slowly fading away into an unknown oblivion. Spittle and blood were smeared across his mouth, which was parted slightly, as though he had been suddenly interrupted in mid-speech. I swallowed hard and staggered forward a little, not quite believing what I was looking at, grabbed hold of his still-warm arm, then rolled his body from side to side and started to go through all of his pockets. All I found was a pearl-handled, retractable stiletto knife, its switchblade smeared with blood. There was no wallet, no identification nor jewellery on him, just a plain Timex watch, which was strapped tightly around his left wrist by a brown leather band. As I let go of his arm, I noticed the edge of a blue-tinged tattoo peeping out from underneath the cuff of his black commando-style polo-neck. I leaned back across the body and hesitantly pushed up the dead man's sleeve to reveal what looked to be an armed forces crown and winged emblem with the Latin words *Utrinque Paratus* underneath it. I stumbled backwards, my head still woozy, and sat on the edge of the bed. My body shook, beads of sweat ran down the back of my neck and down my stomach. I stared down at the bloody corpse, my baffled brain trying to make sense of the madness that had just unfolded. I looked around the room. I desperately needed a stiff drink, but there wasn't a drop of hooch to be had in the place. Out of the corner of my eye, I caught sight of my blood-soaked reflection in the mirror on the wardrobe door and felt myself gag in reaction to my own grisly image.

I got to my feet and went into the bathroom, washed the blood off my face and hands, then quickly pulled on my trousers and vest, walked back across the bedroom and opened up the room door. I poked my head cautiously outside and looked down the hallway. Unsurprisingly, my new-found minders Love and Edwards were nowhere to be seen. I flicked up the latch on the door to stop myself from being locked out, stood in the middle of the hall and looked either way down the empty and quiet corridor. As I turned to go back to my room, I felt something wet soak into the heel of my foot. I glanced down at the floor. Running alongside my little toe and parallel with the length of my right foot were a series of small spots of blood. I looked behind me and saw another five or six drops of deep crimson liquid dotted across the beige-patterned carpet. The final globule was pooled at the very bottom of the door to room 209, directly opposite my own room.

I told myself to get the hell back inside and leave whatever bloody mess was lurking inside room 209 to the cops. I knew deep inside that I should have obeyed my own cautionary inner voice, but my addled, jetlagged brain just wasn't thinking straight. I turned around, stuck my hand in my pocket and pulled my handkerchief out then took the door knob in my hand and opened it up. I peered into the darkness then gingerly leaned into the pitch blackness and let my covered hand slide down the inside of the wall until my fingers located the light switch. I knocked it on and took a couple more cautious steps inside. In the centre of the hotel room were the blood-spattered corpses of both Willy Love and Bumpy Edwards. The two men were spread-eagled out across a large double bed like figures that had just been sacrificed upon an ancient pagan altar. I turned and closed the door behind me then walked over to the bed to get a better look at my gruesome find. Despite the fact that it had been a ruthless death for Sweetness Minton's minders, both men's features were oddly composed, almost as if they were lying in front of me asleep.

Their heads were tipped back over the edge of the bed, each had a single entry wound just above their windpipes. Thick, red rivulets of blood trailed from their throats. The blood had soaked into the bedding underneath their heads and through the sheets then collected in a sticky pool on the carpet below their limp heads.

I knew there was little point in me hanging around any longer. I backed up towards the door, turned off the light and let myself out. Once I was back inside my own room, I snatched up my jacket from off the floor and dug into my inside pocket for the slip of paper that had Evangeline Laveau's telephone number printed on it. I walked across to the bed and picked up the phone from off the table next to it, lifted the receiver, waited to hear the dialling tone, then punched in her number. As I waited for Laveau to pick up her phone, I turned and stared down at the bloody body sprawled out on the carpet behind me. I'd only been in the United States for just over twenty-four hours and there were already nine corpses linked in some way to myself, Conrad Monroe and my damned cousin Vic. As I listened to Laveau's phone ring in my ear, I found myself wishing that I could turn back the clock. I wished I'd never set foot out of Great Britain on this crazy journey. I wished I'd stayed put on my boat down on the Bristol docks and had ignored Vic's telegram for me to come settle family affairs. Most of all, I wished that I'd played no part in any of the bloody mess around me ... but in truth, I knew I was in it up to my neck.

★

Evangeline Laveau had not been happy to be woken by my early morning call. Exhausted by lack of sleep, she'd answered with a quick-tempered "What?" like some bleary-eyed, sleep-deprived ogress. I'd quickly laid bare my macabre account of what had just gone down to her like some predawn harbinger of doom. Laveau cursed to herself repeatedly as I recounted the mayhem that had ensued in the short time she had left me.

"Okay. I'm gonna call Sweetness; git him, Pigfoot and some o' the brothers to you befo' the place starts crawling with pigs. You sure nobody saw you when you went into the other room?"

I slumped down onto the bed and shook my head to myself. "No ... there was nobody. It's as quiet as the damn grave up here." I looked over at the dead man and felt myself wince as soon as I'd uttered my off-hand remark.

Laveau either chose to ignore the stupid comment or it simply didn't register in her mind. "Okay, you just keep your black ass inside that room, you hear me, brother?"

I fell back on to the bed, my body raw and nagging,

smarting from the beating it had just taken. "Yeah . . . yeah, I hear you."

I listened to Laveau breathing heavily into the receiver before she spoke again. "Good. Okay, I'm gonna need you to straighten out that damn room the best you can befo' we git over to you. When you finished, go clean yo' self up and get ready to haul it real quick. We ain't gonna be leavin' thru the front doors this time!"

Just as I was about to thank her, Laveau hung up in my ear. I lay staring up at the ceiling, the phone resting against my face, wondering if I'd still be as thankful once Sweetness Minton and his heavies turned up.

14

I'd spent what was left of the night, struggling to sleep, laid out, shivering on a tatty bunk in a damp room over the top of Sweetness Minton's club on Lennox Avenue. Pigfoot had come along to keep me company. He'd sat himself in an armchair at the foot of the cot, lifted his feet up onto a stool, then lined up a series of enormous joints on the arm of the chair and proceeded to smoke each one, extinguishing the final joint between the tips of his thumb and forefinger as dawn broke. Throughout the remainder of the night, he'd sat in silence, the shotgun which seemed to be permanently attached to his right hand, aimed at the door in the event some other nut decided to seek me out and try and take another chunk out of my scalp with a length of cheese wire. Whilst Pigfoot kept watch, I rolled about the makeshift bed in restless turmoil; my eyes stinging, reliving the horror of what had happened back at the hotel, coughing underneath a choking thick canopy of marijuana smoke. By 5.30am I was up and taking a strip wash in the artist's changing room at the rear of the club.

I stood over a grubby, mildew-covered basin and quickly got myself cleaned up. I shaved, changed into fresh clothes, then walked back out into the club to be greeted by Minton, Pigfoot and Evangeline Laveau, who were all chatting by the side of the stage. Minton shrugged his shoulders at me by way of a reluctant greeting, then offered to make a pot of coffee. The three of us went and sat ourselves in a booth at the rear of the nightclub while Sweetness hacked and sneezed over a tired-looking percolator at the back of the bar. Laveau took out a packet of Camel cigarettes from her jacket pocket, lit one, then took a deep drag, finally blowing a curling trail of fuzzy, grey vapour up into the air. We watched as Minton slouched breathlessly from behind the bar and made his way across the dance floor towards us. He stopped at my side, then unceremoniously shoved a rusting metal tray containing a stained metal coffee pot and three battered mugs across the booth's brown Formica table towards us. Laveau sniffed then looked across at the tray and back up at Minton. The tubby negro took a couple of steps backwards from the booth and glared at Laveau. "What's yuh fuckin' problem?"

"My problem?" Laveau pointed at the tray. "You gotta be kiddin' me . . . three cups o' damn coffee? That's all the breakfast we git befo' we trek our asses halfway across the country; three goddamn coffees? Sweetness, you are one cheap bastard, you know that?"

Minton dismissed her with a wave of his sweaty palm. He turned and slowly walked back across to the bar, finally calling back to Laveau when he'd settled himself on to a high-backed stool and lit up a cigar. "Niggah, dis ain't the fuckin' Waldorf Astoria. Yuh want breakfast . . . go git it on the damn train!"

*

Sweetness Minton drove Laveau, Pigfoot and me across Harlem to Pennsylvania Station personally. The train was due to pull out at 7.30am on the dot and Minton made sure we were there with plenty of time to spare. The three of us said our farewells to Sweetness quickly. The huge nightclub owner sat behind the wheel of his expensive Cadillac looking like a fat negro vampire, scared to be out during the hours of daylight. This was a man who clearly wanted to be elsewhere and who was still in a real bad mood after being dragged out of his bed during the wee small hours and forced to arrange the clean-up of my hotel room and the disposal of yet another pile of blood-soaked corpses.

I was never going to be Sweetness Minton's best friend and I could tell that he was eager to have me out of his life. He turned sluggishly in his seat, stuck his hand into the inside pocket of his jacket and handed over the train tickets and a brown envelope to Laveau. He grunted farewell to Pigfoot, then nodded at me sourly. We climbed out of the Cadillac, collected our luggage from the boot, then watched as Sweetness pulled his motor out into the street, slammed his foot on the gas and sped off up Seventh Avenue.

*

Even at such an early hour Pennsylvania Station was alive with a hefty throng of commuters. Businessmen rushed past our faces, their heads tucked into their chests clutching at leather briefcases, all, I assumed, heading for early morning meetings. Holidaymakers ushered excited children, their little ones clutching on to their parents' hands. Uniformed servicemen and women seemed to be standing and waiting everywhere I looked, their heavy dark green kit bags slung over their shoulders. The military personnel were constantly being joined by other soldiers and sailors, all, it seemed, on their way back across country to various ports and barracks. We pushed on, cutting through the hordes, and finally squeezed into a lift which took us down to the passenger departure concourse.

Penn Station was buzzing with life. I followed Laveau and Pigfoot as they made their way across the busy foyer. Laveau checked which platform we were leaving from, then trudged through the crowds across an ornate marble floor and along a lengthy corridor which finally brought us out into a huge atrium overlooking the platforms and waiting trains.

Laveau, Pigfoot and I were among the first passengers out of the lift and down to the gate of the platform. The huge Amtrak Crescent line locomotive was waiting on the tracks, its engines rumbling noisily away. The platform was dimly lit, humid and emitted the strangely comforting aroma of grease, diesel and wood polish. In front of us, a blind, elderly black man, immaculately dressed in a dark suit and tie, sunglasses and newsboy cap, made his way slowly across the platform. The old man shuffled along with a white cane, guided by a black porter who held him gently by one elbow. Seeing that his own leaden, measured movements were limited by blindness, advanced age and bad knees, I wondered where he was going, and how the hell he ever managed to travel alone.

Pigfoot nudged me with his elbow as we walked. He was carrying a small holdall and a plain brown leather golfing bag was slung over his shoulder, which I was pretty damn sure didn't contain a single club. He looked at me disapprovingly as we headed towards the train. "What yuh starin' at the beaten down ole blind niggah fo'?"

We stopped suddenly to join another small queue to board the train. I looked at Pigfoot and shrugged my shoulders. "I was just wondering that's all."

"Wundrin' 'bout what?"

"'Bout what happen last night. All that damn madness. I'm starting to worry that I may never get to be as old as that poor fella over there. Seems like since I got here, all I've seen is death an' killing."

Pigfoot laughed. "Don't be worryin' 'bout gittin' near ya grave, Mistah Ellington, or 'bout nun o' dem stiffs yuh seen or tha honky yuh 'ad ta kill. Dem already cold in da ground. Befo' now me an' Minton's boys done buried five or six niggahs one af'a da other, all a dem in the same damn suit. Nobody be followin' yuh fo' dem fella's killins. Trus' me."

Pigfoot laughed to himself then pushed past one of the queuing passengers and pressed on in front, leaving me to ponder his dark hellfire words. The grim image of the face of the dead white man I'd killed earlier still hung in my mind as I climbed up the steps and boarded the train.

Laveau and Pigfoot had sleeping berths either side of my own. Laveau had shown our tickets and a porter had led us to our individual carrels. Laveau said she'd let me get some sleep and that she would join me for dinner later that evening. I nodded in agreement, then opened up my compartment door and dragged myself and my heavy case inside. I dropped the bag next to my feet and looked around the small room. The overnight billet was compact but comfortable. A single bunk on the back wall was where I'd be laying my head for the night. On the opposite side were two facing seats that could make up a second bed, and a sink that flipped down over a poky toilet. A young black female steward knocked the door to inform me what time dinner was served in the dining car. She smiled and wished me a pleasant journey and left me to store my luggage underneath my bunk. As we picked up speed, I slumped down into a seat by the window and watched as New York's skyscrapers soon gave way to New Jersey timber homes and high-rise apartments. The seven-car train rumbled through the built-up suburbs, climbing steadily along the tracks for thirty miles or so before passing over the dizzyingly narrow span of a long iron and sandstone bridge. From there, the locomotive cut through the beautiful dense woodlands of New Jersey to the lush green Pennsylvanian forests. The willow and lime backcloth of new countryside was like nothing I had encountered before. The fertile countryside took my breath away with its vastness and rural splendour. The weighty canopies of the trees which shrouded either side of the rail tracks caused the inside of my cabin to darken. My eyelids flickered and became heavy, the uncontrollable desire to embrace sleep gnawing at my insides.

During the next hour I fought to stay awake as we passed through a varying landscape of plantations, timberland, scrapyards and wooded wastelands, each punctuated by an array of decaying buildings. A huge chemical plant that looked like a disused hobo settlement took up a vast swathe of the landscape as the train continued to rattle along. Smokestacks coughed out white fumes from countless foundries. Each elderly-looking smelleding works had a tired, eerie feel to it; all had loading bays and platforms offset by the same decaying intricate latticed scaffolding frontages. Further along the track, huge blue silos erupted out of the earth, a vast interconnecting network of pipes. Most were discoloured deep orange and cracked with rust that trailed along the ground, which was as dark as black sand. Industrial wasteland soon made way for a more welcoming landscape of open fields that was occasionally interspersed between wild and dense brush. Birch trees lined either side of the route and, in the distance, undulant hills rolled out for as far as the eye could see. Outside the loud, hurrying train pushed on and my eyes began to struggle to make out the ever-changing panorama which raced past. The magical and new terrain that had until recently caused me such delight and intrigue now seemed more like topography wallpaper than new-found scenery to delight and amaze. It was a kind of wallpaper that soon became simple and repetitious; one where you looked at the seams rather than the breathtaking design. I rested my chin against my chest as darkness took over inside my head, then drifted toward a long overdue state of welcome slumber.

*

It was just before 6pm by the time Evangeline Laveau had knocked on my cabin door and woke me from what had been a seven-and-a-half-hour hibernation. I'd been dead to the world for the better part of the day and I still felt like I could keep on sleeping until we reached New Orleans. Laveau sat down next to me and laughed at the lethargic state that was lounging next to her. Since I'd last seen her, she had changed out of her leather jacket and trousers into a pretty white cotton dress decorated with blue and yellow flowers. On her feet were a pair of white canvas pumps with no socks, which showed off her dainty feet. Her hair had been drawn back into a tight ponytail; only two single curls had been allowed to escape and hung down either side of her cheeks. Her eyes were the most beautiful that I had ever seen. She wore no make-up and looked all the more stunning for it. Evangeline nudged me with her elbow as I pulled myself up straight in my seat.

"Say there, Rip Van Winkle. I could hear you snorin' ya head off from next door. How you feelin' now?"

I peered out of the window dopily at the fast-moving countryside. "Like my head's in a bucket. Where the hell are we?"

Laveau shrugged her shoulders. "Someplace between Danville an' Greensboro. In the meantime, whilst you were in the land o' nod you missed the Philadelphia skyline, Chesapeake Bay estuaries, Baltimore, the Washington monument and Jefferson memorial. Nothing important. You hungry."

I rubbed at my face with the palms of my hands. "Yeah, starving."

"Good, straighten yo'self up an' let's go eat. Pigfoot, he already bin an' chowed down. He's away in his pit. Catching up on his beauty sleep after babysitting you all night."

The train rattled and jerked as we walked along the narrow corridor towards the dining car, our bodies thrown from side to side by a sudden rocking. A pot-bellied black conductor met us halfway and stepped back and smiled at us, extending his big arms, indicating that we should come on by him. Inside the dining car, Muddy Waters was playing on a crackling blues station, and plates of fried food misted up the windows when we entered. I had to grab onto the back of a booth to prevent myself from falling facedown into a woman's lap as we made our way to a table with a couple of free seats. In my enthusiasm, I had imagined the Crescent to be a faded American version of the Orient Express, sadly it was nothing more than a no-frills commuter train. On the way through, things looked pretty rough. The bar car looked shabby and needed reupholstering and the dining car reeked of fried fish. A middle-aged white waitress greeted us sternly as Laveau and I sat in our seats and continued to boss us around like a canteen matron scolding a couple of school kids whilst we ordered from the menu.

I looked at the bill of fare, my eyes immediately drawn towards the eggs with bacon, sausage, buttery grits and biscuits. Laveau ordered for me, then got herself a plate of fried chicken and a green salad, along with a couple of cold beers. She sat back in her seat and looked out of the window, finally turning back to me and speaking after our beers had been brought over.

"Once we hit Mississippi, that curtain behind you head is gonna separate us from the rest o' the good white folk on board. We'll be doin' our eatin', drinkin' and socialisin' wid the rest o' the niggah's onboard. Our Jim Crow laws still got some clout down south, even if they bin outlawed in the north."

I nodded my head sleepily. "Same kinda thing happen back in Britain, only not quite so bad. Looks like something's never change no matter where you are in the world, Miss Laveau."

"Oh, they gonna change, Joseph ... They gonna be changin' real soon." Laveau took an angry swig of her beer, glared back out of the window and lost herself in the countryside that was zooming by. I sat back and shut my eyes and listened to two elderly black women seated at an adjacent table. The old girls were discussing how they both missed the strong, bitter coffee with chicory that they drank in New Orleans. Eavesdropping on their flighty conversation passed the time while I waited for our food to arrive, and it took my mind off other more weighty, troubling matters. At one point, one of the women snapped at the other sternly and remarked, "You know, I met Elvis befo' he was famous. I wasn't impressed ... His

140

damn neck was dirty." I opened my eyes and saw Evangeline Laveau staring at me. I rubbed the doziness outta my face with the palm of my hand and smiled at her.

"I'm sorry, I'm not being very good company. I'm still real tired." Laveau nodded. I sensed that she was lurching toward a conversation she knew I really didn't want to have. She took another swig of beer then rested her arms on the table just as our food was being brought over. A young black waitress carefully laid our plates of food in front of us and smiled.

"Will there be anything else fo' ya'all?"

Laveau put her bottle onto the table, looked up at the waitress and returned the smile. "No, that'll be it fo' now, honey. Thanks." For the next ten minutes we both ate in silence. The food was excellent: simple and tasty. We finished our meals and the beers and Laveau lit a cigarette before calling over the waitress and ordering two more bottles. She looked across the table as the waitress cleared away our plates and gestured with her head towards me.

"Brother, it's a long damn journey we got ourselves; I hope you're gonna be better company than Pigfoot. That Bajan ain't much fo' conversation."

"That maybe a problem. I ain't what you'd call the talky type either."

Laveau sat back in her seat and shrugged her shoulders. "Shit ... Are all you island folk the same? You niggah's are either yellin' ya mouths off or just plain damn mute."

I laughed and nodded my head. "You ain't far off the mark there ... Bajans kinda choose their words real carefully, Miss Laveau."

The waitress returned with the two beers, placing the dripping, ice-cold bottles on crisp white paper doilies before

141

leaving us again. I picked up the beer and read the label, *Jax, a New Orleans Tradition*, then put the bottle to my mouth and took a sip. The beer tasted good. The cold liquid gripped at my insides as it slid down my throat and settled in my belly.

"Call me Evangeline, will ya? Look, we're gonna have to find sum'ting to talk 'bout. We got a lotta distance to cover, an' I git bored real easy. So, you are gonna need to step up to the plate an' git talking to me, Joseph."

"You make it sound real complicated."

"Ain't nuthin' complicated 'bout it; a long-distance train conversation ain't like no normal small talk you git with most strangers. Most black folk on trains, they wanna talk. Wanna know all 'bout your life. Shit, on a train, you're likely to be sitting with some fool fo'ever. Who the hell wants to go thirty-two hours without talking to anybody? What you gonna do: watch the scenery drift by? Offer the occasional dull comment to the waiter? Compare fuckin' notes with 'em? You may as well spill your guts to me; that's unless you're gonna hide in that poky sleeper cabin fo' the rest of the journey?"

"No, I don't wanna do that, but I had hoped to see some of that scenery drift by after missing so many landmarks earlier, if that's alright by you?"

"Fine by me, I ain't got a problem with you takin' in the views. I just don't wanna spend the entire trip twiddling my damn thumbs an' staring out the window whilst I'm headin' home."

"Home. You're from New Orleans?"

Laveau shook her head and laughed. "Nah, Leflore County, Mississippi. But the Southern states are still home. The South is where I grew up. Made me who I am ... Don't mean I'm in any rush to be going back though."

142

"And that's why you weren't too happy with Minton 'bout making this journey with me?"

"You damn right I wasn't happy. It's still the same shit fo' niggahs in the South. Burnin' crosses in black folks' backyards. All that kinda crap."

Laveau sat forward again and stabbed the tip of her index finger on the table in front of her. "If you is black, once you hit the South then you got yourself a heap a' trouble from the off, whether you like it or not. There's still segregation. There's lynchings and beatings by those fuckas in the pointy white hats. There's po'lice corruption and endemic racism. It's a way o' life down there, and we're about to go stick our black faces into all that."

I shook my head. "And I thought we had it bad back home on Bim an' over in Britain."

"Look, brother, don't matter where a niggah from. It's the same anywhere a person o' colour goes. Nobody wants us, whether it's here or four thousand miles away across the Atlantic. A niggah is still a niggah in white folks' eyes, an' don't you evah go forgittin' it!"

Laveau took another swig of her beer. She held the edge of the glass on the table, agitated, turning the tumbler in her hand as she continued to speak. "In the South, if you black, then you ain't even a second-class citizen in most white folks' eyes. You ain't even a human being ta most o' them damn crackers. That's why I moved to Harlem when I was nineteen. It's why I joined the movement. Got myself organised an' aware o' what's going on in the real world fo' black folks. I got rid o' God an' got myself organised with the brotherhood fo' the cause. The idea I gotta drag my black ass back down to New O'leans with you ain't fillin' me with any kinda joy, that's fo' damn sure."

"But buying dope and guns from my cousin is helping you and your brothers to find joy and better that cause, is it?"

"It's a means to an end, Joseph ... a means to an end. Look, the dope brings in cash; the cash gives us a power base. Shit, most honkies bin carry guns or knives since they jumped off the ship with Columbus. It's took five hundred years for the black man to catch up with them. It's time we was armed. Only way these crackers are evah gonna listen to what we gotta say is if we gotta pistol in our hands and we start using 'em."

"I don't buy it, Evangeline. Do you really think carrying a gun an' killing white folk is gonna get you what you want?"

"I don't give a shit whether you buy it or not. We're on the cusp of a revolution here in the States, brother. Guns is gonna git us heard. It's what's gonna make those bastards sitting in their ivory towers back in Washington sit up and listen. Once they see a bunch a' niggahs armed to the teeth on their precious streets, things are gonna change."

"You really think so? What do you think is gonna happen when your government sees all these black militant revolutionaries armed to the teeth?"

"I think we're gonna have ourselves a heap o' trouble. But it'll be trouble worth takin' on to git what we is due."

"What you're due? It all sounds pretty scary to me."

"It is, Joseph, it is real scary, but that's my point. The cause ain't just 'bout carryin' a piece. It ain't 'bout havin' ta fight with white folk. It's 'bout what's right, an' things ain't bin right fo' me an' every other negro born an' raised in this country fo' centuries."

Laveau stared around the diner then sank back the remainder of her beer in a couple of gulps. "Do you know that most a' the black folk making this trip, they gonna have to sleep in their damn seats? They segregated as soon as they reach the Georgia state line. Black folk, they mo' than likely gonna turn in for the night alongside some stranger an' wake up next to the same fool in the morning, then they stagger their asses down the aisle together for some breakfast. We the lucky ones. Minton, he forked out fo' the sleepers, so we can at least keep outta the way o' trouble and that means any unwanted honky attention. When we finished doin' all this talkin', we git to sleep in one o' them rickety bunks." Evangeline laughed to herself.

I watched as her face suddenly turned sombre. Her eyes had glassed over with a watery film when she looked back across the table at me. "My papa was murdered by a white cop when I was six years old. The town lawman found him playin' dice in the stock room of a general store in Laurel where I grew up. Papa was shootin' craps with the store owner, an old white fella called Walter Arnold. Walt, he got on with ever'body, he played dice and the bones with white folk and niggahs." Laveau shuffled in her seat. She looked suspiciously around the dining car then lowered her voice a little before continuing to speak. "My mama told me that she heard Papa's body had bin dropped into the Tallahatchie river. She said she went out there with my Uncle Clem an' a few other fellas, see if they could find him. Said the place was heavin' with cottonmouths and gators and that after searchin fo' her man fo' more than twelve odd hours, that there was no way all that dirty water or the wildlife were evah gonna give up his corpse, let alone his soul. Like you said a while back, somethings never charge. Sure, didn't fo' my papa. But it ain't gonna be the same fo' me. The cause gonna see to that."

145

Laveau rested her arm on the table, propped her chin into the palm of her hand and looked at me. Her eyes burrowed into me. "So, enough o' me ... come on, let's hear all about you, Mistah Detective Man ... What's your story?"

I smiled back at her then glanced nervously out the window and stared at the darkening sky. Dusk was beginning to fall. I turned in my seat and looked around the diner, which was now filled to bursting with travellers eating their evening meals. I stood up and took some cash out of my pocket to pay for our meal. Evangeline Laveau reached across the table and touched my hand. "Put your money away, honey. Dinner's on me."

"Thanks, Evangeline ..." I took hold of Laveau's hand and watched as she rose up out of her seat and smiled at me. I stood back out of the booth and guided her out into the aisle. "Come on, let's go to the bar, get ourselves another couple of beers then go find somewhere a little more private to sit and chat. The story I got to tell ain't for any kind of audience."

★

I talked until around midnight. In between recounting my entire life story, Evangeline and I drank more ice-cold Jax beer from bottles. We'd settled in two seats in a middle carriage that was practically empty. There I spoke about my late wife, Ellie, and our daughter, Amelia, and our lives back home on Barbados. I retold the tragic story of their deaths in graphic detail, discussed my work as a police sergeant and why I had been forced to flee to a country 4,500 miles from the place I'd been born and called home. I spoke about Bristol, St Paul's, Loretta and my late, much lamented friend, Carnell Harris. I retold my family history, and those

146

who played such an important part in it... I spoke with great fondness about my Aunt Pearl, Uncle Gabe and Vic. Afterwards, exhausted, we walked slowly back to our cabins. Evangeline held on to my arm as we strolled unsteadily along the carriage aisle and told me that, outside, the state of South Carolina was rolling past in the darkness, and that its moonlit fields were haunted with the ghosts of civil war soldiers.

The two of us stood without speaking outside my cabin door. Evangeline smiled up at me then came in real close and I didn't stop her. Her hand caressed the back of my neck, her body only inches from my own. My breathing rose high in my chest, I reached out and put my hands around Evangeline's waist and drew her gently towards me, her breasts touching my chest, the lost curls of her hair brushed against my face as I took her up in my arms and kissed her deeply. Her tongue snaked along the edges of my lips then slipped into my mouth. If she'd been worried that I may have thought her too easy, that signal hadn't yet reached her brain yet. Other signals related to a different part of my body were busy doing overtime. As we continued to kiss, I thought I heard the voice of my long-passed papa whispering the same words of wisdom he had spoken to me when I was a kid, "Pickney, when yuh a man an' you wid a wo'man, 'member it's da motion o' da ocean, not de size a da boat dat matters."

Evangeline's left hand gently touched my neck and her fingers glided along the centre of my back then I felt her arm drop away from my body and, at the same time, heard the door of my cabin creak open. Laveau's lips parted mine and she smiled at me. She took hold of my hand and began to walk backwards, drawing me into the cabin with her. I closed the door behind me and stood in front of Evangeline. She reached up and put her fingers on my face, slipped them through my hair, drew me down towards her, then kissed me again. I wrapped my arms around her slender back and lifted her up off her feet. As I embraced her tightly, I could smell her perfume and the faint scent of baby powder on her skin. I closed my eyes and wondered if her heart was in that very moment as light and as carefree as my own.

15

The rising sun woke me from a dreamless sleep. I lay on my back, struggling to bring the new day into focus, staring up at the train compartment's bare metal roof, my head and aching body unwilling to start the day. Blinking at the early light seeping through a crack in the curtains, I raised my left arm and peered through half-opened eyes down at my wristwatch; it was just after 8am. Evangeline Laveau had left my cramped berth at around 1.30am. I'd spent the rest of the night alone; though dearly wished that I hadn't. I lay thinking about the night before, recalling Laveau's beautiful, dark face smiling at me before we'd kissed. We'd caressed and spoken honeyed words under our breath, held each other in our arms and smooched like a couple of besotted teenagers on a first date. Later, just before Laveau left, she'd stroked my cheek and kissed me on the side of my temple, then spoken softly in my ear: "I better be goin' honey. If Pigfoot catch me tiptoein' outta yo' door, no tellin' what he gonna start thinkin'."

I'd watched Evangeline walk out of my tiny room and whispered, "Goodnight," to her before she'd quietly closed the door. As my simple farewell came out of my mouth, my heart had twitched and my stomach turned.

I suddenly felt bad about my heart racing as I lay there thinking about Evangeline Laveau. A strange sense of guilt and betrayal had crept up on me and had flung an accusatory shadow over my previously buoyant and romantic inner feelings. I told myself to promptly stash away any dewy feelings of attraction for my travelling companion and that it was time to get my bare ass out of my cot and face the day. Hauling myself up, I climbed down out of my bunk, pulled open the blinds then sat and looked out of the cabin window. Overnight, the landscape had got flatter, greener. I looked up into the clear blue sky and watched a hot-air balloon floating over the cane fields that stretched out along the rail tracks.

Although I couldn't be certain, the train looked as if it had recently eased itself into Mississippi state. Tumbledown shacks had replaced the massive industrial buildings of the north. Rusting cars and trucks stood idle in junk-strewn yards, generations of motor parts piled high at the backs of rundown timber homes. It all looked pretty poor and reminded me of the shanty villages back home, my mind reminiscing of my old island life on Barbados. I fondly recalled my childhood and how free I always felt. I thought of my long-dead papa and my mama. In my mind I saw the azure, crystal-clear seas, the miles of golden beaches, the warmth of the afternoon sun kissing the bare skin of my neck and back, the shadowed lakes groaning with bullfrogs, the hours spent fishing and playing in caves and rock pools with my sister, Bernice. I remembered long-suppressed feelings about my idyllic Caribbean home, my mind returning to the long summer seasons which I thought would be always eternal and when the world I lived in was a quiet and gentle, peaceful place; when life was simply there to be enjoyed with the same pleasure and certainty of an evening breeze that carried with it the sweet-scented fragrances of the azaleas and magnolia and watermelons that rose up from many a distant field.

But inside my head there were other darker memories of that time that ached to escape and blot out such calm, pastoral remembrances. My mind cruelly summoned up the desolate, little frame chattel home in the beach village I grew up in with its unpaved streets, garbage in the backyards and ditches full of mosquitoes. The days when the sun didn't shine and the hurricanes out at sea battered against the shore. The countless times I'd been alone as a child, ate scraps and leftovers because there was little else for us to eat, my father's drunken rages and the many times I would have to hide and witness him beat my mama until she bled. Early each morning I'd wake and watch my mama get up with her bruises, her pain and hardships and see her leave for work. She'd walk away from our rickety home with the knowledge of who she was and how little her life was worth to others, and how she spent much of it going to war with my papa and, more often than not, with the rest of the world.

★

I'd spent way too long staring out of the train window at a fast-moving view and dragging up bad memories from my past. I quickly got dressed in the clothes I'd been wearing the night before. I put on my jacket and went back out into the corridor of the carriage and took a slow walk down to the dining car. The diner was practically empty, so finding myself a free seat was real easy. Outside, the sun was shining and the sky cloudless. I ordered a plain omelette and mug of coffee and, when the waitress brought it over a short while later, I sat and ate in silence. Beyond the windows, I caught brief glimpses of small towns where American flags flew and cars and pickup trucks waited at crossings. For an instant, our passage was heralded by flashing red lights and warning bells. I heard the mournful sound of our own horn far ahead from the engine. The journey provided me a view of American towns as they were meant to be, with storefronts facing the tracks on both sides, framing the sometimes bleaker domestic scene. Gone-to-ruin gardens and the uncut lawns of old, tired houses sloped down to the tracks, presenting their ugly dilapidated truths. Abandoned buildings appeared in every other town we passed. The steep ravines at the side of the rail line were littered with old refrigerators, sofas and worn-out tyres, that had been dumped.

Children waved at the train as we passed over a crossroads in the middle of nowhere and I caught the ghostly image of a solitary black man drift by outside, pausing from his task of splitting wood with an axe as he silently noted our speeding passage at the side of his rundown tin-shack homestead. After I'd finished my breakfast and drank the last of my coffee, I looked behind me at the quiet bar area and considered going over and sitting myself down at the counter to order a long-neck bottle of the cold Jax beer I'd been drinking so much of the night before. I decided that booze was not the answer to alleviate my already melancholy mood. I riffled through my wallet and pulled out a five-dollar bill and left it underneath my empty coffee cup. I pulled myself up out of my seat and walked back down the carriage towards my room, my muddled brain still in two minds as to whether I should say "to hell with it", and turn back and go get myself that cold beer.

*

I stood undecided for a moment outside the door of my berth. Something didn't quite feel right. For no apparent reason I suddenly felt my chest tighten and my breathing become strangely laboured. I hesitated a moment longer whilst my right hand balled itself up into a fist, then took a deep breath, turned the handle and pushed it open. Inside, sat in the seat nearest the cabin window, was Evangeline Laveau. I walked inside and closed the door behind me, then leaned against it. Laveau looked up at me and smiled. It was a smile that made her look as beautiful and as happy as she was when she had walked out last night, only now something was different about her; something I couldn't quite put my finger on. Her face had a cool, slightly nervous look about it. Her already high cheekbones had been sculpted with faint dark rouge and she was wearing dark red lipstick, which gave her normally pliable features a crueller appearance. Her thick black hair had been pulled back from her forehead and tied in a bun.

She wore white gym sneakers on her feet, blue jeans, an open short leather jacket and a pale blue, round-necked T-shirt. She sat back in her seat and gestured with her head for me to join her in the chair next to her. I stayed for a moment, my head desperately trying to weigh up what was going on.

"Sit down." Laveau gave it as an order rather than a polite request. I gave her a long stare, unsure of what was about to go down.

"Joseph, sit ya ass down." This time there was a stern authority in the way she spoke. I did as she commanded and sat down next to her, a new fear taking hold of me as the recognition of the woman who had previously held a gun to my head rapidly sprang back into my mind. Laveau sank back a little further towards the window and put her hand into her jacket pocket. I immediately felt the hairs on the backs of my arms and my neck stand up on end. I stared back at her and felt myself frown.

153

"What's going on?"

Laveau stared down at her feet for a moment before looking me straight in the eyes. "Last night . . ."

"What about it."

Laveau cleared her throat. Out of the corner of my eye I saw her hand twitch inside her jacket pocket. "Last night shouldn't have happened?"

"Why?"

"Why? 'Cause it was a damn crazy thing to be doin', that's why!"

"I don't get it . . . why was it so crazy?"

"Joseph, this ain't *Peyton Place* . . . we in the fuckin' real world 'ere. If what went down back in Harlem was anything ta go by, then I don't see it gettin' any better by the time we hit the Big Easy. We need ta cool it now. Understand?"

I looked down at the floor and nodded my head. "Yeah, I understand."

Laveau got up out of her chair and stood directly over me. "Good. We need ta keep things between us just 'bout the business. Any'ting else just gonna lead ta trouble."

Laveau her put her hand gently on my shoulder. "Here, you may need this." I looked up as Laveau pulled her hand out of her jacket pocket and placed her .25 Beretta onto the seat next to me. "They play tough in the South, honey, an' you is gonna need more than your fists to pick a fight down there."

Laveau turned around and began to leave. I wanted to rise out of my seat and snatch her back towards me, but something inside of me held me back. I wanted to put my arms around her shoulders, press her body against mine and hold onto her for dear life. That's what I wanted. As Evangeline Laveau closed the door behind her, leaving me alone in the cabin, I reminded myself of the old Bajan saying: "That what you want, ain't always what you deserve."

★

I'd sat with my maudlin introspective thoughts rolling through my head for over an hour before I reached across and picked the Beretta up off the seat next to me. I held it flat on my palm, studying the weapon that Laveau had given me. It was compact and ugly from the snub snout of its short protruding barrel to the curious curled hammer. The grip was made of black Bakelite and it felt light in my hand. Sat at the butt of the pistol was a lanyard half-loop.

It was a small, well-designed and, from the little I knew, efficient gun. I thumbed the magazine release button on the butt and popped out the clip then took hold of the serrations on the rear of the slide and drew it back. Inside I saw a cartridge in the chamber. I gently let the slide drop back into place, leaving the hammer fully cock, then turned off the safety catch so that it covered the small red dot by the grip and tucked it into the waistband at the back of my trousers. I sat back in my seat and rested both hands behind the back of my head and felt myself sigh. Last night Evangeline Laveau had smothered me with a multitude of passionate kisses, this morning she'd told me to cool it and handed me a loaded gun. Sometimes, I thought to myself, a man's spirit and faith in his fellow human being can sink with a sense of loss and disappointment as abrupt and curt as opening a door to a dark room filled with a thousand whirring clocks.

16

I'd sat alone in my cramped berth for way too long. In my head I'd been going over Evangeline Laveau's earlier speech to me about keeping things professional and cool between us, her icy words lingering in my head like a leftover curse. I had planned to leave my room a lot earlier, but after all the downbeat talk I'd heard from Laveau, I just didn't have the strength to stand up. What she had said to me was true. With all the death and mayhem that was going on around us, it would have been plain foolhardy to consider becoming involved with each other. Once again, I was at odds with myself. My head told me Laveau was right; my lonely heart however felt very differently. Love, they say, makes of the wisest man a fool, and I knew that I had been very close to making a real chump of myself. I'd always known that when you live your life among desperate men and women, any door you open may have an unexpected Pandora's box waiting for you on the other side. Evangeline had locked the door of opportunity behind her before I'd had a chance to open it up. In doing so, she'd probably saved me from a good deal of pain and torment. By 1pm I'd had enough of feeling sorry for myself. I hauled myself up, grabbed my trilby and jacket from off the seat next to me, and felt at my back to make sure the Beretta was secure in my trouser waistband. I tipped the peak of my hat over my brow then walked out of the tiny cabin and made my way down to the bar compartment of the train.

★

I found a seat at the rear of the carriage, parked myself behind the table and waited for one of the bar staff to arrive. It didn't take long for a red-eyed, red-faced white waiter to turn up. His name tag read, Stanley. He stood with a notebook in his hand and smiled, his stubby yellow teeth offering up an insincere greeting that I could easily have done without. I watched as he put pencil to paper to take my order. "What'll it be, sir?" I coughed as I got a sudden whiff of the man's halitosis. I ordered myself a Jax beer and a shot of rum, then sat back in my chair and looked out of the window whilst I waited for my drinks to arrive.

Ol' Stinky Breath didn't keep me waiting long for my liquor. The red-faced waiter leaned across the table and carefully positioned both my beer and the glass of perfume-scented, caramel-coloured spirit on separate napkins in front of me. I thanked him and handed him a dollar bill tip for his trouble. The waiter nodded his head at me in gratitude and walked away. Such wordless thanks came as a great relief. The thought of the man's foul-smelling breath permeating the air around me turned my stomach and I reminded myself to be grateful for small mercies.

I breathed in the fruity aroma of the rum and took a sip. The spirit slid like velvet fire across my tongue. I then downed the remainder in three quick swallows. It tasted old and expensive and deserved much better treatment, but I was in no mood to be a connoisseur. I stood the empty crystal tumbler on the table in front of me, picked up the beer bottle and sank that back in a few swigs. I looked behind me at the bar and resigned myself that I'd have to put up with the stink coming out of the steward's mouth if I wanted more hooch. I reluctantly called the waiter back over and ordered myself another cold beer and I kept on ordering more bottles of the chilled, amber-coloured booze until around 3.30pm. I'd have still been drinking until the train hit New Orleans station, but Evangeline Laveau was about to put paid to that. I watched as she slinked her way down the carriage towards me. I supped the last dregs of my beer and twisted the bottle in my hand. When she finally sat down in the seat opposite, I got a hit of her heady perfume and was immediately transported back to our amorous encounter the night before. She crossed her legs and rested her hand on her knee. Laveau looked across at the empty beer bottle that I was clutching, then smiled at me. It was an unexpected benign grin, which immediately put me on edge again. When she finally spoke, I was almost expecting her to berate me on the demons of daytime drinking. I couldn't have been further off the mark.

"You seen Pigfoot today?"

I rested the beer bottle down on the table and shook my head. "I ain't seen Pigfoot since I stepped on to this damn train. You checked for him in his cabin?"

Laveau gawped back at me. "'Course I checked his damn cabin. He ain't there, ain't in any of the johns takin' a leak, ain't eatin' in the diner and he ain't here with you gettin' drunk!"

I shrugged my shoulders. "What do you wanna do?"

Evangeline Laveau gave me a look that could kill. "I want you to stop behaving like a barfly ass'ole and come and help me find the crazy son of a bitch; that's what I want you to do."

Laveau gestured towards the stinky waiter. "Pay ya damn bar tab and let's get goin'."

Laveau shot up out of her seat, stood in the aisle and shook her head at me while I fumbled in my pocket for my wallet. She turned on her heels and strode back along the carriage muttering quiet obscenities to herself. I pulled out a couple of five-dollar bills and handed them to the waiter then traipsed on after Laveau like a scolded spouse chasing the forgiveness of an ill-tempered wife.

★

We checked both my own and Evangeline's berths before looking again inside Pigfoot's room. Just as Laveau had said, there was no sign of the man. The room smelled of body odour and stale marijuana smoke. The bunk was still made and had clearly not been slept in. On the floor next to one of the seats was an empty plate and a food-smeared knife and fork. I knew that Pigfoot had travelled light. The golf bag, which I knew contained the Bajan minder's trusty shotgun, was nowhere to be seen, and this set my nerves on edge. We backtracked through the bar to the rear of the train, then turned back and walked along the aisle of each of the carriages, sticking our heads in every room door that would open. We checked toilets, a guard's office and looked across at countless rows of seats as we headed towards the front of the train. We let the final door of the last passenger carriage snap shut behind us. In front was the door of the baggage car and our only way forward. I looked back at Laveau, who gestured with her head for me to open it up and push on with our search. I did as she ordered and headed on into the storeroom.

The carriage was lit by a series of tiny lamps that hung

from the walls either side of the aisle at four-foot intervals. The lights gave out a subdued glare. Wooden shelving ran in rows parallel to the central aisle. Each shelf was stacked floor to ceiling with passenger baggage, parcels and mailbags. The shelving ran either side across the full width of the train, separated only by the walkway running along the centre of the carriage. Evangeline began to search along the left-hand side set of shelves whilst I took the right. Halfway along the carriage, towards the end of one of the rows, I was hit with the fusty and all too familiar pong of burnt dope. In front of me, at the very end of the row of shelves, stuffed tight into the right-hand corner, bathed in the shadows of the overhanging luggage and travel trunks, was a hessian mail sack propped up against the wall of the train. I could just make out that it had been turned on its head so that the opening and cord ties were dragged down towards the floor. I carefully inched myself forward and stood over the sack for a moment, my mouth as dry as a bone and my body trembling. I grabbed hold of the top of the sack, then coughed and tried to call back to Laveau to come and find me. I couldn't get the words out. My throat became tight and my power of speech was suddenly lost in the semi-darkness. I took a deep breath, then looked at the floor, deliberately averting my eyes from whatever was underneath, then snatched the mailbag up from the ground, dragging it above my head, then let it drop at my side and immediately staggered backwards. In front of me, jammed into the corner of the baggage car like a ghoulish mannequin was Pigfoot's body. His head was tipped back, his eyes wide open and staring up at me. A blank expression was etched across his lifeless face, giving him the haunted look of a gargoyle awaiting the magical breath of life. I swallowed hard and took a couple of steps towards his corpse to get a better look. On the left-hand side of Pigfoot's neck, underneath his jaw, I could just pick out a single puncture wound. There was very little blood around it, most of it already clotting. A thin trail had seeped down his neck onto his shirt and the lapel of his jacket.

Whoever had murdered Pigfoot had known what they were doing. This wasn't a case of two men going head to head for a simple punch up. This was a professional hit. An assassination. From the little I knew of the Bajan, he'd have been a hard man to put down. His killer would have needed to be strong and swift; just like the fella that had tried to silence me back at my Harlem hotel room. Behind me, I heard Evangeline Laveau call out my name. I reached down to my side and quickly picked the mail sack from off the floor and turned back around, just as Laveau began walking down the aisle towards me. I held out my arm, the palm of my hand outstretched to stop her coming any closer. Even in such poor light, I knew Evangeline would make out the horror that I desperately didn't want her to see. I watched as she held out her arm and took a couple more unsteady paces towards me. Laveau looked over my shoulder, then immediately put her hand to her mouth followed by a sharp intake of breath. I saw her body pitch forward then falter. I reached out and grabbed her elbow, then cupped my hand behind the nape of Evangeline's neck and snatched her close to me. In the Cimmerian shade, Laveau's trembling body pulsed uncontrollably against my own. Her sobbing muffled as she sank her face deep into my chest.

17

My Uncle Gabe had once told me that great kingdoms were lost for want of a nail in a horse's shoe. I think lives perhaps unravel in the same fashion, sometimes over events as slight as an insult, an ill-spoken opinion or being in the wrong place at the wrong time. Whoever had murdered Pigfoot had little regard as to whether his life had mattered to anyone, or if his body was found. I was pretty sure the Bajan minder's killer wanted to link his death to me. And with corpses piling up behind me from as far back as Harlem, I knew that if I didn't start to cover my tracks I'd soon be taking a seat on the electric chair. Evangeline Laveau stood in silence close behind me. I could feel her body trembling against me. I reached down and took hold of one of her shaking hands then gestured with my head down towards the dead Bajun.

"He has to go."

Evangeline squeezed hold of my fingers as she glanced down at Pigfoot's corpse. "What you mean, go?"

"I gotta get rid of him before he starts stinkin' the place out. If somebody finds him before we reach New Orleans we're gonna be in a heap o' trouble. They'll have the cops waiting at the station and swarming all over the train. Nobody's gonna be able to get off; not me, not you, not the train guards, the driver or whoever it was that actually killed him." Confusion and fear was stamped across Evangeline's face. She looked uneasily back down at Pigfoot then straight back up at me.

"Evangeline, the killer either wanted us to find Pigfoot or for some other fool on board to stumble across him an' start hollering. This was planned. It's a warning."

Evangeline shook her head at me in bewilderment. "Whadda ya mean, it's a warning?"

I took hold of Evangeline's upper arms in my hands. I could feel her body quaking in my grip. "Whoever it was killed Pigfoot is more than likely still onboard this train, and they probably have been since we got on at Penn Station. I don't know how many of 'em there are or what the hell they want; I just know that it all rolls back to my cousin Vic, and that they've already killed nine of your people and they nearly had my head took off at the neck with a cheese wire. We need to lessen the odds against us. I need to throw Pigfoot off a' this damn locomotive, then we need to go find someplace safe to hole up fo' a couple hours until we reach New Orleans."

I let go of Evangeline's arms and bent down and quickly ran my hands across Pigfoot's stiffening body, searching for anything that could possibly identify him. I riffled through his pockets and laid the contents out on the palm of my hand. There was no driving licence or identification, no photograph of a sweetheart or proof of who he was, just six crumpled twenty-dollar bills and a little spare change, a packet of Juicy Fruit gum, a book of matches and a half-dozen toothpicks. Not a lot to show for a man's life. Pigfoot had been a ghost in this world and, as I was leaning over his remains, I got the unsettling feeling he'd be a revenant phantom from the afterlife too. I stuffed the few meagre possessions he'd owned into my jacket pocket then picked up the mail sack from the floor beside me and began to pull it over Pigfoot's head, then dragged it down over the rest of his body until I reached his feet. I put my hand behind the back of the hessian bag and eased Pigfoot's body onto the floor, then took hold of his ankles and pushed his starchy legs up into the sack. I pulled at the rope drawstring around the top of the mailbag, closing the dead Bajan into the makeshift body bag. I glanced behind me at Evangeline, who had taken herself down to the end of aisle and was looking uneasily along the corridor back to where we had entered the baggage compartment.

I got up off my haunches, grabbed hold of the unwieldy sack and lifted it up towards me. I rested the heavy mailbag against my chest for a moment, took a deep breath, bent forward a little and heaved the Bajan's corpse over my shoulder. Pigfoot was a dead weight no matter how diminutive he'd been when he was alive. Manoeuvring myself along the tight aisle between the parcel shelves wasn't easy. Evangeline stood out in the passageway of the baggage car then followed after me as I made my way towards the central door in the middle of the carriage. Evangeline reached down and grabbed hold of the release bar on the large sliding door, yanked it up towards her and ran it backwards. The humid carriage was immediately filled with the deafening noise of the train as it hurtled along the tracks. My hat was torn off my head and blown back into the carriage as I stumbled backwards, my legs almost giving way from underneath me as the force of the wind and the speeding momentum of the locomotive pushed me away from the gaping hole in the side of the carriage.

I regained my balance and staggered back towards the open door, the wind pelting at my face and body and howling behind me down the baggage car. I lifted the sack off my shoulder and held it at arm's length beside me then pulled my feet apart to steady myself. I gripped the edges of the mailbag, bent my knees a little then wrenched back my arms, tensed the muscles at the top of my back and shoulders and slung Pigfoot's body out of the door. As the sack pitched itself out into the speeding void I grabbed hold of the side of the door and gripped the metal rim of the frame for dear life. I watched as the mail sack spun violently across the stony ground at the edge of the tracks and was then thrown down the sidings towards the thick undergrowth of the pine forest. The scream of the wind rushed across my head, the violent force of the gust blew my body about in the open doorway like a like a rag doll.

I saw Evangeline fighting to draw the heavy ingress back along its runner. I reeled backwards and grabbed hold of the handle of the carriage door and the two of us hauled it shut. Evangeline and I fell back against the door. We both sat still, allowing the silence inside the carriage to wash over us. My head dropped forward, and I could feel my arms and legs tensing with adrenaline and fear. I took a deep breath and slowly reached across the wooden floor to take hold of Evangeline's hand. When my fingers touched her skin, she snatched her arm back and shuffled her body away from me. I looked across and saw her huddling her legs up close against her shaking body, her face tucked into her chest, her body crumpling up like a tissue. She drew her quaking arm around her legs then rested her chin on her knees. Evangeline raised her head and gazed across at me, her tear-filled eyes searching mine as though she would hope to see in them the reflected image of someone better; a man very different from the one who sat before her now, a soul possessing the

165

decency and virtue which I knew she sought in her fellow mortal and not one who had drawn her into a terrifying world of bloodshed and death.

I watched as Evangeline's dilated pupils flickered then saw her frightened eyes nervously shift from mine and stare disjointedly out into space, her face etched with tormented thought like the silent beating of a bird's wings inside a cage.

18

My mouth was dry and tasted of ashes. I closed my eyes for
a moment, my mind desperately trying to wish itself that the
horror it was living through was just some kind of bad dream.
I rested the palm of my hand on my chest and listened to my
heart beat away like an overworked motor. When I reopened
my eyes, the world came back into focus and offered up the
same nightmare my brain was trying to run away from. I
stumbled to my feet, and immediately felt a sense of self-
loathing nip at the insides of my guts. Evangeline stayed
put. She glared up at me, her nettled expression desperately
trying to mask the hostility and confusion that I knew she
felt inside. I held out my hand, but she refused to take it. I
shrugged my shoulders and left her to haul her own ass up off
the baggage compartment floor. I turned and eyeballed the
ground, searching for my trilby. I found it jammed against
the base of one of the parcel shelving racks. Evangeline had
already begun to make her way towards the door to leave. I
hightailed after her, grabbing hold of the edge of the carriage
door as it swung back towards my face. I caught up and the
two of us walked in silence back along the corridors of six
practically empty cars until we reached our berths. Outside,
it was growing dark by degrees. The trees at the side of the
track were becoming silhouettes against a blossoming cobalt
sky before merging together in the coming blackness.

When we reached our cribs, I told Evangeline to go and

quickly pack her things while I went next door to Pigfoot's cabin and cleaned the place up. Evangeline nodded her head without speaking and went back into her room, leaving me standing alone, staring at the door she'd just snapped shut in my face.

Three short, solitary steps were all it took to get me outside Pigfoot's room. I reluctantly opened up and went inside and was again hit by the sour stink of dope. I tipped my trilby back on my head and looked around the cramped, stinky billet. There certainly hadn't been a struggle inside. There was no blood or damage to the furniture or bunk. I rested my back against the cabin door, my head filled with questions I had no answers for. Why so many dead in such a short space of time, and for what? None of it made sense. Had Pigfoot perhaps known his killer? Had he walked out of his cabin and gone to the baggage compartment with someone he was familiar with, someone he had trusted? And, if so, why? I stared down at the floor. Apart from some old food drying up on a plate and the littered remnants of a little dried leaf tobacco and a few loose cigarette papers, there was nothing untoward. Nothing except the missing golf bag, which had contained Pigfoot's shotgun and ammo. That was gone, taken by his killer, for sure. I put the shotgun to the back of my mind and quickly picked up anything that the dead Bajan had left lying around, stuffed it all out of the window and let it blow down the tracks. I cleaned down anywhere I had touched with my handkerchief, then went back to my own berth and did the same in there. I collected my case and overcoat from the end of the bed and looked around the berth one last time to make sure I had everything. I walked back out into the corridor, took a deep breath and went and knocked on Evangeline's door. I stood back in the aisle and waited for her to open it up, knowing the reception I was about to receive would not be a benevolent one.

★

I knew we couldn't stay in the berths we'd slept in overnight. I was pretty sure we were being watched, but I didn't know by who, or how many, or for that matter where they might be hiding out on the train. Whoever had killed Pigfoot still had to be on board, and Laveau and I had to be their next targets. Evangeline and I needed new digs and quick. It needed to be a berth close to an exit, someplace we could get out as soon as we hit New Orleans Union Station. Evangeline slowly opened the door, a .38, snub-nosed revolver in her hand, pointed directly at my belly.

I smiled back at her nervously, all too aware of the piece stuck only a few inches away from my stomach. "We gotta go."

Evangeline held onto the door tightly then suddenly let the gun drop to her side and nervously gestured with her head at me. "Where we goin' to?"

"I ain't got time fo' explanations. Go get your bag, we're goin' upmarket fo' the last part of this ride."

Evangeline looked at me suspiciously, her body motionless, like a scared rabbit caught in the headlights of a fast-moving vehicle. I snapped at her to bring her out of the statue-like state. "For Christ's sakes girl . . . we need to move right now!" Evangeline's eyes snapped open and shut, my barking at her suddenly bringing her back to her senses. She looked down at the .38 in her hand then quickly stuffed it into the pocket of her leather jacket, grabbed her case from behind her and followed me out into the aisle of the carriage.

There wasn't a soul to be seen as we made our way down to the immaculately restored first-class car that was coupled

169

up directly behind the back of the locomotive. A desolate train carriage had been the only piece of good fortune I'd had since arriving in the damn country. My second lucky break came when I thankfully found a cabin that was unoccupied. I looked up and down the aisle to check if we were still alone, then ushered Evangeline inside and followed her in.

The plush roomette was pink and blue in the shades of a plastic 1950s dollhouse. It had its own tiny bathroom, comfy seats and a fold-down bed rather than a bunk. Evangeline dropped her case at the floor, plumped up one of the pillows and stretched out onto the bed and shut her eyes. As the train rattled gently along the tracks, I sat down on one of the swanky chairs and rested my aching body against its high back and looked over at Evangeline who seemed to be lost in a fearful world of her own. My own head was still in a place somewhere between sleep and wakefulness. I looked out of the window into the blackness and wondered just where we were. With only the occasional street light or platform whirring past, there was little in the way of clues to our exact location or how long we'd still be on board. I reached out my hand and gently touched Evangeline's elbow, but she snatched herself away from me,

"Don't touch me." Evangeline sat up, swung her legs off the bed and stared at me, wild-eyed, pleading in silent panic for some kind of explanation. I shoved the palms of my hands up in front of me, hoping to placate my grudging travel companion a little.

"Hey, I'm sorry ... I just want to ask if you knew where we might be?"

Evangeline's agitation mellowed a little. She turned and looked out of the window at nothing but darkness, then shrugged her shoulders. "I ain't sure. I guess some place close to Hammond. If we are, it'd be another two hours befo' we hit the Big Easy."

I shuffled uneasily in my seat. "Look, I'll be honest with you, Evangeline. I don't know everything that is goin' on ... I'm no closer to finding out the truth than I was the first night we met, but I think I might know who the guys that murdered Pigfoot and the rest of those other poor bastards back in Harlem are, and I sure know how they work. We gotta start thinkin' real smarter than they do. They're well organised, smart, an' they ain't gonna stop until we're both dead."

The hairs stood up on the back of my neck as I watched the slow realisation of my words sink deep into her mind then brush out across Evangeline's face. Her eyes closed as she moved her head back in despair and in acceptance of the pain that she believed was about to follow.

"How do you know 'em, Joseph?"

I leaned forward in my seat, rested my palms on my knees and stared back at her. "When I was a po'liceman back home on Bim, I wasted more than two years of my life trying to put the man who is most probably running these guys behind bars. I never managed to do it."

"You talkin' 'bout Monroe?"

I nodded. "Yeah."

"This Monroe fella, he a honky?"

"Oh yeah, he's white, alright. White as that damn alabaster box I got hidden in my case."

Evangeline leaned forward, stuck her hand into her coat pocket and pulled out a packet of Camel and her lighter. She put the opened packet to her mouth and pulled out a cigarette with her lips then lit it. "And you think maybe this Monroe fella could be partnered up with your cousin Vic?"

171

I shook my head. "Monroe and Vic in partnership, no way . . . no way in hell. Vic may be linked into all this madness fo' sure, but he ain't responsible fo' killing Pigfoot or any of your other people. Like I said befo', it ain't Vic's way. He's been doing business with your organisation without a hitch. He supplied, you paid. There's no reason for him to try an' stiff you as far as I can see. There's one other thing Vic would never do."

Evangeline took a heavy drag on her cigarette and blew a thick plume of grey smoke at me. "Yeah, what's that?"

"Use white fellas to do his dirty work fo' him. Vic would trust a white man 'bout as much as he'd trust a cop."

Evangeline pulled on the end of her smoke then released another curl of hazy vapour from the corner of her mouth. "What 'bout a white cop?"

I cleared my throat and shook my head. "Vic'd sooner kill a white cop than trust him . . ."

Evangeline bit at her bottom lip as she thought to herself. "Was this Monroe fella a lawman?"

"No . . . but he had dirty cops in his pocket. Cops I used to work with. Most of 'em white an' a fair few either former Metropolitan police officers outta London or ex-military types, like the fella I killed back at my hotel room."

Evangeline sighed then slumped back against the cabin wall and stared back at me. "So, Mistah Detective . . . tell me sum'ting 'bout you that ain't ta do with all this madness."

My brow furrowed and my pulse suddenly started to hammer at my temples.

"'Bout me? What you wanna know?"

I watched Evangeline's mood lighten as she took a moment to consider what I'd just asked her. "I don't know . . . Anyt'ing to git my mind off death and dirty cops. I already told you 'bout long train journeys and needin' ta pass the time with decent conversation. Come on, Dick Tracy, spill ya guts fo' me."

"Well, some years back I used to gamble, gambled all the damn time . . . Spent a helluva lot o' my life messin' about at race tracks." My top lip sneered when I thought about what I was confessing. "I always loved dog-racing. Ellie, my wife, she hated it. Hated the dogs as much as me losin' all my money on 'em."

Evangeline smiled at me, her gaze now as unwavering as a cat. "You still gamble?"

I diverted my eyes away from Evangeline's prying gaze. "Nah, not on the dogs, that's fo' damn sure."

Evangeline craned her neck a little, making sure she kept eye contact with me. "On life then?"

I nodded my head to myself and smiled. "Maybe . . . Life's a bit like gambling. You win some, you lose . . . Lost most o' the time. I used to watch the action down at the track; watched the winners and the losers, just like me. I always noticed the bar was empty during the first couple a races. By the seventh race, it was packed with two kinds of folk – the winners, and me and the losers, but there were more damn losers than winners, because compulsive gamblers, they always wins, even when they loses."

Evangeline frowned at me and toyed with her earring, a small cameo, edged in gold. "How so?"

I ran my tongue over the roof of my dried-out mouth. "A gambler who loses more than he wins; well, his scatty head will always confirm a long-held and cherished suspicion that the universe has gone an' plotted against him an' he's got the evidence to prove that he is not responsible for his own failure."

I perched on the edge of the chair and put the palms of my hands together as if I was about to drop to my knees in prayer. "You see, Evangeline, a gambler believes the Fates have done it to him, not him doing it to himself, and knowing it's Fate rather than his own stupidity makes any gambler happy to keep on gambling; he's as happy as a pig rolling in slop to keep spending that dough. An' then, if he wins, he's proven that he can intuit the future he's painted with his own foolhardy sense o' magic."

Evangeline laughed at me. "And you can see into the future can you, Joseph?"

I smiled back at her. "Just far enough to know that back then the magic wasn't real an' that I was losin' on more than just the dogs."

★

It was just after 8.30pm by the time the Amtrak locomotive pulled into New Orleans train station. Evangeline and I waited until a hefty amount of the passengers began to alight the carriages. I took the Beretta from out of my waistband at the back of my trousers, flicked the safety off with my thumb, then squeezed the grip and stuffed my hand into my pocket. Behind me, I heard Evangeline spin the chamber of her .38 then snap it shut. I opened the cabin door a little and peered outside. I wanted as big a crowd as possible to give us a fighting chance to get off the platform and out of the station unharmed. I needed to be calculated, careful, shrewd.

When the train began to rock with the bustle of alighting passengers, the two of us grabbed up our coats and luggage and made our way out of the compartment. I opened the carriage door and we stepped out onto the platform, my eyes strafing left and right along the length of the track. All around us passengers bobbed and weaved between each other as they made their ways through the crowds, everyone eager to be heading home or to book into comfy city hotels in the French Quarter. It was good cover, perfect for getting lost in. I looked behind me for anyone who looked suspicious or anything untoward. Evangeline took our tickets from her jacket pocket, linked her arm through mine, and the two of us joined the head of a dense throng of other travellers making our way towards the gate at the end of platform to show our travel documents. My sweating hand clutched the grip of the Beretta inside my overcoat pocket. I swept my eyes back along every pocket of the platform, but saw no malevolent swagger from any of the passengers, nobody who looked like a cop or anyone I'd consider to be a hostile threat. Once we'd successfully got past the ticket inspectors, Evangeline unhooked her arm from mine and the two of us quickly paced along a wide gangway out into the arrivals lobby. I gestured with my head to Evangeline as I spotted the exit doors. I took another quick look behind me, then headed for the street.

Outside of the station, the humidity hit me immediately; the sticky air smelled of salt and stagnant water and dead vegetation. I spotted a taxi rank only feet from the station's main doors, quickly hustled our suitcases to the side of the road and tapped on the glass window of a waiting cab. The black driver rolled a matchstick on his tongue and barely looked up from his paper to speak. "Where yuh wanna go?" Evangeline pushed me to one side and leaned her hand on the cab roof. "Ninth Ward, the Holy Cross district."

The cab driver dropped his newspaper onto the passenger seat, took the matchstick out of his mouth, rolled down his window and sneered back at Evangeline.

"Yuh say, Holy Cross? Yuh sure yuh wantin' de Ninth Ward, lady?"

Evangeline bent in towards the open window, nodded her head bluntly back at the driver. "Yeah an' if you can keep to the back roads and make sure we ain't got nobody on our tail there'll be an extra twenty dollars in it fo' you."

The driver suddenly smiled, his white tombstone teeth glaring back at us in the night-time gloom. "Shit, for an extra twenty bucks I'd lose da muthafuckin' devil off yo' pretty tail!"

The driver slung his arm out the window and slapped the door panel with the palm of his hand, then looked up at me. "Lady, yuh git outta the rain an' let the brother stow dem cases in the back o' my trunk."

Evangeline climbed in whilst I went around to the rear of the cab. I slung our suitcases into the boot, took one last look around me, then joined Evangeline in the back seat of the cab, slamming the door behind me. The driver spun round in his seat, "Hey, 'easy on da framework, niggah. Dis ole shitbox gotta last me till I retire ma ass. It ain't gonna git there if you fling its muthafuckin' do's off its hinges!"

As we drove off, I listened as the crotchety old driver began to complain about the sudden downfall of heavy rain and how there was a nasty squall coming in off the Gulf. He looked at me in the rear-view mirror and laughed. "Yuh two realise yuh headin' to one o' the biggest crap holes outside a' tha Big Easy? Folk in da Ninth can spot strangers quick as a fox can spot a hen. Yuh sure yuh don't want me to tek yuh someplace with a bit mo' style?"

Evangeline shook her head back at the cabby, who in turn nodded back at her. "Okay, lady, it's yuh ass." The driver peered up out of his window into the night sky. "Sure, looks like yuh gone an' brou't in one helluva storm when yuh got off dat night train."

I sat back against the hard leather seat of the cab and brushed water off the front of my overcoat. The old man didn't know how right he was. The driver ducked his eyes at me in the rear-view mirror one last time before he put his foot down on the accelerator.

I smiled back at him as he sped out of the taxi rank and off along the sodden highway. I breathed in deeply, my baffled, worn-out mind desperate to forget the butchery of the last forty-eight hours. I reached my hand towards the door, slowly rolled my window down a little, and looked out into the murky night. I could still smell the lingering, unwelcome odour of death and the fusty scent of Pigfoot's clothing in my nostrils. I turned my face towards the warm breeze blowing in off the street; raindrops on the wind beat gently against my face, as cool, clean and welcome as the taste of pure dark rum on the tip of my tongue.

19

We drove quickly along back roads and side streets, the storm outside worsening. I had no idea where the hell we were heading. I continued to stare out of the window while Evangeline gave the driver further directions, and let raindrops as big as marbles pelt against my face. The rain on the cab roof was deafening, the windows swimming with water, the surface of the road dancing with an orange glow from the street lights at the side of the highway. In the distance, I could just make out the gaudily illuminated skyline of New Orleans. The limbs of the trees overhead thrashed in the wind and a bright web of lightning lit up the sky as the taxi splashed through flooded dips in the road as it made its way along the desolate expressway into the murky suburban sprawl. I turned to Evangeline. "Where in the name God are we heading?"

Evangeline kept her eyes firmly on the cabby when she replied, "The Lower Ninth."

"What's the Lower Ninth?"

I watched as she shook her head to herself. "Sanctuary, I hope."

"Say what?"

Evangeline turned in her seat and drew her head closer towards me before speaking. "I have family in Holy Cross. It's a small neighbourhood, just outside the city. An aunt and uncle on my mama's side. We can hopefully keep our heads low there for a couple o' days until our business with Vic is in the bag."

"Do you think that's a good idea with everything that's been going down?"

Evangeline shrugged her shoulders. "We don't have much damn choice ... We were booked into the Provincial in the French Quarter ... but I think we should give hotels an' small rooms a pretty fuckin' wide berth fo' now, don't you?"

★

The Holy Cross district in the Lower Ninth was one water boundary short of a true island. The cab took a quick right over a large wooden bridge then drove down a long gravel road, at the end of which was a cluster of houses. The cab driver stopped the taxi on the edge of the long, oak-lined street. Evangeline looked over at the meter and stuck her hand in her hip pocket, pulled out a wad of banknotes and quickly leaned across the driver's seat before he had a chance to turn around and handed him two twenty-dollar bills.

"That sure is some easy money for a job that just 'bout covered six miles."

The cabby turned in his seat and grinned at Evangeline. "Hey, a niggah got a make a dollar sum'how, lady."

I nodded my head in thanks at the driver, climbed out of the cab and continued to listen to him laughing to himself as I pulled our luggage out of the trunk. I stood in the gutter, water washing over my shoes and watched the taxi speed off down the road, then followed Evangeline across the street and along the pavement until she stopped in front of a waist-high gate sandwiched between a length of white picket fence. The night air smelled of damp moss, sage and wood smoke. The moon had gone behind a bank of heavy clouds,

179

the leaves of the oaks flickered with lightning. Evangeline's family's place was a rambling, tin-roofed, shotgun shack with white trim woodwork window frames and screen door which was set back off the pavement by a small lawn.

We walked along a thin concrete slab path and climbed three short stone steps. Evangeline gave the door frame a couple of hard raps and the two of us stood under the porch and waited with the warm wind and rain blowing in our faces, the vault of sky above us exploding with sound.

"Who da hell is dat cranking on ma door in dis damn weather?"

I watched as Evangeline smiled at an elderly black man as he opened up the door. "We drop by at a bad time, Uncle Ernie?"

The old man stood with the light from his hallway illuminating the outline of his fat frame. He squinted through the screen door down at us. "Jesus … is dat yuh, Evangeline?" He shuffled forward, his face managing to fill a grin before he even knew who it actually was.

Evangeline moved in a little closer towards the light. "'Course, it's me yuh ole fool. Who yuh tink it is, the IRS? Yuh gonna leave me ta stand 'ere like a drown rat or yuh gonna invite ya damn niece in?" The old man swung open the screen door, the grin on his face remaining, as though it was incised in clay. He raised his arms out in front of him as if he was about give praise to an unseen higher power.

"Well, I'll be damned … Evangeline Laveau, as I live an' breath. Git yuh ass in 'ere, child." The old man slowly shuffled himself back along the hallway to allow Evangeline and I inside, then grabbed hold of his long-lost niece, embracing her tightly. "Bin way too long, child, too damn long." The old fella lifted his head over Evangeline's shoulder and gave me a long, hard stare.

"So, who we got 'ere, den?" Evangeline stood back out of the old man's grasp, turned on her heels and put her hand underneath her kin's elbow to introduce me. "This is Mistah Ellington, he's a friend o' mine, all the way over from England. Joseph, this is my uncle, Ernest Dejean."

I stuck out my wet mitt. "Pleased to meet you, Mr Dejean."

The old fella reached across and grasped at my palm. For a man in his twilight years, he had one hell of a grip. "Likewise, son, likewise. Come on in outta dat squall, brother."

I edged my way into the hallway and stood next to Evangeline whilst her uncle closed the door behind me. Ernest Dejean must have been seventy-five if he was a day, maybe even older. His craggy black face had the look of creased parchment, his eyes a deep yellow taint, the bags hanging underneath telling of a life that had been hard lived. He wore old brown braces which struggled to hold up a pair of creased off-white trousers and a sweat-stained powder-blue shirt, which was buttoned up to the neck. Tipped back on his head was a pork-pie hat with a navy silk ribbon running around its centre. A cigar stub hung out of the corner of his mouth. He removed his hat and fanned himself, his short, curly grey hair soggy with sweat. He looked at me suspiciously then back over to Evangeline. "So, where the hell yuh bin all dis time?"

Evangeline dropped her suitcase on the floor and stuck her hands on her hips. "Same place I bin this past ten year o' more."

Ernest Dejean shook his head, his face burning with reproach. "Up in Harlem, still? Shit ... why'd yuh wanna hang yo' skinny black ass out in dat den o' thieves fo'?"

Evangeline, not wanting an argument, changed the

181

subject swiftly. She glanced up the hallway then back at her crotchety uncle. "Where's Aunt Harriett?"

Dejean hooked his head toward the street. "Same place da ole fool always is dis time o' night. Cross da road over at Mullatte's cookin' up boudin links fo' the fellas."

Evangeline reached across and took her uncle's hand then kissed him sweetly on the cheek and winked at him. "Git ya coat yuh mean ole goat an' let's go find the love o' yuh life."

The moon was down in the sky and the warm wind blew leaves at our feet and rattled them down the rain-soaked street and up against the trunks of the oaks. The clapboard nightclub called Mullatte's stood in front of a small parking lot no more than five hundred yards from Ernest Dejean's home. The old cinderblock building was painted purple and fringed with bright, burning red and green Christmas lights. The place shook with the reverberations of folk having a good time inside. On the door stood a huge bouncer in an ill-fitting cheap suit. The deep black tone of his skin gave him the ambience of a negro leviathan who had risen out of the depths of the Mississippi just to guard the place. The bouncer gestured at Ernest Dejean with a nod of his thick head then went about biting a hangnail from the edge of his thumb. Instead of taking the front door, Ernest ushered the two of us along the side of the club. In the distance, I could hear the sound of roosters clucking. Evangeline and I followed Ernest out into a huge wood-panel fenced yard. Dozens of candles sat on saucers were strewn across different parts of the dust-bowl floor. In the middle of the courtyard stood a washtub filled to the brim with crushed ice and bottles of beer. A muscular young Creole man with close-cropped hair sat staring at the ground, nursing a beer bottle. At the bottom of the yard, a line of dense myrtle trees separated the land from what sounded like a fast-moving river, the low-hanging branches filled with fireflies. We walked across the yard towards the back door of the club. To the left rear of the building stood a circular pit which had been railed off. The hollow ditch was enclosed with chicken wire, the dirt on the ground hard-packed and sprinkled with sawdust. Around the rails stood a dozen or more black men who ignored us as they waited to watch a cockfight. As I climbed up the steps to go inside, I saw two of the men pass cash from hand to hand as they wagered on the birds who were about to maim or kill each other with their sharpened spurs.

Inside the juke joint, the lighting was subdued, the air grey and heavy and smelled of sweat and cheap perfume. The old building was basically a huge aluminum barn with a bar along one wall, two small bathrooms in the back and a row of pool tables lined up beneath the cellulose-insulated trusses of its corrugated metal roof. A black woman, who looked to be pushing into the final stretch of middle age, walked back and forth behind the bar, smoking a cigarette. The railed bar was interspersed by jars of pickles and hard-boiled eggs with a couple of spittoons at each end for good measure. The wood floor was scrubbed colourless with bleach, the black folk inside the place all happy to be underneath a layer of floating cigarette smoke. A four-piece zydeco band played on a raised stage at one end of the room. The heady sound of a rub board and thimble worked its intoxicatingly hypnotic rhythms alongside an accordion and box drum. In the centre of the stage sat an old black fella who strummed coolly at an electric guitar, the feedback screeching like fingernails on a slate.

The familiar and welcome aroma of soul food cooking hit me as Evangeline and I followed Ernest Dejean across the club dance floor and down a small hallway towards the open door of the club house kitchen. Evangeline's uncle quietly ushered the two of us inside. An elderly black woman stood with her back to us at a large wooden table. Directly in front of her, a huge pot of red beans and rice boiled on the stove. The woman had a red and white polka dot bandana knotted across her forehead to keep the sweat out of her eyes.

"Harriett, look what I got ... I gone brou't yuh a sup'rise."

Harriet Dejean rolled a slow tortoise-like sideways glance at her husband, then went back to slicing the plantain in front of her. "Ernie, what I done tell yuh 'bout bringin' folk in'ta this damn kitchen!"

"Nevah mind dat shit, woman ... will yuh just take a look at who I brou't along!"

The old woman hissed under her breath and slammed the knife she was using down on the table then reached her head round to get a better look at what her husband was rattling on about. When Harriett Dejean first caught sight of her niece standing behind her, she began to sway unsteadily on her feet as if she were about to faint. She leaned back against the table and held out her arms to her long-lost kin. "Lord a' mercy ... It's my baby, Evangeline." I heard Evangeline try to speak, but her voice only cracked with emotion. Then I watched as she ran like a child across the kitchen floor into the unsteady waiting arms of her elderly aunt. The two women embracing each other tightly like drowning souls about to be drawn down into an unforgiving sea. Ernest Dejean nudged me hard in the ribs and smiled.

"Come on, Mistah Ellington, let's go git us a beer. This ain't no place fo' a brother wid a thirst to be."

★

The men who drank at the bar were all black. Most seemed like leftovers from another era. I'd grown up around such lost souls; plain-talking men who rarely shaved, never travelled more than a few parishes from the place of their birth, and who considered events in the outside world unimportant and unrelated to their own lives. These were tough fellas who cussed, drank booze till it freely mixed and ran with their own blood and who smoked weed as if it were a gift from God. Few around the bar acknowledged us, preferring to keep their faces averted, deliberately concentrating on their hooch.

Ernest Dejean leaned across the bar and ordered a couple of drinks, then the two of us headed back across the dance floor. We sat ourselves down on metal chairs in front of a small, circular wooden card table against the back wall across from the bar. An elderly mulatto woman sitting opposite me glanced nervously up at the screen door of the club's entrance when it suddenly opened, as though the person entering was a harbinger of unwelcome change in her life. I rested myself back in my seat and watched as an elderly black fella brought over two bottles of Jax beer on a metal tray to the table. Ernest nodded his head at the makeshift waiter and tipped him a quarter, then picked up one of the bottles and wiped the lip of the bottle with his palm.

I watched as he drank the foam from out of the top of his bottle of beer then sucked at the front of his false teeth.

The old man put his beer down on the table in front of him and smiled at me. "Yuh sure is a long way from home, son."

I nodded my head in agreement and took a swig of my ice-cold beer. "I ain't too sure where home is anymore, Mr Dejean. I originally herald outta the island of Barbados. You could say Britain has become some sort of reluctant adopted abode these past few years."

"That so? Call me Ernest, son. I'm too hoary ta be answerin' to Mistah Dejean any mo'. What brings yuh dis far south?"

I cleared a sudden tickle in my throat before answering. "A death in the family. I'm going back to settle family business."

A crease went across Ernest Dejean's brow and his watery eyes crinkled at the corners. "That so? I'm sure sorry fo' yuh loss, Mistah Ellington." The old man picked up his beer from the table and drank out of it. The bottle was beaded with moisture. I watched as the golden liquid ran down the inside of the neck into his mouth. He spun the bottle in his hand a couple of times, then hit me with another question. "How yuh an' Evangeline git acquainted den?"

I started to utter a lie to the old man and wished that I didn't have to. "Through my cousin, we met a few days ago back in New York." It was at least a half-truth, but it was still a white lie that hung heavy on my lips.

Ernest scowled to himself. "Wha' yuh do fo' a livin', son?"

I turned slightly in my seat and studied Ernest's face, his expression flat. "I do enquiry work . . ."

"Enquiry . . ." Ernest wrestled with the word for a moment, then the penny suddenly dropped. "Yuh a damn shamus?"

I nodded. Denying it would have been another lie, and I was already tired of spouting those.

Ernest Dejean sniffed into the air and smiled to himself. "Gumshoe, eh? I don't 'ole it again' yuh, son. We all gotta earn a livin', an' it sure explains a helluva lot."

I leaned forward in my chair. "I don't understand, Ernest . . . explains what?"

186

The old fella put the beer bottle to his lips and gulped the last dregs out of it then I saw the muted change in his yellowish-brown eyes when he looked across at me. "Explains 'bout how yuh an' ma wife's niece gotta be in a shitload 'a trouble fo' her to be knockin' at my front door fo' the first time in a decade."

Ernest Dejean got to his feet and rested his hand on top of my shoulder. "Son, we gotta 'bout an' hour befo' ma Harriett brings us out a plateful o' hogs links n' rice fo' us ta chow down on. I'm gonna git us a couple mo' beers, then when I git back, yuh can unburden yo'self with whatever the hell it is that 'as brou't tha two o' yuh all tha way down 'ere from Harlem."

I sat back in my seat and smiled to myself as I watched Ernest Dejean make his way back to the bar. I lifted the bottle up to my lips to finish off the last of my beer. As I tipped my head back, I came face to face with the elderly mulatto woman who had been sat across the room from me. I gulped back the last of the beer and snatched the bottle away from my mouth just as the old woman fixed me a stare and rested her hand against my chest. The noise of the band disappeared from the room and I sensed a heavy weight holding me firmly in the chair as she bent down towards my face. Unable to move, her hair brushed against my face as she reached around and kissed my ear then whispered softly into it. "Da Loa, he gonna carry yuh dead to the underworld fo' yuh, brother."

I tried to lift my arm up to push the woman away from me, but it just hung like a lead weight at my side. The woman's wet lips touched the skin around my ear then the warmth of her breath crawled deep down inside as she muttered into it. "Jus' tree coffins is all da Baron gonna need ta put dem in da ground, jus tree."

187

The old woman pulled her head back and smiled at me, then seemed to glide backwards, her frail body suddenly a few feet away from me. At the same time, the weight that had been pressing down on my upper body suddenly withdrew and the room burst back into life with a wail of sound from the zydeco band. I yanked myself forward and dragged my trembling body up out of the chair. The air around me suddenly felt so heavy with ozone I could almost taste it on my tongue. I spun around on my heels as I searched desperately for the woman, but she was nowhere to be seen. I caught sight of Ernest Dejean heading back from the bar, in his hands he held two more bottles of beer, a curious expression etched on his face as he watched me aimlessly scouring the dance floor. As I backed myself up towards my seat, out of the corner of my eye I saw the screen door of the club swinging quietly back and forth, the evanescent presence that had visited me long gone.

20

The next morning, I woke from a bad dream that lingered behind my eyes like a thick cobweb. I heard the bones in my neck crack as I rolled onto my side and immediately felt a warm draft hit the back of my naked shoulder. I pulled myself up off the living room sofa I'd spent the night on. It was a little after 7am. I sat for a moment and let the unwelcome remnants of the nightmare I had been sleeping with seep its way out of my head, then dragged my ass up off the Dejeans' couch. I slouched across their small sitting room, stood at the open window and looked out into the street. The rain had stopped, the air humid and still heavy with mist. The early red sun had just broken above the treeline like a Lucifer match being scratched against the sky.

I grabbed fresh clothes and my washbag from my case, went into the bathroom and shaved, then took a strip wash in water so cold it left me breathless. I quickly towelled myself down then put on a fresh white short-sleeved shirt and a pair of lightweight navy trousers. I headed out into the hallway only to find Ernest Dejean standing directly outside the bathroom door. He wore the same creased white pants he'd had on the night before and a tatty string vest. His shirt was hung over his arm, his shoulders and chest beaded in sweat. His head looked like a cannonball. He grinned with an unlit cigar in the corner of his mouth. "Mornin', son. Harriet, she fixin' up some eggs an' bacon.

189

Come on in ta da kitchen and sit ya ass down." Ernest took a step towards me and looked me dead in the eyes then chuckled to himself and shook his head at me. "Shit, brother, yuh looks like yuh jus' got ya ass up outta damn coffin."

Harriett Dejean smiled warmly at me as her husband and I walked into the kitchen. She was stood at the table with her hands resting on the back of the chair that Evangeline was sitting in. Evangeline, still in her nightgown, looked up at me briefly then quickly stared down at the empty plate in front of her. Ernest, sensing his niece's embarrassment, pulled out a chair for me opposite, then went and sat down at the head of the table. He looked up idly at his wife and winked at her, then slapped his knee and grinned back at me. "Man, I got me a hunger, let's eat."

*

Whilst Evangeline bathed, I helped Harriett dry the breakfast pots. The old woman spoke very little, but her constant smile was warm and welcome in her home. As Mrs Dejean hung washing on the line in the yard outside, I returned to the living room, picked up my case and sat it next to me on the sofa. I opened it up and dug underneath my clothes for the alabaster casket that had been given to me by the Obeah at the church in Harlem. I slipped the cover off the coffin and took out the tiny notelet inside and read it again. I looked at the address at the bottom of the message.

Odell & Bultman Mortuary Service
3338 St. Charles Avenue
New Orleans

I knew that I was going to have to pay a visit to the mysterious city undertakers later that day, but a voice deep inside my head called out to me, advising I'd be better off staying well away from the place. I closed my eyes as the muttering in my head slowly vanished and thought about the strange mulatto woman who approached me in the club the night before. As I sat mulling over the old girl's words to me, I made the sudden decision that I would not share my bizarre experience with either Evangeline or any other person whose lives and vision were defined by daylight and a rational point of view.

I stuffed the note into my back pocket, shut my suitcase, went outside and stood on the porch steps which lead up to the Dejeans' front door. The heavy rays of the sun blazed down on my face as I watched Earnest Dejean rake up and burn leaves in a wire brazier in the middle of his lawn. Since moving to Britain, I'd become strangely accustomed to its colder climate. I may have been reluctantly adapting to the damn cold, but it sure as hell didn't mean I liked it. The sultry Louisiana heat was very much akin to the climate of my island home on Barbados and for a moment I had a shudder of anxiety at the thought of both returning to Bim in the coming days and the icy winters back in Bristol. I wiped the sweat off my face with my handkerchief, unbuttoned my shirt a few notches and stepped down onto the lawn. The pavements on either side of the road were cracked by tree roots and the tiny well-maintained green lawns outside of the narrow, paintless shotgun homes were filled with fragrant hydrangeas, hibiscus and philodendrons.

"Dat's one of my babies ovah by da side o' da house, Mistah Ellington." Harriett Dejean gave me a start as she crept up behind me. She smiled then pointed to a beautiful

191

cypress tree towards the back of her garden. "That tree gotta be over a hunnerd years old. See da base, the size of it. It ain't going any place fo' sure. Shame dat can't be said fo' me an' Ernie ovah there. Seems like all da wrong tings either change, die or jus' disappear in'ta thin air." Harriett eyes looked off reflectively around her tiny front garden. "Yuh know, dis whole damn neighbourhood was built on a swamp. Place was full o' cypress trees when I was a young'un. In fact, dis area was a regular southern Eden: cypress, pecans, fig trees, we had fruits an' mulberry trees an' all dat kinda stuff. Back den we had our'sel's pretty yard gardens, ever'body had dem'selves a garden. But not no more, no, suh."

"How long you lived here, Mrs Dejean?"

Harriett scratched the top of her head whilst she considered my question. "Oh, I dunno. It gotta be coming up fo' nearly ten years, now. Ernie an' me, we move down here from Leflore County, Mississippi state in fifty-eight. Most coloured folk back den, they be headed nort' a' soon as they could git the cash to haul their black asses outta the Sout'. Not my Ernie, oh no . . . he wanted to com' on home, back to da Big Easy."

Harriett Dejean laughed to herself, then took me firmly by the arm. "Come on, Mistah Ellington, I wanna show yuh sum'ting. Evangeline, she back in da house makin' her'sel' all pretty an' all. Yuh come tek a walk wid an ole wo'man down ta da river."

★

We walked a half-mile or so. Harriett Dejean held on to my arm as she greeted neighbours and friends as we made our way downhill. We wandered past jaunty and colourful negro

192

homesteads, a handful of new sawtooth buildings painted in beige and yellow, red and rose tints that stood next to more rundown shotgun and gingerbread wooden ranch houses with rusted iron rails and unkempt front yards. Harriett squeezed at my elbow as we turned a bend in the path. "Yuh know dat da Holy Cross it plain hugs on'ta da Mississippi." Harriett took hold of my hand and led me through a clump of live oaks down to the water's edge. I stared out at the massive expanse of the Mississippi river. Harriett and I carefully walked down the steep bank and I watched in amazement as the fast-moving, dark water inched its way up the levee on the other side and cascaded up against the concrete wall which separated land from water. I looked up and down the huge river and felt my jaw drop at its wonder. Close by where we were standing, bream were feeding among the cattails and lily pads, and in a shady cut by the edge of the bank I could make out the back of a largemouth bass roll just under the surface. On both sides of the river for as far as the eye could see, oil and coal barges floated by accompanied by buzzing tugboats which saddled up to their enormous metal hulls like pilot fish to a whale. My eyes looked down stream and I followed a gravel path atop the levee which headed out to a vast industrial corridor with a pier at its end. Seagulls dipped and wheeled over the water's edge and a solitary blue heron stood among the sawgrass in an inlet pool, its long body and slender legs like an oil painting on the air. Harriett stared up at me and shook her head back and forth as though she were dispelling a troubling thought. I took hold of the old woman's hand and guided her back up the bank on to flat ground.

"What's wrong, Mrs Dejean?"

Harriett looked down at the parched earth then back up to

me. "Son, I don't like ta have no truck with what other folk git up ta, but I'm right in tinkin' yuh mixed up in sum real bad bid'ness, yeah?"

"How'd you know 'bout all that?"

The serious expression on Harriet Dejean's face suddenly broke and she smiled back at me. She patted one hand on top of the other and her eyes became muddy. "How yuh tink, boy? My Evangeline, she tell me 'bout what yuh both doin' down 'ere n' who yuh really are. Ah, yuh really a po'liceman?"

I shook my head. "I was once ... but not anymore."

Harriet nodded to herself. "That a fact ... well, son, Al Jolson, he gone an' blacked him'sel' up, but it didn't make him no niggah."

"I'm sorry ... I don't understand, Mrs Dejean."

Harriett rested her back against the trunk of a pecan tree. "Mr Ellington, yuh need to re'member, down here yuh is just a niggah. Whatever yuh may a bin back home, sum po'liceman or da kind, yuh can't evah be dat in these parts. Black man tink he the law in New O'leans, fo' too long he gonna end up floatin' face down in dis 'ere river. Yuh an' my Evangeline be gator food befo' da sun goes down fo' sure ... Yuh need to keep dat in mind if yuh gonna start pokin' 'bout in white folks' bid'ness."

Harriett Dejean shut her mouth nervously then looked out across the fast-moving, opaque river. She shrugged her shoulders despondently, swallowed then looked at me, her eyes filming. Harriett heaved her back away from the tree and made her way from out of the overhanging canopy of the oak. I watched as the old woman began to walk slowly back along the dust path. The air around me suddenly turned cool. I followed after her, the soles of my feet crunching down on

194

to mouldy pecan husks. All around me I could smell the musky scent of the camellia bushes and the fecund odour of the fish spawning in the river behind me. I chased on up the track, recounting Harriett's sombre warning, unaware that her prescient words would come back to haunt me in the days ahead in ways I could not have imagined.

21

A white flicker of lightning struck out above the trees on the opposite side of the Dejeans' home as I opened the taxi door and joined Evangeline on the back seat. I felt the cold metal of the Beretta against the clammy skin on my back as I leaned forward in my seat and gave the driver the address of the funeral home that was printed on the scroll of paper from inside the alabaster casket. We drove out of one of the poorest parts of the city and quickly entered the wealthier, middle-class areas of the suburbs. Outside of pristine homes and ornate lawns, black gardeners clipped the hedges and watered rose beds. White oleander, azalea and myrtle trees were planted thickly behind the scrolled iron fences that lined the fronts of most of the white-columned properties. It was all far removed from the old wooden row houses and shrub-filled front yards that we had just left less than three miles back in Holy Cross. I turned from staring out of the passenger seat window and glanced across at Evangeline. She looked stunning. Her face had lost the anguished look of the last forty-eight hours and had been replaced with a radiant quality that somehow made me feel a little more buoyant. She wore a white, knee-length cotton dress decorated with tiny red flowers and her hair was tied back in a bun with a short length of red velvet ribbon. A number of thin, silver hoops jingled on her wrist and she held a white clutch bag in her right hand. My heart suddenly picked up a beat in my chest and my stomach had butterflies. The skin around my cheeks warmed. I knew what I was feeling wasn't down to the Louisiana heat. I heard myself sigh, then turned and stared blankly back out of the car window; my inner voice telling me to stick to the job at hand.

Odell & Bultman Mortuary Service was located on the north-west corner of Charles Avenue in the heart of the Garden District of New Orleans. The taxi driver pulled up sharply outside the undertaker's establishment. I looked across the front seat of the cab at the meter, pulled a roll of banknotes out of my hip pocket, paid the driver the three-dollar fee and threw in a dollar tip for good measure. Evangeline swung open her door and the two of us got out, crossed over the street and stood on the pavement outside the gravediggers' swanky-looking joint. The company name was hung proudly in the show window of the funeral home in six-inch-high, white neon script. Enormous trees draped in the haunting southern canvas of Spanish moss shaded the front of the building. On the gable end, the American flag, hung at half-mast, was waving gently in the breeze.

Evangeline and I went inside, and I was immediately hit with the overbearing smell of burning incense which stung the air. A bell tinkled above our heads as I shut the door and took a quick look around. In front of me was a polished oak counter and, behind that, through an open door, I could just make out what looked like a large storeroom. Glass-fronted wooden shelves ran along the far wall and a strip of four fluorescent lights hung from a pressed tin ceiling. Inside the showroom, the swinging of a clock pendulum seemed the only obvious activity in the place. A thick-pile red and black patterned carpet adorned the floor, which had a series of raised black cloth-covered plinths displaying expensive

197

gold- and brass-handled coffins and caskets, all in varying sober colours and varieties of wood.

I was about to shout out to see if anyone was at home when a thin-looking black man with a pointed, sombre face, wearing a tight-fitting black frock coat and matching trousers, came out of an office door at the back of the showroom. His greying, tight afro glistened with oil in the light from the lamp that hung from a rose above his head. I took the nattily dressed negro to be in his late sixties.

"Can I he'p yuh, suh?" Underneath his carefully modulated southern diction lingered the melodic calypso lilt of the Caribbean.

I stepped forward across the expensive carpet. "Yes, my name is Ellington. I was hoping to be able to speak to Walter Odell."

The undertaker broke out into a tombstone grin which immediately set me on edge. "Ah, Mistah Ellington, we bin expectin' yuh, sir. I'm Walter Odell."

He reached out his slender hand. I reluctantly took his palm in mine and we shook. I snatched my hand back as quickly as I gave it; the fear of being drawn closer to my own grave by the mortician very much at the front of my mind. Walter Odell took a couple of paces sideways and offered his hand to Evangeline. "And yuh must be Mistah Minton's associate." The undertaker took hold of Evangeline's hand and shook it in the same creepy fashion. "Pleasure ta mek yuh acquaintance, Miss Laveau."

Odell lifted his hand to his chest and nodded at the two of us, then turned on his heels and headed for the open door which led out back. "If de two of yuh wud like ta follow me."

We did as the odd-looking undertaker requested and made our way across the showroom and behind the counter into a large warehouse. Odell waited at the door and guided us inside, the palm of his hand outstretched in front of him. Once inside, the undertaker closed the door behind us and walked out in front of us. He looked at Evangeline with his fat, milky eyes and smiled. "I have bin instructed ta conduct bid'ness wid yuh first, Miss Laveau."

Odell turned and paced on ahead, coming to a halt next to a baroque glass-panelled horse-drawn hearse. In front of the hearse stood three separate piles of hessian sacks, each pile stacked on pallets rising at least four feet off the warehouse floor. The all too familiar funky smell of marijuana reeked out of the sacking and permeated the air around us. Odell took out a large penknife from his trouser pocket, opened it up and stood back from one of the pallets, then offered the blade to Evangeline. "Dis all fo' Mistah Minton, courtesy o' Victor Ellington, in light o' recent unfortunate occur'ances."

Evangeline took the penknife from Odell then looked at me suspiciously before walking over to the nearest pallet and cutting open the top of one of the bales. Odell joined her, placing his hand on top of one of the sacks as Evangeline pulled out a handful of the ganja and smelled it. "I can assure yuh, every'ting in order wid dis new merchandise. We gonna ship it out later today. Be wid Mistah Minton an' yo' organisation day after tomorrow, fo' sure."

Walter Odell took another step back from the pallet of dope and turned and looked across the warehouse towards a glass-fronted office. He raised his hand and gestured with the fingers at the glass. Moments later, the door opened. My hand reached around to the back of my jacket, my palm resting against the Beretta underneath. A young black man, no more than twenty, and dressed identically to Odell, marched out of the office and presented himself in front of the undertaker. He nodded at the shifty embalmer but didn't utter a word. I watched as Odell turned back and smiled at Evangeline again and, at the same time, my hand slipped underneath my jacket, my fingers clasping at the butt of the automatic pistol.

"Miss Laveau, dis 'ere's Whisperin' Bob. He don't speak nun, but pay no mind ta dat. He gonna tek yuh ovah to my office. Victor Ellington ax fo' yuh to call Mistah Minton an' assure him every'ting in order 'ere." Evangeline turned to me, her face tight with anxiety. Odell picked up her uncertainty immediately, reaching over and touching the back of her arm with his. "Miss Laveau ... ain't no harm gonna come ta yuh from ole Bob 'ere an', fo' dat matter, anybody else under dis roof. Yuh as safe 'ere wid him, me an' da dead as if yuh were in da hand o' da Lord."

I nodded at Evangeline. "It'll be okay, Evangeline. If Vic wants you to make the call, go make it. Tell Minton 'bout Pigfoot and the shipment here and that you're safe."

Evangeline looked at Odell and his minion then back at me. She swallowed nervously and took a deep breath. I watched her chest rise and fall, then saw her grip the handle of the penknife and direct it towards Whisperin' Bob's guts.

"Oh, I'm gonna be safe alright." Evangeline looked at Odell and raised the knife up in front of her. "Mistah, if any'ting happen to me between 'ere an' that fuckin' phone then I'm gonna cut dat mute o' yours a new ass'ole, yuh dig me?"

Odell nodded his head subserviently at Evangeline, then turned to me and grinned. "Mistah Ellington. Yuh can tek yo hand off dat Saturday-night special yuh got tucked under yo' coat. Same go fo' yuh. Yuh safe 'ere. It's time we settled

200

our bid'ness to'gedda." Walter Odell pointed to a door behind the pallets of dope. "Dis way, suh."

I let my arm drop to my side, but ignored Odell's request and let my wary eyes follow Evangeline as she walked across the warehouse and into the office with the dumb gofer. Whisperin' Bob ushered her inside then stood outside the door as if he were guarding a precious cargo. I watched Evangeline pick up the phone and a few short moments later saw her begin to talk into the receiver. Odell called back after me. "Mistah Ellington . . . dis way, suh."

I cut in between the pallets of ganja and joined Odell just as he was opening the door. The undertaker stuck his arm inside and flicked on a light switch. The room was suddenly illuminated with an eerie low-watt incandescence; inside was a small chapel. Walter Odell once again held out his Grim Reaper palm to shepherd me inside. "If yuh'd like ta go on in, suh." I stepped cautiously across the uninviting threshold. Odell walked in behind me, closed the door quietly then came and stood at my side. He looked up at me then gestured across the room with his head. "I'd like ta offa ma sincerest condolences on yuh loss, Mistah Ellington. Deese a fo' yuh." I stared out disbelieving across the strange-looking vestry. Sitting on a raised altar at the back of the chapel sat three coffins, each different in style and design, all crafted beautifully in the darkest mahogany. I looked at Odell and pointed at the trio of caskets. "What the hell is this?"

Odell gestured with his hand for me to walk over to the altar with him. I followed his lead as he spoke to me in a hushed tone. "Dey bin made at da request o' yuh cousin, Mistah Vic. Dey gonna be goin home wid yuh, suh." I looked at the coffins and back across at Odell.

"Home? Whadda ya mean, they're going home with me?"

Odell gave me a hard stare before answering. "Dey bein' flown out ta Barbados in two days' time. Yuh on da same flight out wid dem. Every'ting else be explained when yuh git there." Walter Odell raised his arm, stuck his hand inside his jacket pocket, pulled out a thin white envelope and handed it to me. "Dis 'ere's yuh airline ticket an' the cargo documents fo' the caskets. Every'ting all in order. Mistah Vic wantin' yuh ta know yuh ain't gotta be worrin' 'bout what happens when dem caskets git ta da airport. His fella's gonna tek care o' all dat."

Odell smiled at me then walked back across the chapel and opened up the door. "Am gonna give yuh a moment o' reflection, suh. I'll bring Miss Laveau ovah ta yuh in a short while, den da two a' yuh can be on ya way. Bin a pleasure makin' yuh acquaintance, Mistah Ellington."

I watched the old gravedigger disappear, then turned back and stared in disbelief at the three caskets. A chill struck me across the back of my neck and my head throbbed. I picked over what Odell had just told me and still none of it made a word of sense. I tried to combat my confusion with logic as I walked slowly across the chapel to the altar, lifted my hand up and gingerly touched the edge of one of the coffins. I immediately felt myself flinch, and snapped my arm back to my side. My skin felt clammy and my insides ice cold. I stared back at the trio of coffins and snapped my eyes shut. In the darkness I thought I heard my deceased wife, Ellie, call out my name and a child's footsteps rush past my side. I opened my eyes, stumbled backwards and fell to the ground. My head reeled as I struggled to prop myself up with the flats of my hands on the chapel floor.

Fear ate at my belly as the touch of a heavy shroud was draped over me. The inside of my mouth was stripped of

202

moisture as I tried to fight the woozy sensation going off inside my head. I snapped my eyes open and shut then heard the laughter of a little girl echo out behind me. My brain whirled around uncontrollably inside my skull as the air was squeezed out of my chest, the blood drained from my heart and the light sank quickly from my eyes.

22

The esplanade was shady under the spreading oaks that ran along Charles Street. I don't remember coming to, or how I came to be sat on a boardwalk bench with Evangeline opposite the Odell & Bultman funeral building, I just knew that I was alive and grateful to have been drawn back from the chimerical netherworld that had invaded my waking being back in the morgue.

My head felt like it was stuffed with cotton wool and I could not shake the spectral thoughts and images of my dead wife, Ellie, and young daughter, Amelia, from drifting before my eyes. I knew Evangeline had nestled herself in close to my side and had rested her hand gently on my forearm, occasionally squeezing at the top of my hand to ask if I was okay. I took little notice of her presence next to me, my fuddled mind still desperate to rid itself of the visions, voices and sounds that I knew only I saw and heard.

It was a sharp, sudden gust of a warm breeze that hit my face square on that brought me back to the land of the living and away from the clutches of the dead. I opened and closed my eyes in quick time, regaining my focus, then watched as the gentle wind blew tiny pieces of newspaper over my feet and out along the gutter. I turned and smiled at Evangeline, then watched as the palm fronds and banana trees swayed gently in the courtyards of the surrounding buildings. Evangeline drew herself away from me. I breathed deeply and exhaled, letting some of the tension ease out of my body, then relaxed my shoulders and rested my back against the wooden seat. I squinted lazily across the road and watched a young black man who was stood under a scrolled colonnade selling watermelons, strawberries and ripe cantaloupes from a painted, antique handcart whilst the last residues of the ghostly manifestations of my beloved kin left my waking senses.

Evangeline rubbed at the top of my arm with her hand to get my attention. "You were calling out fo' your wife back in there."

I could feel Evangeline's eyes on the side of my face. I turned to face her and felt my brow frown into heavy lines.

"I was?"

Evangeline nodded her head at me smiled. "Yeah, along with a lotta other weird stuff whilst you was laying down there on the ground."

My cheeks heated up with embarrassment. "I'm sorry ... It happens sometimes. I get light-headed and, the next thing I know, I'm out fo' the count."

Evangeline touched the side of my cheek with back of her hand, "Don't sweat it, man. We all got our crosses to bear, you ain't no diff'rent."

She smiled at me then reached into her clutch bag and handed over the airline ticket that Walter Odell had given to me before I'd fainted. "You had this in your hand when we found you."

I took the ticket from her and stared blankly at it for a moment. When I looked back at Evangeline, she had again lost the streetwise, hard expression that often graced her features; her face now both beautiful and vulnerable in a way that made my throat dry and caused my skin to tingle.

I gazed down sadly at the travel pass in my hand and shook it. "Looks like I'm heading back to home in a couple o' days."

Evangeline, realising my solemn frame of mind and feeling a need for a quick mood change, pulled herself forward across the bench and jabbed me sharply in the gut with her elbow. I yelped as the pain in my ribs instantly pulled me out of the blossoming funk she could see me falling into. "Listen, we can talk 'bout all that later. I gotta call Sweetness back in a couple of hours. Looks like your cousin, he made good on his promise. Those three pallets of merchandise back at Odell's warehouse are the second delivery he's got shipping out to us. Minton expects the first shipment to hit him in Harlem by 4pm today. Once those are stored away in Sweetness's lock-up, every'ting'll be cool. Ole Vic sure moves real fast when the chips are down, don't he?"

I nodded my head and looked down at the floor then back up at Evangeline. "Oh, you can say that again. One thing Vic is good at is moving fast . . . What I wanna know is where the hell is he getting all this damn dope from?"

Evangeline put her hand on mine. I looked at her, then felt another wave of uncertainty wash over me. I couldn't help but notice her breasts rise and fall underneath her pretty white dress as I struggled to maintain eye contact with her.

She studied my eyes before speaking. "That ain't your concern . . . All you need to know is that your cousin is all straight with my guys and that he's locked in with some seriously well-connected people back on his home turf, Joseph. Some real heavy-hitters that linked him in with my organisation and with Minton."

I stared back at her, puzzled by her words, unsure what I should say to her next. Evangeline's face suddenly became hard again, like someone who had been caught unawares by a photographer's flash.

"You don't git it do you, ya damn fool? How'd you tink Vic could afford to git you flown ovah 'ere first class an' put so much cash in your hip pocket? Your cousin, he ain't doin all a' that selling Twinky bars off a back of a truck, honey. Git real why don't ya."

I heaved out a sigh and stared up into the sky whilst I thought about what Evangeline had just said. Overhead clouds that had the dull sheen of steam floated lazily across the piercingly blue sky. The wind had dropped and the humidity hit me again. The atmosphere around me was clammy and thick, like someone had just dropped a steaming hot towel over my face. I could smell the acrid scorch in the air that the streetcars made when they snapped across an electric circuit. My eyes, now acclimatised once again to the bright afternoon sunshine, followed further along the centre of the cobbled street. Iron streetcar tracks, burnished the colour of copper, trembled slightly from the rumbling weight of a tram car that was still way off down the boulevard. Evangeline, recognising the deep, reverberant hum, squeezed at my fingers, got up, stepped out in the road and waved at the oncoming tram to stop. She looked back over her shoulder at me, the expression of playfulness from earlier on now returned to her face.

"Come on, Mistah Detective, let's split. You need to use your last few days here with me in the South wisely, brother. We'll go git ourselves something to eat, then I'll show you around the Big Easy. Whaddya say?"

Evangeline winked and hooked her arm out towards me. I picked my trilby up from off the bench, tipped it on to the back of my head and smiled at her. I lifted myself up off the seat and walked across to Evangeline, linking my arm through hers. Her hand stroked at my forearm, then she pulled me in close towards her as we headed quickly across the road with the sun blazing down on our backs, oblivious to the maelstrom that was to enter both our lives in the coming hours.

23

The sun was high in the afternoon sky and the shadows deepened inside the trees. Evangeline and I rode the five-minute tram journey into town, then we threaded our way through the crowded, narrow streets of the French Quarter. The old port town felt both strangely ascetic and hedonistic in equal measure. The quarter was the city's oldest neighbourhood, sitting on the highest ground, on the banks of the Mississippi. The tropical freshness of the morning had given way to a more oppressive, sticky atmosphere. New Orleans had the same uneasy feel of most of the big cities I'd ever been to. It was a place you could feel safe during the hours of daylight; but once the night set in, its streets, and those unsavoury beings residing in them, became as lascivious as an old man chasing a hooched-up floozy, and as rife with trouble as rats around a rotting dustbin. Evangeline and I walked slowly along the unevenly paved paths and thoroughfares of the Garden District, soaking up the sights and sounds. The dark streets were interspersed with roaming souls of every creed and colour. Lost tourists and city dwellers interlaced themselves with busking musicians, tap-dancing hustlers, panhandlers and pickpockets; the place had an almost biblical sense of its own seedy impropriety. Elegant eighteenth-century carriage houses with ornate, baroque interiors sat at ease alongside backstreet brothels and gambling halls. Old Spanish, French and Creole homes with their cast-iron balconies and pretty-painted fronts were nestled together on stone streets with numerous restaurants, private clubs and bars, whose tables and chairs spilt out onto the pavements. Evangeline became the perfect tour guide as she walked me through a maze of alleys and passageways, past antique shops and galleries, tarot readers, sidewalk artists working behind easels underneath shaded oaks in the afternoon heat, and street performers of every stripe plying their carnival trades.

My ears picked up on the vibrations of a trumpet, tuba and snare drum trio playing "Sweet Georgia Brown" down in the courtyard of one of the hotels. We walked across and listened to the standing trio for a while before heading away from the subterranean avenues and making our way across Jackson Square. Above our heads I saw the Confederate flag waving limply in a fragile breeze across a pocket of clear blue sky. Azaleas bloomed inside large gaudily painted earthenware urns along the edge of the square and purple wisteria hung in clumps from the sides of the identical façades of a row of opulent-looking municipal buildings. The white stone statue of General Jackson atop his rearing horse loomed over us as we made our way through the pretty park and back out on to the bustling street. Evangeline took my arm again and smiled at me.

"You 'bout ready to sample a proper cup o' southern coffee?"

"Do I get a nip o' rum in it?"

Evangeline laughed and slowly shook her head at me. "What is it with you and booze? Don't you know there's a time an' place fo' every'ting, brother?"

I shrugged my shoulders. "I'm Bajan ... back on Bim we say there's always time fo' rum."

Evangeline, still beaming, reached down and took my hand, then stepped off the pavement into the gutter, dragging me along with her. She looked along both sides of the street to see if it was clear, then we ran across the road like a pair of giggling school kids unaware of the dangerous, nameless forces churning all around us.

★

The Café Du Mode sat on the corner of Decatur Street in the Market District close to the banks of the Mississippi and overlooking the splendour of Jackson Square. Riverside streetcars clanged past as Evangeline and I found ourselves a couple of seats with a good view of the busy quarter. The restaurant seemed to be in a constant state of frenzy as servers slipped through a maze of tables to shoo stray pigeons, control crowds, bus tables and greet customers. Evangeline ordered two cups of café au lait and a half-dozen French-style beignets from an elderly black waitress who smiled sweetly at us and offered the kind of look you get from old folk who think they are witnessing the early blossoming of a new love between two souls. When the waitress returned, balancing our drinks on a tray across her arm, she still had that same wistful look etched across her lined, inscrutable face. My cheeks warmed with bashful unease and wished for that shot of liquor to magically appear next to the steaming brew that had just been place on the table in front of me. Evangeline, seemingly unaware of the elderly waitress's interest in us, looked out into the lively street and then back at me. "Well ... whaddya tink?"

I quickly swallowed the dense pastry and took another swig of my java before answering. "They kinda heavy, ain't they."

Evangeline laughed. "Not the donut you fool!" She stuck her hand out in front of her. "All this: the Big Easy?"

"Well, it ain't Bristol that's fo' sure . . . I get the feeling that I'm either gonna get robbed or picked up at any minute."

Evangeline laughed, then picked up her coffee cup and rested herself against the back of her chair. "Baby, the Big Easy got itself a tradition fo' vice and crime that goes back mo' than two hunnerd years when the French used the place as one big dumping ground fo' all its shysters and whores. It don't take much imagination to guess at the kinda offspring those folks bred down the generations. Ain't no place like it in the world."

"Oh, you can take it from me, St Paul's . . . it comes pretty close."

Evangeline drank from her cup then set it back down on the saucer. "You missing Britain and your folks back home, Joseph?"

I shook my head. "It ain't my home, Evangeline, an' I ain't got much to miss, 'part from my Aunt Pearl and Uncle Gabe . . . they're Vic's mom n' pop."

"Ah . . . your elusive cousin Vic . . . When are you two guys meeting up?"

I reached my hand up to the inside pocket of my jacket and touched my palm against the envelope containing the airline tickets that Walter Odell had given to me back at the mortuary parlour and looked across the table at Evangeline. "I fly out to Barbados, day after tomorrow. So, I'm assuming he'll be at the airport to meet me. That said, assuming anything of Vic is a pretty stupid thing to be doin' . . . he's a law unto himself. Never been big on formalities has Vic." I broke out into a smile as I thought of my wayward kin.

Evangeline nodded her head then sat forward in her seat

and reached across the table to me. "And you sure you can trust him, Joseph?"

I gave a sharp, immediate nod. "Oh, yeah ... I'd trust my cousin with my life." I smiled to myself again. "Just not my money ..."

Evangeline frowned at my comment. "Well, he's sent you enough green backs ... I'd say you ain't got no worries on that score. The man's obviously rolling in the stuff."

I nodded. "Sure sounds like it. Vic's always been able to make a buck ... even when we was kids, he'd have some kinda scam on the boil. How the hell he's making the kinda big money he is at the minute scares me."

"I wouldn't be scared 'bout the cash or where it's coming from. You need to be worrin' 'bout those caskets back at the funeral home. Why the hell's Vic got three coffins shipping out with you?"

"I have no idea. None of it makes a damn bit o' sense. Fact, nuthin' has tallied up since I got here."

Evangeline smiled awkwardly, her gaze had become jittery and was fixed strangely on my face, her eyes lit with a bizarre luminosity. I watched her tap her fingers nervously on the arm of her chair then sit back from the table. She looked across the room and raised her arm into the air, called across a waitress and ordered two more coffees, then looked back out at the throbbing crowds in the street outside. I looked up at the towering steeple of St Louis Cathedral across the square, which stood like a sentinel, neither judging nor joining the mayhem below it, and was almost compelled to rush into its shelter, to hide amongst its cooling cloisters and get away from the noise of the street vendors and the afternoon's stifling humidity. Evangeline finished eating the last of her beignet. I watched as she brushed icing sugar off her palms then looked at her wristwatch and fished inside her clutch bag, pulling out a handful of change. "I need to go call Minton." She pushed her chair back across the linoleum and got up out of her seat and winked at me. "I'll be back in just a minute."

Whilst Evangeline made her call to Harlem, I sat and finished my coffee and watched a young white fella clutching a black umbrella ride a unicycle back and forth in the street outside while an old, black juggler tossed wooden balls in the air. A gust of wind suddenly shot through the coffee house, it sucked the air out of the trees and drew the leaves off the ground and sent them soaring into the sky, flickering like hundreds of yellow and green butterflies across the street. When Evangeline returned, she'd lost the carefree easiness which she'd freely possessed as she was showing me around the old town. The phone call to Sweetness had darkened her mood, made her edgy and she was restless for us to be on our way. As I got up out of my chair, I looked down at my wristwatch; it was just after 4.30pm. When I looked back up, Evangeline was already out of the café door.

★

I paid the bill, caught her up in the street outside and we wandered through the French market, down a long boulevard filled with heavy-scented, fresh-blooming dogwood and redbud trees, and headed down to the Mississippi levee path on the edge of the city, both our minds in some way absorbed by the telephone conversation which had just taken place.

The fierce heat shimmered off the tarmac as Evangeline and I strolled quietly along the jetty for a couple of miles, finally stopping by a clump of live oaks to admire the view. The sky over the wetlands across the water was filled with birds that seemed to have no destination or home. I looked out at the fast-moving river, the sticky air clung to my face and suffused with the now all too familiar tang of ozone. I listened to the river's strong current sing as it rolled past. I could almost feel the water's powerful juju speaking to me. I found myself almost in a trance, seduced by its beauty and vastness as I tried my best to put Sweetness Minton and Evangeline's call to him out of my mind. Birdsong echoed out from the trees and the cicadas chattered in the long grass behind where we were standing. Evangeline tapped me on the shoulder and looked at me gravely. "Wakey, wakey there, sleepyhead, you got a face like thunder. What you thinking 'bout?"

I broke out a reassuring smile to her, then turned back to the breathtaking vista that stretched out in front of us. "Oh, nothing much . . ." I pointed out across the water. "I'm just taking all this in."

"Beautiful, isn't it?

I gazed back at the picturesque canvas and felt the wind picking up around me, a hint of salt and rain was in the air. In the distance across the river, towards the bayous and open countryside, I could just make out the edges of a mass of darkening clouds on the horizon. I breathed in deeply and felt the steamy aura fill my insides. "It sure is . . ." I turned back to face Evangeline and felt the question I'd been telling myself not to ask her on the tip of my tongue.

"How's Sweetness?"

Evangeline looked out at the water and I saw her sigh. I watched as she nervously kicked at a clump of dirt with her toe and shook her head. "Same as he always is, mean . . . That niggah's an ornery, sly old bastard. I said I was gonna take you to Tajague's restaurant fo' dinner later on. That really

215

got his damn back up. Sweetness hates to think anybody eatin' better than he is. He is one greedy mutha. He told me that Vic's new shipment o' dope has arrived and is already stashed away in that lock-up o' his. He's waiting on the next like a cripple waiting on a new leg. Says he wants me to git my ass back to New York on the first damn train out tomorrow morning."

"And are you?"

Evangeline sniggered to herself, then gave a defiant gesture by flipping the edge of her jaw up into the air. "I tole him to go fuck himself. Said I'd come back once you'd flown the nest the day after tomorrow. That pissed him off some. Said he wanted me to call him back later."

A nagging sensation hung in my gut. "Why'd he want you to do that again?"

Evangeline shrugged and moved in a little closer towards me. "It's just how we play it. We away from home, we stay in touch. It's a Panther protocol. It's what keeps us safe." I reached down and touched the back of Evangeline's hand with my fingers.

"And do you feel safe?" I saw a wave of sudden hesitation strike across Evangeline's brow as she took in my question to her.

"Not since I met you, brother. All these stiffs you got piling up around you. Shit ... why the hell you tink Sweetness got me on the phone every other hour axin' 'bout our every move?"

I took Evangeline's fingers in my hand and squeezed them gently then saw a glow replace the uncertainty on her face. It was the look of a woman who knew she was beautiful and desired. Her eyes had rediscovered the brightness from earlier in the day, but something still didn't feel quite right.

I put my feelings of unease to the back of my head when Evangeline, resting her head against the top of my arm and her arm linked through mine, drew herself in tight next to me. "Come on, let's go find ourselves some place to relax . . ."

The wind swirled in the trees and wrinkled the river water and, in the rustling of the canebrake as we walked back down the path, I thought I heard the word "Judas" hiss inside my ear.

24

We walked back into the French Quarter in the twilight, just as the rain broke out of the darkening sky. The cobbled streets and courtyards smelled of freshly sprinkled flower beds, spearmint and old brick that was sheathed with mould. Lights from overhead apartment buildings and the stores that were still open for business shone down across the dampening roads and etched shadows across our path like spun lace. Despite the coming storm, customers were still sitting chatting and eating under the colonnades of restaurants, whilst further down the street at a bar, folk were enjoying an early evening drink on the balcony that dripped with bougainvillea and passion vine.

Evangeline and I walked arm in arm to the end of Decatur Street, stopping outside a pretty Creole corner restaurant. She read the menu from a board pinned on the wall then took hold of my hand. "We gonna be welcome in this joint. These folks are serving some fine-tasting soul food." Evangeline pulled me across a red-brick courtyard filled with flower beds blooming with red and yellow roses, irises and hibiscus. Umbrella trees and windmill palms stood either side of the entrance.

Tajague's restaurant was small and most of the customers seated inside were black. There were white cloths on the tables and candles that flickered inside glass vessels that gave the place the feeling that it was existing in another age-old historical dimension. A young negro waitress, no more than eighteen years of age and dressed in a white and blue striped uniform and pinafore, headed across the floor of the diner and welcomed us. The girl smiled sweetly at Evangeline, picked up a couple of menus from a table by the door and showed us to a quiet stall at the furthest edge of the room.

Evangeline and I sat opposite each other in the booth. I took off my hat and placed it on the seat next to me and watched as the young waitress handed out the menus then reached into her pocket and pulled out a tiny notepad and pencil and smiled at me. "Can I git yuh two good folk any'ting ta drink?"

Evangeline winked at me and quickly scanned her menu, nodded her head to herself then looked up at the waitress and smiled. "Can we git twelve oysters on the half-shell, a seafood gumbo, a bowl o' red beans and rice, two bottles o' Jax, and the gentleman here would like a boilermaker o' rum."

The waitress took down Evangeline's order without saying a word or looking up from her notepad. When she'd finished writing, the girl took a step back from the table, reread Evangeline's order back to her then slipped her stubby pencil behind the back of her ear. "Thank yuh all. I'll git yuh drinks."

I watched the waitress as she quickly glided her way back across the restaurant floor and disappeared behind a pair of long-slatted doors into the kitchen. A few minutes later, she returned with our drinks perched on a melamine tray in the centre of the palm of her hand. She placed our bottles of beer in front of us then sat a thimble-sized glass of rum down next to mine.

"Enjoy." The waitress smiled at us both, then spun on her

heels and turned her attention to a middle-aged black couple who were about to leave.

"Cheers, Joseph," Evangeline raised her bottle in front of her and tipped the neck towards me. I picked up my beer and reached across the table and we clinked our drinks together. The ice-cold beer felt great as it slipped down my throat. I took a couple of solid gulps then rested the bottle on the table, picked up the shot glass and downed the snifter of dark rum in a single swallow. I closed my eyes, the warm liquor burning deliciously at my insides. When I reopened me eyes, Evangeline was staring at me, smiling.

"That good?"

I nodded my head. "Good enough to make me want another."

Evangeline called over the waitress and ordered me another boilermaker and another two beers, then reached into her handbag and pulled out a packet of cigarettes, took one out, stuck it between her lips and lit it with the candle on the table. She took in a mouthful of smoke then blew it out above her head and looked across the table at me. "You never smoked, Mistah Detective?"

I shook my head and looked at the booze sat in front of me. "Nah ... this stuff is one poison enough." I grinned, then picked up the beer bottle, put it to my lips, sank the rest and suddenly felt light-headed. I sat back in my seat and stared back at Evangeline, the uneasy feelings from earlier slowly creeping back inside my head. I bit at my thumbnail as I searched for a way to broach the subject of my edgy thoughts with her. I didn't have to search my jittery head for long. Evangeline broke the spell on my troubled musings with a single, short and sweet statement that cut the air between us like a hot knife through warm butter.

"Sum'ting ain't right with Sweetness, Joseph."

I reached forward in my chair and rested the palm of my hand on the table next to the empty beer bottle. "What's makes you say that?"

"He jus don't sound right. Sum'ting's got that brother spooked."

"Spooked? Whaddya mean?"

Evangeline was about to continue when the waitress came over with our next set of drinks. She waited until the waitress had cleared the empties off the table and left before continuing. "I don't know fo' sure . . . Minton was asking all kinda questions 'bout what we were doin' today. 'Bout the funeral parlour, what Odell wanted with you, where we were goin' today. The niggah's always bin curious 'bout bid'ness, but he ain't normally this damn nosey. Says I gotta call him at seven thirty, sharp. Sonufabitch wouldn't tell my why. Made me give my word I'd call him back, said he needs to speak to me, in private, without you listening in. That shit don't fly straight with me."

I reached for the nip of rum, sank it back and thought about what Evangeline had just told me. I spun the bottom of the tiny glass in my fingers as I tried to piece together what Minton and Evangeline may be up to. I put the glass back down on the table and reached across for Evangeline's hand. She held onto my fingers and I could feel her trembling. I looked across at her and smiled, knowing that it did little to settle the insecurities and fears that were eating away at us. Evangeline squeezed my hand as she leaned across the table towards me, nestled her head against mine and whispered into my ear, "How bad do you tink things are gonna get, Joseph?" It was a question I knew I couldn't honestly answer, and one I would sit and brood upon whilst we ate.

★

221

From across the table, at just before 7.30pm, I watched Evangeline walk up to the young black waitress and ask if she could pay to use the restaurant phone. Whilst we'd eaten, I tried to pick up more information from Evangeline about Minton's erratic behaviour. I garnered little, other than to hear Evangeline reiterate that her boss was more interested in our whereabouts than Vic's ganja shipments that Walter Odell was shipping out to him.

I decided the two of us should stay close together until I knew what Sweetness was playing at. I knew that it wasn't a good idea for Evangeline to be heading back out into the street and using a payphone to make her call to him; she either asked to use the diner's telephone or we went out into the street together. Evangeline didn't like the idea of going back on her word to Minton and, against my better judgment, I agreed that she could call him in private.

Evangeline made up some story to the waitress 'bout how she needed to make an urgent call to an upstate hospital to check in on her sick mother and how she'd neglectfully forgotten to telephone earlier in the day. She would have made a great actress, pulling off the "bad daughter" routine to a T. The sympathetic waitress, taken in by Evangeline's lie, went away and checked with her boss, coming back to our table a short while later to say he'd said it was okay to use the phone in his office at the back of the kitchen. I asked if I could get the bill, then watched Evangeline stroll across the restaurant with the waitress and head through the slatted doors into the kitchen. Moments later, the young black girl came back out and returned to my table with the bill on a tiny silver saucer. I took out my wallet and counted out a stack of dollar bills and a tip. I handed the cash back to the waitress and peered around her thin frame towards the kitchen door. The waitress, sensing my nerves, looked over her shoulder and then back at me and smiled.

"I hope your friend's mama gonna be okay, suh?"

I looked up at the girl and nodded my head. "Yeah ... yeah me too." The waitress bit at her lip, not knowing what else to say to me. She backed away from the table without uttering another word, leaving me to worry alone. I finished the last dregs of my beer and rubbed at my face frantically with my palms in a futile attempt to wipe away the shame of having to deceive the young girl so cruelly. When I looked back up, my eyes were watery and my vision slightly blurred. Across the room I could just make out a thick-set white man heading towards me.

Whoever the man was, he'd arrived inside the diner in the time it took me to wipe my face with the flats of my hands. My eyes still struggled to focus for a moment against the candlelight that bathed the softly lit room. I shook my head and wiped my sleeve across my face just as the man reached the booth and slid himself down into the seat opposite.

"Good evening, Mr Ellington."

I looked across to the kitchen doors then back towards the white man.

"I'm sorry, do I know you?"

The man shook his head slowly. "Permit me to introduce myself ... my name is Gatehouse." He didn't offer his hand to shake and I wouldn't have shaken it if he had.

The pit of my stomach tightened suddenly. "And what can I do for you, Mr Gatehouse?"

The stranger sat forward and rested his arms on the table in front of him. He had the all too familiar stink of old-school colonial policing. All Brylcreem and boot polish. I was in the presence of the officer class and he wanted

223

me to know it. I took him to be in his mid-fifties, although he had the physique of a fella who spent most of his time pummelling a speed ball in a gym. His tanned face was like old cigar paper, wrinkled from years in the sun, the hard jawline, freshly shaven and smooth. His short-cut blond hair was freshly trimmed, swept back from his gargoyle-like forehead and stuck down on his skull with sweet-scented pomade.

He wore a light blue seersucker suit, navy polka-dot bow tie and spit-shined shoes. Gatehouse looked like the kind of man who'd never felt the pleasure of a smile. I hated him. I watched as he turned and looked at the rain hitting the windows. He put his hand to his mouth and bit at a thumbnail, then looked back at me. When he spoke again, his voice was cold and controlled, the forceful utterance coming out of his mouth making no sense to me at all.

"V.L.E.?"

I shrugged my shoulders and rubbed at the burning sensation in my eyes with my thumb and forefinger.

"Say what?"

Gatehouse blew up both his cheeks and slowly shook his head at me.

"V.L.E ... Victor ... Ladysmith ... Ellington."

"Sorry, never heard of him."

"That's very droll, Joseph. Very droll, indeed. It's not the correct answer to my question, but not an unexpected one, either. Shall we start again?"

I stared back at Gatehouse, shocked at hearing him use my Christian name.

"What the hell you want with me, man?"

Gatehouse breathed in deeply through his nose and drummed three of his fingers on top of the table. "I want your cousin, Mr Ellington. Or, more precisely, I want you to take me to him."

"Well, you shit outta luck 'cause I ain't gotta clue where the brother's at." I went to get up out of my seat. Gatehouse slid his hand across the table and slowly lifted his palm up from the polished veneer top.

"I wouldn't do that if I were you, Joseph. You need to listen to what I have to say, before people you care about start to get hurt."

I sat back in my seat and looked across the restaurant floor towards the slatted kitchen door. Gatehouse followed my line of sight then returned his beady eyes back on to me. "You're clearly concerned about, Miss Laveau, yes?"

I nodded my head, a red balloon of anger rose up in my chest. I let my right hand sink down towards my side, then leaned back against the seat and felt the metal of the Beretta pistol push against the clammy skin on my lower back.

"That's very wise, Joseph. Very wise. Now, just so we're singing from the same hymn sheet, as it were. I think I need to make something very clear to you from the start." Gatehouse gave a nudge of his head towards the kitchen door. "Your friend, Miss Laveau ... she's not in the kitchen." Gatehouse shook his head at me slyly. "And she's not making that phone call to Mr Minton either." I swallowed hard and let Gatehouse continue. "Miss Laveau is with a couple of my chaps. They're taking care of her whilst we have this chat."

The blood pulsed through the veins on either side of my temples. My left hand balled into a fist and my right reached around to the Beretta tucked into the back of my trouser waistband. Gatehouse looked down over the table towards the back of my seat. He rested himself against the back of the booth and slowly rocked one finger at me like a school teacher about to scold a belligerent child.

"I'd think very hard before doing anything rash, Joseph. We don't need a scene, now do we?"

I shook my head, lifted my hands above the table and placed the palms of my hands flat down in front of me.

"So . . . where can I find Victor?" The tone of Gatehouse's voice was soft, his gravelly timbre precise and unfaltering.

"I don't know where my cousin is."

"Oh, I believe you, Joseph. I really do. But just because you don't know where your cousin is now, doesn't mean you won't know before you fly out to Barbados in a couple of days' time."

I snatched my head back up and was immediately caught by Gatehouse's cruel, almost hypnotic stare. "Yes, you're going home, aren't you? It's amazing how much I know about you, Joseph. I've gone and done my homework on you old son. Very impressive curriculum vitae you have. Former sergeant in the Barbadian constabulary, recipient of the Barbados star for gallantry. Returned to the motherland four years ago after, how shall I say . . . blotting your copybook with your fellow police officers. Widowed too I hear . . . now that was a crying shame."

A hot ball of rage welled up inside me. I clenched my teeth beneath my closed lips. My barely controlled temper coursed through every fibre of my body, desperate to burst out and exact a swift and painful retribution. Gatehouse sensed my inner fury. I saw his left eye twitch, then his face returned to its blank canvas. I could smell his cologne and sweat all around me and heard his rancid breath go in and out between his teeth. He remained quiet for a moment, then, after eyeballing me a while longer, spoke again.

226

"I'm sorry, I can see that last remark touched a raw nerve. I don't want us to be getting off on the wrong foot here." Gatehouse touched the sides of his mouth with his fingers and tipped his head slightly, his face unflinching, his gaze never leaving me.

He sniffed the air around him and I watched his fingers roll out again across the tabletop. "Let me spell things out, so you know exactly where you stand. Your cousin has in his possession valuable items that were stolen from my employer a short while ago."

I shifted in my seat a couple of inches. "What kind of valuable items we talkin' about?"

Gatehouse lifted his hand up in front of him and wagged his index finger at me again. "That's none of your concern. All you need to know is that these valuable items could cause my employer considerable embarrassment if they got out into the public domain. Understandably, he's eager to see the items retrieved. I've been tasked with their retrieval, somewhat, I have to admit, unsuccessfully."

"An' where do I fit in to all of this?"

I saw Gatehouse's shark-like eyes sparkle when I mentioned my involvement. He leaned forward and I winced at the man's breath. "Now, that is a good question, Joseph. I've been searching for Victor for some time now. If it wasn't for Mr Minton back in New York, we'd still be much further in the dark than we are this evening. Sweetness Minton already had dubious connections with your cousin way before he started to purchase narcotics from him. Minton also has business connections in Barbados, those very same commercial connections are shared with my employer. Let's say we put two and two together and we applied a little pressure on the tubby, little darkie. He told us about your

227

visit and how you were going to meet up with your relation back home ... The Ellingtons are grieving it would seem. There's been a death in the family I hear?"

I nodded my head and let Gatehouse continue with his patter. "Well, my condolences, Joseph." I heard him continue to suck in air between his pursed lips, then watched him roll his shoulders stiffly, as if he was knocking an unwanted spectral irritation from his being. "We thought we'd try and lure your cousin in ... get him to stick his head above the parapet, as it were. We stole his drug shipment, knocked off a few of Minton's men, put the frighteners on you back at the hotel room and then killed the man called Pigfoot, to try and get his attention. All this information kindly passed on to your cousin via Sweetness Minton to wherever you kin is holed up ... I must add at this juncture that we don't know what Victor looks like and, of course, we don't know where the little blighter is, either ... and that's where you come in."

A lick of fear rose up from the back of my throat and a sour taste tainted the inside of my mouth. My stomach knotted as a sudden wave of sickening revulsion surged up from deep inside me. My jaw locked tight as I fought to suppress the unbidden savagery that I longed to unleash. Gatehouse inched forward and I got a better whiff of his stale halitosis and the unusual lavender scent coming off his polished hide. I set a hard glare back across the table at him. "Why'd don't you spit out what the hell you want from me."

I watched him curse under his breath then close his eyes as if he were taking a moment of reflection. When he reopened them, I could have sworn they flickered back at me like a lizard's. "Like I said a moment or two ago ... we want you to bring your cousin out into the open. He made you a player in my problem. You took his money. I believe I'm correct in thinking you're taking orders from him. The way the dice are rolling, you're gonna be taking the fall with him too."

I was breathing deeply now, the tendons trembling deep inside my chest. I watched Gatehouse wet his lips before speaking again.

"Victor Ellington is an enigma. He's been more than a few paces ahead of us since I first began to hunt him down some weeks ago. You see, your kin has asked my employer for an exorbitant about of money for the return of the items he has already stolen." Gatehouse's eyes became dark and unsettlingly malevolent.

"We're talking about blackmail, Joseph . . . that's what your cousin is playing at: blackmail. It's a dirty game and I'm having to be just as dirty in stopping him from making good on his promise to release a lot of unwashed linen that would damage both my employer and a number of his associates."

Gatehouse put his hand into his jacket pocket and took out a pack of Pall Mall cigarettes. He pulled one out and lit it with a silver lighter. He removed tobacco from his tongue with his fingernails then blew smoke out of the side of his mouth.

"I need you to tempt Victor out from wherever he is hiding. Let the dog see the rabbit as it were. We can do the rest once he shows himself."

"An' how am I supposed to do that?"

"Well, you get on that plane in less than forty-eight hours' time and you go home, Joseph. You go back to Barbados knowing that we'll be watching you. You'll be the bait that brings in my elusive quarry."

"How do you know Minton won't let the cat outta the bag to Vic? Tell him 'bout you and all the killing you and your men have been doin'? I get a feeling he'd happily spill the beans if he thinks he's gonna lose out on getting his merchandise."

Gatehouse took another drag on his cigarette. He looked down at his wristwatch then back up at me. "Oh, we've cut those ties with Sweetness ... As of twenty minutes ago, Mr Minton sadly ceased to exist. You could say that we're covering all the bases, Joseph. I like to work tidily. I'm the product of a sound military upbringing and twenty years serving as a Metropolitan police officer. Order and no loose ends, that's my mantra."

"Why the hell do you think I'd help you put the finger on Vic?"

Gatehouse shrugged his sizeable shoulders. You could have struck a match on his cold eyes and I don't think he'd have blinked. "Oh, that's simple ... you either do as I say or you'll be dead as soon as you set foot outside of this scabby restaurant's front door."

I looked at Gatehouse and licked my tongue across my lips. I could feel the skin around my mouth tingling. "Perhaps I'd rather be dead than betray my own flesh and blood."

"And perhaps your flesh and blood isn't exactly on the up and up with you."

"What the hell are you talkin' 'bout?"

"Monroe ..."

I glared back at Gatehouse, my eyes filling with water. "What 'bout him?"

He stared at me blankly with his lips parted. I watched as the edges of his nostrils discoloured, a look of pure glee rising in his eyes. "Monroe is my employer ... He's also your beloved kin Victor's business partner."

My ears rang and I stared back at Gatehouse, dumbfounded. A squall of my own unforgiving wrath was bursting to be released from my pent-up body. My mouth began to tremble and my limbs tighten as if they were being drawn together by piano wire. "You're a fuckin' liar."

Gatehouse shook his head. "Oh, I wish I were, Joseph. But every word I'm telling you is the truth ..." He shifted himself across the table towards me and whispered. "It's the gospel truth, my old son. Your cousin, who I'm sure you've always loved and trusted, is without doubt working with the man who had your poor wife and child killed, and, I'm very sad to inform you ... your sister, Bernice, too."

The tears began to fall from my eyes and stream slowly down my cheeks. I snatched my face away from Gatehouse's cruel stare and looked out of the window, but still felt his ferine gaze burning into the back of my head.

His hand touched at my lower arm. His palm pressed down hard on the fabric of my jacket. I tried to pull myself away from his grasp, but all my strength had suddenly been sapped from me. I could feel a fiery heat seeping down through my skin as if I was being touched by the devil himself. Gatehouse pushed down on my arm a little harder, the burning sensation driving along the rest of my arm into the centre of my chest. "Help me find Victor and the items he's stolen and I'll see to it that you can have the opportunity to settle some old scores. You have my word."

Gatehouse lifted his hand off me, but the heat still coursed through me like poison shooting through my veins. Through my tears, I watched the rain swirling out of the sky, saw it glisten on the red bricks outside in the street. I heard a tram car whistle blow as it ran through the town and saw the fleeting images of racing tourists, their speeding frames picked out by the glare of the amber street lamps as they darted each way across the water-logged road. I turned and stared back across the table at Gatehouse.

"Do we have a deal, Joseph?" He puffed on his cigarette and widened his eyes in the smoke.

My head nodded up and down, but didn't say a word. I could taste blood in my mouth and felt the wetness of my eyelashes against my skin when I finally spoke.

"Where's Evangeline?"

"Ah, of course . . . Miss Laveau." Gatehouse put his hand inside his jacket and pulled out a folded piece of white paper and slid it across the table towards me. He kept his finger on top of the paper and continued talking. "Miss Laveau was always going to be a problem. You see, she's what you might call a loose end in all of this. She's been part of the smaller picture but never a real player in our game."

Inside my head was a sound like the roar of the ocean in a conch shell. My eyes were watering uncontrollably, my face hot and twitching; there was a pressure band across one side of my head as though I had just been punched in it. My breath felt sour and fluttered in my throat as I breathed. Gatehouse could see my discomfort and was revelling in it.

"Now, I can't believe that during the short space of time we have been sitting here together that you haven't come to your own conclusions about what you are intending to do when you leave here. You're a bright chap, I know that. I just wouldn't want you to feel you're being anything less than honest with me, Joseph. Perhaps you may be thinking you can try and operate your way out of this with Miss Laveau. Be a policeman again, start bringing people to book."

Gatehouse's eyes didn't show any more feeling than a corpse. He looked down at his wristwatch again, then back at me. "You're going to be a good boy and do as you're told.

I need you to be certain that you have no choice other than to do as I've asked. Do you understand?"

I nodded my head again, then felt a sharp pain surge up from inside my stomach and travel up towards my throat.

"That's good to hear my old son. Right . . . do you know what the City of the Dead is, Joseph?"

My body become icy cold. I looked down at the notepaper in front of me and back up at Gatehouse and slowly shook my head at him.

"It's a cemetery, Joseph . . . Just a short few blocks away from where we are sat." He pressed down on the notelet with his finger. "Inside this slip of paper are printed a very precise set of directions to get you to the Number One St Louis boneyard. It's a carefully plotted course for you to locate Miss Laveau."

Gatehouse leaned across the table and pushed the paper to the very edge of it. "Now, take care to follow those instructions very closely my old son, for time is of the essence here and the clock is ticking for your lady friend." He sat back and stubbed out his cigarette on the top of table and flicked the butt across the restaurant. He looked back down at his wristwatch, tapped at the face then stared back up at me. The skin around his eyes was stretched tight. His pupils like black marbles. He shook his wrist in front of me.

"Tick-tock, Joseph . . . The Cities of the Dead are legion in New Orleans. Make sure you get the right one."

I snatched up the piece of paper, grabbed my hat and rose to my feet. I heard my own voice inside my head sound out with an animal cry as I stumbled out of the booth. Gatehouse pointed his finger up at my face.

"Whatever you should find in that graveyard, no matter how abhorrent, remember it's for your own good. Any blame you choose to apportion should be laid solely at the feet of Victor Ellington . . . Tick-tock, now."

I ran across the restaurant into the courtyard and bolted out onto the street. The rain pelted against my face, a sulphurous tang was in the air and I felt the barometric pressure dropping around me. My head reeled as I tore open the tiny slip of paper and stared at the diagram that had been handwritten on it. Unsure of which direction to head in, I raced back down Decatur Street. As I sprinted towards the unknown, I thought I heard Gatehouse's voice shout out the words "Tick-tock" behind me. I sped into the darkness with any further intelligible sound lost in the howling wind, the splatter of the rain and the rumbling of the thunder above my head.

25

The terror fuelling my racing heart urged me to run faster. My throat was dry and burned with the sour aftertaste of rum, raw adrenaline streamed through my shaking body. The rain hammered down onto my hat and soaked through into my clothes. The air smelled of sulphur, and white electricity jumped across the night sky as I raced down to the end of Decatur Street. I zigzagged in between parked cars waiting at a red light at a crossroads and finally clambered to a halt underneath the candy-striped colonnade of a general store. Rainwater poured in a heavy stream down from the store front veranda and collected at my feet in brown pools that were filling with floating leaves and litter. The fast-moving deluge rattled across the wet sidewalk and fell away from the edge of the pavement, then surged in a torrent down into the street and ran noisily along the gutter. My chest heaved as I gasped for breath, the air around me thick and muggy. I opened my fist and pulled at the edges of the crumpled map that Gatehouse had given to me with my clammy fingertips. My hands trembled as I held it up in front of the dull green-grey light that hung idly on the other side of the condensation-smeared shop window. I rubbed at my face with my sleeve and squinted down at the paper, a bilious sensation spiking at my guts as I tried to make out where Gatehouse's men had taken Evangeline. The handwritten map instructed me to turn left at the bottom of Decatur

Street onto North Rampart Street then, after what looked about a quarter-mile, I needed to take the first right into Basin Street and the St Louis cemetery. My face burned as my finger followed the black arrows that had been drawn on the simple road map. I looked around me frantically, my eyes straining through the downpour as I struggled to get a bearing on where I was, finally making out a street sign with the fading word Rampart just a few yards away from where I stood.

I bolted back out into the rain-soaked street and coursed towards the end of the road, my percussive heartbeat crashing in my ears, my nerves screaming. In the darkness, I heard a tram car bell clang out. I ran out into the centre of the street and sprinted along the wet tarmac. An overwhelming sensation of blind panic was driving me towards the nocturnal resting place of a thousand lost souls, an unwelcome destination that I only ever strayed towards in my nightmares.

*

The rain swirled out of the blackened night and danced off the red brickwork road and drummed down onto my body. A dim glow from an amber street light hung over the open gate of the St Louis Number One Cemetery on Basin Street. Above my head, the graveyard's name hung in large scrolled ironwork lettering. Carved stone angels stood either side of the black-painted entrance. Inside, low-wattage lamps suspended from thick wires criss-crossed the interconnecting paths and lit up the interior of the burial ground with a phosphorous incandescence. I took the Beretta from my trouser waistband, pulled back the receiver, slid a round into the chamber, then stepped across the unwelcoming threshold. I looked cautiously around me then walked quickly past the first decrepit tombstones and glanced back down at the map, my pulse racing in my neck. I followed the path along the edge of the cemetery and made my way past a series of sunken brick crypts, the white plaster cracked, the open-air graves sunk down into the earth and wrapped in vines that had rooted into the mortar. Glass jars and rusted tin cans filled with withered flowers littered the ground. At the end of the footpath, lit up by one of the overhanging lamps, I saw, tied at waist height from the central stem of a crumbling iron railing, a length of thick red cord. I took a deep breath and ran the tips of my fingers nervously along the taut rope, then followed its route deeper into the graveyard. Around me more tilted stone angels brooded over lost souls amid a grove of marble crosses.

Old vaults stacked like alabaster filing cabinets lined the inner walls, their brass plaques identifying the remains of those housed within. The red cord led towards the open doors of a tiny red-brick burial chamber. I raised the Beretta out in front of me. The pistol suddenly felt heavy and warm in my hand. My arm stretched out into the night, dead leaves clicked under my feet as I followed the red rope and edged closer towards the catacomb. I swung the pistol in all directions as I closed in on the tomb. At the entrance, protected from the rain by an overhanging stone canopy, were a row of fifteen or so large candles that had been lit and placed in jam jars. Written in white chalk on the lintel above the door of the mausoleum were the words *Tick-tock*. I walked inside and pointed the Beretta down towards the shaded opening at my feet. A set of stone steps corkscrewed into the darkness, each lit by a single candle. Dreading the descent, I followed the red cord down the stairwell into the unknown, one step at a time. The stairs wound out into a long, candle-lit whitewashed crypt that had to have been twenty feet underground. The crimson rope had been threaded along the centre of the stone floor and was then pinned to the wall at the end of the short crypt-lined passageway. I could feel my heart tom-tomming underneath my ribs as I made my way slowly along the damp corridor, the backs of my legs quivering, flashes of colour popping like lesions behind my eyes, the Beretta cautiously sweeping from side to side in my jittery grip. Each step I took felt as if I was being drawn back down towards the fiery Hades that I visited, reluctantly, in my sleep. A grey blanket had been hung over the entrance of the last vault. Pinned to it was a large piece of white paper which had the words *The blame layeth at the feet of Victor Ellington* printed on it in black ink. I held my breath as I let the tip of the Beretta's barrel graze the blanket. My hand shook as I reached out and grabbed hold of the damp fabric with my fingers and snatched it back from the wall.

A small lantern that hung from the low ceiling of the crypt blazed back at me with iridescent humidity. The inside of the dank tomb reeked of damp, warm fetid urine and the unmistakable musk of death. My eyes forced themselves shut for a moment, then snapped open as my squinting vision struggled to focus on the horror inside. My unsteady grip immediately loosened on the blanket, but my brain did not register it falling to my feet. I started to retch, my body staggering backwards, my knees buckling with shock. Tears welled in the lids of my eyes and a sudden, violent wave of nausea propelled itself up from the pit of my gut. I became light-headed and, at the same time, strangely disconnected from the inhuman carnage in front of me, as though what I was seeing belonged somehow inside the world of another wretched being's unwanted nocturnal hallucinations.

I stared inside the oppressive tomb at Evangeline's lifeless body, which was still bathed in sweat. Beads of perspiration ran slowly from her forehead and dripped from the tip of her chin and jawline. Her bottom lip was swollen and crusted in freshly drying blood. Her wrists and ankles had been bound tightly together with the same red cord that had led me to her. She'd been pushed back inside the crypt, her body pinned up against the back of the damp clay wall. Her head had been tilted backwards, her hair matted with dirt and small leaves. Two small brass coins had been rested carefully on the lids of her closed eyes. I reached inside and touched her tear-stained cheek with my fingers, gently caressing the side of her face with the back of my hand before pulling out the saliva-soaked rag that had been stuffed cruelly into her mouth. The damp cloth was pitted with specks of blood. I reached down and stuffed the rag into my trouser pocket then pulled out my Puma pocketknife and cut the ropes that bound her.

I staggered forward like a sleepwalker not quite believing what I was seeing. My stomach lurched again as I brushed my palm across her curly hair and then put my hand around her fingers and squeezed them. I hooked my arms underneath Evangeline's still warm, but quickly stiffening, legs. Her clammy skin brought on renewed waves of nausea as I pulled her body close to my chest and drew her out of the crypt. I held her tight against me and closed my eyes, the tears streaming down my face. The ground seemed to move underneath my feet as I sobbed uncontrollably. Then the shaking started, like rough bone and sinew ripping apart inside me. I pressed my face against Evangeline's cheek, muffling my weeping, then slowly slid my body down the wall and sat with her in my arms. The brass coins had fallen from her closed eyes. Her beautiful face looked like a flower cut unexpectedly from its stem. I held her chin and kissed each lid, before resting her head against my chest. A silent scream coursed from deep inside me; my wailing stifled as I sank my face against the side of Evangeline's broken neck.

★

I don't know how long I stayed there. A numbness took over my body and kept me tucked against the fusty sarcophagus wall, along with my grief-stricken reverie. The passing of time was eradicated by an all-consuming sorrow which had rendered me powerless to move. I don't remember what brought me back to the living world, or finally getting to my knees and carrying Evangeline back along the candle-lit passageway, up the spiral stone stairs and out of the underground tomb. The crypt behind me felt palpable in its silence and reluctant to allow us to leave its subterranean world. All I could hear as I reached the final step was the sound of my own pitiful sobs echoing back at me.

Outside the mausoleum, the rain had stopped and the wind was blowing a dense mist across the graveyard. The cemetery lights glimmered hypnotically above my head, the weak beams from the overhanging lamps cutting through the approaching fog and picking out the wisps of the air vines and flickering cobwebs that were strung from the cypress moss and live oaks along the length of the path in front of me. I took a few unsteady steps forward towards the footpath then felt a heavy pressure pushing down hard against my chest. I couldn't draw enough air into my lungs and my head began to reel, my heartbeat pounding in my ears. My knees suddenly gave way from underneath me and I sank to the ground, my weakening arms still clinging to Evangeline's

240

limp body. I lifted my head and drew Evangeline towards me.

Shadows danced out of the fog. I thought I saw two faceless figures walking towards me. I closed and opened my eyes in quick succession and tried to focus on the approaching shapes that moved in between the headstones and sunken, marble sepulchres around me. I saw one of the apparitions pick up speed and cut across my line of sight as if he was making his way around the back of the crypt. I pulled Evangeline's body closer towards me and, as I did so, saw a cloaked man striding towards me out of the mist, the hem of a priest's robe raised into the air, buffeted by the quickening breeze. Then, to my left, out of the corner of my eye, I saw a pair of legs of rush across the grass and immediately felt something hard rake off the back of my head. A white light went off inside my skull and a feeling of total paralysis encased me like concrete. My mouth hung open, my eyes could not focus and my ears roared with a high-pitched sound. As I began to fall forward into a cloudy abyss, I saw a black hand reach out to try and catch me. Evangeline slipped from my weakening grasp as an all-encompassing blackness wrapped itself around me and drew me towards a far off resting place I knew I had no name for.

26

I awoke in darkness, stretched out across a damp camp bed. My head was pounding, the sweat pouring down my face. The air was hot and breathless, like steam caught under a glass bell, and dense with humidity. Whilst I'd slept, I'd been haunted by nightmares, most of them thankfully lost as soon as I'd opened my eyes. I tried to raise my head off the pillow, but was suddenly hit with a sharp wave of pain that pulsed from the back of my skull to the front of my forehead. I winced, sank back and put my forearm across my face, my breathing shuddering in my throat as I slowly came to. I rolled off my side and lay on my back with no idea where I was. I was weak, my arms and legs hot and heavy, as if they'd been set in lead. I closed my watering eyes and felt myself keep fading towards sleep, then coming awake again. In that strange dream state, I suddenly remembered the St Louis cemetery and finding Evangeline's body. I saw myself being lifted from the ground by men with no faces who pitched me through a door into a wet, stone-paved alley that reverberated with the clatter of dustbins. I recalled a sharp stabbing pain in my arm, the back doors of a truck being flung open and being thrown inside. As the vehicle sped away, I thought I saw a partial moon shining down on me. The night sky was lit up with violent bolts of white lightning as I submitted to an insentient dominion.

"Joseph." I heard my name being called and recognised the man's voice immediately. I lifted my head from the pillow and saw Vic sitting in a rocking chair at the foot of the bed. His lips didn't move when he called out my name again. I watched as he smiled back at me, then felt a shiver of pleasure and fear at seeing him again. The chair and the floor creaked as he moved slowly back and forth. I tried to raise my arm off the bed and reach out to him. Vic stared at me and smiled, then shook his head when I tried to pull myself up onto my elbows. A hand touched my shoulder, then pushed me back down onto the mattress as I struggled to rise. I heard my cousin's voice call out to me as I slipped backwards, and closed my eyes, his words echoing all around me, "Rest now, JT, every'ting gonna be al'right, brutha."

The only image remaining in my head, as I fell back into a dark realm of unconsciousness, was of Evangeline calling out to me, her face contorted in fear, her trembling fingers reaching out towards me; the scarlet cord that held her wrists dripping with blood.

*

A thin beam of multicoloured sunlight crept in between a crack in a pair of barely parted drapes. I was sitting on the edge of the camp bed, my mouth as dry as sandpaper, staring at the empty rocking chair. I squeezed my temples between my fingers and tried to shake away the images that were still springing up inside my mind, each one more disturbing than any of those from my sleep. The panorama of my hallucinatory journey called out to me to return. I wanted to close my eyes again, drift back off to sleep and rejoin the pain-riddled memories I'd been existing with until just a short while ago. Across the room I heard a door handle being turned. I looked away from the chair to see an elderly mulatto man coming through the door in a burst of hot sunshine. The man walked across the squawky wooden floorboards towards me, carrying a suitcase, and let the door slam hard behind him, drawing the room back into semi-darkness. My fingers balled together to make a weak fist and tried to raise myself up from the camp bed, but felt the room begin to whirl as I attempted to stand. I looked into the shaded light. My vision was still playing tricks on me. I could see the man, but the room around him was still blurred, without specific detail or special form. I heard the case being dropped on the floor and the swish of the curtains being drawn back. My eyes snapped shut as the room was suddenly filled with a rainbow of bright light. When I finally reopened them, I saw the room I was in properly for the first time. I was in some kind of small church or chapel. Old timber walls reached up around me towards a high-beamed plaster ceiling. A large brass crucifix was nailed in the centre of one of the walls and a fading portrait of the Virgin Mary hung over the head of the bed. In front of me, the sun shone down through a large and ornate stained-glass window, creating a multicoloured light display that stretched across the bleach-scrubbed floorboards towards me. I sat still for a moment and let the last of the phantoms which had been plaguing my mind ease away, then picked up on the sour smell coming from underneath my arms. The old man was dressed in a black priest's cassock, which was fastened up to his thick, muscled neck. He picked up the suitcase, which I now recognised as mine, and walked over to me, dropping it at my feet.

"Dis fo' yuh." The accent was backwater Bajan and reminded me instantly of my deceased father's. "I had to club yuh pretty good wid dat sap last night . . . Yuh mem'ba any'ting?"

The question almost brought me to tears. I concentrated on what had happened to Evangeline the night before with such ferocity that I began to tremble. I nodded my head. "Yeah, I remember." My voice was hoarse and congested, cracking hard enough that I thought my windpipe was about to split open. When I spoke again, my vocal cords felt like they were about to snap. The old man standing in front of me was no more a member of the clergy than I was. I stared up at him and felt a bubble of hot anger well up inside my chest.

"Who the hell are you?"

The man pointed to himself and smiled. "Me? . . . Am a friend'a da family."

The elderly Bajan was perhaps in his late sixties and no more than five and a half feet tall. His thick-set body looked in good condition for a man of his advanced years, his muscular shoulders and arms straining inside his ill-fitting clerical attire. The fella's eyes were watery and red along the rims, his face unshaven and shiny with sweat. His teeth were yellow-coloured and thin at the ends, almost as though they had been filed. A light grey afro was cut short on his head and looked like a wig on top of a black mannequin. He looked down at me, then reached into his trouser pocket and screwed a cigarette in to his mouth, lit it with a Zippo then crumpled the empty packet and threw it on the chapel floor. I watched as he sucked on the cigarette, then blew a plume of thick grey smoke into the air. He scrunched up his nose as he sniffed the air then turned and walked back across the room and out the door. When he returned a few moments later, he was carrying a blue and white wash jug and bowl and had a towel hooked over his arm. He sat the pitcher and basin on a white-painted table in the corner of the room then rubbed his sleeve across the face of a dusty oval mirror that was attached to the back of the washstand and made his way back over to where I still sat.

"Yuh looks like you could use dis, Mistah Ellington." The mulatto man pointed back at the jug and bowl. "Dey is plenty hot water fo' yuh ta tek a wash an' shave. Den we git yuh sum'ting ta eat."

"Who's we?"

"Yuh'll soon see, once yuh sweetened up a bit." The old Bajan chuckled to himself and backed away from me to leave. I raised my arm up and felt a twinge in the muscle close to the top of my shoulder. I held out the palm of my hand to stop him from leaving. I looked at the washstand then back up to the old man.

"What do I call you?"

The Bajan's shrewd, bloodshot eyes stared down at me. They held onto mine suspiciously for a second or two whilst he sized me up. He took another drag on his cigarette then began to walk back across the room, finally calling out to me when he was just about heading through the door. "Ma name's Worrell ... Everton Worrell, but most folk dey jus' call me Bussa. Yuh can call me Bussa ... like yuh papa did."

27

I stood underneath a wisteria-covered iron trellis on the back porch at the rear of the chapel that overlooked the lush green everglade. I stretched my arms out either side of me and felt the bones in my neck crack as I rolled my head and yawned. The dilapidated old church sat at the furthest edge of the bayou, the brown current of its slow-moving waters drifting close by. On the far side of the water was a heavy border of willow trees, and, beyond them, a vast expanse of marsh filled with moss-strung dead cypress, whose tops were as pink as newly opened roses, as the sun broke through the low mist that rolled in between the overhanging branches. The sky above the wetlands was clear and blue, the day warm and windless. Earlier, I'd been standing over the bowl Bussa had brought me as if I'd been drugged. I washed and shaved myself slowly, then changed into a fresh, white, short-sleeved cotton shirt and a pair of navy trousers. Everything in my suitcase was just as I'd left it back at the Dejeans'. My money was untouched. How the case had found its way to be with me was anyone's guess. Evangeline's trusty Beretta had been wiped down, oiled and left on the seat of the rocking chair. Next to it was my penknife and trilby, which had been carefully dried and brushed clean. I reached around to the back of my scalp and felt at the bump on my head. I smarted as I ran my hand carefully across the bruised skin underneath my hair. My body suddenly lurched forward and I became dizzy again. I sat myself down at a wooden bench by the back door of the chapel and, after regaining my balance, looked down gingerly at my wristwatch. I patted my fingers gently on the glass and read the hands; it was just after 8.30am.

I gazed back out at the marshy landscape. It was like being back home by the coast on Ginger Bay in St Philip Parish. My distant ancestors were akin to the slave negroes who would have worked the plantations, sawmills, sugar cane and cotton fields of the Southern region I was now admiring. That thought sent a cold shiver through me. Not only was the terrain similar, but so was its unsavoury history. Those same maltreated black men and women, like my own island people, had been forced into bondage and endured years of miserable oppression. My own forefathers had lived lives that had mirrored those of the Southern chattels of Louisiana. Like them, Bajans had been weighed down with the daily toil of hard labour and the burden of the lineage of their captivity. We too had used the surnames of our white owners to be recognised by others. We had done so for so long that the early tales that had been passed down by our slave descendants had faded slowly over time. Stories of those first slave ships that had appeared innocuously at the foot of our ancestors' West African river homes amidst the fertile lands of plenty in which they lived, had also, over the intervening years, become the stuff of oral legend, confusing itself with biblical history and then, finally, forgotten.

Since I was a child, I had been constantly touched by the ugly hand of racism and bigotry. I knew what it was like to live inside my own black skin and realised that my colour dictated how most white folk treated me; but now, sitting in the verdant, tropical home of such long-lasting historical

248

slavery, I finally felt inside me just a faint whisper of what it must have been like to be owned by a fellow human being, white slave owners and their brutal overseers who would have had little, if any, regard for my person, other than to beat a good day's work out of me. I looked out across the bayou and wondered if history might not be waiting to have its cruel way with my people once again and, as I continued to contemplate such a bleak world, felt another icy shudder run through my veins.

★

Bussa brought a hot pot of coffee and a plate of grits and biscuits and sat them down on the table in front of me. The elderly Bajan stood over me with a half-smoked cigarette stuck at the edge of his mouth and watched me like an overeager prison guard as I reluctantly spooned in the first mouthful of the insipid, porridge-like breakfast. Eating was nearly as difficult as it was to get myself washed and dressed. My stomach felt tight and it ached when just a small mouthful of food made its way down. Bussa nudged the top my shoulder with his hand.

"Don't yuh like, man?"

I swallowed the grits in my mouth and felt a lie edging its way out of my lips.

"Yeah, it tastes great, but I think my guts are on strike."

Bussa laughed and sucked on his cigarette. "Dat be da curare still floatin' 'bout inside yuh."

"Curare ... did you damn well drug me too?"

The old man grinned and put one of his fingers up to his cracked lips and whispered back at me. "I 'ad ta keep yuh still an' hush-hush, Mistah Ellington."

I pushed the plate of mush away across the table, rubbed

249

at the top of my arm and shook my head in disgust. "Where the hell are we?"

Bussa laughed and pointed out across the bayou. "Dis 'ere's Black Lake, 'bout t'ree hunnerd mile north o' New O'leans."

I picked up my cup of coffee and took a sip, then gestured with my head out towards the boggy water. "Why here, in the middle of nowhere?"

Bussa shrugged. "Cause dey got no room fo' our kind in no swanky hotel ... Dis swamp da next best ting fo' yuh an' me, brutha."

"You said earlier that you knew my father, Clifford?"

Bussa nodded his head and looked out across the water. "Yeah, me knew da man. Wuk wid 'im at da Portvale sugar factory. Me nevah call 'im, Clifford. Ever'body know yuh papa as Fitz." The old man took a last drag on his cigarette, then pitched the dog end into the air with a flick of his finger. I followed the butt as it flew through the air and watched it fall into the smoky green swell. When I looked back at Bussa, he was gone. I touched the tender inflammation at the top of my arm and then felt a wave of fatigue roll through my body. I closed my eyes and rubbed my hands across my face, then heard the creak of the screen door swinging open and rattle shut.

"S'appenin', JT ... I t'ought I could smell a pig back here." The hearty laugh that ensued was all too familiar and sent the hairs on my arms and the back of my neck up on end. I could almost feel the smile that followed it burning through my clothes and into my skin. I heard my voice crackle as I spoke his name.

"Vic?" I could feel the tears wanting to come from my eyes as I snatched my head around to face him. My head felt addled, my thinking almost working in slow-motion. Torn between the two powerful sensations of love and hate, at that moment my woozy head and sunken heart just couldn't go either way. I stared at my cousin, open-mouthed. Vic grinned at me and began to chuckle. It was the kind of controlled laughter that only politicians and killers had mastered. My cousin could have easily taken up the first role and was born the other. Knowing that made the anger rise up from deep inside me.

A ball of rage seethed in me. I clenched my right fist, rested my left hand on the table, pushed myself up from the bench, and immediately began to stumble. Vic held out his arm and started to rush forward towards me, but came to an abrupt halt when he saw the look in my eyes.

"Hey now, cus, yuh ain't in no fit state ta be flingin' yuh fists 'bout. Jus' sit yuh arse back down, befo' yuh fall on it!"

I felt any strength I may have had dissolve in an instant, the fiery sense of anger remained though and burned at every fibre of my being as I sank back down into my chair. I breathed in deeply and glared back up at my cousin's rugged profile as he walked slowly across and sat on the seat opposite me. Vic was dressed in a sharp, black linen suit and black cotton shirt. A starched cleric's dog collar rested against the front of his throat. Vic crossed his arms, leaned back against one of the wooden porch posts and offered me a cheeky grin. We stared at each other, each weighing up the other's thoughts, my head still groggy, a sharp throbbing pain pulsating behind my eyes. I could feel the last of the Curare drug reluctantly working its way out of my dazed mind and weakened body. The draining after-effects were like nothing I'd physically endured before. I wiped a string of sweat beads from my brow and took another slug of my cooling coffee, then focused my weary eyes over towards Vic.

For a man who had less than two years ago fallen nearly three hundred feet from the top of Clifton Gorge down into the murky depths of the River Avon, he looked surprisingly fit and well. There was not an ounce of fat on his six-and-a-half-foot muscular frame. The black silk patch he had worn when I'd last seen him at Southampton docks aboard the TSS *Camito* still covered his right eye.

A neatly trimmed salt-and-pepper goatee graced his top lip and chin. His greying hair was now much longer. It had become thickly matted and was dreadlocked in tight braids and tied back away from his handsome dark face in a ponytail.

"So, why'd you decide to show up now?"

"Now?" Vic slapped the top of the table and laughed. "Fool, ma man Bussa bin followin' yuh in da shadows since yuh got off da damn plane back in New York!"

I pinched at my eyes with my fingers and slowly shook my head in disbelief. "You gotta be kidding me?"

Vic shook his head back at me. "Nah, that mean ole bastard bin my eyes n' ears. He a snaggle-toothed muthafucka, but he's loyal, jus' like Pigfoot was." Vic kicked irately at the ground with the toe of his shoe.

"That wus a damn shame 'bout that ugly nigger. He would'a had yuh back fo' sure if he a lived. Some fucka gonna pay fo' sendin' him to an early grave. I had Bussa follow the men that bin following yuh, JT. Soon as yuh got into that damn taxi at New O'leans Union Station, he was on yuh tail. I tol' him to keep it all real low key. Bussa an' Minton bin feedin' me info, keepin' me in the picture. Shit, I knew if tings got nasty along the way that yuh'd handle it, cus."

252

"Handle it; I was nearly torn to pieces back at that hotel room in Harlem. Do you realise there are corpses stacked up over three damn states because of all this madness you've gone an' created? You know Minton's dead, don't you?"

Vic shrugged his shoulders. "That greedy bastard was bound ta end up dead. If Gatehouse's fuckin' guys hadn't pulled the plug on his double-crossin' fat black ass, I would'a done eventually."

I felt my heart sink when I heard Vic mention the white man from the restaurant. "Tell me 'bout Gatehouse."

Vic, irritated by my question, opened and closed his hands on top of the table. I could hear his feet tapping at the floorboard underneath the bench. "He's Conrad Monroe's honky hatchet man. He's a dirty cop, the kinda nasty albino whose shit jus' don't flush."

I felt the wind pick up from across the water, the air suddenly smelled of sour mud and decay as if it was picking up on the death and destruction that had been following me. I felt my pulse throbbing away in the vein of my neck as I desperately tried to stay calm. "Vic, I got so many damn questions I need to ask you." I saw Vic's face change suddenly; his mouth formed a seamed, crooked line, the scar above his left eyebrow tightened against the bone. His chest swelled and he began to breathe more deeply as he shook his head at me. "Well, yuh gotta be patient . . . I ain't got all the answers ta give ya, jus' yet, JT."

"Patient my ass . . . Where's Evangeline?"

Vic's head dropped towards the ground; the ball of one finger worked at the corner of his mouth. When he looked back up at me again, I could see the unease in his face, a thought suddenly translating into words from behind his eyes, his voice box crackled as he cleared his throat, his lips

253

parted, the words he was about to expel already painful to my ears.

"She wid ole man O'Dell back at da funeral home, in New O'leans. We left her wid him befo' we headed out here. I tell ya, JT, Bussa, he couldn't 'a reached her in time to make a blind bit'a difference to what went down fo' that po' woman. I tell yuh straight. She would'a bin dead befo' she evah reached that graveyard."

I felt the tears begin to sting and well up in my eyes. "I don't care ... She didn't deserve to end her days like that Vic ... She'd have been petrified ... She was alone, damn you." I felt myself push the words out of my chest, felt my lips moving, my eyes blinking madly with each syllable as I spat them out at my cousin. Vic stared back at me coldly. I heard him ease out his breath, then watched as he lifted the dog collar away from his neck with the hook of his thumb.

"Look JT, when Gatehouse showed up at the place yuh two was eatin' at. I hadda make a simple choice. Either stay an' watch out fo' yuh, or follow the damn skirt."

I felt my face flush, the blood rushing to my temples. "The skirt, is that all she was to you? Just some floozy in some sick game you're playing? You callous bastard!" I saw Vic try to suppress the twitch of anger that suddenly invaded his face. He bit at his bottom lip, his chest rising high as he reined in his wrath. He leaned across the table and stuck a finger in my face.

"If I'd'a jumped in back there all guns blazin', every'ting I bin workin' on would'a bin fo' nuthin'. Yuh gotta trus' me, man."

I felt my stomach flutter and the pain in my head pinch at my temples like it was clamped between a vice. "Trust you ... You got some nerve, asking me that. I knew something stunk as soon as I opened that telegram. I've been in this damn country for less than a week an' I find out you're up to your neck in every kinda underhand crime. Blackmail, drug dealing, selling guns and Christ knows what else . . ."

Vic raised his eyebrows at me. "What's yuh problem with how I mek a buck?"

"My problem is you! You contacted me outta the blue to tell me Bernice was dead. I'm beside myself with grief, an' in case you forgotten 'bout 'em, so was your poor mama an' papa too. After breaking the news to them, I get on a damn plane, paid fo' by you, an' I fly over four thousand miles to come settle her affairs."

Vic nodded his head at me. "Yeah, an' even wid every'ting that's goin' down, that's what yuh gotta come do."

I puffed up my cheeks in desperation, then blew out a mouthful of warm air across the table. "Well, I ain't settled nuthin' up to now. Thanks to you. I got more cash flying round me than they got stashed in reserves at the Bank of England. All of this dough ending up in my back pocket with your name on it. I hit the airport stateside an' get hooked up with a bunch o' crazy revolutionaries from Harlem, then as soon as my ass hits my hotel room every nigger around me starts to get bumped off like it was a new-found national sport . . . You think after all that shit that I should trust you?"

Vic sat back and scratched at his gut, then hunched up his shoulders. "Well, when yuh put it like that. I can see why yuh ain't perhaps in the best o' moods."

I swallowed hard, my fingers biting deep into my palms in a desperate attempt to prevent myself lunging out at my cousin's face with my fist. "Best o' moods . . . You gotta be fucking kiddin' me. Vic, I've bin beaten, threatened an', in case you just forgotten, I've bin watchin' negroes dropping like flies fo' days ... What kinda mood you expectin' me to be in?"

Vic raised up his hands, his palms outwards towards me. "Okay, okay, I hear yuh, fo' fuck's sake ... Now why'd don't yuh git off that high horse yuh on an' cool it befo' I git vexed wid yuh an' I do sum'ting I might regret."

I saw Vic's eye drift away towards the screen door for a moment. When he turned back to look at me he'd clearly taken a moment to calm himself and I could see he was hankering to change the subject. He slid his hand palm down across the bench towards me and feigned a smile. "Listen, yuh didn't really tink I was jus gonna leave Laveau back at that manky cemetery, did yuh? What kinda cheap brutha, yuh tek me fo'?"

I dropped my head and ran my hand through my hair, then spoke down at the ground. "I don't know anymore, Vic ... I really don't."

I heard my cousin hiss through the gap between his teeth. "There ain't nuthin' I say to yuh that's gonna change how yuh feelin' 'bout me at the minute, is there?

I looked back up at Vic and shrugged my shoulders weakly. Despite everything he'd said, I could see that his one good eye had a familiar light of rare honesty sparkling in it, but I wasn't gonna tell him that's what I saw staring back at me. My cousin stood up and kicked the bench back away from him, his face pinched with anger. He stabbed his index finger down on the table. "Well, fuck dis shit ... Yuh need to hear the trute from another fool's mout."

He began to walk back towards the screen door. "Come on, move yuh black ass ... Yuh ain't gonna like what yuh 'bout to see, but it's gonna set tings straight between us."

Vic swore under his breath and spat a wad of white spittle

on the decking of the porch, then continued to grumble to himself like a petulant child. He looked back at me, his eye hollow and lustrous with a dark knowledge, as though he had just seen the future.

28

The two-storey wooden boathouse that stood at the rear of the chapel was partially collapsed and covered from its roof downwards in thick strands of woolly cypress moss. The iron grillwork around the rusted guttering was torn loose from its fastenings and the decaying ventilated wooden shutters hung at odd angles on the windows. Sweet pea vines wound up the loose timbers of the walls and a swathe of purple passion fruit flowers knotted through the low-hanging cedar branches that surrounded the secluded old building. I stooped down underneath a clump as Bussa opened the door for Vic and me to walk inside.

The interior of the boathouse looked worse than the outside. The wooden roof had grown dark with lime and rainwater, and was caving in; all four walls leaned inward. The air inside was moist and smelled of damp and rotting vegetation, the humidity thick and warm, like a wet towel hanging in front of my face. Bussa picked up an old oil lamp from a beat-up workbench by the door. He took out his Zippo from his back pocket, lit the wick, put it on the ground, then did the same to a couple more kerosene uplighters, positioning them back on the old table. The old Bajan held up one of the lamps in front of him and headed towards the water, seemingly carrying the shadows that hung around us along with him as he moved. The burning tallow cast a dull yellow glow across the boathouse, eventually picking out the planks that led along a low pier that reached out into the bayou. At the end of it, picked out by the ashen glimmer of the lamplight, sat a naked white man. He had been tied to a chair with thick rope, his mouth and eyes wrapped in brown duct tape. The chair had been positioned at the very end of the wide, wooden jetty, its thin back legs only inches from the motionless, sludgy water.

The man's face was caked in dried blood, his neck and shoulders marbled with bruises the colour of rotting plums. He turned his head towards the sound we made as we entered, like a blind person, his nostrils dilating with fear. He tried to talk through the tape as he heard the three of us approach him. Vic stood quietly over the bound man for a moment, then grabbed a handful of his hair and wrenched his head backwards. He yanked the duct tape first from his eyes, and then his mouth. The man writhed in fear, panic etched on his bloody face. He stared wildly up at Vic as Bussa hung the lamp close to his face. One eye was swollen shut, the inside of his lips gashed, his teeth pink, as though they had been painted with cochineal. I felt a revulsion go through my body as though I had been spat upon. Vic turned to me, his gaze fixed, his face empty of expression. He looked across at Bussa and then back at me and winked then, without missing a step, raised his arm in the air and whipped the palm of his hand down hard on the back of the man's skull, sending his head and neck flying forward. "JT, this 'ere is Jerry. Bussa found this bastard hiding out at Laveau's folks' place after he'd gone an' shot 'em both ... he was probably waiting fo' yuh black ass to turn up an' shoot it too!" Vic grabbed hold of the man's jaw and jerked his face toward me. "Jerry, say 'Hi' to my cus, JT." Vic jabbed his fist into the side of Jerry's ribs. The man yelped out, his eyes rolling backward in his

259

head, a thin streak of blood trickled out of the corner of his mouth down his neck and onto his perspiration-soaked chest. He coughed up more blood before staring up at Vic, his face contorting with a strange mixture of anger and dread as he tried to focus his vision on his captor. I watched Jerry cower in his seat as he plucked up the courage to speak.

"You're making a bloody big mistake, you know that, don't you? ... I'm a police officer. You can't do this to me." Jerry's accent was pure Queen's English; his clipped colonial diction pitch perfect.

Vic shrugged his shoulders at Jerry's futile threat. He leaned in close toward the frightened policeman, his nose almost touching the man's face, then pointed his finger over toward me and grinned. "Yuh 'ear that JT, Jerry 'ere's a po'liceman. We can all sleep safe in our beds to'night, cus Jerry's ploddin' the beat."

Vic stood back and hammered his fist into the side of the white copper's face. A thick string of crimson saliva shot out of his mouth and flew out somewhere into the pitch. Vic grabbed hold of Jerry's ear, twisting it backwards sharply and making him scream out in agony. Vic bent forward again toward Jerry's face and sniffed at the man's skin like a bloodhound picking up the scent of its pray; there was ice in his voice when he finally spoke again. "Now, Mistah Po'liceman ... JT, he's lookin' to git some answers to a shit load 'a questions. An' yuh ... well, yuh gonna start answerin' him pretty damn quick. Yuh 'ear me?"

I watched as Jerry quickly nodded his head back at Vic in agreement. The policeman looked up at me, waiting for me to speak. My eyes and ears still struggling to assimilate the savagery that was taking place before me. I cleared my throat, then heard a rumbling sound behind me in the darkness.

I looked across at Bussa. "What's that noise?"

Bussa took the glowing dog end of his cigarette out of his mouth and rubbed the hot ash between his fingers until it was dead, then flung the butt at his feet. "Dat a yerp."

"A what?"

Bussa coughed and spat a mouthful of phlegm into the water. "Noise de gator meks."

I snapped my head round towards Vic. "He talkin' 'bout a damn alligator?"

Vic nodded his head at me then laughed and slapped Jerry's arm, making him flinch.

"Ah, ah ... an' it a mean, big fucka too, Jerry. Didn't know that did yuh, fool. Yuh bin in dis shithouse all night, strapped to that damn chair an' sweatin' yuh nuts off wid that mean-assed gator sleepin' back there."

I heard the reeds rustling behind me in the dark followed by the rumbling sound again. I glanced nervously over my shoulder then quickly moved closer toward Vic.

Bussa laughed and lifted the lamp out at arm's length across the water, then back over towards Jerry's face. "Mistah, best yuh know, if a gator feel dat a human or sum 'uther gator intrudin' on dey territory, or if sum'ting git too close to da nest, dat gator, she'll sound'a bellow, dat's wha' dey call de yerp. Dat's what we just 'eard. Dat gator sounds pissed."

Bussa looked at the petrified man strapped to the chair and gestured with his head out across the dark water. Bussa stared up at me then back at Jerry. "Now, honky ... dat gator tellin' yuh she fuckin' hungry an' yuh need ta start talkin' quick ta ma man 'ere."

Jerry looked up at me, bloodshot eyes bulging in their sockets, his body shaking, his breath escaping from his mouth in fearful gasps. "For Christ's sake, man . . . Wha . . . what you wanna know?"

The air around me suddenly felt cold. I could smell an odour like gas from a sewer main creeping up from underneath my feet. I pinched at my eyes with my fingers and stared back at the bound copper. When I finally spoke, my words rang around me head like a death knell.

"Who are you working for?"

Jerry looked up at me with an almost stunned expression on his face.

"Wha? . . . What do you mean, who am I working for?"

Vic grabbed hold of the top of Jerry's skull and jammed his index finger down into his right ear, making him scream again. "Jus' answer the man's fuckin' questions!"

Jerry nodded impotently. He breathed hard through his mouth, his face dilated with pain as the words his throat couldn't fight to form finally came out. "I work . . . work with Gatehouse . . . Chief Superintendent Silas Gatehouse."

"An' is Gatehouse part of the Barbados force?"

Jerry nodded his head. Vic smacked him across the bridge of his nose with the flat of his hand, quickly forcing a blustering answer out of his mouth. "Yeah, yeah . . . he's with Central Division . . . Bridgetown station."

I felt myself rub at my mouth with my fingers. A dozen memories flooded into my head, all of them bad. Bridgetown had been my old hunting ground, the place where I'd once carried a warrant card and the rank of sergeant. "And how is Gatehouse connected to Conrad Monroe?"

Jerry looked up at me, his fearful eyes squinting in the poor light. He suddenly fixed on mine as I stared back at him blankly. "Monroe had a break-in at his home about six weeks ago. He had paperwork and photographs stolen from his safe. He asked Gatehouse to deal with it personally, get back what had been taken, and quickly."

"Gatehouse told me that my cousin there was blackmailing Monroe ... What's he got on him?"

Vic began to chuckle to himself like a mischievous school boy. Jerry suddenly looked away from me and stared up at Vic, the policeman's battered face, grave and the colour of ash.

Vic tapped repeatedly at Jerry's cheek with his palm. "Go on now, Jerry ... tell the man, what it is I got on ole Conrad that he wants back so bad." Jerry swallowed hard then looked back at me.

"Your cousin has a diary, cinefilm reels, negatives and photographs ... explicit photographs." The skin on my face felt tight when I heard the word *explicit*. I could feel a dryness, a constriction in my throat that would not shift when I pinched at my neck with my fingers. I looked at Vic and moved a little closer towards him. The leaves and desiccated twigs under my feet crunched like tiny shards of glass.

"Film and photographs of what?"

Jerry shook his head, blood trickled from his nostrils, a high wheeze coming out of his throat, his blossoming betrayal of his master clearly gnawing at his professional conscience. "Of people."

Vic slapped Jerry's face with the back of his hand. "Don't git smart, Jerry."

Jerry was looking deeply into my eyes. He stammered his words a couple of times before finally breaking back into fluid speech. "Monroe held parties up at his home ... special parties where his guests could indulge themselves in whatever they wanted to."

I felt my lips and the skin around my mouth quiver. "What kinda parties?"

Vic squeezed the bottom of Jerry's chin and tilted his head up towards me. Sweat dripped down the policeman face. I watched him as he quickly opened and closed his eyes several times as he tried to pinpoint my exact positioning in front of him. "You know the kind of thing, skin parties."

I shook my head. "No, I ain't too worldly-wise, why don't you try an' enlighten me."

Jerry's eyes continued to strain up at me. "Monroe liked to keep his business partners sweet. He held sex parties, supplied booze and drugs on the night to them. It was all very discreet."

"But not discreet enough to stop Monroe taking photographs of his guests, yeah?"

Jerry nodded his head slowly. "He told Gatehouse it was his insurance if any of his partners got out of line at any time."

"Out of line, in what way?"

"Money stuff... you know, contracts that may get reneged on, deals falling through, all that kind of thing. Monroe's been expanding his island organisation. He needs other businesses for his own to thrive outside of Barbados. If a company executive isn't playing ball or wants to move on, Monroe's got the films and photos to apply that little bit of leverage and keep the bosses in line. He's got it all tied up with some real heavy hitters. He's shipping out just about anything you can think of to the US and Europe. He's making a fortune."

"By shipping anything, you really mean he's into drugs an' guns."

"Yeah ... there's all of that, but Monroe owns more than

half of the sugar plantations on Barbados, it's a perfect front for all the other stuff he doesn't want people to know about. He's got Barbadian, American and European shipping companies in his back pocket. The fellas who run those companies, they get invited to the skin parties he puts on."

I breathed loudly through my nose, shaking my head in disgust. "And all these fellas end up in Conrad's home movies an' get their ass plastered across a bunch of seedy snapshots that he gets taken?"

"Yeah ... that's about the measure of it. I heard that some of the photographs that got snatched had shots of both Monroe and Gatehouse in them. That's why they've been so eager to have them retrieved without any questions being asked, except by us."

I looked across at Vic and shook my head at him. "An' I suppose you found out 'bout Monroe and his sordid parties an' had his safe riffled, then you tried to muscle in on him for a fast buck ... You really have sunk to the bottom of the bloody barrel this time, Vic."

Without warning Vic stuck his hand inside his jacket and pulled out an all too familiar Colt. 45. He pistol-whipped Jerry a couple of times across the back of the copper's scalp with the gun; every blow made a sickening thud. Jerry's head sank forward, dark blood fell from his head and rolled down his face onto his knees. Vic rested the barrel of the .45 against Jerry's right temple. "Now, tell him the rest o' yuh fuckin' story, pig."

Jerry hesitated for a moment. He sucked at a droplet of blood that was about to drip from his bottom lip then stared down at the floor before nervously gazing back up at me. I could hear his speech crackle as he tried to get his words

265

out. "It was your ... it was your sister who stole the damn photographs and films from Monroe."

I closed my eyes, not quite believing what I was hearing. I swallowed hard and felt myself try not to grimace when I spoke again. "Bernice ... how the hell did my Bernice get mixed up in all this madness?"

"Tell him!" Vic pressed the gun hard against the top of Jerry's face.

"She worked for Conrad ... he took her on as his housemaid about two years ago."

I shook my head in disbelief. "How would a black housemaid manage to get inside'a Conrad's safe? Bernice, she weren't no thief."

Vic slowly ran the barrel of the Colt underneath Jerry's blood-soaked chin and jaw and nudged his head savagely at the policeman for him to continue. "Your sister was more than just Conrad's damn housemaid. She wasn't just doing nigger jobs like cleaning up and gardening for him."

"Hey, rasclat! Watch how yuh slingin' the word *nigger* 'bout ..." Vic stabbed the end of his gun into the soft part of the flesh underneath Jerry's chin. There was a bleak bloodlust ringing through my cousin's voice. I took a couple more unsteady steps closer to Vic and the trussed-up policeman. The side of Jerry's face twitched nervously. He tried to speak, then stopped himself for a moment, his eyes pleading up at me.

"Your sister, she was bed-hopping with Monroe. He likes dark meat ... She'd been his floozy for nearly eighteen months. She got real close to him. He didn't know it at the time, but she had access to his study, saw business files, contracts, all that kind of stuff. She even had the combination to his fucking safe."

Jerry stopped for a moment. He looked at Vic's gun next to his face and began to gasp in mouthfuls of air. He spat out more blood then began to speak again, his voice fluttering with anxiety. "Your sister, Bernice, she knew more about his private life and his business dealings than she should ever have done. For some damn reason, she broke into his safe and took the photographs and cinefilms then scarpered. Monroe had Gatehouse start up a police search across the island. The two of them cooked up some story about her stealing a large amount of cash out of the safe. Put up a reward. Some drunk from Crab Hill gave her up. We found her hiding out in a backstreet dive on Blacksage Alley."

I felt my stomach turn. A wave of nausea ran up from my guts towards my throat. I gagged, then swallowed hard to suppress myself from being sick.

"How in the name o' Christ do you know all this?"

I smelled a sour, rancid stench rise up from Jerry's armpits and saw the panic race across his beaten face. He spat out his next set of words as if they had been force-fed him and coated in acid. "Because ... because, I was there when your sister told Monroe everything. Once Monroe got what he wanted, he told Superintendent Gatehouse to get rid of her. It was Gatehouse who killed her then took her back to Crab Hill and dumped her body."

The policeman's voice echoed blankly around my face as a shifting red haze dropped over my eyes. My palms rang with rage and I could hear my heartbeat pounding away inside my head. In my mind, I saw an image of Bernice as a little girl as I lunged towards Jerry. I drove my fist into his mouth, throwing all my weight into the blow, snapping the copper's head back as though it were on a spring. I saw his lip burst against his teeth as I hooked him a left, catching him hard on the jaw. I heard Vic bellow at me from behind, then felt him grab hold of me and pull me back along the jetty, his grip tightening around the tops of both my arms as I kicked out at Jerry's deadlocked body. I saw Bussa standing in front of me, staring into my eyes, his mouth moving, his words like the muted sounds of submerged rocks beating against a fast-moving riverbed. I felt his hand touch the side of my arm then heard Vic's voice speaking close to my ear.

"Easy, Joseph, easy now, brutha . . ." My cousin squeezed at my arms again, then I felt him release his grip on the top half of my body. Vic rubbed the palm of his hand up and down my chest, like a mother comforting her distressed child. He put his mouth against my face again and whispered into my ear. "I tole yuh, yuh wouldn't like what yuh were gonna hear, JT. I'm jus' sorry yuh hadda 'ear it from that honky pig."

I yanked myself forward away from Vic and walked back over to Jerry's hunched up body. I kneeled down beside the policeman and lifted his head up with one hand and drew back my fist to hit him again. Jerry focused on a neutral space behind me, his blood-smeared mouth agape, his face now ashen white with fear and shock. I felt a hand grab hold of my wrist and squeeze it tightly, making my fingers pulse inside my clenched fist. Vic's sombre words seemed to peal down onto me as if they were being spoken to me by the Grim Reaper himself.

"That pig Gatehouse, he beat on Bernice till she'd told him every'ting . . . Well, that's what he thought."

I looked up at my cousin, the tears welling up inside my eyes. "Whatta the hell you talkin' about, Vic?"

I bit at my trembling lower lip as Vic eased the pressure

on my wrist. He held my arm firmly in his grip and smiled down at me sadly.

"Bernice, she lied to that sonufabitch Gatehouse befo' he did fo' her, Joseph. She tole him an' Monroe that she'd already mailed out those films and pictures to you, in the UK . . . but in trute, that girl already gone an' sent 'em to me."

I felt the tears begin to fall from my eyes and I started to shake from head to toe. A burning pain was ignited deep inside my chest and pulsed through my body, erupting out of my mouth in a single ear-piercing scream. I sobbed uncontrollably and kept on crying until my aching, grief-stricken soul had no more tears to give.

I felt my cousin's hand rest gently against the side of my arm; he left it there for a while. The smell of the lingering blood on his fingers seeped up inside my nostrils, making me retch. I wiped at my face with the backs of my hands and tried to regain what little composure I could muster. Vic reached down and held onto the tops of my arms and helped me back up on to my feet. I thought I saw him smile at me as he put his arm around my shoulder and guided me back along the jetty path toward the door of the boathouse. Behind me, I heard Bussa's voice echo out through the darkness and bounce off the decrepit, moss-soaked wooden walls; his foreboding words and Jerry's sudden futile pleading followed me outside into the bright sunshine and hung over my broken spirit like an executioner's axe.

"Mistah, dat gator she gonna roll yuh round down there in da bayou. She gonna tenderise yuh ass fo' a while. Mek yuh good eatin'."

Then I heard the rasping sound of chair legs scraping across wood and Jerry scream out all too briefly as Bussa kicked the policeman into the black water. I snatched myself away from Vic's arm and turned around and looked back inside. In the shimmer from one of the oil lamps dimming flare, I watched the elderly Bajan walk towards me, his face expressionless, his eyes fixed on mine, as empty as death. Behind him, as he began to close the door of the boathouse, I could have sworn I saw the water rippling from its furthest edges. My eyes catching, only too briefly, the pale underbelly of a brutal prehistoric force as it sank down into the depths.

29

A flicker of dry lightning and a rumble of thunder echoed out of the night sky. I looked out of the passenger window from the back seat of a rusting 1950s Dodge town wagon, that Bussa had quickly ushered me into just a few minutes earlier, and watched as the elderly Bajan and Vic loaded up my case and their meagre belongings into the back of the truck. I'd tried to stay mad at Vic for dragging me into his labyrinthine world of madness for a long as I could, but my acrimony at both his deceit and duplicity towards me had slowly waned by nightfall. Vic was Vic. He was blood kin and my cunning relative knew how strong my own loyalties were towards him. Vic saw the world he inhabited as a dark place and saw fit to behave in an equally opaque manner. Despite his, at times, playful and humorous exterior, I knew my cousin to be a deeply complex man; quick-tempered, cunning, dangerous, and I suspected that more than one soul perhaps lived deep inside his skin. The one sure thing I knew about Vic was that I could never quite fathom what was exactly going on inside his head, no matter how intimate our family bond. My brethren knew that, and that's how he wanted it to stay.

For most of the day, Vic had left me alone with my temper and mean thoughts, only meeting up with me again just after midday to eat a simple lunchtime meal of rice and peas. We'd both sat outside at the table at the back of the chapel and, after a few minutes of brief, awkward silence, my cousin had gone on to carefully explain his next set of serpentine moves. Vic had uncapped the tops off a couple of cold, long-necked beer bottles, handed one to me and told me that we were hiding out in a backwater place called Black Lake; an unmapped and remote everglade region stuck dead centre between the Cajun town of Breaux Bridge and the larger Louisiana city of Lafayette, just over a hundred miles to the west. Vic had said that we'd be leaving the wetlands after nightfall and that we'd be on a plane and heading back to Barbados before sunrise. He imparted all of this important information to me whilst shovelling spoonfuls of food into his mouth, his jaw swollen with rice, and washing it down with mouthfuls of frothing beer. When he'd finished eating, he'd pushed his plate across the wooden table then casually stuck his hand underneath his jacket and drew out his trusted Colt .45 from the back of his trouser waistband. The gun was rust-pitted, the blueing on the cylinder worn, the sight had been filed off and the wooden grips wrapped in black tape. I'd watched as Vic expertly worked the well-oiled mechanism, snatching back the slide and inserting a round into the chamber before weighing up the pistol admiringly in the palm of his huge hand. When he looked back up at me, his face was expressionless; the muscle in his jaw knotted tight. I watched him wet his lips and saw a flicker of hesitation tic at the edge of his mouth before he spoke. When he finally did, his foreboding words felt like iced water being poured into my ears.

"Tings, they gonna git bloody when we git home, yuh know that, don't yuh?"

I stared down at my feet and felt the humid air around me suddenly become cool. I nodded my head in response, like a child about to accept a painful punishment from a vexed parent. I knew that my uneasy silence would say more to my cousin than any assenting utterance I could try and muster. Out of the corner of my eye I saw Vic slip the .45 back underneath his coat.

I felt an uneasy weight lift from my shoulders knowing the gun was out of sight. I looked up gingerly at my cousin as he rose from the bench seat. I felt myself smile and shook my head as I examined the austere clergy get-up that he was dressed in. "So, what's with the priest's dud's, Vic?"

Vic shrugged his shoulders and laughed, "Shit, why not, JT ..." My cousin took a step back and brushed admiringly at the lapel of his black clerical jacket with the back of his hand, then took a couple of steps backward towards the chapel door. Vic let his muscular arms drop to his side, the palms of his hands splayed open. "Niggah dressed like a man o' the cloth gonna git less ovah rough time offa the backwater shit-kickers 'bout these parts than a niggah in a sharp suit would. Kinda made sense ta me, cus."

As Vic walked away chuckling to himself, I reached across the table for my beer and lifted the bottle to my mouth. I sank the remaining dregs while I watched my cousin's huge frame stride across the wooden boards. I spun the glass bottle nervously in my hand a couple of times, then put it down on the floor by my feet. I stared straight ahead, my eyes following Vic as he disappeared back inside the old chapel. When the screen door had swung to and he was out of sight, the unusually glacial atmosphere around me seemed to lift and was replaced by the familiar clingy humidity. As I sat gazing into space, I could feel my pulse beating in my throat, my heart throbbing in my chest. A single bead of sweat ran from my temple and trickled down the side of my face and neck. I rested my trembling hands on the tops of my thighs and sighed deeply, like a man beaten by the troubles the world was constantly throwing at him.

For the rest of that afternoon I'd sat alone with my uneasy thoughts and Vic's ominous words rattling around in my head. I'd tried unsuccessfully to hold back a wave of tears that stung behind my eyes as I thought about Evangeline and the way she had died. I'd wept as I berated myself at not saving her, reliving in my mind the terrible moment I had found her lifeless body back inside the crypt. Wracked with guilt and self-loathing, I held my head in my hands and continued to sob; a sense of impotent rage hung over me, finally coming to rest across my brow like a crown of piercing thorns.

By six that evening, the leaves had begun to whip up in circles at my feet and were swept up towards the highest limbs of the oaks. Spiderweb-like forks of electric light burst inside the clouds in the far-off distance. From the bench, I watched dusk slowly gather in the trees along the bayou and saw the water darken. As the light began to soften, I listened to the fish roll in the shallows as egrets flew in to feed on the bank opposite me. Out in the distance, the western sky became red and black and I could smell the approaching rain on the cooling breeze that had picked up and blown itself in across the swamp. I looked out across the water and watched the darkness begin to creep further out of the cypress trees on the other side of the marsh and roll across the still waters. My body ached, and perspiration rose up from my clammy skin and prickled underneath my clothing and on my head and face. I stumbled onto my feet and felt a warm shudder run up through me. As I looked back at the approaching blackness, a sharp sensation bit into the pit of my gut, like a flame burning a hole in paper. Inside me, its fiery kindle spread quickly inward, blackening everything it touched. The unwelcome conflagration surged through my frame, making me unsteady on my feet. I held on tightly to the edge of the wooden bench with my sweating fingertips as the burning feeling continued to course its way deeper up into my body; its dark volcanic presence edging closer towards my heart, the unseen flames searing at my broken spirit, its scorching embers seeking to incinerate any of the remaining courage that I may still have possessed within me.

30

It was just after midnight. The sky was pitch black and laced with stars, the bayou resembling a strange ethereal kind of heaven; clusters of fireflies glowed white, their bodies glittering in a startling array of yellow, blue and green. The Dodge drove slowly across rough ground, past a network of canals, oxbows and sand bogs, its headlights bouncing off the vine- and cobweb-covered trees that bordered each side of the dirt track. Two or so miles down the swamp trail, the old pick-up truck rumbled over a drawbridge across the coulee then motored along a maple-lined gravel road and back out onto the highway. Out in the open, there wasn't a soul on the roads and I knew that would unsettle Vic. Three black men driving about in a rundown motor in the early hours of the morning was the equivalent of a moth to a flame to any eager night-shift traffic cop sitting in his squad car by the side of the road. Bussa, sensing Vic's unease, drove swiftly, but carefully. Out in front of us, veins of lightning pulsed in the sky, the air thick with the heavy odour of pond water and sour mud.

I'd never liked being a passenger in a car, especially not jammed into the back seat. I'd always thought of driving as an escape, and night driving was the ultimate distillation of my belief. Taking a car out in the dark removed me from what I thought of as normal and placed me in a happy world of my own definition. I believed no bad ever existed in a car while I was driving, and that was especially the case for motoring at night. I used to tell myself, "If you can't see it, you can almost pretend that it doesn't exist." For a few precious hours, I'd hoped, as we headed out into the darkness, that life would become simpler, less dangerous, and that I would feel like I was in control again, but I knew I was kidding myself. The nagging doubt in my gut and the uneasy feeling that ran hot through my veins told me that the journey home was going to be anything but pleasurable, whether it was dark or not.

I looked over the seat at Vic as he sat up front smoking a joint. Even though he'd never admit as much to me, I could tell that he was on edge.

On the superstition-riddled island of Barbados, most folk Vic and I had grown up around did not have a positive image of the night. Ask an elderly Bajan woman, a young girl or a four-year-old boy preoccupied with the monsters under their beds, and you'd most likely get different versions of the same damn answer: when the sun goes down, the potential for bad things goes through the roof. I knew night time to be a world of dark corners and fuzzy edges; a place I was happy to reside in and which my people tolerated, but rarely preferred.

The view out of the windshield rarely changed for the next few hours. Small towns buzzed past us in a fleeting wash of amber light as we headed towards Lafayette. Bussa stopped briefly for gas at an all-night petrol station and we were back on the road as soon as Vic had stuffed a wad of banknotes into the white attendant's hand. Neither Bussa nor Vic spoke for the next hour. I sat quietly and avoided forcing any kind of conversation with them. A cloak of pitch black hovered over the rest of the journey, forcing me to sink deeper into my own maudlin thoughts about Evangeline. As we pushed on down the highway, only the moon or the odd street light picked out the hard-to-make-out landscape.

Everything around me suddenly acquired a kind of eerie feel to it; the roads turned a liquorice black and the fields stretched broader and flatter than in the daylight hours. The night sky had become impenetrable in its inky vastness, and its unwelcome gloom seemed to draw itself inside the vehicle. The shadows in the coulees and the woods seemed to reach out towards us as Bussa drove; the branches on the trees hung like gallows, the wind blowing the glassy leaves across the road and flinging them against the bonnet and roof of the truck.

The unrelenting bleakness seemed to pour itself into my head and the wall of silence inside the old Dodge set my already prickly nerves further on edge. I felt myself shiver with cold and pulled the lapels of my jacket around my neck and face and hunched myself down on the back seat and closed my eyes. I held onto my coat tightly and tried to dismiss any further bad thoughts from entering my head. Like a child, I sought a lullaby to call me to slumber. Instead, a distant voice, like that of a young woman, called out to me. Her indecipherable mutterings continued to hum inside my ear as I drifted towards the uneasy realm of broken sleep.

I woke with a start to see Vic hanging out of the passenger window of the car looking at a large billboard that hung away from the roadside between a row of trees. The sign simply read, Lafayette Aerodrome. A large white arrow pointing left through a light mist guided us in the right direction. Heavy rain poured out of the sky, droplets as big as marbles pelted down against the windshield and roof of the truck.

Bussa swung into the unlit entrance of the airfield and drove down the uneven asphalt drive, the stones clicking up from behind the tyres against the underside of the vehicle. I grabbed hold of the back seat in front of me and reached forward. As I peered around Vic's head, I noticed the warm glow of a series of arc lights illuminating the airfield. Bussa swung the Dodge a hard left at the end of the driveway and pulled up alongside a dimly lit Nissen hut. I climbed out of the back of the Dodge and was immediately hit by the humidity. I looked at my wristwatch: raindrops splashed against the glass. The illuminated hands said it was just after 2.30am. Even at such an ungodly hour and in such miserable weather, I could feel the heat reflecting off the tarmac. It was hard to breathe. The air was heavy and smelled of diesel.

Vic climbed out of the truck and looked at me sternly, his face already wet with rain. "Go he'p Bussa haul our stuff." He turned and stabbed his hand across the aerodrome towards an aircraft on the edge of the runway, then began to walk towards a hangar on the other side of the airstrip. He called back to me as he paced off into the darkness.

"Looks like we's headin' home on that pile o' shit!"

I felt Bussa nudge me in the back with his fist and turned just as he was throwing my suitcase at me. I snatched the case in midair and heard the old Bajan laugh as he lifted the two canvas holdalls belonging to Vic and him out of the trunk. I looked back at the creaky aircraft and shook my head. Bussa came and stood beside me, his leathery face soaked with rain. He smiled at me, even in the bad light his teeth looked like yellowing tombstones. He nodded towards the airplane. "Dat a Dakota DC-T'ree." It look like it 'bout ta drop ta pieces, don't it?" Bussa burst out laughing. He

279

slung the two bags over his shoulder and began to walk across the tarmac, his laughter carried back towards me on the hot, wet wind.

The plane looked more like a battered steel coffin waiting to pitch me into the hungry ocean between the States and home. It was more like a tin can with wings than a proper plane. It was maybe thirty years old and, even in the poor light, looked fit for the scrapyard. I felt my stomach flip as I followed after Bussa and climbed up a ladder into the rear cargo hatch of the Dakota and looked around me. At the front of the plane, in the cockpit, two white men, the pilot and co-pilot, sat chatting behind a panel of gauges and lights, both ignoring my or Bussa's presence as we came onboard. A row of seats ran six deep backwards from the cockpit and directly behind them, strapped down to the floor with thick stowage ropes, were the three coffins I'd seen at Odell's funeral home back in New Orleans.

I shuddered as I walked past them and watched with surprise as a grizzled, black mechanic with a bag of spanners wandered out of the cockpit and made his way towards me. He nodded his head by way of a greeting to Bussa and me as he squeezed past us, then tugged at the ropes that were securing the three caskets to the floor. I followed Bussa up the short aisle and sat down in a seat by one of the windows. Bussa stowed the canvas bags on a seat behind him and sat down opposite me. I looked back at the old black man and half expected to see him pull out a stethoscope and start listening against the fuselage. Ten minutes later, Vic climbed on board and waited as the rear door was closed shut behind him. In a very short space of time, he'd lost the clerical suit and dog collar and replaced it with a black silk shirt open at his chest, black trousers and a mid-length, black leather jacket. A gold clenched-fist medallion, identical to the one Evangeline had worn, hung from his neck. His oiled dreadlocks were swept back tight away from his forehead and tied in a neat ponytail. The silk eyepatch he now wore had been replaced by a black leather one, the ties almost invisible as they ran across his glistening locks and around back of his head. As he walked along the aisle towards me, I could see again the old Vic I knew and loved. When he sat down next to me and hitched out a hip flask from his jacket pocket, I was left in no doubt that it was my trusted kin at my side. I felt a flutter of excitement burst inside my chest as I watched him unscrew the cap, put the flask to his lips and take a couple of hefty swigs.

Vic pointed at the flask with his finger and nudged me in the ribs with his elbow then handed the canteen over to me, "Now that, JT, that's some fine Bajan shit, in there. Knock it back, brother. Sounds like we's in fo' a bumpy ol' ride." As I took my first sip, the engines of the aircraft fired up and the Dakota suddenly came to life. I tipped the hip flask back and swallowed a couple of mouthfuls of the strong-tasting rum. As I went for a third glug, I felt Vic's hand wrestle the canteen out of my quaking fingers.

Vic glared at me and tutted to himself as he screwed the silver cap of the flask back on. I watched as he teased the bottle of booze in front of my face, shaking it gently from side to side. "Easy, brutha, that fuckin' hooch yuh sinkin' back gotta last me fo' the rest o' the damn night." The Dakota began to lurch forward and I saw, out of the corner of my eye, Bussa's arm reach out across the aisle towards the flask. Vic saw the elderly Bajan's wrinkled hand heading towards him and quickly jammed the hip flask back in his pocket. He looked back at the elderly gofer and sucked through the gap in the middle of his front teeth, "Yuh can fuck off if yuh tink yuh is sticking yuh scabby ole mout' anywheres near this damn canteen!"

I smiled to myself and watched as Bussa began to mumble to himself, his words suddenly drowned out as the DC-3 started to taxi off down the runway, the pulsating roar of the two radial engines throbbing either side of the hull of the craft. The wings of the aircraft yawed suddenly, the airframe juddering around us as it picked up more speed on the tarmac. I snapped my eyes shut tightly as the Dakota sped along the runway, then lurched and leapt free of the ground. I felt my fingers grip onto the armrests either side of me as we began to climb, the wind buffeting the body of the plane as it began to gain altitude. Next to me, I heard Vic howling with laughter as the DC-3 continued to climb. I opened my eyes and looked across at him just as he bellowed out above the engine noise.

"Bussa, yuh 'ear me, brutha?"

I heard the old Bajan bawl back at my cousin over the din. "Yeah."

Vic grinned at him, looked down at his jacket pocket then back at the old man. "If this shitbox drops outta the sky any minute an' crashes ... then yuh can have ma rum."

Half an hour later, the Dakota DC-3 had climbed out of the wind and rain and was rocking its way through the night sky. Across the aisle, Bussa was sound asleep in his seat, his snoring masked by the engine noise. I sat looking nervously out into the blackness. It felt as if time had suddenly stood still. There was no cloud and the moon shone cold, gleaming off the wings, turning the propellers into arcs of pale silver light. It was bitterly cold inside the cabin, the darkened hull almost pitch, save for the dim glow of the overhead passenger lights dotted above our heads. The noise of the two engines was deafening. Everything inside vibrated, as though the plane was about to tear itself apart. I looked back out the window of the plane and watched as the wings were semi-illuminated by the moon: the lower half shining around the rim, the upper half several shades darker. As the plane dipped, the line between shadow and light moved and I felt my stomach roll again as the aircraft was buffeted by light turbulence. I felt Vic's hand rest on the top of my arm. When I looked at him, his expression was grave. I watched as his cheek twitched, the spasm arcing across his face up towards his one good eye. Vic reached back into his jacket and pulled out the hip flask, he unscrewed the cap and took a hard pull of liquor, then handed the canteen to me. I took a swig and held tightly onto the flask for a moment as Vic stared back at me. He moved his head towards my ear and spoke into it. His voice crackled as his rum-soaked breath hit my nostrils.

"Yuh evah tink why Bernice was the chocolate colour she was?"

I lifted my face away from his and shrugged my shoulders at my cousin. "No ... why should I? Mama was Bajan Creole, Bernice had her colouring."

Vic shook his head knowingly and coughed into his clenched fist before speaking.

"Monk Monroe."

"Who?"

Vic gritted his teeth, his temper rising across his face. He put his face closer to mine and raised his voice above the engines. "Jesus, JT ... yuh bin hit on the fuckin' head, not lobotomised. Monk Monroe ..."

Confused, I snatched my head back again. "You talking 'bout Conrad Monroe's father?

Vic nodded his head at me. "Yeah ... that's who I'm talkin' 'bout. Welcome back, cus."

"So, what about him?"

I watched as Vic swallowed hard again. "There ain't no easy way o' sayin' this, JT ... Monk Monroe, he raped Aunt Cora."

I felt every muscle in my body tighten when I heard Vic say my mother's name. I took a deep breath and tried to make sense of the appalling horror that my cousin had just spoken of. "Say what?"

Vic pulled at his mouth and jaw with his fingers and nervously spat his words back at me. "Yuh fuckin' heard me, fool ... I ain't repeating this shit!"

I took another slug of rum. Vic watched me gulp at his hooch and let me do it without complaint. I gripped at the flask as if it was breathing new life into my tormented soul then stared back at my cousin. "I don't know what the hell you're talkin' about."

I watched Vic bite down onto his bottom lip, an anguished look now etched firmly across his face. I felt his hand tighten on my arm. "Yuh mama, she had Bernice, but she weren't yuh papa's pickney. Bernice was Monk Monroe's kid."

I shook my head in disbelief and sank another mouthful of my cousin's rum. "Nah, that's bullshit ... No, I don't wanna hear this ... This is madness, you got it wrong, Vic."

Vic kept his eyes straight ahead, locked on mine. I saw their edges suddenly well up with water and, in that very moment, knew that he was telling me the truth. He shook his head sorrowfully at me again, then let his head slump towards his chest, the words that he spoke back at me barely audible. "Brutha, I wished I had." Vic continued to rock his head back and forth. I watched as he wiped at the side of his face with the sleeve of his jacket, then look back up at me. "I surely wished I had got it wrong."

I could feel the heat on my face and arms, the stink of my body odour rising up from underneath my clothes. I struggled to fully take on board what I'd just been told, my head and heart fighting against the abhorrence of my cousin's words. I stared back at Vic, the rum burning at my insides, my head thumping, the blood pounding through the veins in my temples. "But ... but that copper, the one back at the boathouse, he said that Bernice had been Conrad Monroe's floozy."

Vic shook his head in agreement, then reached across and placed his hand on my shoulder. "It gits worse ... yuh don't know the half o' it, brutha. Ain't nuthin' worse than having to lay this kinda shit on yuh kin. The Monroes bin a sorry sack o' shit to our family fo' years ... they still are being."

I pinched at my eyes with my fingers and glared back at Vic. "What the hell are you talking 'bout?"

"When I said yuh needed to hear the trute back on the bayou ... I hadn't the heart to tell yuh the whole picture ..." I watched Vic take a breath before speaking again. "Ting is, JT, yuh still ain't got no idea where that trute is gonna be leadin' yuh an' me, cus." Vic lifted his hand from my shoulder, sat back in his seat and looked back at me. "Like I said, tings 'bout ta git real bloody. Yuh need ta prepare yuh'self fo' some bad shit."

I lifted the flask back up to my mouth and drained the contents inside. The rum stung my tongue and burned at my throat, then finally lit a cruel torch down in my aching belly. My entire body shook with rage. I dropped the hip flask at my side and balled up my fists so tightly that I felt the blood drain from my fingers. I looked at Vic. He had rested his head back against his seat, his eyes closed, his steady breathing rising and sinking deep inside his chest. In the time it had taken him to utter those fateful words to me, my cousin had successfully set a bitter hook inside of me, and he'd set it deep.

31

I woke with the sound of the Dakota's engines ringing in my ears, a familiar nightmare still coursing through my listless head. The dawn light had just broken, its gentle rays shone through the window of the aircraft and warmed the side of my face. The seat next to me, where Vic had been sitting, was now empty. Across the aisle, Bussa was still sound asleep and snoring heavily. The remnants of the cruel night-time succubus was reluctant to leave me, even though I was awake. When I closed my eyes again, I could still see the chilling images of my dead wife, daughter and my sister; their waxy, soot-marked features uniform and no longer individually defined as the people I had known and loved. I could see myself sitting next to Ellie, Amelia and Bernice's charred bodies as two elderly black men with spades dug a deep grave. I was sitting on a mound of earth, my eyes covered by my forearm, weeping. I rubbed at my face with my hands, blinked my eyes repeatedly and peered through the gaps in my fingers. As always when these moments of dark reverie occurred in my waking day, there was no way I could think my way out of them. The unwelcome apparitions would often stay with me until they deemed it the appropriate time to leave, their spectral presence perhaps haunting me for only the briefest of moments, for an hour or so, on occasion for the remainder of my waking day.

I closed my eyes again and watched as the images of

my three loved ones began to fade. I breathed deeply then slowly opened them and saw Vic strolling out of the cockpit of the plane like he'd just finished flying the damn thing. A huge smile broke out across his face when he saw that I was awake, which was quickly replaced with his usual grimace, the one he'd usually express before unleashing another of his course, cutting remarks.

He stood in the centre of the aisle and tutted to himself, "Brutha, how long yuh bin asleep fo'? It's a six-hour flight an' yuh bin away wid the fairies fo' five o' the fuckas!" Vic looked across at Bussa, still fast off in his seat and shook his head in disgust. "Jus' look at that ole muthafucka there, he ain't no better. That niggah bin snorin' and fartin' fo' the last two an' half thousand miles. Bin like sittin' next to a shittin' pig." Vic kicked at Bussa's seat with his foot. The elderly Bajan grunted, his face contorting at being disturbed, the old man sniffed and blew air through his cracked lips, then turned in his chair and continued to snore, oblivious to my cousin's vexation at him. One of the pilots called back to Vic from the cockpit. His laidback American drawl immediately reminded me in some way of Evangeline's accent.

"We're heading into Paragon now, better get strapped in."

I looked up at Vic. "What's Paragon?"

"Place this crate's gonna be landing."

"We're not going into Seawell Airport?

"Hell no! Seawell? Yuh outta yuh fuckin' mind? Yuh want every honky copper to know we is back in town? We going in'ta Paragon."

"You still ain't told me what Paragon is?"

"It's a US military base."

"A what? How the hell you worked it so you can land a damn plane on a US Air Force runway?"

Vic shook his thumb towards the open cockpit and leaned down toward me. "See those fellas flyin' this ole ting, they the key ta makin' this trip so easy, JT. They bin shipping out a shitload o' merchandise on my behalf fo' a while now."

"You mean, they've been running drugs fo' you?"

Vic snapped his head back and shrugged. "Yeah ... drugs, booze, guns, rubbers, so what? Them Yanks bin shifting any'ting comes ma way. I bin making a heap o' the folding green since I hooked up with these guys an' I've had ta t'row in a fair few dollars to git ma operation movin'."

I shook my head and signed heavily. "Oh, I bet you have ..."

Vic looked back at me, a hurt, dumbfounded expression on his face. "Wha? ... Why should me t'rowing a few bucks 'bout git you so fuckin' prissy?

I stabbed my finger up towards my cousin's face, "'Cause when you start throwing cash about, it's normally to meet only a couple of ends."

Vic began to laugh, the creases in his cheeks furrowing up towards his brow, his expression reminding me of the once cheeky adolescent cousin I'd grown up with and loved. "Yeah, an' what's them?"

"To either make you some more damn money, or get me outta trouble!"

"Yeah, well, yuh is in trouble, like yuh always is, an' I ain't got no interest in bein' fuckin' poor!" Vic rubbed at his chin with the palm of his hand and cleared his throat before speaking. "Look, JT ... those fly boys back there, they is running some operation called Air America, it's all real hush-hush ... I he'p them out and they do the same fo' me."

"An' how you helping out the US military?"

I watched as Vic's left eyebrow rose up on his brow. "Monroe."

My stomach knotted into a tight ball when I heard Vic say Monroe's name. "Monroe ... what's Monroe gotta do with the Yanks?"

Vic looked out of the window and pointed his finger down towards the ground. "The Americans, they gotta ting goin' on down there called Harp."

I shrugged and opened out the palms of my hands. "Harp ... what the hell is Harp?"

"High Altitude Research Project ... they gotta big fuckin'g gun they is always shootin' up in'ta the air."

I reached behind my head with my hand and tried to massage a knot out of a muscle in my lower neck, then looked back up at Vic as I rolled the tension out of my shoulders. "How'd you know all this stuff?"

Vic's nostrils flared in temper. "'Cause I hear the damn thing goin' off, that's why ..."

"Not the damn gun, I'm talking 'bout what Monroe has to do with this Harp thing?"

"Monroe greased the pole with a few local bigwigs. He smooth-talked the right fellas in sum back room at the parliament buildings ta git the Yanks the permission to start firin' these huge fuckin' shells up in the air an' out across the Atlantic Ocean."

"Is that it?"

Vic sucked air angrily through the gap in his front teeth. "No, 'course it ain't it! ... Yuh 'memba them photographs Monroe liked to be takin'?"

I nodded. "Yeah, how could I forget ... what 'bout 'em?"

A broad smirk broke out across Vic's face. "Turns out some them skin snaps ole Monroe took was of a couple o' Yankee generals wid their dicks hangin' out. Those top-brass honkies bin caught having a good time with sum dark meat at one o' Monroe's nasty all-nighters."

My brow tightened as I slowly frowned. "Dark meat?"

Vic shook his head and rubbed at his face with the palm of his hand. "Jesus, JT . . . I worry 'bout yuh sometimes, brutha, I really do . . . where were yuh fuckin' born, in a convent?" My cousin wet his lips before speaking again, the skin around his mouth tightening, a sly grin suddenly curling out at the edges of his mouth.

"These four-star troopers in the photographs, they like ta git it on with black fellas . . ." Vic smiled at me, then chuckled to himself, "An' the younger the better from the look o' sum o' those snaps Monroe bin takin'."

I shook my head as the penny suddenly dropped. I looked back up at Vic and saw him chuckling to himself. "And Bernice gave those photographs to you before she was killed."

Vic snapped his finger and thumb together in front of my face. "Give that detective a cigar. Exactly!"

★

The entire fuselage of the ancient Dakota began to shake as we made our slow descent into Bim. A sudden throb of excitement and fear coursed through my body as the plane broke through the clouds and I saw Barbados again for the first time in over three years. The DC-3 continued to lurch and roll as it made its final approach, circling twice above the airstrip before straightening off and preparing to land. I looked out of the window, down at the blue ocean and out towards my beloved island home, and smiled to myself. Vic had sat down next to me and lit a joint. The air around us thick with the scent of ganja. I turned and looked over

Vic's shoulder at the three caskets strapped down on the hull floor, then brought myself back round to face my cousin. "What about those things back there ... who they for?"

Vic blew a cloud of grey smoke out in front of him and turned in his seat. He looked blankly at the coffins then stared at me. "What yuh tink they fo', fool? They fo' dead folk ..." The Dakota jumped in the air as a sudden headwind hit us full on. I shuffled nervously in my chair and squeezed my palms around the ends of the arms of my seat and looked across at Vic. His face had become flat and expressionless. He turned to face me, his left eye watering slightly at the base of the lid, his teeth gritted as he spoke again. "Yuh don't have to be worryin' yo'self 'bout those damn caskets, JT."

Vic grinned and gestured with his head back towards the lacquered boxes then fixed his eye on me. "Yuh gonna find out soon enuff what I got planned fo' 'em ..." I turned away from looking at my cousin and stared at the back of the seat in front of me. I suddenly felt colder than I had done throughout the flight, my hands trembled and my mouth became dry. The shock at hearing such spine-chilling words from my cousin had sent an icy wave of nausea from the pit of my guts up into my throat. As the Dakota's undercarriage began to drop down beneath us, Vic reached across and gripped tightly at my forearm, then started to speak again, his next bitter utterance more terrifying than the one that had just come before. "Brutha, by the time all this bullshit is ovah, I tink one o' us is probably gonna need it."

32

I used to think that the swaying tropical allure of the island of Barbados was like being hooked onto a strong drug or some kind of heady booze; you could never use it all up or get enough of the damn stuff. Now, as I walked down the steps of the DC-3, my feet firmly planted on the lush, green turf that I'd once played and run across as a young boy, there was little to quash such staunchly simple reasoning. As a child, I'd truly believed where I lived resembled the earth as it would have been on the first day of creation. In those days I'd known little of the greater world around me, and cared not to enquire. Hot sun, warm seas and my family were all that had ever mattered to me as a kid. As I'd grown, my love for family and my island home had never left me, despite both being cruelly taken away many years later. Now it was the love of family that was dictating my sorrowful return, back to bid a final farewell to the last of my own immediate family.

I'd left Barbados in the March of 1964 without fanfare or salute; my departure was then shrouded in secrecy and fear. Today, I was returning in exactly the same clandestine and faltering manner. The reality of my lamentable and backstairs homecoming was about to rain down on my already shattered spirit like a curse cast down from a cruel Obeah's hand.

The warm Barbadian air caressed my face and body as

I walked across the tarmac in the heat and humidity to join Vic and Bussa. I opened another button on my shirt, wiped my forehead on my arm and looked at the long streak of sweat on my skin.

Vic had already given the elderly Bajan his orders before getting off the plane. The old man was to get our luggage and organise the transportation of the three coffins to a place in St Andrew Parish called Hillaby. It was a remote rural area, tucked away in the interior of the island where few people lived or visited. It was the perfect hideaway, and my wily cousin knew it. Vic told Bussa we'd join him once he'd sorted out "bid'ness" with the Yanks.

In the tree line behind me, I heard a green monkey call out to its mate, the harsh cry was yet another reminder that I was actually home. Vic was waiting for me at the edge of the runway. He tapped at the ground with the toe of his foot, his face careworn and tense. My cousin rarely expressed any kind of anxiety and never showed fear. To see him look so unsettled immediately put me on edge. I smiled at him as I walked across to join him. "You okay?" Vic shrugged his shoulders at me, then turned and pointed towards a long, single-storey building which ran almost along the entire length of the perimeter of the base.

"Bernice, she in there."

I looked across at the stark, grey brickwork of the military barracks and felt my blood run cold and my thinking become woozy. My body was taut and immobile, every muscle locked and tense, my feet heavy on the ground, as if my shoes had been filled with lead weights. I gestured weakly with my head towards the foreboding prefab billets. "Bernice ... is inside'a that place?"

Vic nodded his head and smiled sadly at me. "Yeah ..."

My cousin held out the palm of his hand encouraging me to join him and waited. "Come on wid me, I tek yuh ovah to her. I got sum people who work here ta look after Bernice till yuh could git back." Vic reached out and cupped his hand underneath my elbow and drew me a couple of steps towards him. His voiced became hushed when he spoke again. "Bernie, she bin cared fo' real well, Joseph, yuh got my word on it."

Vic took a couple more steps forward and I followed after him like a lost and confused child searching for his vanished parents in the throng of a fast-moving crowd. Vic and I made our way across the asphalt landing strip then walked onto the grass that separated the runway from the main buildings. Every step felt as if I was taking it in slow motion. Above my head, as the sun shone brilliantly in the sky, the evanescent colour of another day in paradise seemed offensively bright and cheerful. It was as if the beauty of such an idyllic place had somehow conspired to show me how the world would go on without my sister in it. As life went on around me, it felt as if Bernice's death had been nothing more to the world than any other everyday occurrence that happened all over the planet. To Mother Nature, it was an unimportant event, one that ebbed and flowed in and out of each twenty-four hours, marked only by those it mattered to. I thought that everything around me should have been as grey and foggy as my own emotions. I told myself that it should be cold and damp, the sticky air silent and respectful, but I knew that could never be the case. Above my head, the birds sang, the monkeys in the trees called to each other and the flowers at my feet bloomed still.

The grassy area was filled with yellow and red hibiscus and, at its furthest edge, brilliantly coloured azaleas. A white wooden sign, stuck into the soil with the word Hospital printed above an arrow pointing left, told me where we were heading. Purple wisteria grew on an overhanging trellis above a walkway which led down to an austere flat-roofed building. Vic strode off in front, opened the door of the hospital and waited for me to catch him up. I was hit immediately by the heady bouquet of surgical spirits and bleach as it filtered up the pathway to greet me. I looked at my cousin, who was now staring down at the ground. "You not coming in?"

Vic looked up at me and shook his head. "Sorry, brutha . . . I see her once, I ain't got no reason ta wanna see her like she is in there again. This gotta be one trip yuh gonna have ta mek on yuh own."

The smell of castor oil and methylated spirits caught the back of my throat as I walked inside. Warm air touched the back of my neck as Vic closed the door quietly behind me. I immediately cranked my head around and looked back through the small pane of fire glass in the centre of the door, but my cousin was nowhere to be seen. I turned and looked back down the short corridor. Waiting at the end, was a small white man with greying hair dressed in a white surgeon's gown. I took a reluctant first step towards him, then stopped again for a moment as I tried to take in what was actually happening. Was Bernice's body really inside this godforsaken place? The skin on the backs of my hands felt tight and my left eyelid fluttered nervously as I continued to walk down the corridor toward the man, the heels of my shoes clicking on the tiled floor. As I neared him, the man took a couple of paces towards me and stuck out his hand in greeting. I took his open palm in mine and we shook; his grip was firm and warm without a hint of the usual clamminess that came when meeting the kind of folk who generally brought you bad news. "You must be Mr Ellington..." The doctor spoke quietly and slowly, his accent well-bred North American and rich with it. He offered a perfunctory smile, then quickly released me from his grasp. "I'm Dr Burkhardt. I'm the base's head of field medicine, amongst other things. I'm sorry to be meeting you under such very sad circumstances." I looked around at the stark walls; the place gave me the creeps and so did Burkhardt.

The doctor held out his hand again and directed me towards another, longer corridor to my right. "If you'd like to follow me, please." Burkhardt began to make his way down the hallway. For a small guy, he held himself upright like a man born into the military. His gait was precise and perfectly paced. His tan service slacks dropped in straight lines from underneath his surgical gown and looked a good three inches too short in the leg. I could tell that he wore his bedside empathy like his white overcoat, just for work.

The doctor's craggy face was a perfect picture of controlled sadness. I knew Burkhardt, for all his creepiness, would have to find a way not to be drained by the constant grief of others. I learnt during my time as a police officer that stepping into the bleak world of death and the bereaved, even just for a fraction of your time, day after day, wiped you out emotionally. Dr Burkhardt would have been the same. He'd have seen more bodies on his mortuary slab than he would have cared to consider. He'd have witnessed more lifeless cadavers sent down into the cold ground, more souls returned to the Lord, more deaths than most people saw sunsets. Today was gonna be no different for him, and I knew that. As we approached the end of the hallway, I saw an elderly Bajan nun dressed from head to toe in black gothic clothing standing outside of a large double door. She greeted me cautiously by nodding her head and smiling. I returned a faint smile and looked across at Burkhardt. The air force doctor nodded matter-of-factly at the holy black woman before introducing her.

"This is Sister Jackson, from the Ursuline convent at Collymore Rock. Sister Jackson will be assisting in transporting your sister's remains and her interment at a later date." Burkhardt reached up, took hold of one of the stainless-steel door handles and pushed it ajar a few inches. Even from such a small gap, the all too familiar aroma of death was unmistakable. I closed my eyes briefly and took a couple of deep breaths.

A high-pitched buzzing whistled quietly between my ears, the dull piping sound formed a loop of white noise inside my head as if it was attempting to lullaby me and draw me away from a place it knew I did not want to be. When I opened my eyes again, Burkhardt was on the other side, he was holding the door to the mortuary wide open for me, the noise in my head now gone. The fingers on each of my hands pumped open and close, then tightened into balls. My arms hung at my side, my body trembling inside my clothes. I took another breath, then warily crossed over the dark, unwelcoming threshold into a gaunt realm I'd hoped I'd never have to enter again.

★

Inside, everything was white. The albumen walls and floor were tiled and scrubbed until they gleamed. The room reeked of strong detergent, its sole purpose to mask the spilled blood, decaying matter and bodily functions that would have fallen on or spattered across all its washed-down surfaces. Bernice was waiting for me on a table in the centre of the room, her body covered in a pristine white sheet. Beside her corpse, on a trolley, were a selection of surgical tools, each laid out neatly on a white cloth, all of them sparkling underneath the pristine beams of lamps that hung from the equally white ceiling. Scissors rested themselves against scalpels, forceps, needles of various sizes, artery tubes, a rubber bulb syringe and a glass jar containing a couple of gallons of embalming fluid. On the shelf below was an assortment of cosmetics. Burkhardt stood at my side and cleared his throat before speaking. "Family members rarely come into the mortuary. Your relative insisted you have access to the body. I fully understand if you prefer to leave, now that you've had a chance to see that Miss Ellington has been cared for in the appropriate manner."

I shook my head, the tears stinging the skin at the edges of my eyes. I looked at Burkhardt and felt one of my incisor teeth briefly bite down onto my bottom lip. A single tear fell from my right eye and trickled down my face, collecting in a thin pool in the stubble underneath my chin. "No ... I'll be fine, thank you. I'd like to stay a while longer, if that's alright with you."

The doctor nodded at me and smiled, "As you wish, Mr Ellington." Burkhardt took a couple of steps backwards, I could still feel his presence as I began to walk toward the hospital gurney and felt my hand reach up to my mouth as I stood over Bernice's body, my eyes barely able to take in the horror of what I was seeing. I moved in closer, reached out my hand and stroked the side of Bernice's temple with my trembling fingers. Her pallid skin was icy to the touch and felt like damp leather. I closed my eyes and saw light dancing behind my lids like electricity trapped inside a black box.

Then the shaking began, like sinew and bone being pulled apart inside me. A torrent of tears forced me to reopen my eyes; they fell down my cheeks and seeped into the front of my shirt as I sobbed. Then time seemed to stand still. I don't know how long I'd stood there and cried. I know that at some point the skin on my face started to burn as though someone had splashed it with acid; that I couldn't draw enough air into my sobbing chest; that the bright lights above me were like a flame caressing the back of my head; that every muscle inside of me seemed to lock; and that my hands felt like stone.

Burkhardt had somehow managed to transform the bruised and battered features that had once been Bernice's face and head into something that was at least vaguely human. In the past, as a copper, I'd reluctantly spent way too much time inside many a mortuary and knew that the doctor had achieved this minor miracle of restructuring my sister's features by packing the skull with cotton gauze, then very carefully moulding the facial bones back into something that resembled her own normal human face, closing the wounds with some very intricate stitching. My once beautiful sister would never again, as she once had, be the winner of a beachside beauty contest, never turn a fella's eye as she walked down a sunny street. Monroe and his cronies had seen to that. As I stood over Bernice's body, I thought of my long-deceased parents and imagined what they, in the half-light of the viewing room and behind glass, would be feeling on seeing their beautiful daughter beaten to a pulp and stretched out on a cold mortician's slab.

Dr Burkhardt moved quietly from behind me and came and stood at my side again. I could hear the rasp of his unsteady breathing before he spoke. "Death sometimes has a horrible way of leaving a person looking unpeaceful. I hope that isn't the case for your sister today, Mr Ellington?" I shook my head and swallowed hard. To ensure that Bernice's eyes remained closed, Burkhardt had placed tiny pieces of cotton on top of each eye and then her eyelids had been drawn down over it. It was a macabre fact that I'd hauled up from somewhere in the furthest reaches of my memory. Knowing and recalling it, as I had just done, brought me little comfort. If Bernice was now at peace, you would never have been able to tell it from the way she now looked. The light in the mortuary seemed to harden and grow cold and a strange sensation like a ribbon of icy water slid down my back. Burkhardt touched the top of my arm. I turned to face him. I wanted to thank him for everything he had done, but the words simply would not rise up from my throat and out of my mouth. The doctor looked up at me and nodded, my unspoken gratitude somehow connecting with him in some way. Then, in a split second, I saw the solemn expression on his face change to one of fear and watched him suddenly take a step away from me. I looked down at the mortician as he gazed back up into my red, tear-soaked eyes, then saw how he reacted as he watched the muscles in my arms and legs turn to rocks, my nostrils start to flare with anger and the pulse jump in the side of my neck. It was at that moment I realised that Dr Burkhardt had never seen such blind rage and fury as great in either man or beast.

33

The day was wending into early evening by the time Vic had taken care of his business and had returned to the hospital wing to collect me. I'd spent the better part of eight hours alone, sat in a dingy back office behind the mortuary, the whiff of methylated spirits and decay crawling up into my nostrils and sinking its way into my brain like a deathwatch beetle burrowing into rotting wood. My time alone with a head full of vitriolic thoughts had further fuelled my deepening sense of rage towards Monroe. My bitter brooding had left me feeling morose and baying for blood. My body had remained taut and edgy, but inside, my waning spirit was fast draining away into a bleak abyss filled with the all-consuming aura of the violence and retribution I was determined to rain down on my sister's killers in the coming days.

My mouth was dry, the skin on my lips stuck to each other. My head throbbed with pain. A swirling red mist sat in front of my eyes. The wall clock that had been ticking loudly above where I sat hadn't helped matters; the second hand had clicked inside my head, each reverberating stroke sending a throbbing haze of pink pain through my body. As each hour slowly passed, the grip of a string of invisible tentacles encircled my dour being and drew me towards a hidden subterranean pit filled with rancour and requital. Alone in that dark place, the veins at my temples slowly tightening, I pushed unconsciously at my scalp with my fingers, like a man who feared his brains were seeping out of his skull. Most of all, during that long wait, I felt ashamed for again not being able to protect those I loved. Inside I felt impotent and, worse still, old. Advancing age had offered me little insight into the greater world and the mysteries and wonders that inhabited it. At that moment, apart from my burning desire for revenge, I was no wiser as to what the coming days were about to bring.

*

At just after 6.30pm, Vic drove the two of us out of Paragon airfield in a battered, olive-green 1955 Land Rover. A canvas canopy tied tightly to "D" rings on the floor behind our seats separated the cab from the rear of the motor, the nefarious cargo that I knew had to be stashed behind it adding to my already heightened sense of unease. The air around us was still humid and breathless, the stench of the stagnant water in the gullies by the roadside mixing uneasily with the hibiscus and blue lotus blossom. Above our heads, the dying sun had begun to drop over the bay into a darkening magenta sky. In the near distance, I could see the blue waters along the west coast and the white breaking waves rolling in onto the dusky sands. Vic looked across at me as he headed along the coastal road, an uneasy expression etched across his face. I said nothing as he gave me the once over, and watched as he reached up his hand to the side of his face, took a thickly rolled joint from behind his ear, and lit it. When he finally spoke, it was through a fog of cloying, grey marijuana smoke.

"We meetin' Bussa an' a few utha fellas up in St Andrew's. Got us a place we can lay low in just outside 'a Hillaby." Vic began to cough and splutter as he took another long drag on his joint. He turned his face toward the open side window and hacked up a wad of phlegm into his throat then spat it out towards the hedgerow.

I leaned my arm on the sill of the open window next to me and stared back at Vic suspiciously, "What other fellas?"

"Wha...? They jus' some bruthas I trust..." Vic shook his head at me and spat out of the window again. Clearly agitated by my remark, he sucked on the end of the joint, then snapped his head back round and blew a thick plume of smoke at my face. "That mean yuh can trust 'em too, Mistah Detective."

I pushed my cousin a little more, "Trust 'em for what?"

Vic sniffed at the air and sighed, his eyes becoming thin, restless slits as he held in his vexation at my questioning him. "Ta git us a job done! Wha' yuh tink I'm talkin 'bout?"

I gestured my head indignantly towards Vic, aware that my questioning was irritating the hell out of him. "You're talking about Monroe?"

Vic shuffled in his seat, a growling sound catching under his breath, "'Course... who the hell, yuh tink am talkin' 'bout?"

I shook my head like a spoilt child. "Monroe's my business. I'll deal with him and his mess my way."

Vic sniggered to himself, "Yuh way? Shit... listen ta yuh an' yuh doh'tish mout'. We do tings yuh way, we all end up dead."

"What ain't you telling me, Vic?"

"Same shit I bin tellin' yuh since we got on that damn plane. Only yuh ain't bin listenin', like yuh never do... Look, the Yanks want Monroe outta the picture. They come ta me to do the job fo' 'em... It's as simple as that, brutha. Monroe, he bin one massive pain in the ass to 'em.

Blackmailin' n' killin'. It's time sum niggah put his ass in the ground. That niggah be me, so yuh jus' better git used ta that fuckin' idea!"

Vic's fingers gripped and unfurled around the steering wheel as he began to accelerate along the road. I watched as he stared out of the windscreen, trying to hold in his mounting temper. "Monroe bin the source o' all yuh misery. Well, it 'bout time fo' it to stop, don't yuh tink? I brou't yuh out here ta finish the job wid me. We take him out at the neck. Game over. Yuh git ta find sum peace, an' I git to carryin' on wid ma bid'ness as usual."

"What business?"

Vic cursed under his breath, he slammed his foot down hard on the brakes, bringing the Land Rover to a dead stop in the middle of the road. He leaned out of his seat and put his face close up against mine. A palpable tang of rum, dried sweat and dope rose from his skin and clothes. "Same bid'ness it always bin, JT . . . Import n' export." The muscles along Vic's jaw tightened with temper as he lurched back and stabbed his index finger at my face. "Wha' the hell yuh care anyways? Yuh wantin' that honky dead as much as the next fella . . . Monroe bin steppin' on both our toes as well as the damn Yanks. That muthafucka got it comin' ta him. Yuh know he do!"

I cut my cousin off before he could utter another word. "I told you, I can clean up my own mess . . ."

Vic frowned deeply and rubbed at the stubble under his chin. He fixed his eye on me and let his anger well up into his face. "This ain't a mess yuh can clear up, JT. Monroe an' that muthafucka Gatehouse an' his po'lice boys gone an' proved that already. They kill a niggah like it's sport. Killed Evangeline wid'out as much as a second thought!"

305

My stomach sank when my cousin spoke Evangeline's name. For all my bleating and hypocritical griping, I knew Vic was right. Every sound instinct that filtered down to the very core of my soul told me that I could never take on Monroe and his men and come out of it alive. Vic was the answer to prayers I wished I never had to go down on bended knees and make. The truth was staring me in the face and still I felt the need to argue and fight the matter bullishly with him. Despite knowing these facts, I continued to resist the stark realities I faced, and like a mongoose nipping at a spitting cobra, I foolishly continued to keep biting at my already maddened cousin. "So, you're still happy the Yanks got you doing their dirty work for 'em...? Ain't they got their own damn assassins?"

Vic didn't flinch at my choice of words. He rubbed at his chin with his thumb and glared back at me. "Sure, they have ... but they also got a shitload 'a problems o' their own. Ain't yuh evah heard o' Vietnam? I bin doin' dirty wuk all ma life, bit mo' shit ain't gonna matter ta me. These prissy Yankee politicians n' generals come ta me 'cause they lookin' ta git this mess sorted domestically."

"Domestically? Vic, this ain't a cleaning job. You talkin' 'bout murdering a white man here."

Vic shrugged and looked across at me blankly before putting his foot back on the gas and speeding off down the road. "Fuck it ... Still looks like cleanin' ta me."

34

Twenty-five miles out of Bridgetown, we were in open country and over halfway to Hillaby. I was having real trouble keeping my eyes open and felt tired to the bone. I'd been okay on the twisting two-lane sea road but now, as we climbed higher into the interior of the island, the air thinned and both my body and mind began to tire as a wave of fatigue set in. As the Land Rover eased off the asphalt road onto more gravelly terrain, the soporific rocking of the hulking vehicle lulled me further towards the welcoming arms of sleep, the toing and froing of the chassis as it drove over uneven ground gnawing at my wakefulness like ants in a dead tree. I yawned and rubbed at my face, forcing myself to stay awake, as the strain of the last few days caught up with me.

Heavy rain had set in during the last half hour of our journey and I hadn't seen a light in the last five miles. There were no other vehicles on the road, which was now rapidly turning into a mud track. Vic had turned on the radio, a far-off island station played calypso music in between bursts of the Puerto Rican announcer's machine-gun Spanish. By 8pm, we were heading up the north side of Mount Hillaby. In the dim light above us lay the mountain peak which hung over St Andrew Parish at just over one thousand feet high, like a silent protector. As we headed deeper along the dirt roads, we passed the occasional small cattle farm dotted between the many sugar cane fields strewn over the fertile hills. Even at dusk in the rain it was a beautiful, picturesque view through the palms and lush green vegetation.

Five miles further along the same steep incline, Vic turned off down a thin scrub lane that was protected by a dense arc of thick baobab trees. The overhanging limbs were in full leaf and shaking in big, wet clusters as we drove toward the hazy glow of what looked like oil lamps, which appeared to be hanging in mid-air on the other side of the undergrowth. After being thrown about for another half-mile, we finally broke out of the scrub and pulled up outside a walled yard; behind it was a dimly lit, rundown plantation house.

The only entrance to the yard was through an eight-foot-high rusting wrought-iron gate. A crumbling stone wall roughly the same height as the gate ran around the perimeter of the property. Even as dark was falling, the ramshackle place looked more like a prison than a farm. On the other side of the gate, a skinny young black kid was standing talking with Bussa.

The old man walked a few lazy paces down towards us and stood in front of the vehicle's headlights, waved at us, then shouted to the younger man to open up the gate. Vic, cursing to himself, drove in and pulled up next to a light blue Bedford van which had been parked underneath a battered mahogany wood lean-to with a corrugated iron roof. Four slavering, feral dogs were chained up on thick wooden posts either side of the porch of the house. I watched Vic as he sneered at the dogs through the windscreen of the Land Rover. He murmured something under his breath then got out and spat on the ground. I swung open the passenger door nervously, got out and stretched my arms, my body trembling at being so close to the snapping dogs. My limbs ached, stiff from sitting in the cramped passenger seat.

Bussa nodded at Vic then across at me. The young black fella who had opened the gate sidled up beside the elderly Bajan and smiled at my cousin then at me. Vic ignored the kid's greeting, leaving Bussa to make the introductions. "This 'ere's my sister's boy ... Name's Dead Man."

The kid called Dead Man smiled again. He had a tight afro and skin the colour of tanned leather, which looked like it had been left out in the sun for too long. His scrawny facial features gave the impression that he was either in need of feeding up or somebody needed to tell him to get back inside one of the three caskets that Bussa had brought along with him.

Dead Man reached across and took hold of my hand and began to shake it. His grip felt weak in mine, as if his skinny fingers were about to slip out of the middle of my palm and crumble into ash. He continued to grin excitedly across at me, like a man who was meeting a member of the aristocracy for the first time. "Pleased ta meet yuh, suh."

I smiled back at the kid. "Please to meet you too, Dead Man."

Bussa grunted and nudged his nephew hard in the ribs, forcing him to let go of my hand. Vic took a couple of paces and leaned in close towards Bussa's ear and spoke quietly under his breath. The old man listened without speaking, nodding his head occasionally.

After Vic had finished, Bussa took Dead Man by the elbow and yanked him across the yard. I watched as the two headed for the Bedford van. They climbed inside the back of it, shutting the doors behind them as if they were closing themselves inside an ancient, cursed sarcophagus. I turned and looked around the grounds of the dilapidated plantation and wondered what the hell we were doing there. The rain

309

had stopped, thankfully, and been replaced by a warm breeze. The air smelled of night damp, the sweet fragrance of the bougainvillea plants that hung from the tamarind trees, and faeces. A black man opened the front door to the house and began to walk slowly towards us.

Vic turned to me and smiled. It was the kind of smile I'd seen a thousand times before. One that told me that I was heading into trouble. The four words he spoke afterwards left me in no doubt of the fact.

"Yuh 'memba Bitter, JT?"

I nodded my head at Vic and felt my heart sink as I turned to face the approaching behemoth. Grantley "Bitter" Lemon was a huge man, at least six feet six tall, and a good 350 pounds of solid muscle to back up his considerable height. His head was shaven, his arms a maze of purple prison tattoos, and his hands too big, even for a body of his size. He was wearing torn, blue overalls over a bare chest. Many years back, I'd arrested the angry, oversized Bajan more times than I cared to remember and I got the distinct feeling I wasn't about to get a warm welcome. Worryingly, he had a smile on his face as he strolled over to greet me, and that put me immediately on edge. I remembered just how mean Bitter could get and began thinking how I was in no physical state or mood to get into a ruck with him over his past crimes and misdemeanours and his need for retribution against me. Grantley Lemon's eyes bored into mine as he drew closer. He finally stopped toe-to-toe opposite where I stood and looked down at me, the skin on his face and shoulders splattered with perspiration and he stank of stale reefer, hooch and sweat. His lips broke into a half-cocked grimace which offered me a glimpse of his gold top row of front teeth. He growled at me over the howling and barking of his dogs.

"JT Ellington ... So, da wandrin' niggah po'liceman return."

I looked up at the big Bajan and stuck out my hand. "Yuh ain't gotta worry, I ain't a copper no more, Bitter."

Lemon shrugged and ignored my offer of a handshake. "Niggah, I ain't worried 'bout shit. Vic tole me yuh is some kinda shamus ovah in da mutha land now."

I nodded my head, eager to placate the big man. Bitter Lemon looked me up and down suspiciously, his eyes were too small for his big, bald head. "I tou't detectives sup'pose ta be older fellas, yuh know, retired fro' da force, like in da movies?"

I breathed in and immediately got a whiff of Lemon's cheesy body odour, his pungent scent happily mixing with the heady perfume of the blossom and dog excrement that was wafting up around me. I opened my hands and swallowed hard. "I retired early. They wouldn't make me chief o' po'lice by the time I was thirty, so I told 'em they could stick the job up their arse."

Bitter Lemon grumbled and nodded his thick head at me. His dogs seemed to sense my fear of them and began snarling in a different key. Bitter spun his thick neck round and stomped on the ground with his giant foot. "Git tha fuck back on dat stoop yuh noisy bastards!"

The mongrels dropped their hands, whimpered and obeyed, skulking off back up the steps of the porch into separate kennels on either side of the door. Vic's face had turned to thunder. He sniffed the air and stared at Bitter. He stared down at the ground, then gestured with his head towards the kennels on the far side of Lemon's property and pointed at the dogs.

"Bitter, yuh know how much I hate those fuckin' dogs."

Vic stuck his thumb in my direction and stared up at the big Bajan. "JT there, he bin bit by one them kinda mutts a while back. Made him real wary. Keep 'em on those damn chains whilst he's 'ere, yuh 'ear me?"

The earlier violence in Bitter Lemon's demeanour suddenly melted into shaky subservience when Vic started barking at him. He nodded his head apologetically. For all the big man's size and fearful reputation, he was clearly scared of my cousin and he had good reason to be. Bitter looked back at his dogs, then sheepishly at Vic.

"Why'd yuh hate ma hounds, Vic?"

Vic grimaced, then bit at his lip before exploding at the big man. "Why? Cos you don't clean up behind the muthafuckas, Bitter, that's why. This damn yard, it full o' their shit. Yuh got every sweet in flower, herb an' plant growing up round this place an' it still reeks like a goddamn sewer."

I watched as Bitter Lemon's head sank towards the ground, his frightened eyes eager not to make contact with Vic's volatile gaze. He stuttered back at Vic like a child who was about to take a beating from an angry parent. "Yuh know how ma hounds keeps thievin' folk out an' away fro' ma stuff, Vic."

Vic kicked a clump of earth angrily with the toe of his boot. "Keeps 'em out? Too right it keeps 'em out. No niggah gonna be damn fool enough ta wanna climb ovah yuh scabby walls ta git in ta 'ere ta thieve. They stupid enuff ta try, they gonna have ta step thru a heap 'a shit ta git ta yuh or any o' yuh fuckin' stuff."

Vic moved in closer towards Lemon and stabbed his finger at Bitter's chest, pushing the giant back a couple of paces. "Clean up ya damn yard, Bitter!"

Lemon nodded obediently and stood staring at his feet.

Vic pushed him out of the way and began to head for the house. He waved at me to follow him and bellowed back at Bitter as he strode away.

"Git it all shovelled befo' sun-up or am gonna have ta teach yuh a lesson yuh gonna have ta carry down ta yuh grave wit' yuh."

I watched Bitter Lemon nod his head anxiously up and down before calling after my cousin that he understood what was expected of him. By the time Lemon had finished talking, Vic was already on the top step of the porch, waiting for me to catch him up. I hesitated for a moment and looked across at the kennels either side of the door. Vic turned and looked at the dogs, whose snouts were sticking out, clearly picking up on my jittery scent.

"Will yuh git yuh ass up 'ere? These mangy mongrels ain't gonna do a damn ting."

Vic kicked at the side of one of the kennels and I heard one of the dog's whine then scramble backwards towards the furthest reaches of its shabby domain. I walked up the steps of the porch and took hold of Vic's arm just as he was about to open the door. Vic turned on his heels and glared back at me. "What the hell's a matter now, JT?"

I turned and stared at the closed doors of the Bedford van then looked at Vic. "That kid back there ... why they call him Dead Man?"

Vic shook his head and laughed. "You a superstitious muthafucka, yuh know that, don't yuh?"

My face reddened as I began to nod my head. Vic scratched at the top of his scalp with his fingernails then smiled. "When ole Dead Man there was ten, he fell ill wid sum kinda palsy. Death's door in a day they say he was. Brutha went in ta a coma and the doc pronounced him as dead as a vicar's dick. Now, come the day o' the funeral, his kin be singin' hymns an' sayin' prayers. All that shit. That boy he laid out in the coffin an' he only go an' opens up his eyes and climbs out the damn box. Fuckin' mourners 'bout shit themselves round the hole."

Vic began to howl with laughter. I looked back at the van and felt myself shudder. My cousin suddenly stopped chuckling and prodded me in the back. "Since then, that boy always bin called Dead Man."

Vic laughed again and slapped my arm then opened the door. As he did, I was hit by the pungent scent of burning incense. Vic looked inside then back at me. "Right, brutha . . . yuh ready ta meet a couple mo' o' them ghosts that yuh git so riled up about?"

I watched as Vic walked on in then waited for a moment as he held open the door for me. I followed after him nervously, his peculiar words slithering underneath my skin as I crossed over the rotting wood sill into another uncertain dominion.

35

Bitter Lemon's home had the closed musty atmosphere of a Victorian parlour and about as much charm as an abattoir. Blue cotton drapes hung at the windows and what little furniture there was had been covered with tatty sheets. A solitary gas lamp lit up the inside, otherwise the place was in darkness. It was as if night-time had walked in behind me and cast its nocturnal shadows across every nook and cranny in the place. I watched Vic as he looked disapprovingly around him, then down at his feet. I then heard him curse to himself. He turned and looked at me, his expression sour. "Watch yuh feet, probably mo' dog shit on the floor than there is out in the damn yard."

Vic kept on chuntering to himself as we edged our way further inside, past the sitting room and then along a narrow corridor. At the end of the hallway I could see a door which had been left ajar. A faint light burned through a slit between the door panel and the frame, and from underneath the bottom rail. The muffled beam cast a dull glow out across the floor, its hazy glare inching closer toward our feet as Vic reached hold of the handle and opened the door. He walked on through, and I followed him.

The air inside the kitchen was thick with the smell of smoke, stale beer, expectorated snuff and reefer. Rising above the stink was the familiar and welcoming aroma of rice and peas cooking on the hob of a wood-fired stove on the back wall. The kitchen windows shone as they reflected the amber candlelight flames that burned in the centre of old saucers resting on the sills. In the corner of the room a bright bead curtain covered the entrance to the larder. Out of the corner of my eye, I watched as a thin black hand poked between the strands, the frail fingers of a woman gently pulling the curtain to one side.

I took a couple more unsteady steps and stood next to Vic, my body trembling as the woman stared back at me and smiled. She was small and ebony-skinned and, to my reckoning, had to be at least seventy, though she sure didn't look the three score years and ten that I believed her to be. The elderly woman was barefooted and wore a long, light green dress, the frayed hem resting just below the ankle joint. Her greying hair was pulled away from her forehead and tied back in a neat, long ponytail. A visible aura of beauty leftover from a long life still radiated brightly around her slight frame and burned far more brightly than the candles in the windows. Behind her, on a shelf over the fireplace, were various dusty bottles and coloured jars, the contents of which I knew were a secret known only to her memory. Pinned to the walls and ceiling hung sheets of dried snakeskin and old John the Conqueror root, and cast across the floor were the skulls and bones of different kinds of animals. Vic had spoken to me of ghosts. The old woman standing on the other side of the kitchen was a welcome phantom from my past; a spectre from my childhood whom I'd feared I would never see again.

Mama Esme had always lived in hidden places; this evening the powerful voodoo priestess and shaman had come out of the shadows and granted me a rare and unexpected audience. The Mama had stood by a table piled high with dried plants, hessian bags filled with seeds and a stone pestle and mortar. Mama Esme had, for most of her life, made medicines and potions for poor superstitious black folk and was renowned for her fortune-telling abilities. A witch by anyone's definition, and a soul that, as a child, I had always been petrified of, and who had treated my late wife, Ellie, as if she were her own daughter. Mama Esme gestured for me to approach her. "Joseph Ellington . . . com' on ovah 'ere, ma son. Let the Mama's eyes see yuh a'gin." A moment's fear held me back, but an unspoken sense of joy then began to draw me toward her. Instead of taking one step after the other, my body felt as if it were gliding across the wood floor.

Mama Esme reached out her arms toward me and it felt as if I was being spirited across the room to her like the spiritually unclean are drawn toward the cleansing baptism of holy water. She lifted her hand up to my face and grazed the side of my cheek with the backs of her fingers. A sudden whisper of warmth began to seep through my skin and then softly cascade down throughout my body like a benevolent kiss.

"Sit down, Joseph . . . Yuh look tired, son."

I looked back at Vic, who was now leaning against the kitchen door, his hip flask tipped toward his mouth as he sank back a mouthful of rum. I pulled a chair out from underneath the table and did as Mama Esme had asked. The old woman perched herself on a wooden stool next to me and rested the palm of her hand on to the back of mine. She looked across at Vic and waved him away with the other. "Victor . . . Go an' drink yuh damn firewater out in the yard. Leave me an' yuh kin alone a while."

It must have been over twenty years since I'd last heard

my cousin referred to as Victor. I was as surprised as he was to hear his Christian name spoken in full. Even more surprising was to see Vic doing as he was told. I watched as he gave Mama Esme a petulant glare. He sucked air through the gap between his front teeth, then took another slug of rum from his flask and walked out. Mama Esme frowned and began to shake her head as Vic closed the door behind him.

"That boy still as much vexation ta the world now as he was when yuh was both chirren."

I smiled to myself then at Mama Esme. "Ain't that the trute."

I watched as the old woman's nostrils flared and her eyes caught the light and flashed like gemstones. "Trute a funny ole ting, Joseph. Trute the reason yuh sittin' here now."

I could feel my heart working away inside my chest. The inside of my mouth had dried out and I struggled to speak. "It is . . . I don't understand?"

Mama Esme's face became hard and she squeezed at the back of my hand with her fingers, her long nails biting into the skin. "Victor, he brung me the trute a few weeks back, now. Yuh gonna 'ear that trute in the days ta come, Joseph. Yuh gotta believe in that trute an', hardest o' all, yuh gotta trus' that cousin o' yuhs ta show yuh it better than I can."

Mama Esme reached down toward the floor, lifted a brass oil lantern up onto the table then picked up a box of matches and lit the candle inside. Shadows jumped around the room as the wick fluttered for a moment. Mama Esme leaned forward on her stool, her piercing green eyes holding onto mine.

I watched as the voodoo priestess's eyelids fluttered. Her pupils seemed to grow larger as I stared back at her. When she spoke, the words I heard seemed not to emanate from the old woman's lips. "Ellie an' the chirren, they still visit yuh when yuh sleeping?"

I looked down at the table and nodded my head solemnly, then cleared my throat and looked back into Mama Esme's eyes. "Yeah ... I see 'em in my sleep an' in my waking day, Mama."

"Ain't nuh sup'rise ... Evah since yuh woman was a pickney, she had sum strong juju inside o' her. That kinda power, it ain't evah gonna settle in no grave, not tha way she wus sent down ta it. No matter how deep that 'ole bin dug, Ellie ain't evah gon' be at peace till dem that put her in the ground be restin' next ta her. Yuh un'astand me?"

Mama Esme quietly got to her feet. Her hand touched the back of my head and stroked my hair. She ran her hand down to the nape of my neck and held it there, her palm hot against my skin. The old woman bent forward and whispered into my ear, "Yuh got sum diggin' ta do, Joseph ... Got sum blood ta shed fo' yuh woman ta git that peace she deserves. Yuh, trus' yuh kin, now. When this madness all done, I want yuh come visit Mama Esme ... I gotta gift fo' yuh."

Violent, agonising tremors shot through my body as Mama Esme's words sank in. My arms and legs became heavy, my head thick, as if I was drunk. A black, slumberous fog draped itself over my listless senses. I closed my eyes then saw the playful image of my pregnant wife and child laughing together as they sat on the golden dunes of the beach behind our old home. I blinked and returned to the dark, only to find their spectre lost from my view. I heard Mama Esme whisper my name again, then there was silence. Once again, I was lost in my own grief, bitter memories of a wonderful life erased by an all-consuming fire in an instant.

Everything I'd ever loved was gone in a heartbeat. I'd wished then, as I still wished now, that I'd died with my family; comforted by the truth that in heaven I'd feel no lingering regrets, no never-ending grief, and that my days would not be blighted by a cruel, lifelong sadness.

36

I woke from a dreamless sleep. I was stretched out on a
large double bed I had no memory of climbing into. My
jaw clicked as I yawned, then I rubbed at my face with the
tips of my fingers and peered down at my wristwatch; it
was a little before 8am. I kicked off the single bed sheet and
walked across to the window, wrestled with the rusting brass
catch on the ledge, and eventually threw up the sash. The
early morning heat hit me immediately. Outside, the trees
were loud with birds. The air was humid and windless and
smelled of the watermelons that were growing in the field
next to the house. I looked across the yard toward the early
pinkish light that cut through the roughbark trees, the moon
still visible in one soft corner of an already aqua blue sky.
Below, two of Bitter Lemon's dogs strained on their chains
as they stared up at me and growled. I spat down a wad of
spittle at them then stood back from the window and turned
and looked around the bedroom. Like downstairs, the place
had an eerie, unlived in feel about it. Everything around me
looked dusty and old, like the place had been sealed up on
a whim and put into cold storage. I couldn't imagine a man
like Bitter Lemon living in the place, let alone crashing on
the ornate bed I'd just climbed out of. On the bedside table,
I noticed a small slip of white paper with Vic's practically
illegible handwriting scratched across it. I picked it up, then
struggled to make out what he had written.

You clothes in wardrobe.
Be water for you to cleans up.
It was me that carry you heavy fucking ass
to bed last night
Vic

I found a towel at the foot of the bed, grabbed my washbag from my case, then walked out of the bedroom and found the bathroom at the end of the landing. I shaved, brushed my teeth, showered with hot water until there was none left in the tank, then kept my head under the cold water for as long as I could stand it. I went back to the bedroom and put on a fresh pair of navy cotton trousers and a light blue, short-sleeved shirt, splashed a palm full of aftershave across my face then went downstairs to the kitchen. Vic was sitting at the table, drinking a cup of coffee. He was dressed head to foot in his usual black attire. Black T-shirt, slim-fitting pants and ankle boots. His dreadlocks had been tied back in a knot on top of his head and he had at least three days of salt and pepper stubble growing across his cheeks and jowls. The ebony leather patch across his right eye pulled at the skin at the side of his face, slightly distorting his normally handsome features. On either side of him sat Bussa and Bitter Lemon and, behind them, Dead Man stood at the stove, frying links of sausages and eggs. Dead Man cranked his neck round to greet me. "How yuh doin', suh?"

I nodded at the kid and pulled up a seat across from Vic and the two other men. "Cut it with the sir stuff, Dead Man. Joseph do just fine."

Dead Man smiled. "Jus' as yuh say, Joseph. Mama Esme left breakfast fo' me ta cook. Yuh want sausages?"

"Sounds real good, Dead Man."

Dead Man looked down at the frying pan then across at Vic. "'Bout yuh, Vic?"

Vic sipped at his coffee and tipped his chair back on its hind legs before answering the boy. "Wha' 'bout me?"

"Well, yuh bein' Rastafarian n' all now, yuh ain't wantin' tha pork, no?"

Vic almost fell off his seat as he turned on Dead Man. His face a mixture of mild rage and disbelief. "'Course am want me sausages, yuh fuckin' goat head!"

Bussa and Bitter Lemon began to snigger. I knew better than to make fun of my cousin so early in the morning. Vic immediately turned his vexation away from Dead Man and onto the chuckling men either side of him. He gave Bussa the evil eye.

"Wha' yuh laughing at, yuh ole prick?

Bussa began to cough nervously. "Nuthin', Vic."

Vic, agitated, looked Bussa up and down, his eyes drawn toward the garish-looking sleeveless, multicoloured tropical shirt the old man was wearing. "Wha' the fuck yuh got hanging off yuh scrawny ole back?"

Bussa cast an admiring eye down at his chest. "It's ma bes' dress shirt, Vic."

"Bes' dress shirt! Yuh gotta be kiddin' me, Bussa." Vic slapped the palm of his hand on the kitchen table and began to laugh. "Niggah, yuh tellin' me that ole rag is the bes' ting yuh got ta wear? Shit ... I wouldn't dress one o' Bitter's fuckin' flea-bitten ole dogs in that git up!"

Bitter Lemon continued to smirk like an imbecile. It was a bad move. Vic turned his venom on the big Bajan. "Yuh tink this is funny, niggah?" Bitter clamped his hand tight across his mouth and shook his polished head, his huge shoulders rising and falling as he tried to hide his mirth from my cousin. Vic, filled with enough venom to cripple a big cat, let his poisoned tongue lash out at the giant a while longer. "Yuh tek a look at yuh'self in the mirror this morning, Bitter?" Lemon shook his head at Vic. "No? Well, yuh ought'a, brutha, 'cause yuh look like yuh al'ways do ... A stinky-assed, overall-wearin', reefer-smokin' muthafucka."

Vic glanced across at me angrily, his one good eye telling me that he'd meant every word that he'd just said. To have intervened on the men's behalf would have only spelled more trouble for them. I reached across the table and grabbed hold of the coffee pot and poured myself a cup, then sat back and took a sip. I looked over at Vic and winked at him as he sat muttering to himself, then recalled an old saying my mama used to tell me when we was kids. "Chirren, yuh go invitin' trouble, it usually quick ta accept!"

They say that wise words are spoken by sages ... That was true of my mama. It was fair to say she had the wisdom of Solomon; and, like the great Hebrew king, she had never asked for reward or favour from God or man.

*

My cousin normally only ever had two things on his mind: money and women. Revenge ran a distant third and I'd always known since I was a child that you never wanted to get on his bad side. Vic had been itching to talk business with me. When Bussa, Dead Man and Bitter Lemon had finished their breakfasts, he had swiftly banished them outside to the yard. It was money and revenge that were high on Vic's agenda this morning. I knew that the women would wait till later. My heart began to race when he started to speak.

"JT, yuh know what Monroe is scared o' mo' than any'ting else?"

I shook my head dumbly "No . . . what?"

"Yuh, brutha."

"What you talking about?"

Vic folded his hands across one another and leaned across the table toward me. "When Monroe found out I knew 'bout those dirty photographs that Bernice had stolen from outta his safe and what he'd done to her for thieving 'em, I made sure he also got wind that yuh knew 'bout it too."

"Why?"

"'Cause I knew he'd reach out ta me an' mek a deal, that's why."

"What kinda deal?"

"The kind that's gonna bring him yuh black head on a plate."

"I don't get it, Vic."

My cousin sighed heavily. I watched him pinch at his eyes with his thumb and forefinger then rub at his nostrils with the back of his hand and sniff. "Look, there ain't no easy way o' tellin' yuh this shit, JT."

"What shit?"

Vic sighed again, his fingers suddenly drumming in quick succession on top of the table. "Befo' Bernice got herself killed, I was doin' bid'ness with Monroe."

"You were doing what?"

Vic shot back in his seat. "Yuh heard me!"

"An' yuh knew he was carrying on with Bernice?"

"What yuh tek me fo'? I didn't know a damn ting 'bout that shit!"

"How long have you been in cahoots with Monroe?"

Vic shrugged. "'Bout as long as my black ass bin back on

the island. He got wind I had a ting going with the Panthers stateside. I bin supplyin' the drugs to Evangeline's people. They asked me 'bout gittin' hold'a some shifty firepower. That's where Monroe came in. He had a line on gittin' cases o' guns thru from the Yanks ovah at Paragon. Like I said, he'd already bin openin' doors and greasin' palms over at parliament buildin' fo' the Americans. Ting is he got greedy. He started axin' fo' a bigger chunk o' cash, boxin' the Yanks in'ta corners they couldn't git dem'selves outta. That crazy honky starts holding parties, lotta free skin floatin' 'bout from bedroom ta bedroom. That's when he starts takin' pictures and blackmailin' folk on the general staff."

"An' the Yanks begin to panic when he starts making trouble for 'em?"

Vic nodded and smiled. "Ah, ha ... Few weeks later, Bernice is found dead and I git an envelope stuffed to burstin' with a load o' mucky pictures from Mama Esme."

"Esme?"

"Bernice gave that ole witch the photos after she'd been rifflin' through Monroe's safe."

I squinted and sighed, half my mind thinking about Bernice and the other still trying to fathom out what Vic was telling me. "I don't get why Bernice was going through Monroe's safe."

"Money."

"Money, why the hell was Bernice stealing money outta Monroe's safe?"

Vic dismissed my question with a wave of his hand, his voice suddenly edged with agitation. "That don't matter now ... Ting is Bernice found them photographs and a shitload o' evidence that would'a put Monroe in the pokey fo' the rest o' his life. That's why he had her killed. When I

326

got hold o' the envelope an' I tole Monroe yuh had it, that's when he made me that deal I bin tryin' to tell yuh 'bout."

"Go on . . ."

"Monroe offered me a shit load o' cash if I got yuh ovah 'ere and with that envelope."

My brow creased as I frowned with confusion. "But I never had the damn envelope in the first place."

Vic blew up his cheeks in frustration, then released the air out of his mouth and continued to drum his fingers on the top of the table. "I know that . . . but that honky bastard didn't! I played the muthafucka . . . Got him ta believe yuh was comin' fo' him. Made him sweat. I tol' him Bernice she'd gone an' sent yuh the photographs an' that yuh was comin' home ta nail him."

"But why all the killing . . . Evangeline, Clefus Hopkins, Minton and the rest of his men?"

"I went ta ground an' that spooked Monroe. That's when he sent his goons across tha water ta either clean up, kill or mek yuh an' the Panthers tink I'm jus' another double-crossin' niggah . . . In fairness, he got the double-crossin' right."

"What you talking about?"

Vic grinned and slouched back in his seat. "As soon as I'd got Monroe in the palm o' my hand, I went ovah ta the Yanks an' brokered me a whole new deal."

"Why do I not like the sound of this."

Vic's eye focused in on me. His expression filled with an intensity that made me shiver. "Oh, brutha . . . it's the sweetest part."

"None of this sounds sweet, Vic . . . just scary."

Vic kept on grinning. "Scary, my ass . . . I got honkies sittin' in Washington, DC that have signed this shit off. I take Monroe an' his men outta the picture fo' 'em an' they leave me ta git on wid bid'ness as usual."

My voice rose, its pitch reaching toward hysteria. "Business as usual ... Vic, people have died because of your double-dealing and damn greed!"

Vic reached out his arms, opened up the palms of his hands and sniffed into the air. "People dying all the time, JT ... This time the right folk gonna be headin' fo' the grave."

"I don't believe you. This is madness ... Who the hell made you judge, jury and executioner in all this?"

Vic pulled himself forward violently and shot to his feet, kicking the chair back against the wall. He leaned across the table, his fists knotted up in balls in front of me. "Ma damn niece an' yuh wife when Monroe burned 'em to a cinder ... that's who!"

Vic slammed his fist in front of me and spat on the ground, then swung his arm across the table, sending plates, cutlery, mugs and the coffee pot flying across the kitchen. He stormed across the room and slammed the door after him. The room shook as if the house had just been hit by an earthquake.

I stared back at the door as it rattled on its hinges and listened as Vic stamped down the hallway and out into the yard. I sank forward in my seat, put my head in my hands and listened as Bitter Lemon's four dogs barked and howled outside. For as long as I could remember, my cousin had been a solid fixture in my life. He was a crook by any other name. A thief, philanderer and, when the occasion arose, a stone-cold killer. Apart from being family, my cousin was probably the best friend I ever had. He was the kind of man who stood by your side through fire and rain, blood and death. No one in their right mind would ever choose to live in a world where they'd need a family member or friend like Victor Ellington. Now, as I sat alone, I realised for the first time that you don't choose the world you live in or the colour of the skin you inhabit.

37

I found Vic standing with Bussa by a wall of rotting wooden planks in the barn on the other side of the yard. The two men were watching Bitter Lemon and Dead Man as they lifted one of the three coffins from the Bedford van. Three sets of carpenters' trestle tables had been arranged in three-foot intervals in the centre of the barn. Bitter Lemon and Dead Man carried the coffin past me and rested it across the first two trestles, then walked back to the van to collect the next. Thin shafts of light streamed through the jagged-edged gaps in the old walls, and dust swirls danced through the hazy beams of sunshine that hung in the air above our heads. The barn had seen better days. Thirty years of hard Caribbean rain and baking summer heat had taken its toll. The original structure that once kept the weather off the crops of sugar cane and sheltering animals was long gone. Now the walls and doors were a patchwork mess of botched carpentry. The roof had been cedar shingle, the same as the old house, with holes in it that were worse than a gap-toothed sailor's. Tiles were missing, rotten or sticking up at awkward angles. In places a stubborn patch of sun-bleached red paint clung to the wooden sides, but otherwise it was as brown as the rutted mud around it. A ladder, used to get up to the hay loft, sloped at an angle on the far wall, the decrepit rungs sagging after years of use and warning that only a fool would be stupid enough to attempt to climb it. The strong smell of ammonia that crept up my nose and stung my eyes came from Bitter Lemon's dogs pissing all over the place rather than any kind of livestock the big Bajan might have kept in the past.

Vic ignored me as I came and stood by his side. His gaze fixed on the coffins as each one was lined up in front of him. The back of his neck looked oily and hot, his forehead coated with a thin thread of perspiration. Bussa felt the edgy atmosphere that had shot up around us and quickly made his excuses to leave. I watched the old man wander off to Bitter and Dead Man by the back of the van doors, then rested my hand on Vic's shoulder. It felt as hard as a rock. "So, are you gonna tell me what these creepy damn boxes are for, or what?"

Vic turned to look at me. His eye moved carefully over every inch of my face, no doubt studying for weaknesses and ways to bite at me with either his cruel wit or bitter temper. His expression was blank, devoid of the anger he'd expressed earlier. I watched as he raised his arm and point towards the three ornate, wooden palls. "One's fo' Bernice, the others fo' Monroe." Vic hesitated for a moment. He looked somberly at the last casket then walked across and stroked the coffin lid with the palm of his hand and turned to me. "An' this one's fo' yuh."

The skin on my face suddenly felt tight and prickly, like I'd just walked through a cobweb. "Say what?"

Vic's expression remained stony. "Yuh heard me."

I could feel a vein of black electricity crawl through my body as I tried to make sense of what Vic was saying. "What the hell do I need one o' those things for? I ain't planning on croaking it just yet."

"I know . . . But that's how Monroe wants yuh delivering ta him."

"In a coffin?"

331

"Yeah ... it's kinda out there, ain't it? But yuh know Monroe, that sucker's one crazy honky muthafucka!"

I took a sharp step backwards. "Why the hell's he want me in a coffin?"

Vic held out his hands. "Hey, whatta I know? Fucka's out to prove sum kinda point. Most probably wantin' ta mek yuh suffer."

"I ain't gittin' in no damn coffin, Vic." I spat on the ground, the inside of my mouth drying out before my lips had shut.

"Damn it, JT, I ain't jiving yuh. Monroe wants yuh in that box, an' he wants yuh breathin' when I hand yuh ovah."

I pointed at the casket, my hand trembling with a mixture of anger and fear. "This ... this is part of your deal with that mad bastard? To nail me up inside some coffin and hand me over like a birthday gift to him!"

Vic grinned. "Nah ... we ain't gonna be nailin' yuh in, brutha."

"Oh, thanks a lot ... that's a real comfort."

Vic slapped the top of the coffin lid with the flat of his hand. "No ... but we's gonna tie yuh ass up an' leave the lid loose, jus' like he asked."

I shook my head. "You're as mad Monroe is, you know that?"

Vic shrugged his shoulders at me. "It gotta look like we mean business, JT."

"So, you in the undertaking business now?"

"No ... but I may tink 'bout it when we git back ta Bristol."

I stared back at my cousin, shocked by what he had just said, the surprise crackling in my voice. "So, you planning on coming back?"

Vic shook his head and grinned. "Yeah ... bringin' the boys wid me too!"

I looked down at the ground and rubbed at either side of my temples with my thumb and forefinger. "That's great ... you're gonna be importing the island's criminal great and the good. Gabe an' Pearl are gonna be real happy when they hear all 'bout that."

I looked back at the coffin that Vic wanted to lay me out in. I hesitated for a moment before walking across to my cousin, my legs felt weak and an odd pain shot along my shoulder, down my left side and through my back and chest as I took the first step. I ran my tongue across my dry lips and looked nervously at the casket then at Vic.

"An' what happens when I'm in here and we get to Monroe?"

"Then yuh gotta trus' me, brutha."

I remembered what Mama Esme had said to me the night before, took a deep breath and tried to restore some kind of coherence to my thinking. I knew I needed to drive the gargoyles that were chipping away at my reasoning back toward that unlit place in my mind where I kept old terrors. The place in my head where I stored my unwanted memories of Monroe. A tight cord of tension wrapped around my chest and pressed the air out of my lungs before I spoke again.

I held my gaze on my cousin and tapped the coffin lid with my finger. "Other than me trusting you ... what else you got up your sleeve?"

Vic smiled mischievously and slapped me on the arm. I watched as he walked out of the barn and headed back across the yard. He was climbing the steps onto the porch of the house before he called back to me, his voice laced with impish excitement. "I gots me a Doctah Lickrish ... that's wha' I got."

38

By one that afternoon, the sun had already gone behind the house and the trees in the yard were in full shadow, and clattering to the sound of dozens of mockingbirds. The air outside was dense and humid, the scent of salt and seawater caught on the wind as it blew through the house. Bussa had heated up the rice and peas that Mama Esme had cooked up and the five of us had sat at the kitchen table and chowed down on platefuls of the rice, along with fried pork chops and plantain. Bitter Lemon opened up bottles of cold Banks beer he'd fetched from the larder and passed them round to each of us. I found myself speaking in the patois of my childhood; my speech and accent changing to accommodate my fellow Bajans as we chatted. Afterwards, I'd taken another bottle of beer and sat on a wooden stool out on the back porch by the kitchen door and watched an emerald green hummingbird flit from flower to flower. The lawn, such as it was, had become overgrown with high weeds and wild evergreen shrubs. A row of baobab trees separated the old property from the sugarcane fields that stretched on, acre after acre, down toward the village of Hillaby.

After Vic had finished eating, he'd gone upstairs and returned a short while later dressed in his priest's garb. He said that he and Bussa were going to drive down to a village called Carrington and that he'd be back within a couple of hours. I'd watched him walk out of the kitchen and down the hallway. The wind blew in from the front door, fanning the tail of his jacket, whisking it away from his back to reveal the Colt .45 pistol he'd tucked into the waistband of his trousers. The urge to call out to my cousin, to ask him what he was up to, bloomed in my chest; the question rose up towards my throat, aching to be released from my mouth, but something inside prevented my enquiry from being fully expressed.

I clammed up quicker than a Venus fly trap. Perhaps my better judgement warned me that Vic never liked to be questioned, or maybe it was the fact that sometimes it was better not to know what dark path my cousin was about to take, or who he was going to cheat or hurt next. The word "trust" had just started to take on a whole new and scary meaning to me. I sat back against the kitchen wall and looked back out toward the sugar cane and heard myself curse under my breath. I lifted the beer bottle to my lips, then drained every last drop from inside it. I closed my eyes and squeezed my fingers around the neck of the bottle; the glass felt as cool and damp as a serpent in my palm.

Vic's couple of hours down in Carrington had turned into five, and it was just after seven that evening by the time he pulled the Land Rover back into the yard. I stood on the front porch and watched Bussa hold open the passenger door and a thin, elderly black man get out. The old man was frail and had to be in his late seventies, his grey afro was clipped close to his head, his face gaunt. A top set of craggy, yellowing choppers protruded over decaying bottom teeth. He walked slowly around the front of the vehicle to join Vic, and the two men headed across the yard toward me. As they climbed the steps of the porch, Vic grinned at me and slapped the old fella on his back, sending him shooting forward. I quickly grabbed hold of him as he lost his footing and started to take a tumble, his feeble body falling against mine. I held him by either side of the tops of the arms, the man felt as if he was made of skin and bones and little else.

"JT ... this 'ere's Doctah Lickrish."

I steadied the doctor onto his feet and saw him wince when he looked up to greet me. "Pleased ta meet yuh, son."

I smiled at the old man, then stood back to give him a chance to compose himself. "Likewise, Doc." In spite of the evening heat, the doctor wore a heavy navy blue suit and white dress shirt and a dark polka-dot tie; the warmth collecting in his suit climbed visibly up his neck, making him hook his finger round his collar and tug at it to let out some of the stifling sultriness that was brewing underneath his clothing.

Vic, oblivious to the damage he'd done, pushed past me and Lickrish, waded into the house and stood on the bottom step of the stairs. He clasped the bannister with both hands and nodded at the doc. "Tek that old fucka in ta the front room, JT, sit his ass down on one 'a Esme's recliners."

I looked at Vic in surprise. "This is Esme's place?"

Vic, about to start climbing the stairs, turned and frowned at me. "'Course it's Esme's ... Who yuh tink this ole joint belong ta anyways?"

"Bitter Lemon."

"Bitter Lemon! Shit ... yuh kiddin' me? That raggedy-assed niggah live wid the other trash down in St Lawrence Gap." I heard Lemon grunt and saw him stick his head dozily around the kitchen door.

"Wha yuh say?"

Vic hung his head over the rail of the banister and shouted down the hallway at Lemon. "I din't say a goddam muthafuckin' ting ta yuh, Bitter. Jus' haul yuh lazy black

336

ass an' go git Dead Man." Bitter Lemon grunted again and started to walk across the kitchen toward the back door. Vic bellowed after him, bringing the hefty Bajan to a sudden halt. "An' while yuh at it, bring us in some cold beers on yuh way back!"

I watched Vic take the Colt from out of his waistband then run upstairs without saying another word. I walked the doctor into sitting room and showed him to a seat, then went across to the hearth and took a box of matches from out of the fireplace and lit two oil lamps that stood either side of the mantlepiece. The room came alive with a comforting amber glow, but became frosty when I turned around and saw Bussa walking in carrying one of the coffins. I backed up and leaned myself against a dark-wood dresser; I instantly felt my blood throbbing in my wrists and a taste like copper coins coating the inside of my mouth as I watched the casket being ceremoniously laid out in front of the hearth. Bussa plonked himself down into an armchair opposite the doctor, a cloud of dust blew up into the air and fell back down onto Bussa's head and shoulders. He waved his arms around above his head and cursed and spluttered as lint and tiny grey flecks floated around his blustering face. Through all Bussa's commotion, the elderly doctor had remained silent. I watched as he reached into his inside jacket pocket and pulled out a pair of gold wire-rimmed glasses. He perched the spectacles on the bridge of his nose and stared inquisitively down at the coffin on the floor. Lickrish seemed more gravedigger than quack and that sent my guts rumbling. The doctor peered over his glasses at me, as if he had heard my thoughts, his gaze travelling across the room to meet mine, his dark eyes unreadable in the light of the oil lamps.

337

Lickrish smiled at me crookedly. My palms became damp. My breath loud in my chest. I rolled my tongue inside my dry mouth and was about to speak to Bussa and break the awkward silence when Vic barrelled into the living room carrying a rolled-up length of rope, his one good eye twinkling with a liquid glee. He stood next to the coffin and rolled the muscles in his shoulders, flexing the stiffness out of his back, and grinned at me and the doctor. "Yuh two boys got acquainted?"

I looked at the old man sitting quietly in the armchair then back at Vic. "Kind'a ..."

Vic, sensing my exasperation, paused for a moment before going on to make more formal introductions. "The doctah 'ere, he ain't yuh usual medicine man ... Ain't that right, Doc?"

Lickrish nodded his head in agreement and stared up at me over his specs.

I turned and gawped at Vic. "Then what the hell is he?"

Vic stabbed his finger toward the doc. "The doctah bin in jus 'bout every damn t'ree-ring circus an' big top fro' 'ere ta Kingston, ain't that right, Lickrish?"

The doc nodded his head slowly. "Yuh cousin right."

I smiled at Lickrish. "Doing what?"

Lickerish was about to continue, but was swiftly interrupted by Vic's enthusiasm to spill the beans: "Knots."

A surge of blood rushed to my head. I rubbed at my face with my hands in disbelief. I stared back down at Lickrish through my splayed fingers, eventually speaking to him from behind the palms of my hands. "Knots ... you're a doctor o' knots?"

I saw Doc Lickrish's eyes move over my face and watched him slowly shake his head at me. "No, suh ... I'm wha' dey

338

call a' escapologist... 'mongst utha tings. Tha doc ting is jus' ma stage name."

My hands dropped weakly to my sides, my face numb. "Stage name ... say what?"

Vic blew air out of his mouth. He pushed me out of his way and went and stood behind the armchair Doc Lickrish was sitting. He leaned forward, resting his arms on the back and dropped the rope he was holding into the old man's lap. "This buck-tooth old fucka can break loose outta boxes, sacks, cuffs n' chains. He yuh saving grace, JT!"

"My saving grace! You gotta be kidding me... You're telling me that this plan you got to wipe out Monroe an' his boys boils down to you sending me to him hog-tied an' boxed up with a seventy-year-old circus act?"

"Not quite... the doc ain't coming wid us ... Look, we gotta tie yuh up, an' it gotta look real convincing, else Monroe gonna know he's bein' took fo' a fool. The doc 'ere gonna fix it so yuh ain't bound up too tight an' yuh can git outta them ropes round yuh wrists n' ankles quicker than shit tru' a goose!"

Doc Lickrish picked up the rope from his lap and sat forward in his seat. He held up the rolled length of cord for me to take from him, his frosted brown eyes fixed on mine with the lidless glare of a bird's. "Yuh gon' have ta trus' me, son." *Trust.* I was growing pretty sick and tired of hearing that damn word. Hearing it spoken again just made me want to trust nobody. My nostrils quivered when I breathed, I took a couple of unsteady paces and nervously reached down and took hold of the coil of rope Lickrish was offering me. The old man continued to stare wide-eyed at me, his grasp on the cable far stronger than I'd imagined a man of such advanced years could possess.

★

By ten that evening the air in Mama Esme's living room was thick with cigarette smoke and the smell of dried sweat, fried food, flat beer and dope. The musky odour of marijuana struck at my face and made me feel sick. Worst still, the man responsible for saving my neck not only liked to knock back the rum, but he was fond of the herb too. For the better part of two hours I'd been laid out in the coffin by the fireplace whilst Vic watched the Doc as he tied my wrists and ankles in a series of knots, each one carefully designed to be easily loosened at breakneck speed. Bussa, Bitter Lemon and Dead Man had sat around the room drinking booze, smoking and stuffing pork and leftover rice and peas into their faces whilst the doc got me to break free of the different restraints until I'd found one I had any confidence in. By eleven, Vic was happy he could truss me up like Lickrish had shown him and he'd then stuffed an envelope filled with cash into the old boy's eager mitt and bundled him back into the Land Rover and had Bussa drive him back to Carrington.

I stood on the porch and watched the car drive out of the yard, then felt Vic's hand on my shoulder. I turned to face him, my head bent slightly toward the ground, my jaw clenched to keep it from shaking.

My cousin squeezed his hand around the nape of my neck and whispered into my ear. "Come wid me, brutha, yuh look like yuh could do wid a shot o' rum." I followed after him, back down the hallway toward the kitchen, my head spinning, feeling like a sacrificial lamb about to be drawn towards its own slaughter.

39

They say a man who lives fully is not afraid of death. I wasn't too sure about that sentiment or whether it applied to me. I sat in one of the armchairs opposite Vic, sipped my rum, nervously surveyed the coffin that still sat by the hearth, and wondered about the kind of life I'd been living and whether I'd actually lived it to its fullest. The macabre-looking box was stained cherry with a cushioned and quilted silky lining. It had been quite comfortable to lay down in, almost inviting ... but not that bloody inviting. Lying in the casket earlier, I'd had time to ponder my own demise and I was certain of one thing: I was afraid to die. Over the years, as a policeman, I'd seen plenty of death and, in my experience, it was never straightforward, and often bloody. I'd never believed that death brought you to the pearly gates of immortality or to the arms of long-deceased family, but simply that it was a departure from life. I knew there was no pattern nor control in the manner of how a human being died. Nor was there a God or supreme being to choose or discriminate when your time was up. Death just happened. Death was neither fair nor unfair in who it took to the grave and was unmoved by the prayers of the living.

Vic had been silent whilst I was lost in my bleak reverie. I watched as he picked up the rum bottle from beside his chair and filled up his glass with another four fingers of the golden-coloured spirit, then reached across and topped me up. He sat the bottle back down by the side of his seat then slouched back in the armchair and stretched out his long legs. He was still dressed in the clerical dog collar. Underneath his black shirt his chest barreled out, his flat stomach corded with muscle. He let his breath out quietly and smiled at me, then pulled on his earlobe before speaking.

"So, this is how it's all gonna pan out in the morning."

My stomach knotted. I lifted my glass away from my mouth, a small amount of rum burning at my lips and tongue. "That soon?"

The brow over Vic's left eye raised slightly as he nodded his head at me. "Monroe wants to meet at daybreak."

"Where?"

Vic rubbed the knuckles on his right hand unconsciously. "Gun Hill."

"The signal station . . . why there?"

Vic drank from his glass, a slow, steady gulp that showed neither need nor pleasure on his face. "It's outta the way an' that honky bastard owns the land now. I gotta hand yuh and the photographs over to him outside'a the barracks befo' six thirty."

I swallowed hard before I spoke. "And then what?"

"Monroe's gonna git one o' his stooges to put a bullet in me an' then they probably gonna bury yuh alive."

I pointed at the casket on the floor. "Hence the coffin?"

Vic chuckled to himself. "Weeks ago, when I first tol' Monroe yuh was on ta him 'bout killin' Bernice and that yuh was comin' home . . . he said then that he'd pay me handsomely if I was ta bring yuh in ta him alive an' in a casket. I tol' him he was mad. Damn fool said he din't give a damn 'bout wha' I tout, jus ta bring yuh like he said."

Vic bit at a hangnail on his thumb and spat it across the

room. "Look, Monroe's gonna have all his shit worked out. Deep down he knows he can't trus' me. He's playin' the game, same as I am. I bin givin' him the run around fo' weeks. New York, Louisiana, now 'ere. He bin settin' me up an' me him every step o' tha way. Tit fo' tat killin's, Gatehouse tryin' ta scare yuh inta givin' me up. I bin one step ahead of 'em since this charade began. Stringin' 'em along all this time. Monroe knows he ain't got no damn choice uth'a than ta tek me out at the neck. 'Cause, he knows if he don't then 'am gonna do the same ta his ass …" Vic took another mouthful of rum and pulled the dog collar away from his throat with his thumb and undid the top button of his shirt then gestured at me with his near-empty glass. "I called Monroe when I was down in Carrington earlier. After he'd finished hollerin' down tha phone at me, I tol' him I'd got his dirty pictures an' that he could have yuh so long as I got my cut o' tha cash we bin mekin' together outta both them Panthers an' the gun-running deals."

"And he believed you?"

"That muthafucka only gonna believe what he need ta believe. He knows I'm as shifty as a ten-speed clutch an' the fool tinks I'd sell my mamma fo' a case o' rum. He can keep on tinkin' all'a that shit fo' all I care." Vic leaned across the arm of his chair and pointed at my chest with his finger. "I don't want yuh ta wash or shave, an' sleep in yuh damn clothes tonight. I need yuh ta look like yuh bin put tru' tha ringer. By the time we git ta Gun Hill tomorrow mornin' he's gonna have that place locked up tighter than a drum. He's gonna have every crooked copper he can lay his hands on hangin' 'bout that place. There ain't gonna be any wiggle room once I make my play. Once Monroe has the lid o' the coffin hauled off at some point yuh gonna see me wipe my

343

hand across ma face wid the back o' ma hand. That's the sign, brutha. Sign that means tings are 'bout ta git damn serious. Means yuh gonna have ta haul yuh ass outta tha fuckin' box an' git bloody wid tha rest o' us. Understand?"

I nodded and felt a ball of fear knot deep inside my stomach. I watched as Vic sank the last of his rum then pulled himself up out of the armchair, walked across the sitting room and shouted down the hall for Bussa and Dead Man to come and join us.

"So, how much blood money is my hide worth to Monroe?"

Vic leaned against the door jamb and ran his tongue over his front teeth then winced. "Sixty thousan'."

"Sixty thousand pounds!"

"Guineas . . . yuh tink I sell yuh ass cheap?"

I knocked back the last of the rum and watched as Bussa and Dead Man returned to the sitting room through the bottom of my glass. Both men were carrying large olive-green duffle bags in their hands with the words US ARMY printed on the sides. The men dropped the bags onto a table which stood by the closed drapes. Dead Man unhooked a rifle bag from his shoulder and laid it next to the hold-alls. Vic walked across to the table and opened the duffel bags and began to pull out a dizzying array of firearms, laying them out in front of him. "So . . . we git ourselves two Thompson M1s, two Remington 1100 pump-actions, four .45s, couple o' snub-nosed .38s, ten ANM8 smokes grenades an' enuff ammo fo' tha five o' us ta hold out at the Alamo fo' a month." Vic picked up one of the 12-gauge shotguns and snapped open the breech. The gun had been sawn off at the pump, the stock shaved down and honed into a pistol grip. He stared down the breech then blew into the barrel, closed it, and snapped the firing pin on the empty chamber. He placed the Remington back on the table then pick up one of the Colt automatics and threw it to me. "We gonna need ta stuff that in the box wid yuh … someplace it ain't gonna git seen."

I weighed the .45 in the palm of my hand. It was a heavy gun, far weightier than I'd have preferred. I clasped the grip then released the magazine from the butt so I could see the top round and inserted it back in again, then chambered a round and set the safety. I stared at the gun and ran my trembling hand down the barrel. I looked up at Vic who was watching the gun quivering in my hand. He turned back to the table, unzipped the rifle bag, pulled out an impressive-looking gun and held it up in front of him admiringly. This 'ere's the M40 bolt action sniper rifle, telescopic sight an' a sound suppressor fo' the muzzle. Yuh can shoot the dick off a donkey from nearly t'ree thousan' foot away." Vic threw the rifle across to Dead Man. The kid smiled at Vic and snapped open and shut the bolt-action in quick succession, then raised the gun up to his slender shoulder and squinted into the sight. Vic shook his head and began to laugh to himself. I watched as he walked back over to the armchair he'd been sitting in and pick up the half-empty bottle of rum from off the floor. He pulled out the stopper, put the bottle to his lips and swigged back a mouthful of spirit, then looked down at me and grinned.

"That boy's namesakes 'mounts ta mo' than him jus' cheatin' tha grave, brutha. He git Monroe in his sights … then he a dead man."

345

40

By 4.30 the next morning, a heavy mist had settled in the trees. It was raining hard, the water sluicing off the gutters down into the front yard filling it with floating leaves and twigs. Vic didn't need to worry about me dropping off during the night; I'd not slept a wink. I was nervous, my palms moist, and I'd walked about the bedroom for hours, aimlessly waiting for the sun to finally come up. I'd done as my cousin had instructed, and not washed or shaved. I was still in the same clothes I'd been wearing for the better part of twenty-four hours. I didn't need a mirror to tell me that I looked a mess, and my nose was crying out to me that I smelled like a polecat sitting on a heap of its own dung.

I slumped down on the edge of the bed, stared out of the window and watched the rain pelt against the glass, the burning ache of fear gripping at my insides. My body felt wooden, my arms and legs disjointed. The muscles around my neck and across the tops of my shoulders knotted with tension, my pulse leaping in my neck. I lifted my hand up to my forehead and felt my eye twitch involuntarily, then touched at the scar tissue on my brow with the tips of my fingers and thought of Bernice. With all the madness that had been going on around me this past week, I'd pushed to the back of my mind my true reason for returning home; the death of my sister. In his telegram to me, Vic had called it 'settling family affairs', I now realised that those so-called family affairs would turn out to have included theft, blackmail and a trail of dead bodies littered across thousands of miles. Bernice's life had been snubbed out by a ghost from not only my past, but also my closest family member's. She'd been murdered on the orders of Monroe, and Vic had made it his sworn duty to seek bloody retribution for our kin's death and, in turn, had drawn me back into a world I'd hoped I'd never be a part of again.

I'd continued to ponder on the past; Bernice's death and my almost narcissistic absorption with my own mortality for longer than I should have, lost in a desolate world of my own making. I never heard Vic when he walked into my room at a little after five. I turned to find him standing at my side, a large mug of coffee in one hand and eating a round of toast with his other. My guts rolled as I looked up bleary-eyed and watched as he began to stuff the remaining thick wedge of crust into his mouth.

"How the hell can you eat at a time like this?"

Vic shrugged his shoulders, poured coffee into his already full mouth and chugged it all down in a single swallow. "Ain't no point dyin' on an empty stomach."

I nodded silently, unable to muster up the words or energy to disagree with him. Vic looked like he hadn't got a care in the world. He was dressed in a black lightweight polo-necked jumper and black corduroy pants, his favourite Colt .45 hanging from a chamois leather Berns-Martin shoulder holster that was tucked underneath his left arm. Killing came easy to my cousin and today I knew he'd be looking to use some of those deadly skills on Monroe and his men. Knowing that still didn't make me feel in any better. I watched as he slugged back the last of his coffee, then put the mug on the dressing table and sat down on the bed next to me and squeezed his greasy palm over the back of my neck.

"What yuh tinkin' 'bout, brutha?"

I shrugged my shoulders and felt Vic's hand loosen its sticky grip on my neck a little. "Oh, I dunno ... everything n' nothing ... Mainly whether I'm gonna see another sun come up, and if I've got the backbone to make it through the day."

Vic started to speak, then stopped and looked down at the floor. "JT, look, brutha, yuh can beat on yuhsel' fo' the rest o' yuh life if yuh wanna ... but no matter how yuh cut it, yuh ain't no coward. Nevah have bin."

I bit at my lip and shook my head. "You gotta a helluva lot of faith in a frightened man."

Vic looked at me and smiled. "Yuh bin scared befo' an' handled it jus' fine." Vic patted my shoulder and got up off the bed and stood over me. I lifted my head and stared up at his expressionless face as he made a motion toward the door with his thumb. "Com' on, let's git the hell outta 'ere an' git tha damn job done."

★

Downstairs, the place was as deadly quiet. Vic told me that Bussa, Bitter Lemon and Dead Man had left hours ago. I pulled on my jacket, stood at the bottom of the stairs and watched whilst Vic stuck a slim colonial throwing knife into the inside leg of his left boot and covered the bottom of his trousers over his ankle. He reached down and picked up a roll of duct tape from off the floor then stuck his hand into his back pocket and pulled out Evangeline's old Beretta. "This gonna be lighter than using a Colt an' it's easier ta conceal." He clicked the magazine out of the butt and showed it to me, then snapped it back into the grip, chambered a round and left the safety off.

"Yuh got one up the pipe and another seven in the mag. Yuh git the chance, go fo' a head shot with this pop gun 'cause it ain't gonna dent shit utha'wise!" Vic spun me around on my heels and pulled up my jacket and shirt and rested the Beretta in the small of my back with one hand then began to bite off lengths of tape with his teeth and moulded the pistol to my skin with it. When he'd finished, he yanked my clothes back down, grabbed his leather jacket off the ball of the stair bannister and headed for the front door.

"Shit, JT... yuh ain't gonna have to worry 'bout firin' no pea-shooter. Tha' stench comin' off yuh hide gonna kill Monroe an' all them utha' honkies befo' either o' us can loose offa round!" Vic began to bawl with laughter, his cutting jibe to me clearly trying to disguise in the cheapest fashion the painful realities of the danger we were about to face.

It was still raining when I came out of the house, the sky rolling with blue-black clouds, the thunder rolling in over the mountains in the distance. Vic was waiting for me inside the back of Bussa's Bedford van. I pulled up the collar of my jacket and walked down the steps of the porch, then ran across the yard and climbed inside to join him. Laying on the floor directly in front of me was the cherry wood coffin, its shiny lid resting up against the wall of the van just behind where Vic stood. I looked at my cousin and forced a smile, my head finally realising that I no longer had time to worry about life, death and whether I could summon up the courage to take on Monroe and his men.

The rain drummed down on to the roof of the van as I stepped into the coffin. I got down on my haunches slowly, then stretched my body out along the full length of the

349

casket. Vic kneeled down over me, then picked up two short lengths of rope from beside him and tied them just as Doc Lickrish had shown him. The thick brown cord looked as if I was bound tight but, in reality, I could feel the give in the rope and felt fairly confident I knew how I needed to twist and turn my wrists and ankles to release myself from their phony hold.

Vic reached down inside his hip pocket, pulled out my old Puma pocketknife and stuffed it deep into my sock inside my right shoe. He smiled at me. "Just in case, hey." He slapped me on the calf a couple of times then got to his feet and picked up the coffin lid from behind him and began to lower it over me. "I'll see yuh in the daylight in thirty minutes; sit tight, cus."

As the lid closed, the darkness hit me like a punch in the face. It was an extreme kind of darkness; scary, immediate, total. My heart began to beat furiously and I had to stop myself struggling for breath. I raised my hands instinctively, my palms touching the lid of the coffin inches above my face. I heard Vic slam the back doors, get into the cab and fire up the ignition, then felt the Bedford reversing across the yard and drive out onto the mountain road to begin its twenty-mile journey down to Gun Hill signal station in St George Parish. As Vic accelerated, the silk and wood base of the coffin jolted underneath me as the van ran over divots and bumps in the track. I could hear the sound of my heart beating in my ears. The smell of my body odour clung to my skin like damp wool, an all-enveloping odour that was like a salty tangle of seaweed and fish eggs and pork gone green with putrefaction.

Ten minutes later, it was getting warmer inside the box. The sweat trickled off my chest and stomach and ran round to my back, soaking my shirt.

Somewhere deep inside me, I recognised that panic was now my worst enemy. I needed to slow down my breathing; I was snatching in too much air and that was making my head go light. I touched the lid again and felt it give underneath my palms. I rested my arms at my side and shut my eyes. I wasn't underground, I told myself. I was in the back of a damn van, which Vic was driving. I was safe, at least for now. I pressed my back down onto the base of the coffin, felt the Beretta dig into my back and immediately felt better. I lay still and thought of Evangeline and everything she'd sacrificed so that I could still be alive today. My hands balled into fists and, in my mind's eye, I saw the image of Monroe and, in the darkness, swore to myself that I would end his life within the next few hours.

41

The drive to St George Parish, and then the climb up to Gun Hill signal station, seemed to take for ever. I peered down at my wristwatch and saw the illuminated hands shining back at me. I'd been encased inside the coffin for a little over fifteen minutes, but it felt like hours. The heat inside the wooden box was almost unbearable. Sweat ran out of every pore of my body, soaking my clothing. Any sound outside of the casket was muted and flat. My feelings of claustrophobia had diminished little as I was continually buffeted about inside the coffin as Vic navigated the old vehicle over the rough terrain. My cousin's driving and the roads had begun to calm down a little as the van's wheels finally hit the asphalt roads and began to inch its way up what I assumed to be Brigg's Hill and the last part of the journey up towards the old military outpost, which was now owned by Monroe.

It was about another ten minutes before the van finally came to a halt. I heard Vic get out of the cab and slam the door behind him, then listened as his feet began to walk across gravel. Way off in the background, I thought I could hear the low, mumbling voices of men, then everything fell eerily silent. I pushed my ear against the side of the coffin and listened. I caught the muffled sound of two, maybe three, men's voices speaking briefly outside, then things went quiet again. Moments later, I heard Vic's voice and the other men speaking, then the handle on the back of the van turn and the doors being flung open. The tail of the Bedford sank down as the group of men climbed inside. I listened as they shuffled about above me, the studded heels of their boots tapping on the metal floor. The casket was suddenly pulled forward, as I was lifted off the ground, and then carried out of the back of the van and walked over the noisy aggregate. Raindrops tapped noisily on the coffin lid as the box was carried across open ground.

My head cracked against the top of the casket as it was slid down toward the floor and slowly tipped forward so that I was in upright position. The base hit the gravel and the coffin was then dragged backward and rested against something solid. I stayed in the dark, staring into the black for maybe another thirty seconds, my body trembling from head to foot, then, finally, felt the lid of the coffin slowly being prised open. As it was pulled away, the light stung at my eyes, making me blink repeatedly. Tiny teardrops welled up in my lower lids and began to trickle down the sides of my face, stinging my cheeks. The humid air around me suddenly became heavy with the smell of ozone, damp moss and my own fusty perspiration.

Monroe stood directly in front of me. His thin pasty face broke out into a wide smile when I made eye contact with him. His white hair was combed out of his tanned face and stuck back against his scalp with sweet-scented pomade and rainwater. I watched as he rested the palm of his left hand against the top of a gold-handled black cane, his eyes, a distant, ethereal blue, continued to gaze into mine. He wore a light blue candy-striped suit with a white dress shirt and crimson tie. His expensive ruby cufflinks glinted and peeked out from underneath the sleeves of his jacket. Monroe was over six feet tall and could not have been called a soft man, but, at the same time, there was no muscular tone or definition to his body, as though in growing up he had bypassed physical labour, exercise and sports as a matter of calling. Staring at him now, I realised just why I hated him.

Monroe had been born into an exclusionary world of wealth, segregation, private schooling and membership of the island's finest clubs. He'd been born, raised and still lived in an enormous white-columned home close to the village that I and my sister, Bernice, had been brought up in. From the veranda at the back of the family mansion, Monroe would have looked down the slope of the immaculately cut lawns, through the widely spaced cedar trees and down across his papa's enormous estate toward the shanty village where we lived.

Most of the occupants of Ginger Bay had descendants who at one time had been enslaved and owned by the Monroes, including my own family. The Monroes had thrived on the sweat, toil and bondage of my brethren. My meeting with him today would have no doubt pleased him; the witnessing of a black man bound and subjugated in the manner his ancestors had been accustomed to. Standing close to Monroe's left was Silas Gatehouse, who had the same oily smile written across his smug face as his fulsome boss. He was kitted out in an ill-fitting beige safari suit with thin brown stripes running through it, a white shirt and brown knitted tie. A small red rose was stuck in his lapel, giving him the look of a ponce more than a policeman. He winked at me, then put a cigarette in his mouth, worked the lighter out of his waistcoat pocket and lit it. Gatehouse blew a cloud of cigarette smoke into the air then stood to one side and yanked Vic towards him by the collar of his leather jacket. A thin streak of blood ran from a gash on the right side of Vic's forehead where he had been hit by one of Monroe's men. Directly behind Vic was a hard-looking, heavy-set white fellow with a black crew cut. The man's height and breadth, and the corded tension in his body, were not to be taken lightly. His right arm was stretched out in front of him. He held a Webley revolver to the back of Vic's head, the tip of the barrel only inches away from his skull. Another four white men were spread out across the grey shingle ground, each armed with automatic pistols. Monroe looked at Vic and shook his head, then took a couple of paces towards me and smiled.

"Joseph ... Tremaine ... Ellington, as I live and breathe."

A sour-tasting bile rose up in my throat, an unpleasant mixture of anger and hatred that I hawked up and spat out onto the gravel at the foot of the casket. "I was kinda hoping you'd a bin neither, Monroe."

If his feathers were ruffled by my spitting at his feet, Monroe was sharp enough not to show it. He sniffed and tapped the handle of his cane with a manicured fingernail. It was easy to imagine his pampered hands gripping at a whip. He stretched his wiry neck forward and scrutinised the ropes tied around my wrists and ankles, then looked back up at me. "I'm not sure how to take that, old chap."

I let my eyes drift off Monroe's face for a second or two, then return again. "Take it any damn way you want."

Monroe shrugged his shoulders nonchalantly, leaned back against his cane, then turned to look at Vic. Gatehouse was patting my cousin's body from top to bottom. He reached into his jacket and pulled out Vic's Colt .45 and a large manila envelope. Gatehouse opened it up then stuffed Vic's gun in his trouser waistband and handed over the envelope to his boss. Monroe reached his hand inside and pulled out a handful of eight by ten photographs. He leafed quickly through each of them, then stuffed them back inside and shook the envelope in front of him. "Your cousin here has been a rather slippery chap these past few weeks ... led me and my men here on a bit of a song and dance."

My lip broke into a sneer. "That makes two of us then."

Monroe turned back to face me. "Well, I'm sorry to hear that, one would expect a little less cloak and dagger when dealing with one's family."

I looked at the envelope in Monroe's hand, then back up at him. "Sounds like most of the stuff you've been peddling over the years with my family has been all cloak and dagger, Monroe."

Monroe's face flushed. I watched as the skin at the side of his left eye twitched. He brushed the side of his face with his fingers, as if he were trying to knock the irritation of my comment away from him, his dead eyes returning their gaze to me. "I seem to remember being treated with the same repugnance and disrespect every time we meet."

"Well, you know how it is, Monroe ... old habits die hard, an' all. I start respecting you now, I'm gonna find it hard to sleep at nights."

"You needn't worry about sleep ... You're going to have plenty of time for slumber very shortly, my friend." Monroe was enjoying himself. Gloating back at me like a spoilt child with raw, unconcealed pleasure.

"I ain't your fucking friend, Monroe."

Monroe shook his head and tutted quietly to himself. "Really, Joseph ... you disappoint me. There's no need for such pagan language. You may have gone to school and fumbled your way into the police force, but you wear your lack of education and breeding like a cheap suit."

356

He looked back at Vic, then gestured with his head at Gatehouse. The blond-haired copper took a final drag on the end of his cigarette, threw it to the floor and stubbed it out with the toe of his shoe, then reached inside his jacket with his left hand and withdrew a wooden truncheon, slamming it into Vic's stomach, dropping him to his knees. My body arced forward instinctively, then remembered Vic's words about staying cool. I sank myself back into the casket and watched on helplessly as my cousin hacked and writhed on the ground in agony. Gatehouse reached down and grabbed hold of Vic's dreadlocks and heaved him up onto his knees. Vic hunched forward and tried to wrestle himself out of the policeman's grip. Gatehouse yanked him back towards him.

Vic grimaced and gasped in mouthfuls of air as he fought to catch his breath, his hands balling themselves up into fists at his sides. He spat at Gatehouse's feet and glared up at him. "Fuck yuh, yuh honky pig!" Gatehouse raised his truncheon over Vic's head and took aim then glanced across at his boss.

Monroe's brow furrowed. He shook his head slowly and wagged a disapproving finger back at Gatehouse. "Ah, ah, superintendent . . . I think that can wait till a little later, don't you?"

Gatehouse's face flushed as, reluctantly, he reined in his temper and, slowly, lowered his arm. Monroe smiled down at Vic then turned and pointed his cane up towards my face. "You know, I wouldn't have expected any less from Victor . . . he's like the rest of your family . . . pig ignorant negroes. Nothing more."

Monroe's voice had little trace of an accent, it sounded like polished metal, smooth and clean, as if it had been buffed with banknotes from the day he'd been born.

A cold chill ascended my spine and raised the hackles

along the back of my neck. I gestured with chin down toward Vic. My mouth was dry, my lips stuck as I spoke. "Is that how that bastard beat down on my sister?"

Monroe sniffed the air around him, then grinned back at me. "The superintendent can be a trifle hot-headed. Sadly, Bernice got his dander up. If she'd just been honest with him, he'd have been a little less extreme. Bernice's light fingers were the catalyst to this entire fiasco, Joseph. Don't you forget that."

Monroe turned to Gatehouse and clicked his fingers at him. "Your lighter please, superintendent." Gatehouse let go of Vic's hair and glanced across to his subordinate to make sure that the crew cut copper had once again trained his Webley back onto Vic's skull.

Satisfied that he had, he reached into his waistcoat, took out his lighter and handed it to Monroe, who repeatedly clicked at the roller and struck up a flame, then held it to the corner of the envelope and watched as it slowly set light to the brown paper and the photographs inside. Monroe held the envelope up in the air, one eye watering, and smiled as the flames burned through to its centre. Once the fire had engulfed most of the contents, he dropped the envelope to the ground and continued to watch it burn, the remains rolling up into coiled ashes to be extinguished slowly by the rain. Monroe flicked at the dying embers with the tip of his cane and looked up at me. "If I'd have been in receipt of the contents of that envelope some time ago, you may not have been standing inside that coffin today, Joseph old chap. Did Vic tell you the reason why I'd asked for you to be delivered to me in such an unusual manner?"

I looked down at Vic, his face was hanging forward, his chin resting against his chest, his breathing was shallow and controlled, his left hand pitching at an angle, lazily towards his ankle. I stared back at Monroe. "He said something 'bout you wantin' to bury me alive."

Monroe laughed, his voice wheezing like there were pinholes in his lungs. "What a crude little imagination your cousin has. Nothing of the kind crossed my mind. Burying alive ... how philistine." Monroe moved a little closer towards me and, as he did, the four other white fellas in the background with the automatic pistols crept in with him. He pointed the tip of his cane at the coffin. "The Cubans call this form of casket display *el muerto parao* ... 'Dead man standing', Joseph. Quite apt, all things considered, don't you think?"

"What's your point, Monroe?"

Monroe stiffened; as if someone had touched the back of his neck with an ice cube. "Good question ... my point is, Joseph ... that you are not the first Ellington to find themselves ..." Monroe hesitated for a moment as he considered the correct terminology. "To find themselves on display in this unusual manner."

"What the hell are you talking about?"

Monroe shifted his weight back onto his cane and looked down at the last of the ashes as they were blown across the gravel, then brought his gaze back up to me. His face had become stony. The pupils of his eyes, large and black like a shark's. "I'm talking about your great-grandfather, Joseph."

My jaw slackened, and I shook my head, my ears not quite believing what I was hearing. I saw the feverish shine in Monroe's eyes and pulled at the rope around my wrists, loosening the break-knot just a little.

"Your great-grandfather was in the employ of my great-grandpapa, Cephus Monroe ... By all accounts, grandpapa

359

Cephus was a fair man. A Quaker, so I'm told. God-fearing wife, father of three beautiful daughters. Quite a progressive fellow for his time. My family history says Cephus treated his negroes well; no punishment collars, shackling, branding or the whip for those niggers. Christian fair even-handedness was meted out, so I hear ... But your great-grandfather changed all that, Joseph. Changed all the pious goodwill in a heartbeat, he did."

"You ain't making a damn bit o' sense, Monroe."

Monroe scowled at my belligerence. His skin tightened against the bone as I watched his body tense. He cleared his throat softly and tightened his hand on the top of his cane as if a sliver of pain was working its way up his back and was about to be pitched out of his mouth. He moved in closer, his voice almost a whisper so that the men behind could not hear what he was saying.

"Your great-grandfather took rather a shine to one of grandpapa Cephus's daughters and he ... he actively pursued her in what can only be described as an ungentlemanly fashion. It would seem that your kin had unhealthy passions that he clearly found hard to control, Joseph; passions for an innocent white girl's flesh. He obviously won over her affections and, unfortunately, for your great-grandfather, he was found with her ..." Monroe sniggered to himself and rolled his tongue around the inside of his mouth lasciviously. "He was found with the poor child *in delicto flagrante,* as we say. You can imagine the uproar ... the shame of it. Great-grandpapa Cephus was left with little choice in the matter. Your great-grandfather was stripped, whipped and then strung up from one of the cedars that separated the slave quarters from the big house, then his body was stood in casket and he was left by the gates of one of Cephus's sugar cane fields for the rest of Ellington's kin and the other slaves to bear witness to."

The skin on my scalp receded against my skull. My heart was racing. "Bear witness ... you gotta strange way of describing murder." I watched Monroe's eyes hesitantly leave mine for a moment then return.

"It was a public outrage. The punishment befitted the crime."

"Bullshit!"

Monroe's mouth parted and he bit at his bottom lip with his incisor tooth, his eyes stayed fixed on mine and narrowed. "Bullshit or not, Joseph ... We Monroes have been carrying on with the Ellington strain *in flagrante delicto in occulto* ever since. Great-grandpapa, grandfather, my father, Monk, and your mother, Cora, and ..." Monroe hesitated for a moment, the skin around his eyes became bone white as his cheeks suddenly flushed. He leaned his face toward me, his eyes becoming brighter as he spoke under his breath. "And, of course, your sister and I."

I swallowed hard and felt the cartilage knot inside my jaw. "You mean your half-sister, you sonufabitch!"

Monroe's gaze slipped immediately from mine, his body taut with anger. I heard him mutter something under his breath before he lunged forward and knotted my hair in his fist and wrenched back my head. He pushed his face inside the coffin, his mouth only inches from my own. Monroe edged closer, then his lips grazed mine, the smell of stale tobacco and Parma Violets barely masking the halitosis coming off his warm breath, then a quiet hiss rose from his throat. "Bernice was special to me ... like your mother was to my father. Furtive boudoir companions make such exciting lovers, you know."

361

Monroe's fingers grazed the inside of the top of my thigh and his eyes roved over my face. His nose touched mine then he ran his tongue across my lower lip and flicked out a tiny blob of spittle across my mouth and slowly stepped away from me. The thin string of saliva clung to my chin. Monroe wiped his mouth with the back of his hand and smiled back at me furtively. "It was such a shame that your sister felt the need to betray me in the manner that she did and, sadly, she had to pay a high price for her foolish duplicity ..."

"I can see you're real broken up about it!"

"The loss of one of the faithful is always regrettable."

I spat at Monroe's feet. "Fuck you!"

"Charming ... Is this what it's come down to, Joseph? You bawling obscenities at me because you have nothing else left? I expected better of you, old son." Monroe grinned, looked back at Gatehouse and Vic, then leaned against his cane and I watched as his mouth opened breathlessly before speaking again.

"You know, with regards to Bernice, I was comforted by something my father would say when he was broached on the subject of disloyalty: *Proditoribus itur ad ignem* ... The traitor's path leads to the fire ..."

Monroe's face was bright with sweat, his nostrils suddenly flared and whitened around the rims. He breathed deeply, then spoke through his gritted front teeth. "I'm going to watch you and your traitorous cousin burn, Joseph, just like I watched that pretty little wife of yours burn."

A red rage enclosed me. An almost overwhelming desire to surge forward coursed through every fibre of my being. My eyes daggered into Monroe's. I'd seen enough death in the last week not to recognise it staring back at me now. I took a small, hot breath and drew my wrists together and let the rope loosen around my skin a little more. I glanced out over Monroe's shoulder down at Vic kneeling on the ground at Gatehouse's feet. My heart was racing. I blinked sweat and water out of my eyes, then saw my cousin slowly raise his arm up from his side and lift his head a couple of inches in the air. I watched as he wiped the back of his hand across his nose and cheek. In the distance, steel-grey clouds rolled across the sky. Below them, from the dense canopy of the cedar trees at the edge of the lawn, I saw a rifle's muzzle flash in the rain. There was no sound as the bullet entered the back of the gunman's head behind Vic. It exploded just above his left eye; the exit wound in his face the size of a tennis ball.

Gatehouse staggered back, his suit jacket and shirt splattered with the man's blood and brain matter, a look of pure horror etched across his face. I saw his blue eyes jitter frantically and the words he was about to shout out rise in his throat then transform into a piercing scream. Gatehouse's face contorted in agony, his hands dropped toward his legs, his frenzied fingers clasping at the hilt of the throwing knife that had just been plunged into his groin. By the time the policeman had realised what was happening to him, Vic had yanked the blade out of his flesh and was on his feet.

42

Monroe's unblinking eyes went quickly from me to the maelstrom that was unfolding behind him. As soon as I saw Vic rising to his feet, I'd thrown myself out of the casket like a greyhound out of a trap, the rope around my wrists unfurling just as Doc Lickrish had promised. The cord around my ankles was another matter. As I began to lunge at Monroe's back with my flailing arm and fist, the rope around my ankle bones bit into the skin and brought me to the ground. I saw Monroe spin himself around and look down at me, his face filled with a new-found expression of bewilderment and fear. He turned on his heels and began to run along the wall of the barracks towards the station's signal tower. I rolled across the gravel, reached around and ripped the Beretta from the small of my back. I clasped the pistol grip with both hands and stretched my arms out in front of me to fire at Monroe, but he was nowhere to be seen.

I rolled my body back toward the casket, kicked it to the ground and flung myself behind it; my legs wrestling frantically to unravel the rope around my ankles. I pulled up my knees and reached for the Puma penknife in my sock. I snapped open the blade and sliced through the tangled cord, just as a door on my left-hand side was kicked open. I grabbed the Beretta and rolled again toward the wall as two previously hidden men surged out of the barracks. I raised the gun instinctively and took aim at the first man out of the door and fired. What took place then seemed like something out of a nightmare, as if the fire fight I was now part of was happening to somebody else. A bloodlust unlike any rage I'd ever felt spread through every part of me.

The ringing in my ears became a high-pitched squeal as I pulled the trigger. Rather than the deafening burst of the pistol firing, what I heard were dull thuds as I shot the first man in the face and watched fragments of his bone and brain spray out from the other side of his head. The second man turned to fire on me and I squeezed the trigger and felt the Beretta jam on me. My hand froze on the pistol's grip and a cold wave of terror ran through me. The gunman, his face speckled with his partner's blood, took a step towards me and took aim. Then I saw his mouth suddenly open and his neck fly backwards as one of Dead Man's bullets again found its mark. The .308 calibre round caught him square in the forehead, slamming his body back against the wall of the barrack house.

My hearing suddenly burst back to life. Above my head I heard a low rumble of distant thunder then the flat popping sound of Dead Man's silenced M40 whipping across the grass followed by the return fire from Monroe's men, the heavy report of their pistols cracking in my ears as it was carried across the flattened grass toward the treeline. I looked up and saw one of the men shot through the eye and a second in the throat. The men both dropped to the ground and made no noise that I could hear through the heavy rainfall.

I hitched myself up and crouched behind the open door, quickly working the slide on the Beretta back and forth, clearing the jam. I chambered a round, then swept my eyes out across the parade ground in front of me. I saw Vic still wrestling with Gatehouse at the edge of the asphalt. He was pummelling the copper's face and upper body with a series of hefty blows. I lifted the Beretta and aimed it towards one of the gunmen who was pinned down by Dead Man's hidden fire. As I squinted down the sight of the pistol, I saw Vic snatch Gatehouse up from the ground by the lapel of his jacket and slam the blade of the throwing knife up underneath the policeman's ribs then watched as he plunged the blade into Gatehouse's stomach several more times.

Vic flung himself off the top of Gatehouse's body and moved quickly over the open ground, closing the space between him and one of the fallen men in front of him. He somersaulted over the body and snatched up the dead man's gun then straightened himself up onto one knee and opened fire on the third man in the group. At the same time, to my right, Bitter Lemon had closed in and risen up out of a coulee and began to charge across the grass, the Thompson machine gun at his hip. He loosened off a volley of automatic fire at the fourth man, hitting him across the chest, the bullets almost tearing him in two. I watched as Lemon's gaze swept across the parade ground in front of him, then saw the big Bajan throw himself onto his stomach as another three of Monroe's men burst out of a rear door at the end of the barrack room and began to open fire. The men spread out along the side of the building behind a hail of automatic gunfire. Bitter Lemon reached behind him and yanked a smoke grenade from his belt. He pulled on the pin and lobbed it across the grass toward the gunmen, then began spraying the area in front of him with machine gun fire. Vic had found himself some cover behind the front wing of the Bedford van. I fired off a couple of rounds towards the smoky ridge to my left and made a dart for the inside of the barrack house. As I began to run, I saw Dead Man make a break from the tree line and dart across the grass, throwing himself underneath the Bedford van and start to open fire on Monroe's remaining men.

The barrack room was in total darkness. Outside, the rain had suddenly died and the air that blew into the barracks had grown close and hot, with a smell of burnt flesh and sulphur on the edge of it. Thunder continued to rattle in the distance and the light of a thin streak of lightning flashed dimly through a window above my head. I crawled on my haunches along the wall of the barracks until I could just make out a door. I rose slowly to my feet, raised the Beretta out in front of me, then took hold of the handle and swung it open. On the other side of the door was a short corridor that looked as if it led back out into the open and up towards the signal tower.

I held on to the pistol grip with both hands, sank my shoulders down a little, then slid quickly along the wall, and, at the end of it, swung my body out into the open. In front of me was a short stone path that led to the wooden stairs that then climbed up to the old signal tower. Nervously, I edged my way along the path, my eyes sweeping either side of me as I searched for any sign of Monroe. At the foot of the steps I could see the door to the signal tower had been left slightly ajar. A wave of prickles went down my left arm. Sweat sprouted from my palms. I took hold of the bannister rail with my left hand and clenched the grip of the Beretta in my right. I held the gun out straight in front of me, aimed at the door and began to climb. At the top, an open padlock hung by its shackle on the hasp staple of the frame. I took a step back, stood to one side, kicked at the foot of the door and watched as it swung inward. I couldn't see Monroe, or a great deal else for that matter. The inside of the circular tower was empty of any kind of furniture and was only illuminated by the thin strips of early morning light that shone down toward the floor through four large windows that were set into the brickwork above my head. Directly in front of me I could see a wooden ladder that led up to a balcony that ran the entire circumference of the tower. I took a deep breath, clasped my left hand underneath the grip of the gun and stepped inside.

As soon as my foot touched the floorboards, I felt a sharp pain at the back of my right knee. I let go of the pistol grip with my left hand and tried to swing my body around and save myself from falling. Another swift kick, this time above my left knee, sent my legs out from underneath me. I dropped backwards onto the ground and, at the same time, felt the Beretta being kicked from my hand. I lashed out blindly with my right leg and pressed the palm of my left hand down on the floorboards to try and push myself up. I saw Monroe's shadow circle to my left. I rolled to my right side and scrambled onto my knees.

As I pulled myself up, out of the corner of my eye, I saw Monroe's polished shoe come at me and graze the top of my right arm. I stumbled backwards, the top of my head hitting a low beam. I began to panic and glanced down at the ground, my eyes desperately searching for Evangeline's Beretta.

"That little pistol of yours went underneath the ladder, Joseph. Bit of a tall order to try and make a run for it now, old son." I looked up and saw Monroe walk out of the darkness. "You shouldn't have bothered to come looking for me . . . this is going to end in tears."

Monroe raised his cane up in front of his chest and pulled

at the top of the handle, slowly withdrawing a long, thin silver blade. My body sank forward, my shoulders dipping low, my hands balling into trembling fists. Monroe danced to his left, threw the scabbard end of the cane to the floor and rushed toward me, slashing the rapier in criss-cross movements in front of his face. I darted to my right, my back still in the shadows. The blade cut through the air in front of my face, Monroe laughed and edged forward, his feet stomping on the wooden floor with each move he took. I lunged at him, kicking my leg at his upper thigh but missing him by a mile.

My heart hammered away underneath my ribcage, then I saw the sword arc above Monroe's head and, instinctively, I shot backwards; the blade came in across my chest, slicing the fabric of my shirt, missing the skin under it by half an inch. I kept backing up into nowhere, weaving my body out of the light and back into the shadows. As Monroe teased the blade of the sword out in front of him, my foot stood on the blade's scabbard. I bobbed low and snatched it up of the floor and came back out into the open. Monroe, seeing the makeshift weapon in my hand, brought the fight to me, unleashing another series of hefty blows at my chest, forcing me to stagger backwards.

When Monroe came at me again, he came in hard, swinging the cane sword at my face. I arced my body further backwards towards the wall, then spun myself around on my heels, bringing myself close in towards Monroe's body. I raised the stick and slammed it across the back of his neck, sending him careering into the side of the ladder. Monroe's eyes burned with anger. He raised the sword in front of his face and screamed at me like a petulant child who'd just had a favourite toy snatched from him. He spat on the ground and ran at me. The next two blows came in close across the top of my head, but Monroe's third, a backswing off the one before it, found my flesh, cutting into the top of my shoulder. I cried out, my hand instinctively covering the wound. Monroe had got his first taste of blood, and, like a baying wolf, he wanted to gorge on a hell of a lot more. I heard his breathing become heavy, when he spoke, his voice sounded like it had gone up in pitch; the words he uttered, icy and shrill to my ears.

"Stings a little, doesn't it, Joseph."

I hadn't the strength, will or desire to reply. At that moment, all I knew was I wanted the madness to end. I wanted Monroe out of my life and gone. I wanted him dead. A blind rage suddenly exploded inside my brain and my vision blanked with a misting red cloud. I saw the blade flicker in front of my face and swipe across the top of my scalp. I dipped down low, my body bobbing and weaving, my mind remembering the boxing moves I'd learnt from my father as a child. My calves tightened and my feet become light. I clenched my fists and charged towards Monroe, my head and torso making contact with the lower half of his body. I heard the sword slice down close to my head and right ear, but did not realise that my body blow had released it from Monroe's hand and sent it flying across the floor. Monroe hit the ground with me all over him.

The first punch glanced his chin; the second, square in the centre of his face, broke his nose. Monroe's warm blood splattered the back of my fist and I hammered him with another couple of short arm jabs to the face. Determined to keep him in a weakened state, I brought my knee up deep into his groin as I pulled myself up onto my feet. I kicked at Monroe's side and legs repeatedly. If he screamed out in pain, I never heard him. I reached down and grabbed at his jacket lapels, hauled him up onto his feet and yanked him towards me. Monroe's arms flailed either side of his head as I swung in from my left and kidney-punched him, doubling him over and expelling the choked air out of his chest. My right fist hooked into his face again and caught him across the eye socket. His head snapped sideways, and, in the glare of the breaking sunlight, I saw the white imprints of my knuckles on his skin and the watery electric shock in his eyes.

I watched as Monroe's bloodied face and body seemed to recede into the darkness behind him, the disbelief and injury in his expression shaping and reshaping itself in the dim overhead light. His body slumped forward and his lips moved, and I knew he wanted to curse or wound me in some fresh way, but his breath rasped like an old man whose lungs were perforated with cancerous legions. I drove my body forward and swung at his jaw with my right fist, sending him sprawling backwards. Spittle and blood arced into the air. He hit the ground hard and I heard the last solid breath go out of him. I kicked at the inside of his legs and stood over him and, once again, smelled the all too familiar odour of fear. I turned and looked down at the floor and saw the faint glimmer of Monroe's blade glint back at me from off the floorboards. I reached down and wrapped my fingers around the handle and scratched the tip of the blade across the ground. I stepped back over Monroe's sprawled-out body and swung the sword in front of his face His eyes, wet with tears, glared into mine in the same way a snake's might if it were trapped inside a burning woodpile. His arms and hands shook and were spread out across the ground as if he was about to be crucified.

I put my foot across one of his wrists and pushed down

on it. Monroe hollered out in pain, but I didn't care. I stood over him and looked down at his petrified face and let the tip of the blade touch his skin. I scratched at one of his eyelids then pressed the metal into the fleshy part of his cheek. I heard the saliva catch at the back of his throat as he tried to cry out for me to stop, then smelled the urine as it seeped out of his bladder, through his trousers and trickled out across the wood floor.

In my mind's eye, I saw a multitude of souls gather around me before I plunged the tip of the blade through Monroe's face. I saw Bernice's mutilated body laying on a cold, white mortuary slab; Evangeline Laveau in my arms with the red cord tied around her neck; I saw the lifeless body of Stella Hopkins hanging from the iron curtain rail in my old flat on Gwyn Street; then once again heard the pitiful, horrific screams of my wife, Ellie and our daughter, Amelia, as they were engulfed in a fiery inferno. My fist tightened around the hilt of the sword as I began to press down harder onto Monroe's terrified face. Then I swore I heard my wife call out my name and cry, "*No!*" I turned to see where the voice was coming from. Standing at my side was Vic.

I watched as he drew in close to me and felt the palm of his hand touch my back softly. I saw him shake his head at me. He leaned across my chest and wrapped his hand around the top of mine as I grasped the handle of the sword. Vic prised the blade gently from my fingers. He put his arm around my shoulders and drew me back out of the darkness of the tower room and out into the blossoming early morning sunshine. Vic turned me around so that I faced the staircase.

At the foot of the steps stood Bussa. He smiled up at me, then reached out his hand and gestured at me to begin walking down the stairs. When I turned back to look at Vic, he was already closing the door behind him. I heard him turn a key bluntly in the lock. I called out his name, over and over again, and hammered at the door with my fists, my fingernails clawing at the wood panels to get inside. Suddenly, I felt weak. Every ounce of strength was drawn from my body as swiftly as water siphoned from a well. My legs gave way and I slumped to the floor. I closed my eyes and lifted my face up into the sun, then opened my mouth and screamed. My wretched cries were lifted up into the air by the warm mountain breeze and carried out across the treetops toward the sea.

EPILOGUE

They say time heals all wounds. I don't believe that to be true. All wounds remain. Time may cover our hurt with scar tissue and lessen the pain, but the hurt is never gone. Returning home had reopened old, hidden injuries, and ignited bitter reminiscences which I would have much rather have left in a cold, dark recess in the furthest reaches of my already troubled mind. I found that the Barbados of my dreams held as many bad memories as it did good, and that my loyalty and fondness for my home was connected more to the people I had loved than to the place itself. It was with the sinking of a very heavy heart that I now realised the once bucolic world in which I had grown up was almost gone, and that the idyllic days of my childhood would not be returning to offer me the solace I sought.

Vic had made sure I laid low in the days after the killings at Gun Hill. He'd put me up in a tiny, backstreet chattel house in the remote village of Four Roads in Christ Church Parish. The old, wood-framed house was set on cinder blocks away from the rest of the village and reminded me of the home I once shared with my late wife and daughter. There, I began to let my physical wounds start to heal and I tried to mask the hurt that nagged inside my head by filling my belly with rum. My cousin had done another of his usual disappearing acts and it was his friend Bussa who patched me up, stayed with me during those long, hot days and listened to me scream at night when the nightmares and old ghosts returned to haunt me as I slept.

I knew that Vic had wanted to shield me from the pain of another wound; that he wanted to protect my already damaged spirit from the misery that came with the act of extinguishing the final breath from a man's lungs. Death and killing came easy for my cousin, but the taking of another soul's precious life would always have weighed heavy on my heart and mind.

Vic knew that if I'd killed Monroe, it would have taken me further towards the endless darkness and the demons that inhabited such a pestilent, unforgiving and bleak empire. It was a perpetually nocturnal and bestial realm that, in Vic's mind, belonged solely to him.

Monroe never saw the daylight again, Vic made sure of that. Toward the end of that week, I was alone with Bussa, who told me exactly what had happened after he had walked me down the steps away from the signal tower, back to the Land Rover and had Dead Man drive me back to the house at Hillaby. We had sat in the tiny garden at the rear of the house after the elderly Bajan had spent most of the day slow-cooking pig's feet and rundown stew. He had been quiet for most of the day, and kept himself to himself. At the time I thought little of it, but, on reflection, I now realise that the old man was searching for a way to explain the horrors of what he had taken part in and witnessed. The bodies of Silas Gatehouse and his men had been collected and put into black rubberised body bags, which, conveniently, had been supplied to Vic by the US Air Force, then taken deep into the forests in the interior of the island and buried in deep, lime-filled graves. Monroe's demise had been an altogether different, far crueller, matter.

In the signal tower, Vic had been alone with Monroe for longer than any man had the right to, when his heart was filled with hatred and vengeance. He'd continued to beat down on Monroe, inflicting terrible injuries upon the man's already broken body. Bussa said that you could hear the white man's screams from as far back as where he stood on the parade ground. When his avenging temper had been partially sated, Vic had hog-tied Monroe by his wrists, legs and ankles, had dragged him back down the staircase and then thrown him into the cherry wood coffin that I had been placed in earlier. He then stood over the casket and watched whilst Bitter Lemon nailed down the lid.

Bussa, Lemon and Vic had carried the casket back to the Bedford van and the three men had driven further up into the mountains, to a place where Vic had already been and prepared a funeral pyre. The coffin was placed on top of the bonfire in a shaded clearing surrounded by tall, bearded fig trees, then doused in gallons of petrol. Vic had told the two men to go back to the van and leave him alone a while. As they had left, Bussa said he turned back to look down the thin forest path. He watched my cousin light a gasoline-soaked rag with a match then throw the cloth torch down into the base of the pyre and saw the casket engulfed in a ball of blue and orange flame. Vic did not move. He stood at the edge of the clearing and watched Monroe burn slowly to death.

*

At eleven on the morning of Tuesday, 11 April 1967, we buried my sister, Bernice, close to where our parents had been interred, in a small cemetery in Ginger Bay in St Philip Parish. Her funeral took place six days before her birthday.

377

Had she lived, she would have celebrated her forty-second birthday. Vic, Bussa, Bitter Lemon, Dead Man and I were her only mourners. We had stood at her graveside whilst a minister offered the brief committal service. There had been no hymns, and our prayers were both hushed and fleeting. *"I am the resurrection and the life"* seemed like such a scant tribute to bid a last farewell to a loved one who had, in truth, been sorely treated in life. Bernice's coffin, the second of the trio of caskets Vic and I had brought over from Louisiana, had been draped in pretty white orchids and red and yellow hibiscus flowers; the flowers she had always loved as a child. Bernice's body was lowered slowly into the ground to the song of the cicadas in the trees around us and the whisper of our tears.

That evening, the sky over Four Roads turned a deep purple and the humidity heightened. I went out into the street and watched as a solitary streak of lightning danced out on the horizon. At first the rain fell lightly through the oak trees opposite the house, then, a short while later, the heavens opened and a storm raged for the next twelve hours. Later that evening, as I lay on my cot listening to the rolling thunder overhead, I thought for the briefest moment that I heard my sister Bernice's voice call out to me, but her words were no more than a murmur and they were quickly lost; carried off through the mist outside to a distant place inhabited by those who, like me, sleep little and find comfort in the night.

Two days later, just after sunrise, Vic paid me a visit. I'd already washed and shaved by the time I heard the Land Rover pull up outside in the street, and listened as he lumbered in through the back door, his dreadlocks hanging around his face, barefooted, wearing pale blue shorts and a white T-shirt and carrying a large white envelope. He sidled up against me and slapped his arm across my still smarting shoulder. Despite knowing I was in pain, he hugged me closer and grinned, his face flush with a cheery youthfulness that I'd not witnessed for some time. Vic called for Bussa and kept his arm wrapped around me until the old man joined us. My cousin tossed the envelope over to Bussa. "Git these ta Bitter Lemon an' Dead Man, tell 'em we all's leavin' on Sunday." Bussa tipped the contents of the envelope out into his hand and held up three polished, blue British passports in front of his face. The elderly Bajan smiled at Vic then began to laugh. Vic gestured toward the front door with his head. "Come on, I gotta delivery ta mek ... yuh can gimme a hand."

"What kind of delivery?"

Vic turned and winked at me then grinned. "Wait an' see."

Outside, strapped to the roof of Vic's Land Rover was the last of the three coffins we had brought back from New Orleans. Vic climbed inside, stuck the key in the ignition and began revving the engine impatiently.

"Come on, man ... I ain't got all day!"

I opened up the passenger door of the old motor and stared up at the casket before getting in. "Where the hell we goin' with that?"

Vic slapped the palm of his hand on the steering wheel, his patience quickly wearing thin. "Jus' git yuh ass inside and stop axin' so many damn questions!"

I did as he asked and hauled myself in next to him. My cousin was already speeding off down the street before my backside had time to hit the seat, the coffin rattling on the roof above my head an unwelcome reminder: when you

379

knew a man like Vic, the shadow of death was never too far away from your soul.

★

We drove in silence along the coastal road for around three miles before Vic turned off down a dirt track that was shielded by a thick canopy of overhanging palms. I'd wanted to ask him about the aftermath of Gun Hill, Monroe and the other dead men, but something told me that now wasn't the right time. I'd not seen my cousin this excited for a very long time and it seemed churlish to pull the rug from under his feet by bringing up recent events that he clearly wished should remain shrouded underneath a dark veil of his own making.

Half a mile further down the track, I could smell the sharp ozone tang of the sea air on the breeze. In a fork in the road, Vic swung the Land Rover left into a steep gully and pulled up sharply outside a pretty beach house that stood in front of the dunes. Vic smiled at me then turned off the ignition and climbed out of the cab and waited for me to join him. He pointed his finger toward the wooden shack. "Tek a wander thru' that gate an' go on inside." He took a couple of steps back and smiled at me again, then waved his hand toward the beach house.

"Go on, man . . . trus' me. Ain't nuthin' inside'a there gonna hurt ya." I watched for a moment as he began to walk slowly back toward his car, then I turned and stared at the old shack, the front door wide open. For some reason, the house and the surroundings felt familiar, but I knew I had never been to the place before. As I strolled down toward the white picket fence that ran around the front of the beach house and opened up the gate, I noticed twin candles flickering in jars on either side of the doorstep, when I looked up, Mama Esme was waiting to greet me.

"Joseph ... 'S good ta see yuh, brutha. That no good relation o' yours bring me ma pine box he promised me?"

I nodded my head. "Yeah, we brought it."

Mama Esme smiled. "That's good ... I ain't plannin' on needin' it jus' yet, but the day gonna come sooner or later, may as well be prepared fo' it." Esme waved me toward her with a curl of her nimble fingers, then turned and began to walk back toward the entrance of the beach house. "C'mon ... git yuh'self on inside wid me, I bin waitin' fo' yuh."

I followed Esme into her home and was immediately hit by the pungent, warm aroma of incense burning in the hearth. Coloured fabrics hung from the walls and ceiling, and candles burned on saucers which had been placed across the sandstone floor in every possible nook and cranny of the tiny house. A polished, timber rocking chair sat by the fireplace and, next to that, perched on the top of a small, three-legged wooden stool, was a leather-bound Bible. Esme raised her hand in front of her face and gestured with a flick of her fingers that I follow her. She guided me towards the rear of the house, out onto a tiny porch with steps that led down to a small garden. A stone path cut through its centre, the borders either side blooming with four-o'clocks. Esme stood out on the porch and waited for me to join her. As I came and stood at her side, she linked her arm through mine and pointed across the garden towards another gate that opened out on to the dunes.

To the left of the gate, laid out across the ground was a white blanket. Sitting on the blanket was a small mulatto child, perhaps no more than two years old. Confused, I stared back at Esme. The old woman looked back at the child then back up at me. "There's ma gift ta yuh, Joseph."

I looked across the garden, confused by her words. "Say what?"

Esme smiled at the child. "That pickney, she yuh niece."

I stared back at the child and then at Esme. "My niece?"

Esme nodded her head softly. "That's Bernice's child . . . she called Chloe."

Tears welled up into my eyes. "I didn't know . . ."

"It don't matter none." Esme smiled and let go of my arm, then walked down the steps of the porch and held out her hand. "Why don't yuh come an' say hello ta tha pickney?"

I followed Esme down the path and watched as she bent down and lifted the little girl up into her arms. She cradled Chloe in the centre of her chest, then turned her toward me so that I could see her face. The little girl stared at me, her blue eyes searching into mine, her tiny round face the image of my sister. Esme caressed the little girl's hair with her fingers.

"This redbone child need a home, Joseph." Esme looked at the little girl, then at me. "She need a family ta tek care n' love her . . . That's what they'd be wantin'."

I shook my head. "Who'd have wanted, Esme?"

"'Ere, boy, tek'a off a me an' come see." Esme reached over and held the child out to me. "Com' on, tek tha pickney!" I lifted my arms nervously, and did as she said and took hold of Chloe, then smiled at the little girl. Unsure of me, she turned and held out her arms for Esme, but the old woman had already opened up the gate and had begun to walk out across the dunes and along a shaded sandy path close to the rear of her garden. I followed her and found her standing opposite a small rectangular white fence, behind it, directly in the centre, was a gravestone, no more than three feet high. A single bunch of freshly cut jasmine lay in front of it. Esme turned and looked at me. "Aft'a Monroe an' dem po'liceman ran yuh off, there weren't no'body ta tek care o' tings. I had Ellie an' young Amelia brung ta me 'ere. I bin lookin' after 'em evah since." Esme walked over to the small gate and opened it up. "They bin waitin fo' yuh, Joseph."

My arms became weak, my eyes swollen with tears. I reached down and stood Chloe next to me, then gently took hold of her hand, her tiny fingers clasping onto mine. I looked back at Esme and down at the grave and hesitated for a moment, then walked on in and stared down at the simple inscription on the granite stone.

Eleanor & Amelia Ellington
Ever Loved

I kneeled down next to Chloe and ran my finger along the engraving, my tears falling down my face and collecting underneath my chin, before dropping onto the sandy ground at my feet. I turned and looked out to sea, then back along the pretty beach, and out toward the high coral cliffs which ran the entire length of the south shore, then turned back. Standing over me was Vic. He smiled at me, then stuck his hand into his back pocket and pulled out two British passports. He reached down and handed one to me. I sat back onto the sand and looked once again at the headstone, then wiped the tears from my eyes with the back of my hand and lifted the little girl onto my lap. I opened up the back of the passport and looked at the black and white photograph. Directly underneath, printed in bold black letters was the name, Chloe Cora Ellington. I drew Chloe next to me and looked up towards where Vic had been standing, but he was gone. I crooked my head around and saw him walking slowly back along the path towards the beach house, arm in arm with Esme. When he reached the garden gate Vic turned, waved his passport in front of his face and called back to me.

"Let's go home, Joseph."

ACKNOWLEDGEMENTS

"Why just the three books?" It's the question I have been asked most often by readers or in interview. Back in 2014, when *Heartman* was first published, I was quick to confirm that my Bajan detective, Joseph Tremaine Ellington, would return in two further novels. True to my word, JT came out of the shadows in spring 2016 for *All Through the Night*. At the time of that book's publication I had already written the first draft of *Restless Coffins* and was about to polish the manuscript to bring Ellington's 1960s tale to an end.

During those final weeks of work on *Restless Coffins*, two things became apparent. The first was how much I'd enjoyed writing the third book and being back in JT's world and second, how sad I was at the thought of bidding farewell to the characters who have been part of my life since the summer of 2003.

In spring 2017, with the *Coffins* manuscript posted off to my agent, Phil Patterson, I returned to my desk to begin work again. For many weeks, while I tapped away at the keyboard, lost in a new work, I didn't think once about Joseph, his cousin, Vic, or their world of 1960s Bristol. But favourite characters are often like one's first love … hard to forget.

I'd thought I was done with Ellington and his world, but it became apparent that my wily Bajan detective was far from done with me. Wherever I was, old JT would often creep back into my consciousness and whisper in my ear, "Where we goin' to next?"

Something inside of me knew that my writing journey with Ellington, Vic et al. was far from over. There was more to write about … another tale to tell. And so I hope *Restless Coffins* offers the reader a fitting conclusion to the story that began in *Heartman*.

The next question to ask myself was, "If I'm to write more, then where do I take Joseph in the future?" It took me a good while to answer that question, but now I have the answer, I am delighted with what the future holds for Mr Ellington. Unfortunately, dear reader, you will have to wait until early 2019 for more on this fourth book, but the good news is – Ellington will return in *The Rivers of Blood*.

And after that … Well, let's just say, "Never say never."

★

Writing can be a lonely profession. Hours on hours sitting at a desk, alone with your imagination, a headache, sore fingers, a numb bum and, in my case, dozens of empty cans of Dr Pepper building up as I work into the wee small hours.

I'm a grumpy old git normally and enjoy my own company: perfect, some would say, if one chooses to write for a living.

Now, writing alone is one thing, but producing a book for publication requires a huge behind-the-scenes cast who are rarely seen and rarely get the credit they deserve. Can I please take a moment of your time, dear reader, to rectify that? There are many thanks to offer up …

First up, thank you to my literary agent, Philip Patterson of the Marjacq agency. Phil puts up with my writerly insecurities, constant emails and bad jokes. He is a gentleman. These three books would not be in print if not for Phil's belief in me as a writer and in my characters. Thanks also to Marjacq's director, Guy Herbert, and to foreign rights manager, Sandra Sawicka. Much gratitude also to my film and TV agent, Luke Speed, at Curtis Brown. A huge thank you to Simon Heath, Jake Lushington and the World Productions team, and to the wonderful scriptwriter, Tony Marchant.

Thanks to everyone at Black & White Publishing for their untiring support and commitment to bringing Ellington to readers here in the UK and around the world. Also, many thanks to my editor, Graham Lironi, and to all the staff at Leicester-based large print publishers, Ulverscroft, and to all the gang at Bolinda Audio.

I am indebted to many other writers who have offered kind words and support. A big thumbs-up to you all, especially to Mark Billingham, Martina Cole, James Lee Burke, Nick Quantrill, Howard Linskey and Ken Bruen.

Many thanks to crime writer and dear friend, Tony R. Cox, and the wonderful crime fiction historian and author, John Martin, for their tireless enthusiasm for my work. Cheers, gents. I'll get the next round in.

I have been very lucky to receive the support of a fantastic crime fiction family. I am indebted to the many reviewers and bloggers who have been integral in getting my books out to readers.

Thanks to Ellington's number one fan and book blogging supremo, Abby Jayne Slater-Fairbrother. You are a star.

My gratitude also to Noelle Holten, Sarah Hardy, Amanda Oughton, Richard Latham, Nicola Hodges, Graham Paul Tonks, Sandra Robinson, Linda Wilson, Robin Jarossi, Liz Barnsley, David Prestidge, Robb Dex, Jane Jakeman at the *Guardian*, Marcel Berlins at *The Times*, and to the crime fiction maestros, Ayo Onatade, Ali Karim and Mike Stotter.

Thanks also to Jonathan Lampon and all the guys at BBC Radio Leicester and to Dermot O'Leary for the Instagram snaps of *Heartman* and *All Through the Night* and the book-plugging that he has generously undertaken. I am indebted to you, sir.

Thanks must also go to Simon Farrow at Acerte Design for the stunning teaser poster and online artwork he has created and to dear friends Alex Kettle and Ken Hooper for their support.

Love and thanks to my family. My sister, Sally, brother-in-law, Darren, and my parents, Ann and Pat. I love you all. These three books are dedicated to each of you. You know the reasons why.

Lastly, thank you to my two daughters, Enya and Neve, who bring such daily joy to their daddy, and to my brilliant wife, Jen, who puts up with me on a daily basis and who has thankfully not yet turned to the gin bottle ... I couldn't have done any of this writer's stuff without you. I am truly blessed to share my life with such a beautiful soul. Thank you, my love.

M.P. Wright
November 2017

ABOUT THE AUTHOR

M.P. Wright was born in Leicestershire in 1965 into a family farming home that can be traced back through seven generations. When he left school, he pursued his first love, music – not as a musician, but in a variety of support roles before he became a private investigator. But when he realised that excitement and adrenaline were not a good substitute for a proper career and a steady job, he retrained in the mental health sector. His role was at the sharp end of an intense, often dangerous profession, and he was promoted into the probation service and eventually the Home Office, where he was responsible for offender risk assessments.

M.P. Wright has retained his deep love of music, especially film scores, both modern and vintage. He is an aficionado of real ales and is the Writer In Residence at the Criterion Free house in Leicester.

M.P. Wright has two daughters and lives with his wife, Jen, and their two large Rottweiler rescue dogs.

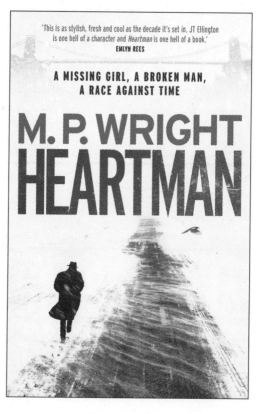

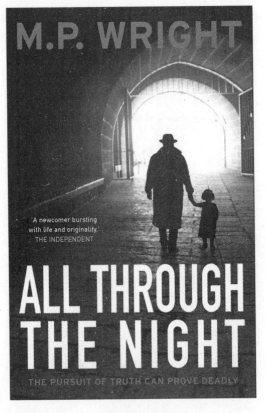